Soft warmth against his lips. Silky heat on his tongue. Spice and flowers. Curves.

The sensations rocketed through Dayn. Gone was any hint of reserve or control. Growling low in his throat, he crowded Reda back against the tree until their bodies were aligned, touching from knee to chest. He kept his hands on her face, willing them to stay there with the last threads of his control, knowing that if he touched her—really *touched* her—he would be truly lost.

It had been two decades since he had held a woman out of anything other than necessity. But now, as their tongues touched and slid, as his body went tight, tense and hard, he wasn't just kissing a woman. He was kissing a dream he hadn't been aware of having.

* * *

"Added Bonus: Two Books in One! Don't Miss Jessica Andersen's Harlequin Intrigue *Twin Targets!*"

Books by Jessica Andersen

Harlequin Nocturne

Harlequin Intrigue

JESSICA ANDERSEN

has worked as a geneticist, scientific editor, animal trainer and landscaper...but she's happiest when she's combining all of her many interests into writing romantic adventures that always have a twist of the unusual to them. Born and raised in the Boston area (Go, Sox!), Jessica can usually be found somewhere in New England, hard at work on her next happily-ever-after. For more on Jessica and her books, please check out www.JessicaAndersen.com and www.JessicaAndersenIntrigues.com.

JESSICA ANDERSEN

LORD OF THE WOLFYN
& TWIN TARGETS

ROYAL HOUSE *of* SHADOWS

TORONTO NEW YORK LONDON
AMSTERDAM PARIS SYDNEY HAMBURG
STOCKHOLM ATHENS TOKYO MILAN MADRID
PRAGUE WARSAW BUDAPEST AUCKLAND

Recycling programs
for this product may
not exist in your area.

HARLEQUIN BOOKS

ISBN-13: 978-0-373-83774-8

LORD OF THE WOLFYN
Copyright © 2011 by Dr. Jessica S. Andersen

TWIN TARGETS
Copyright © 2008 by Dr. Jessica S. Andersen

CONTENTS

Dear Reader,

Blood drinkers, werewolves and warlocks, oh my! Welcome to the Royal House of Shadows.... Do you dare enter this dark, dangerous and sexy world?

I loved, loved, loved writing the story of a secretive magical prince and a redheaded cop with a penchant for archery and no luck with men. When sorcery plucks them from their rightful homes and prophecy throws them together, mayhem, adventure and a hot, sexy romance ensues...and asks the age-old question: Who's afraid of the Big Bad Wolf?

Lord of the Wolfyn follows Gena Showalter's *Lord of the Vampires* and Jill Monroe's *Lord of Rage*, and next month comes Nalini Singh's *Lord of the Abyss*. It was an absolute blast working with these talented ladies and imagining how these royal siblings would avenge their parents and save their kingdom.

Happy reading,

Jessica Andersen

To lone wolves and life mates.

PROLOGUE

ONCE UPON A TIME in a magical land, a dark sorcerer—the Blood Sorcerer—coveted the only power denied him: the right to rule. So he led his army in a vicious attack on the Royal Castle of Elden, vowing to wipe out the royal family and take the throne. But he hadn't counted on the king and queen's love for their children, particularly the rebellious, headstrong Prince Dayn....

BRANCHES STUNG DAYN'S face and lashed at the bloodred chestnut stallion he rode, but neither of them flinched. They were trained for this, had been born for it: Dayn was the king's second son, Hart a royal warhorse descended from generations of beast-chasers. Together, they guarded Castle Island and the villages surrounding Blood Lake, and kept the foul monsters of sorcery trapped in the Dead Forest.

It was a noble role, a dangerous calling...and an incredible rush. At least, it usually was. Tonight, though, he rode in anger with his reins white-knuckled in one hand and his loaded crossbow in the other, his mind not on protecting his castle or the country folk, but on the kill itself.

Full of his master's mood, Hart snorted, grabbed the bit in his teeth and leaped a thorny tangle they normally would have dodged around. Dayn shouted and grabbed the sturdy beast-chaser's flowing mane, and the two landed together and pounded away, now with a clear view of the monster they pursued.

The bristling, pony-size gray creature could have been one of the giant wolves that hunted the high country beyond Elden, save for the saddle of reddish fur at its heavy nape and the golden stripe that ran along its spine. Those things marked it as something else entirely: a wolfyn.

The older hunters told of the wolfyn taking human form and seducing the most beautiful women they could find…and then killing and eating them. Those were just stories, though. And the legendary shape-shifting was a way to explain why, back when they first set out to exterminate the creatures, the ravenous beasts would retaliate by attacking at a village's weakest point and go straight for the strongest warriors and then their beautiful wives, as if they were at war, not hunting.

Those days were gone now, the wolfyn nearly wiped from the kingdoms. The few that remained, though, were deadly and had to be killed for the safety of all.

At the moment, though, all Dayn cared about was riding hard enough to leave everything else behind— his father's anger, his mother's disappointment…and the look on Twilla's face when he'd broken it off with her after hinting at marriage.

His father's words echoed in his mind. *You must wed a proper princess. You are the protector of the royal forest and your brother's right hand.* And the gods knew that dark, seductive Nicolai wasn't settling down anytime soon, so the king and queen—and their advisers—had pinned their hopes for profitable alliances on Dayn and his sister, Breena. The very thought of it—and the argument he'd had just now with his parents—had Dayn riding hard away from the castle and its politics. He was twenty and six, and his kind lived for hundreds, sometimes thousands, of years. Yet his parents wanted to sell his life to whichever royal house bid highest. Gods and the Abyss, he wished he had been common-born.

But he hadn't been, so he kicked on until the wind stung his face and the ground blurred beneath Hart's hooves.

His man-at-arms, Malachai, who was riding well behind them on his sturdy gray gelding, whipped around the thorny brake Dayn and Hart had just sailed over, bellowing, "Damn it, wait!"

Dayn's former-tutor-turned-companion said something more, but it was lost beneath Hart's loud snort as the trees thinned and they caught another glimpse of the wolfyn. The stallion accelerated after the beast, which looked back at them with too-intelligent amber eyes, and Dayn gripped with his knees and raised his crossbow as the gap narrowed. The trees opened up around him, but he focused on the reddish saddle mark, which outlined the target for a kill shot.

The wolfyn gathered itself for a last burst of speed, and—

Mindspeak screamed suddenly in Dayn's skull, filling him with pounding emotions that weren't his own: *rage, defiance, fear, betrayal.* Before he could do more than jerk with surprise, wind whipped up around him, squeezing him in a giant's fist of spell-power, and then yanking him clear out of the saddle and up into a rapidly forming whirlwind that suddenly spun overhead.

"Ambush!" Malachai shouted, his voice winddistorted and quickly growing faint as the tornado sucked Dayn inward and air screamed past him.

He fought the magic that held him, but it was too powerful, too all-encompassing, a physical force that roared and keened, and then flattened, reverberating in his soul as he reached the calm at the center of the whirlwind. There, he hung suspended—seeing nothing but the moving wall of gray-brown surrounding him, feeling nothing but the magic. His pulse hammered and his muscles screamed for him to fight or run. But there was nothing to fight, nowhere to escape. Gods. What was happening? Mindspeaking was usually nothing more than shared thoughts between blood-drinking kinsmen. He and his father shared the bond most strongly, though he also had it with Nicolai. But this was something different entirely. "Hello?" he shouted. "Father? Are you doing this?" Maybe his sire sought to punish him for refusing to—

The chaos of battle sounds suddenly rang clear in his head: terrible screams, bloodcurdling roars he couldn't place, the clash of steel on steel, bow-twangs and bellowed battle commands. And his blood ran cold at the realization that this was no punishment. It was a warning.

"Alvina!" he heard his father shout to his mother, "Go back, damn it!" Then there was a wrenching jolt of magic and Dayn was suddenly *inside* his father's head, seeing what he was seeing, feeling what he was feeling.

Horror and grim determination thudded in Aelfric's veins as he slashed at the creature confronting him on the narrow open staircase. He didn't know how the Blood Sorcerer had gotten his army onto the island undetected, but the castle was overrun.

Monstrous scorpion creatures filled the great hall below the curving staircase, knocking aside elite guard-soldiers with their poison-tipped tails, then slicing through their armor with razor-sharp claws. As blood splashed and men screamed and died, the king slammed a bolt of magic down the stairs, driving back the ettins that were trying to win their way up the steps to the upper level. The huge three-headed ogres stumbled back, dazed, but not for long.

Aelfric spun to charge up the stairs and found himself on his wife's heels. Which didn't surprise him, because his lovely Alvina was a fighter, fierce and powerful in both love and war. What surprised him was the panicked ache he felt at the sight of her rushing up the stone steps ahead of him, the inner whisper of, Please, gods, no. I'm not ready for this.

Worse, he saw the same emotions reflected in her eyes when she ducked into an alcove just short of their chambers and turned to him, holding out her hands for his. "We must act quickly," she whispered as the stones trembled beneath their feet with the force of the battle. "We can still save the children."

He wanted to argue, but knew in his heart that it would only waste time.

Folding his hands around hers, he moved in close and laid his cheek on her brow. "Ah, my queen. My love. I am sorry." Sorry that he had waited too long to go after the Blood Sorcerer. Sorry that he had no hope to offer. Sorry that they had so quickly gone from talking about little Micah's fifth birthday to this.

Her next breath was a sob, but she said only, "We must hurry."

He eased away, keeping hold of her hands, which trembled in his. "Tell me what to do."

"No!" Dayn shouted, pain searing through his chest as the vision dissolved. "Gods, no!" More, as the mind-speak faded he heard the distinctive buzz that said it was a memory, that what he saw had already happened. He struggled against the invisible force that held him at the center of the whirlwind, lashing at it, cursing it. "Malachai!" he shouted. "To the castle!" But there was no response, and the forest suddenly seemed very far away.

Dayn. The word was spoken inside his head, in a familiar low, rumbling voice.

"Father?" Hope burst through him. "Thank the gods. Get me out of here. I can gather the villagers and—"

It is too late. The castle has fallen, and us with it.

"Don't say that." His voice went ragged, his breathing choppy. "Hang on. Just hang on. I'll get Nicolai. If we work together—"

The spell is cast, our lifeblood gone. I don't even know how much longer I'll be able to reach you, so you must listen.

"*No!*" Dayn shook his head wildly, denying both the statement and the whisper of echoes that said his father had passed on to the psychic space between dead and alive. "Father... Mother... Gods..." He felt no shame in the sobs that tore from his throat, jumbling his words with terrible, awful guilt. "I shouldn't have lost my temper, shouldn't have ridden out. If I had been there—"

Cease! Aelfric snapped, much as he did to his men in battle.

Dayn came to attention, but his voice shook when

he said, "I await your orders." He had said the words many times before, though most often lately with resentment. Now it took on a new, sharper meaning, because he didn't know what to do next. Find Nicolai? Muster an army? A magical attack? A retreat? Never in his wildest dreams had he imagined the castle taken, his parents gone. But he couldn't waste whatever time his father had left in the in-between, so he whispered, "Speak, Father. I will do whatever you tell me."

Good, then listen well. Because of our wounds and the sorcerer's power, the spell turned warped as your mother and I cast it. The magic has sent you and your brothers and sister far away, as we intended, but it has also tied the four of you to the castle and begun a countdown. When this count enters its final four nights—and not before then—you must all return to the island, retake the castle and kill the Blood Sorcerer. If you do not, you will die and Elden will be lost. But you must wait until the time is right.

Dayn's breath rasped in his lungs; his mind spun. "How will I know?" Gods, was this really happening?

A woman will come to guide you home. The countdown begins when she arrives and ends on the fourth night. You must let her guide you, but remember: stay true to yourself and know your priorities. Promise me that.

A sob backed up in his throat. "I promise. Gods, Father—" He was cut off as the tornado suddenly accelerated with a roar. Seconds later, he was flying away from the calm center and back out toward the whipping wall of air. "No!" he howled as the wind grabbed him, latched on and flung him forward into the spin. In an instant he was moving, tumbling over and over, leaving him to shout into the roaring wind, "I'm sorry I wasn't there to help fight!"

Thunder cracked and energy detonated inside him, searing his flesh and driving the breath from his lungs. Pain consumed him, convulsed him, as his body suddenly sought to tear itself apart from the inside out. Flesh and muscle ripped; sinews snapped from one place to another and his bones *bent*. There was a sharp jolt, and agony javelined through him, so terrible that he screamed and his senses went dim for a few seconds.

Then, between one second and the next, the howling stopped and the tornado disappeared, blinking out of existence as if it had never been. He hung for a second facedown in midair, eight or ten feet above a grassy clearing surrounded by strange stone pillars. Then his weight returned and he fell.

"Son of a—" He hit hard, with a rushing *boom* of impact that made his eyes blur, his ears ring and his brain spin. Surely that explained why, as he struggled to his hands and knees, the world around him seemed too bright, the sky too pale, the trees too tall. But no head injury could explain the cold that cut through his tunic or the way he could see his breath on the air. Or why the sky was a strange color and the ringed stones and tall, thin trees didn't look like anything he'd ever seen before.

Where was he? Had the spell sent him to the High Reaches? Even farther? Gods, what if he was all the way out by the Barrens? It would take him months to get home. His father had said he needed to wait for a woman guide and a four-night countdown that started when she arrived, but impatience stirred at the thought. What if he didn't wait? What if he returned on his own?

He was a hunter, a Forestal. If anyone could make it safely through the kingdoms alone, it was him. What if—

He jolted when movement blurred in his peripheral vision, and his pulse thudded thickly in his ears as he turned, hoping to see his guide.

Instead, men emerged from the trees. One was a gangly youth in his late teens, while the other appeared to be in his third or fourth decade. They shared long-nosed, forbidding features that suggested they were related, and they wore brightly colored clothing that wasn't made of any hide or textile Dayn had ever seen before. The strange fabric crinkled like parchment when they moved, coming toward him.

Dayn dragged himself to his feet, belatedly realizing that the magic had stripped him of everything but his clothing, leaving him unarmed and wearing only the common laborer's homespun he favored. But if he was in hostile territory, that was probably for the best. He needed to lay low and keep his true identity hidden until he knew whether it was safe for him to reveal himself as a prince of Elden.

"Ho, there," the older man called. "Don't be afraid. We're here to help you." Aside to the younger man, he said, "Okay, pop quiz. What do you make of him?"

Dayn frowned. He understood the man's hard-edged, almost guttural accent, but what was a "pop quiz?"

"Well, the outfit says he's from the kingdom realm." The teen's teeth flashed. "Or maybe a human renaissance faire. But I'm going with the kingdoms. Homespun, nothing fancy, no weapons? Probably just a regular guy who stumbled into a vortex with zero clue what just happened. I say we drug him and send him home, no harm, no foul."

"I'm not sure about that. There's something in his eyes."

"You know how most of them are when they come through. Hell, half of them are so whacked from the trip that they don't need the drugs. I bet that's his deal. I mean the kingdomites don't believe in science, never mind the realms or realm travel, so it's not like he's got any point of reference to start from."

"Maybe." The older man paused at the edge of the stone ring. "You, there. What is your name, and who is your king?"

"King—" Dayn broke off as his throat closed on the knowledge that the answer wasn't "Aelfric" anymore. His older brother was the rightful king now. *Gods, Nicolai. Where are you? What has happened to us all?*

"See?" the youth said. "He doesn't remember jack shit."

"Language, youngling," the older one chided. "You've been spending too much time with the human guests again."

"Better to borrow from the humans than the kingdoms. They're backward, their magic is unpredictable and half of them are led by those foul bloodsucking parasites." The teen made a gesture near his heart, as if warding off evil.

Dayn was suddenly very glad that he'd been unable to name his king. Where was he that blood drinkers were reviled so?

Before he could figure out how to ask the question, a blur flew out of the woods and came toward the men: a gangling, puppyish creature with gray-buff fur. It wasn't until it skidded to a halt, furiously wagging its tail in greeting, that Dayn saw the pale reddish saddle and the hint of a golden stripe. He couldn't hide his flinch at that, or his gasp when the young wolfyn reared up on hind legs that became suddenly fluid as its outline stretched straight and tall and its fur shimmered all over...and then became strange, shiny blue fabric, glossy black boots and gloves and the pale oval of a boy's face.

Dayn stared, stunned. Dear gods, it was true. The wolfyn *were* shape-shifters. Did that mean that the other stories were true, too? Was this their homeland?

The child's eyes were alight with curiosity, his features a younger version of the others'. "Aw, I missed a vortex? Bummer. Where did he come from? Is he staying?"

The teen tousled the youngster's reddish-buff hair. "We're working on it. Though I'd say from his reaction just now, we can safely say he's from the kingdoms."

The older man's eyes narrowed. "Question is whether or not he's one of those murderous bloodsucking bastards or not." He and the others moved forward, stepping into the circle drawn out by the standing stones.

Dayn's heart thudded but he held his ground and willed his secondary canines deep into hiding, so not even their small bumps could be felt if the men checked his gums. Because if they figured out who and what he truly was, he wouldn't live long enough to return home.

CHAPTER ONE

Twenty years later
Human realm

REDA WESTON STALLED on the sidewalk outside the Cat Black Curiosity Shop with her hand on the latch and her stomach in knots.

The wide-eyed reflection that stared back from the tinted window wasn't anyone she recognized. Yes, the stranger had a wavy red-shot ponytail the same as hers, and she was wearing the ratty jeans and beat-up leather jacket Reda had pulled out of her closet that morning because there was no reason for her to dress like a cop these days. And yeah, those were her deep blue eyes at the back of the dark hollows that had taken up permanent residence. But if that was her, what the hell was she doing?

Normally, she wouldn't go anywhere near the kitschy magic, witchcraft and whatnot shops that lined the Salem waterfront unless someone called 9-1-1...but then again, normal circumstances had hit the bricks six weeks earlier. And she *had* asked MacEvoy, the owner of Cat Black, to find the book for her.

"It's here," his phone message had said. "And if you liked the picture you bought, you're going to *love* the rest of it."

Like it? Heck, she'd spent the past four days staring at the framed woodcutting of a dark, eerie forest of gnarled and twisted trees, with just a hint of eyes in the shadows. More, she had dreamed about the image... and others like it.

A clatter startled her and she flinched for the weapon she wasn't carrying, then winced when she saw that the noise had come from the shaking of her hand on the door latch. Worse, she didn't know how long she had been standing there.

"Don't be surprised if you have sleep disturbances, panic attacks, behavioral changes, even compulsions," the department shrink had told her. And yeah, she'd had all of the above...except for the last one. This was her first full-blown compulsion. Or rather, the strange urge that practically dragged her into the creepy-ass store earlier in the week had been the first. This was her second. And it was much stronger.

It's not the same book, she told herself. *It's just another copy.* Except that her *maman* had said it was one of a kind. *You're just transferring, trying to solve something that's solvable because you know the real stuff isn't.* That was the practical part of her talking, her father's daughter. And suddenly she saw the major in the shape of the blue eyes that stared back at her, and in the ramrod posture that made her look taller than her true five-six. Inwardly, though, her mother's voice whispered, *At least take a look. What have you got to lose?*

"My sanity," she muttered under her breath, ignoring the ache that fisted beneath her heart. She hesitated another moment, then shook her head and pushed through the door, causing a distant bell to ring in the back of the cluttered shop.

As before, the place smelled disconcertingly like foot powder—gritty talc with a cloying perfumed undertone that made her think of funerals. Display racks near the door held the usual suspects: artsy postcards, books on the witch trials, copies of *The House of the Seven Gables* and such. But the racks themselves were made of wood rather than the usual cheesy wire, and the sides were carved with strange, sinuous curves and the hint of scales and teeth. The walls were painted black, with greenish-white accents she bet glowed in the dark when MacEvoy turned off the lights. It would make the perfect backdrop for him to pull out the three-foot-high grim reaper statue that was locked in a glass case behind the register at the back of the store, and which she'd bet a hundred bucks converted, Transformerlike, into a giant bong.

Yeah. This was so not her scene. She should just leave.

"Miss Weston!" MacEvoy came through an employees-only door with his hands outstretched and his red-rimmed eyes holding an expression of pleasure that might or might not be faked.

A middle-size, middle-age grasshopper of a man, he was all arms and angles inside a faded black suit that made him look like a Victorian mortician and, she suspected, had come from the clearance rack at Cosby's Costumes a few doors down.

Don't be bitchy, she told herself as she shook his hand and returned his greeting. *It's not like he came looking for you.* And it wasn't his fault she felt totally out of place. The problem wasn't with the location, or with him.

"Right this way." He headed to the register area,

where a wood-and-glass case held a collection of impressively ugly silver-and-moonstone jewelry, along with a sterling frog whose garnet eyes seemed to follow Reda when she moved. But that was just her imagination.

Right?

Holding back a shiver, she reminded herself that she didn't believe in magic, that this was all just a put-on for the tourists. If the atmosphere was working on her, it meant that MacEvoy was better at his shtick than she would've thought.

Disappearing behind the case, he rummaged around for a moment, then made a satisfied noise. When he straightened, he was holding a black, metal-edged cardboard clamshell box that was marked Acid-Free Archival Storage on the spine.

Reda's mental cash register went *cha-ching* and she wondered whether she should do a "thanks, but I've changed my mind," and have another session with the shrink instead. *Certainly be cheaper.* Or she could go home and fill out the paperwork on her desk—applications to the forensic-science programs at Colby and New Haven. That wasn't the same as saying she was wimping out. It was just exploring options.

But those practical thoughts exited stage left the second MacEvoy set the box on the counter and flipped it open…and a skim of heat washed through her, followed by a prickle of gooseflesh that made her feel suddenly awake, though she hadn't been aware of being sleepy.

The shopkeeper grinned. "You like it?"

"Oh, yes," she breathed. "Yes, I do." Because it wasn't just any book. It was *the* book. It had to be.

The cover was intricately carved with another forest scene, this one with an achingly lovely girl front and center, running along a narrow path. She was wearing a long, flowing cloak over a peasant dress, and was looking back over her shoulder with an expression of mingled terror and excitement. There were no authors' names, just a title that stood up a little taller than the rest of the carving. *Rutakoppchen.*

"Red Riding Hood," she whispered, hearing the words in her mother's voice. *Not just one of a kind,* her *maman* had said on that long-ago birthday, *but yours alone. It was sent to me, darling, to give to you when the time is right.*

MacEvoy looked surprised. "You speak the language? The paperwork says it's some obscure Western European dialect, and doesn't make any promises on the translation."

"I don't need a translation." She already knew the story by heart. Pulse thrumming, she reached for the book.

The shopkeeper hooked the box with a spindly finger and tugged it back an inch. "You going to buy it?"

Her plastic was on the counter before she was even aware of having made the decision. More, she didn't yank it back when MacEvoy two-fingered it, even though her smarter self was inwardly screeching that they hadn't talked price.

She didn't care. She had to have it, regardless of whether it was really the same one or not, really one of a kind. Not because of the strange, fragmentary dreams she'd been having every night since she brought home the print—*a circle of stones like Stonehenge only not, a sense of pounding urgency, a flash of green eyes that brought heat and left her to wake up alone and aching*—but because it was a missing part of her past. And if that was transference, she didn't give a crap right now.

As he swiped her card, she brushed her fingertips across the carved wood, and got a jolt of strange excitement. Nerves jangled and her smarter self asked what the hell was going on here, why was she acting like this?

"Is it true that the wolf doesn't just eat Red in this version?" MacEvoy asked as he waited for the slip to print. He glanced over at her, getting a gleam in his red-rimmed eyes. "The paperwork said that he seduces her first, enslaves her, plays with her until he gets bored… and *then* he eats her."

"Something like that," she said. She was dying to page through, but didn't want to do it in front of him, though she didn't know why, just as she couldn't explain the sudden pounding of her heart and faint clamminess of her hands, or the liquid churn low in her belly. All she knew for sure was that her hands were shaking as she scrawled on the slip, and then flipped the clamshell shut and tucked it under her arm. "Thanks. See you around." *Or not.*

"Wait," he said as she headed for the exit. "I wanted to ask you… Aren't you that cop? The one—"

She put her head down, clutched the box and bee-lined it out of the shop.

The short walk to her apartment on the outskirts of the "cool" district where the old houses were still getting restored seemed to take forever, especially when two of her neighbors pretended they didn't see her. Guilt stung, but Reda told herself—as the shrink had told her—that they weren't acting that way because they thought she was to blame for her partner's death in a liquor-store robbery gone bad. Like most of her friends and family, they just didn't know what to say anymore, given that Benz had been dead for months now, and she was still ghosting around looking as if her best friend had died.

Except that he had. And it was her fault. Not because she'd done anything wrong, but because she hadn't done *anything.* She had frozen. Just stood there while a strung-out meth head looking at his third strike opened fire.

The news reports had said she was lucky to get away. The other cops hadn't said anything, really. Just like her neighbors didn't now as she hurried past them. But for a change the uneven thudding of her heart didn't have anything to do with the sidelong looks and whispers, or the knowledge that her father and brothers had been right when they said she wasn't the save-the-world type. Instead, it was the heavy weight of the box she held clutched to her chest, gripping it so tightly her fingers had gone numb.

She was breathing so fast she was practically light-headed by the time she let herself into her small, homey apartment. Not even pausing to shuck out of her leather jacket, she dumped her purse near the door and crossed to the narrow galley kitchen. The hollow sound the box made on the butcher-block counter reminded her that she hadn't looked at the credit-card slip, didn't know how much she had dropped on the thing. Didn't care.

"So open it," she told herself, the words sounding far too loud on air that had gone still around her, like the world was holding its breath. Or maybe—probably—

that was just her. She was turning this into a way bigger deal than it needed to be.

Still, her fingers trembled as she flipped open the box, then reached in and touched the wooden cover. She told herself the faint tingle was her imagination, just as the hot dreams she'd been having the past few nights had been nothing more than memories of her girlish rescue fantasies with the temperature turned up by her adult experiences.

She traced the raised lettering. *Rutakoppchen.* A version of Red Riding Hood with the wolf as both sinner and seducer, the woodsman as the hero who saves the girl and takes her away from her old life to a new, better one. Seeing the book, touching it, made her mother feel closer than she had in years. Even if it turned out to be just a copy, it was worth whatever she had paid.

But she had to know, so she opened it. The cover creaked like an unoiled door, her throat became suddenly parched and tight…and then her eyes filled at the sight of a blank page with two lines of elegant script right in the center, done in blue ink that had faded over the past two decades.

To my sweet Alfreda on her eighth birthday, with the rest of the story to come when you turn sixteen.

—Your *maman*

Reda's heart *thudda-thudded* in her chest as she brushed her fingers across the last word. *Maman.* Her older brothers had teased her about putting on airs, calling her "princess" and poking at her because there was nothing remotely royal about any of them. They were army brats and proud of it.

You'll never get anywhere by looking backward. The major's voice suddenly came so clear he might have been standing right behind her. Which he wasn't; he was overseas. It was just that the words were such a familiar refrain: *eyes up and ahead; one foot in front of the other; look ahead, not back.* Words to live by.

"You're right," she said softly. "I know you're right." She should put the book back in its box and set it aside, maybe even lock it in the fireproof safe where she kept her unused passport. She should take comfort in knowing she had a cherished memory back, and then focus on more important things—like filling out those applications.

But she turned the page anyway, unable not to glance at a picture of the young, innocent girl with her hamper. Then one of a huge wolf—her *maman* had called it a wolfyn—stalking her along the pathway and watching with too-human eyes as she entered her grandmother's cabin, only to find it empty. The next few pages showed the wolfyn and girl together, the story relying on the text more than pictures. But then the huge beast morphed to a shaggy-haired man with hot, feral eyes, and the girl looked up at him, face bright and excited, like she was looking at a handsome prince, not a leering wolfyn. But now Reda saw something she hadn't before: the girl looked disconnected, and she was almost smiling past the wolfyn, not at him.

Reda's stomach dipped. She had seen that look on the faces of roofie victims.

She skimmed the next few panels, realizing that her *maman* must have skipped some pages. Or had she seen the pictures as a child and not really realized what they meant? Because now, looking at them with an adult's perspective—and that of a cop who had worked rape cases, though mercifully far fewer than would be the norm in a larger, grittier city—the girl's vacant, glassy expression and rag-doll compliance to the wolfyn's G-rated yet highly suggestive demands smacked of drugs or brainwashing. Or both.

She hadn't been seduced. She had been compelled.

Reda shuddered. "That's not really the way I remembered this part." But then again, most fairy tales had started out dark and bloody, rarely reaching mainstream puppies-and-kittens territory until Disney got hold of them.

Something buzzed in the back of her brain, like a trapped bumblebee of a thought that wouldn't land long enough for her to catch its meaning.

"Poor girl," she murmured, touching an image of the young woman lying heavy-lidded near the hearth of the cottage, where a fire burned low. The wolfyn was halfway between his two forms, looking out a window with the fur at his nape erect as if searching the shadows for danger. It was hard to tell if he was protecting her or holding her captive. Probably both, depending on who you asked.

Reda found herself getting far too caught up in feeling sick for a two-dimensional character who had suddenly become a stand-in for too many of the victims she had worked with. She was so wrapped up in that theme, in fact, that when she turned the next page and saw the woodsman looking up at her from the page, she simply stared for a few heartbeats.

Then she whispered, "There you are." Which was

ridiculous because, just like the girl, the woodsman wasn't anything more than a picture in a storybook.

Only he was more than that. He was the hero.

Standing in the cabin doorway with a long-handled ax held across his body, he should have looked like a lumberjack stereotype. Instead, he looked strangely out of place, as if a knight errant had been dropped into this story from another. His forearms, bared by rolled-up sleeves, were corded with a tension that carried from his taut-knuckled grip on the ax handle throughout the rest of his big, rangy body and up to his face, which was etched with disgust and determination as he took in the scene within the cabin.

Reda's perceptions tunneled down to the tousle of dark hair atop his noble brow and wide cheekbones, his narrow-bridged, aristocratic nose, full lips and square jaw, and his eyes...dear God, his eyes. They stared out of the page and cut right into her, seeming alive even though it was just an illustration, and a black-and-white one at that.

She knew those eyes, though. "Green," she whispered, suddenly yearning in a way that made no sense, for a man who didn't really exist. "His eyes are green."

Help him. The thought came in a voice that sounded like her own breathing turned into words that weren't hers.

A shudder coursed through her body.

"Great, now you're imagining things while you're wide awake," she said aloud, trying to use the words to chase away the sudden crackle that laced the air.

It didn't work. The air stayed heavy and thunder rumbled, hollowing the space beneath her diaphragm and stealing her breath.

This time it was the whistle of the rising wind outside that said, *Help him. Save him.*

Her heart stuttered when she looked out her apartment window and saw that the sky was as clear and bright as it had been when she left MacEvoy's shop. Yet thunder rumbled again, vibrating through the soles of her boots and up through her body, making her feel suddenly empty and alone.

He is alone, too. Help him. It was the sound of wind, yet the neighborhood trees weren't moving and the light, fluffy clouds hung motionless in the sky.

A whimper lodged itself in her throat, the weak noise unuttered, but the panic that spawned it remained, bringing a memory so deeply buried that she didn't remember even having it until it was right there, full-blown in her mind.

"So what do you think—is she nuts?" her father asked the doctor. She could see them both from the waiting room through the partly open office door, could hear them clearly, though their voices were hushed.

"We don't use labels like that," the stern-faced doctor said, but that made her father nod as if he'd gotten the answer he expected. The doctor sighed. "Look. The mind has a sort of framework it uses to deal with trauma and loss, a way of rationalizing how it happened, why and what it means. In this case, Reda's mind has chosen an atypical framework, one where she believes that her mother is not dead, but rather trapped in a land of magic beyond our own. Things like this can happen following the loss of a parent, especially in children her age. Usually it goes away on its own."

"How long?"

"Months, sometimes longer. In the meantime, it's basically harmless."

"You call sleepwalking out the back door and into the woods 'harmless'? What if she got lost? Or, worse, got found by the wrong sort of person?" The major's voice gained volume at the end, but then he glanced out at her and lowered his voice once more to say, "Help me out here, Doc. I need this to stop. The boys need it to stop. We all need to move on."

The doctor didn't say anything, and Reda's heart went bumpity-bump *at the thought that he was going to tell the major that she was right, the kingdoms really did exist, and that sometimes visitors accidentally fell through the gates connecting the realms. Suddenly excited, she leaned forward in her chair.*

"There are a few things we could try," the doctor said finally. "The first thing I would recommend is getting rid of the book."

The memory wavered and disintegrated, but the heartache remained, along with Reda's dull surprise at remembering how it had happened. Not because the major had tried to pretend otherwise, but because the months of therapy that followed had trained her not to think about the book, magic or monsters.

Or, really, even her mother.

The police shrink had wanted to talk about her mother's death, of course, but Reda had just shrugged and said, "It was a long time ago." And it would have stayed that way…if she hadn't found the book. Or rather, if it hadn't found her.

Thunder rumbled, closer now, though the sun still shone. Unbidden, her eyes went to the picture of the woodsman standing in the doorway, staring up out of the page at her and making her yearn. "Repressed memories," she said softly. "That's what this is all about, isn't it?"

Benz's death had put a crack in the dam, and the strange, cosmic coincidence of her seeing the wood-cutting in MacEvoy's shop had washed out its base of support, meaning that now the entire construct was poised to come crashing down on her. Oddly, considering how much she used to pride herself on control and self-discipline, she didn't really mind. Since the shooting she had felt like she was running in place, or maybe hunkered down inside herself, waiting for something. And this was it.

Or was it? What if this was all just happening in her head? What then?

The rational, logical part of her said to call the shrink and have herself checked in somewhere. Instead, reaching out with a hand that suddenly didn't shake at all, she touched the page, resting her fingers on the wood-cutter's chest.

It didn't take any effort now to remember the magic words her *maman* had taught her. The two of them used to sit on a mossy bank down by the duck pond, cross-legged, knees touching. "Concentrate," her *maman* would say, over and over again, though somehow it never seemed like a lecture, never like work. "Close your eyes, visualize the doorway and say the spell, and when you open your eyes again you'll find yourself where you were meant to be."

The words weren't magic, of course, wouldn't conjure some strange passageway to a magical realm. But they were exactly what her mind needed in order to wash away the dam once and for all.

So she thought, *What the hell?* And she said the words.

Crack! Lightning split the air around her and incredibly, impossibly, wind whipped past her, around her, though she was standing inside her apartment. Panic lashed through her and she froze, paralyzed by the fear. Her heart hammered in her ears, but that inner pulsation was the only movement she could manage.

She tried to call for help but couldn't, tried to tear her eyes from the book but couldn't do that, either. She was snapping, losing it. She screamed but made no sound, fought but didn't move. The woodcutter's eyes grew larger and larger in her vision, until she saw nothing but the inky-black, heard nothing but the wind, and felt...

Nothing.

Kingdom realm

Moragh snapped out of her trance as the divination was interrupted by magic of another kind—a blood-linked power the likes of which she hadn't sensed in many years.

"The prince!" she hissed, excitement firing in her veins as she recognized the signal's source. Finally— *finally*—after all this time she could feel the spell that had snatched her prey from her. More, she could follow it. Even after the first flare of power leveled off, the connection remained inside her, throbbing like a heartbeat. One that said, *This way. I can lead you to him.*

The spell had reactivated. Thank the dark lords.

Her lips curved in a smile that the ornate, gilt-edged divination mirror showed as feral, with a hint of fang gleaming from behind the lips of a coolly gorgeous brunette in her forties. She had survived the Blood Sorcerer's wrath over her failure to kill Prince Dayn the first time, and had eventually won her way back into his graces. But she hadn't ever escaped the failure. And now… "Redemption," she said, the word echoing off the cool stone walls of the castle's upper reaches.

Over near the hearth, her servant, Nasri, looked up from his mopping. The old, crooked-fingered gnome— who now had only seven of those crooked fingers, having recently been caught filching a meat pie he'd had plenty of coin to buy—was cleaning last night's bloodstains up off the stonework. The water in his bucket was dark, the gray mop gory. "Mistress?"

"Send word to the bestiary. I want the largest two ettins ready to hunt in an hour." The three-headed giants were pure rage wrapped up with hunger, killing machines that need only be pointed toward their target. "And have the beast master reinforce their collars and control spells. I'll be handling them myself, with you along to help tend them."

He cringed and whined low in his throat. "Wouldn't you rather—"

"Go," she snapped with enough force to have him squealing and bolting out the door. When he was gone, she smiled again into the warped mirror. "By my life and blood, I'll get him this time."

She had missed before. She wouldn't miss again.

CHAPTER TWO

Wolfyn realm

As THE BLOOD MOON EDGED over the dark tree line, a perfect blue-white circle visible through the windowed wall of the big bedroom, Dayn did up the last button of his plaid shirt and shrugged into his fleece-lined bomber jacket.

"You could stay, you know. Be here when I get back."

He glanced over. A cut-glass lamp shone from the bedside table—a Tiffany knockoff that had been imported from the human realm and converted to run off the quasi-magical energy that powered the wolfyn's gadgets. The pale glow lit the room's earthy brown walls and finely carved furniture, both of which were subtly worked with the Scratch-Eye pack's sigil: four parallel bloodred slashes crossing an amber wolf's eye. The bed was piled with luxurious crimson-dyed furs, but the room's true centerpiece was Keely. The pack's alpha bitch lay stretched, sinuous and satisfied, her scent musky with arousal and the magic of the blood moon. Graced with the toned body of a huntress and the ruddy hair of a bitch in her prime, she was unmated and independent, just like him.

Except that she was nothing like him. Not really.

They met and mated this one night each year, when sex sparked the strongest of changes and the wolfyn stayed largely in wolf form for the next three days, running together, renewing their magic and making or breaking new alliances. She didn't dare mate with a male of her kind during the blood moon lest he claim the Right of Challenge for the pack leadership, which had gone to her brother, Kenar, rather than down through her as was traditional. So, as the Scratch-Eye pack's "guest"—that was the name given to the few accidental realm travelers who by some quirk of the vortex magic couldn't return home through the standing stones—Dayn had become Keely's choice. She had laid it out with the blunt practicality of a wolfyn: sex once a year, nothing more or less. Which worked just fine for him for a number of reasons.

Their relationship might have begun as a transaction, but over time it had mellowed to friendship. Or what did the humans call it? Friends with benefits. But, friends or not, he didn't tell her that he was almost certain this had been the last time. He didn't dare. Instead, he said, "Thanks but no thanks on the staying over. And you wouldn't have asked if you didn't know that would be my answer."

"You understand me too well. So…same time next year?"

"Of course," he said, and then added, as he always did, "unless you're mated by then."

Her eyes flashed. "Kenar is a good alpha."

That was debatable, but Dayn wasn't going to get Keely or any of the other pack members to admit that their alpha was more interested in himself than the pack or its traditions. Or that it had been wrong for him to

twist those traditions around in order to run off the
male Keely's father had brought in from an outside pack
to be her mate and his successor. Granted, the male—
Roloff—shouldn't have left. But that didn't make Kenar
right.

Since there was no point in picking the fight,
though—"been there, done that" was a particularly apt
human saying in this case—he blew her a kiss. "Until
next year, then." Which was a lie, but a necessary one.
In the entire wolfyn realm, only the pack's wisewolfyn,
Candida, knew who and what he truly was, and that it
was almost time for him to go home.

"Of course," Keely agreed. "That is, unless *you* find
a mate between now and then."

He had his hand on the door, but looked back, surprised. "Me? No. Not in the cards."

"The Stone-Turn pack's new guest is pretty."

"I'm not interested in taking a mate." Besides, the
newcomer wasn't the woman he was waiting for, the
one he'd been dreaming of more clearly every night
over the past week, waking each morning with the
image of a heart-shaped face, dimpled chin and go-
to-hell attitude topped with curly, red-streaked hair.
Hurry, he wanted to tell her. *Please, hurry.*

Keely looked at him quizzically. "If that's not it, then
what's bothering you?" To the wolfyn, problems always
boiled down to politics or family. Since he wasn't involved in pack politics, that left family—or, in his case,
his lack of one.

"I'm fine. I promise." Sketching a half salute in her
direction, he said softly, "Have a good run." Already,
he could see the amber fire at the back of her eyes. And,
as he let himself out of her place, he could feel the hum

of change magic on the air. It crinkled along his skin, stirring the restlessness that had been riding him harder and harder as the days passed and there was no sign of his guide. Frustration gnawed at him, making him feel itchy, twitchy. He wanted to race through the darkness, pick a fight, howl at the moon....

Instead, he headed for the small log cabin he'd built near the standing stones, zipping his jacket and shoving his hands in his pockets as he hiked along the two-mile path. The blood moon lit the night with the eerie blue-white light that was almost as bright as day, though monochromatic. By the time his cabin came into view, the air already carried a chorus of excited yips and deeper, spine-shivering howls.

His cabin, little more than a single long room with a central chimney and big hearth, was laughably rustic as far as the pack members were concerned. He had used human-style insulated windows, though, and had a wolfyn-tech generator for power. He had left the lights off tonight, though, and the moonlight that bathed the cabin lit it blue-white, making it seem like it was...

Oh, shit. Glowing. Dayn's pulse kicked, because he knew from past experience that it wasn't the cabin doing the glowing. There was a vortex forming in the standing stones!

He took off at a run. As he came around the corner, thunder rumbled, vibrating up through the soles of his boots even though the sky was clear. He nearly cheered at the sight of blue-white lightning sparking among the standing stones. The electricity lit the air, charging the ozone and making his hair bristle as if he, too, were going through the change.

Magic surrounded him as he charged up the hill, suffusing him and running fox fire glows along his skin when he came to a halt just outside the circle. Electricity arced from one stone to the next and the next, lighting the entire circle with blue-white power. Then, suddenly, the grass and empty air within the circle grew blurry and started to move, making a slow inward spiral at first, but then spinning faster and faster, tightening within seconds to a gray tornado of everything and nothing.

Magic tugged at him, beckoning. *Come,* the vortex seemed to be saying. *Say the words and come.*

Dayn hesitated, though. The vortices had never worked for him before, even with the spell that should return him home to Elden. But what if it was finally time? Maybe his guide wasn't supposed to come to him, but rather the reverse. *Please, gods.*

Thunder boomed and magic churned as he pictured the forest he had been snatched from and said the spell. Then, braced for anything, he stepped into the stone circle.

The wind surrounded him instantly, grabbing him up and tumbling him head over ass in a whirling maelstrom of power. Excitement seared through him. It was working! Thunder roared and lightning arced and snapped, and the universe seemed to hold its breath for an instant. In that moment, he glimpsed a modern, human-style kitchen and jolted with dismay. *No, not the human realm. Take me to Elden!*

Even as he thought that, pain flared behind his eyes, lashing through his skull…and everything winked out.

For a second, there was only darkness. Stillness. Silence. He couldn't even hear his own heartbeat.

Then everything jolted back into existence around

him, and there was blue-white light in his eyes and the springy press of grass-covered earth beneath him. He blinked into the light, gut fisting on disappointment as things came into focus and he recognized the full moon pouring down on the familiar ring of standing stones.

"Son of a bitch." He hadn't gone anywhere, after all. He was still in the wolfyn realm. "Son of a sucking—"

A soft moan cut him off. A soft, very feminine moan.

His heart started to *thud* in his chest as he turned toward the sound, telling himself not to hope, but hoping nonetheless.

And there she was. After all this time, there she was.

She lay curled on the grass with her cheek pillowed on her hands, but he recognized the oval of her face, the stubborn dent in her chin and the strong yet subtly curved lines of her body. More, he knew without seeing it in the light of day that her wavy hair was red-shot, her eyes a clear blue, like the deepest part of the Elden sky after a rainstorm. Not that it mattered whether or not she was beautiful—she was his guide, and he had his priorities well in mind.

Her clothes said she was human, which surprised him. Of the three known realms, the human realm was the most technologically advanced and used the least magic, which put them the farthest away from the pure magic of the kingdoms. Given that, how was she supposed to guide him?

Have faith, he told himself. His father had promised a guide, and here she was.

Which also meant that the four-night countdown had begun, and they needed to get moving. But there was a problem with that: she was out cold, and the Scratch-

Eye pack was gathering for their run, which would include an hour-long serenade at the stones. Although the wolfyn were largely civilized on a day-to-day basis—in their home realm, at least—the blood moon unleashed the other aspects of their personalities. And while Keely probably wouldn't have a problem seeing him with another woman during the blood moon, others wouldn't be so forgiving.

Making a snap decision, though he would have rather stayed and called a new vortex right away, Dayn gathered the woman in his arms. She was lighter-boned and smaller than Keely, and seemed to fit naturally against him as he carried her from the circle, with her head tucked against his neck and her curly hair brushing his cheek.

Inside his cabin, he put her gently on the couch near the hearth, where the remains of the fire were still warm. Then he shucked out of his too-hot jacket and knelt beside her, part of him still unable to believe that he had dreamed of her, and here she was. His eyes lingered on the fullness of her lips, and the faint blush of color on her cheeks. He reached for her, intending to try again to wake her, but instead he found himself easing a few fallen strands of her hair away from where they had caught on her eyelashes. Her skin was soft and warm, and although he told himself he shouldn't be touching her, not like this, he couldn't make himself pull away.

She stirred beneath his touch, and let out a soft sigh. He caught his breath, then held it as her eyes opened and locked on his. The entire universe telescoped down to those blue, blue eyes and her look of shock…and then recognition.

THE WOODSMAN SMILED down at her. "Thank the gods you're finally here."

Reda stared mutely up at him as her head spun and the world tilted a few degrees away from normal.

It was the same dream she'd been having all week, where she would wake in a log cabin to find this man crouched over her while a fire *hiss-popped* nearby. He looked like she had dreamed him: rumpled dark hair fell forward over his brow and curled below his ears, accenting his sharply defined features and emerald-green eyes. He had a rawboned yet powerful body, wide-shouldered and long-limbed, with lean, loose muscles that folded economically where he knelt beside her. His skin was smooth and bronze, with a light dusting of masculine hair visible where the top two buttons of his shirt were undone. And, as in her dreams, the air smelled of wood, smoke and cinnamon. Fluid warmth coursed through her body, concentrating at the point where his fingers rested softly on her cheek.

But as the spins settled, nerves took their place... because the overall picture was right, but the details were wrong.

The cabin was made of rough-hewn logs, yes, but she was lying on a plush sofa rather than a cot, and on a nearby end table, a mosaic lamp gave off muted amber light. And the man was wearing clothes straight out of the L.L. Bean catalog rather than homespun. More, even the details of the details were off. The couch she was lying on had the soft nap of velvet, but the fabric moved oddly, as did the stuffing beneath. And the lamp didn't have a cord.

What the hell?

"I'm going to kill MacEvoy." The idiot must've

juiced the shop's incense burner with something really funky and hallucinogenic.

Like, say, acid.

"Who is MacEvoy?" The woodsman's voice was a smooth baritone with a raspy undertone that seemed to stroke her skin. But the question put another dose of nerves into the mix, as did the look in his eyes as he rocked back on his heels and stared down at her with a wary, confused air.

He'd never spoken before, never looked baffled before.

They were way off the script, and she didn't like it.

"He's… It doesn't matter." She pushed herself upright on the couch, waving him off when he made a move to help. "I'm good. I'm fine." Only she wasn't fine. This was all wrong, because whatever the hell was going on, the dream—hallucination?—seemed way too real.

"Fine enough to get moving?"

"Moving?"

He nodded. "We have four nights counting tonight, so we should get started as soon as possible."

Reda breathed deeply and told herself not to panic. There was some logical explanation for this. There had to be. "I'm not having sex with you." And oh, holy crap, she didn't know why that had been the first thing out of her mouth. Or, rather, she did: it was because of the dreams.

His eyebrows rose. "Of course not. You're my guide."

She flushed, but pushed on. "Seriously. I don't have a clue what you're talking about." And she also didn't know why she was arguing with a figment of her over-stressed mind.

"Don't even joke about that."

"Who's joking?" She wasn't kidding around; she was confused as all hell. "Wait. Am I being punked?" Who would bother?

Expression suddenly clearing, he said, "Damnation. Vortex sickness."

"Vor-what?"

He rose and started to pace. "Sometimes when travelers come through the vortices from one realm to another, they become confused or even forget pieces of their past."

A low burn fisted beneath her heart. "I'm not crazy."

"I didn't say you were," he said, which she guessed was true as far as it went. But then he continued, "Memory loss and insanity aren't the same thing. I believe you call it 'apples and limes,' yes?"

"Oranges. Apples and oranges." His speech pattern was an odd mix of formality and slang, which just added to the weirdness. "Who *are* you?"

He stopped pacing and looked slightly shamefaced. "Sorry. I'm Dayn. Well, Prince Dayn, Forestal of Elden. But if anyone here knew that, they'd rip me to shreds." He said it so matter-of-factly that it took a moment to register. As her jaw dropped, he held out a hand. "So let's just go with 'Dayn,' okay?"

"I'm Reda." Head spinning, she took his hand on autopilot, registering the warm strength of his wide palm and long, elegant fingers. But instead of shaking, he lifted her hand to his lips and brushed a kiss over her knuckles. It was an unselfconscious move, as if he'd done it a thousand times before and it meant nothing

more than a fist bump on the T platform or a cuff on
the arm between buddies at Downtown Pizza. But her
gasp brought his eyes to hers and made it far more than
casual, as did the sizzle that tightened her skin and reminded her that this was a dream. More, it was her fantasy. *He* was her fantasy, had been since she was a little
girl and dreamed of someone coming to her rescue.

He dropped her hand and took a big step back. "I'm
sorry. I shouldn't have done that."

Why not? It's my fantasy. But he wasn't playing his
part. He should have been whispering sweetly to her,
kissing her, stroking—

The cabin door blew open with a bang, making her
jolt as a cold gust of wind puffed ashes into the hearth
and swirled smoke into the air. But that wasn't what
had opened the door. Because as Dayn spun toward the
commotion, a huge figure darkened the doorway. Reda
shot to her feet. Then she froze and a three-headed giant
stepped through.

So tall that it had to duck through the door, the monstrous creature had the body of a man, huge and muscular, but its skin was cement-gray and its broad shoulders
supported three ogre-faced heads with protruding lower
jaws, curved upthrusting teeth and fierce black eyes
framing moist, snubbed noses. The thing was dressed
in a leathery loincloth, boots the size of mailboxes and
studded wristbands and neck collars, and it carried a
huge, blunt-headed club that was ringed with spikes
and banded with iron. When it caught sight of her and
Dayn, all three faces grinned horribly.

Dayn lunged for a rack of weapons her mind had
initially dismissed as decor, grabbed a crossbow and
yelled, "Run!"

The middle head locked on him while the other two stayed leering at her. Which made it tough to figure out who was the target as the creature bellowed a roar, drew back and swung its enormous club of death.

"Down!" Dayn plowed into her. They slammed against the back of the sofa, which overbalanced and fell, taking them with it.

The club screamed over their heads and crashed into the chimney above the hearth, sending chunks of brick spattering around the room. Nearly flattened beneath Dayn—he might be rangy, but he was *solid*—Reda struggled to breathe through the white-hot grip of panic. *This isn't happening, can't be happening. It's just a dream, not real, none of this is real.*

Heavy footsteps thudded as the creature came toward them, growling low in its three-way throat.

Not real. A dream. I'm waking up now. On the count of three, I'm going to open my eyes and everything will be back to normal.

"Stay down," Dayn whispered in her ear, shifting as the monster stumped nearer, shoving furniture and knocking things crashing to the floor.

One.

Three heads came into view, six eyes locked on and the creature roared, reared back and swung. Dayn shouted something, lunged to his feet and fired his crossbow from the hip. The bolt buried itself at the top of the giant's middle throat.

Shaking, Reda flattened herself. She couldn't breathe, couldn't think, couldn't do anything but count.

Two.

The monster screeched, tossed the club, grabbed for its blood-spurting throat and reeled back. The club smashed into a window and hung up on the frame as Dayn fired a second bolt into the same head, turning the creature's roar into a high-pitched mewl that grated on her soul.

Please, God. Three.

CHAPTER THREE

REDA DIDN'T WAKE UP.

Instead, she watched in frozen horror as the three-headed giant staggered and went to its knees, and Dayn methodically fired bolts into the other two heads. As if that had finally hit the kill switch, the creature plummeted to the cabin floor, where it lay for a moment, twitching in its death throes, and then finally going still.

The sudden silence rang in her ears as she stared at the monstrous corpse, which smelled like chicken breasts gone very bad.

She yanked her eyes to Dayn, who stood looking down at the creature with an expression of pity, but also excitement, as if the attack had been partly a good thing.

Who was he? What in God's name was going on? She wanted to ask him but couldn't get out the words. She was locked in place. Frozen. Once and always a coward under fire. Was this, then, what her subconscious wanted her to see?

Maybe. But she'd seen it and the dream wasn't ending.

"You can get up now." He said it without looking at her, but she thought she saw the twitch of a smile.

"There's a bag in the pantry. How about you load up some provisions while I take care of the other stuff?"

As he turned away, she slowly levered herself to her feet, suddenly wishing that a herd of pink elephants would walk past the broken window, so she could point at them and say, *Ha, I told you so. It's a dream.* Hallucination. Whatever. What mattered was that this wasn't really happening. It was all in her mind.

Except there weren't any pink elephants. Which left her with a stinky dead giant with two too many heads, and a really hot guy who thought they were going somewhere.

MacEvoy, when I get through with you, you'd wish you just mailed me the damn book for free, she thought. And then, because she couldn't think of a good reason not to, she went to pack some food.

The bag proved to be a single-strap rucksack, and the provisions at hand were heavy on the hard rolls, dried protein—she didn't ask, didn't want to know—and trail mix. She loaded up whatever she sort of recognized, trying to focus on the similarities rather than cataloging the differences. Her brain, though, kept a running tally that twisted the knots in her stomach increasingly tight.

And all the while, she was entirely aware of Dayn as he pulled on a sweater followed by his heavy leather coat, loaded a rucksack with his crossbow and bolts and strapped on a narrow leather belt that held an unusually short sword on one side, pouches on the other. As she finished up her packing, he slung a sloshing crescent-shaped leather pouch over his shoulder, glanced over at her and nodded.

He didn't seem to expect a reply, though, because

his attention moved on to the overturned couch and smashed end table, the broken window and the scattered other things that defined a life: a journal bound in what looked like nylon but wasn't, a bunch of interesting rocks in a jar, a huge antler with a picture of a beautiful stallion carved into it, only half-finished. And while he looked at the room, she was looking at him. Decked out in a strange mix of modern clothing and archaic equipment, he should have looked as if he was late for Halloween. Instead, he appeared utterly comfortable in his own skin and—as evidenced by the giant's corpse—deadly capable. She couldn't take her eyes off him.

He turned abruptly toward the door. "Let's go."

She held her ground. "Go where?" They were the first two words she had managed to utter since the attack. Her mind might be racing but her body was still mostly vapor locked. That was the way it worked when she went into curl-up-and-die mode.

He tipped his head toward the dead creature. "That was an ettin, which isn't native to this realm. It had to have come from the kingdoms, which means the vortex has probably opened back up. And that means we need to go. Now."

Vortex? Realms? How could he stand there wearing a crossbow and sword and talk about things that belonged in science fiction? It didn't make any sense.

Of course not, her rational self said. *It's a dream, or a hallucination or something. But since counting to three didn't work, maybe this vortex will.*

So she nodded and followed him out of the cabin, her boots crunching on broken glass and then echoing on the short steps leading down.

"This way," he said, urging her along a wide path. His breath fogged the air. "If we can get back through the stones— Shit." His face fell. "It's not glowing."

"Which means?"

"The vortex is already gone." He glanced at her. "You know how to call one, right?"

"I…" She thought of the whirling wind in her kitchen, the spell her mother taught her. "Yeah."

"Then let's go. If we hurry we can be gone before the pack gets there." But he hadn't gone more than a few paces before a wolf's high, eerie howl rose into the clear night air, coming from very nearby. First one, then another and another joined in, swelling the note to a harmony, then to a chorus, as if they were intentionally singing together.

The hair on the back of her neck shivered at the sound, which was wild, feral and hauntingly beautiful. But at the same time, nerves twined through her, turning her skin to gooseflesh.

Dayn stopped in the middle of the pathway. "Damn it, we're already too late to get ahead of them, and we *really* don't want to interrupt the blood-moon ritual." He paused, considering. "Given that I don't want to cross paths with them tonight, especially not with you, we're going to need to hole up somewhere out of sight." He glanced back at the cabin.

"Not there," she said quickly.

He nodded, then pointed off to one side, where the trees ran up a steep, rocky hill. "There's a cave I use sometimes. We'll be okay there for an hour or two."

"A cave," she repeated, apparently only able to string together two words at a time, preferably one syllable each. Suddenly very aware of the cold that bit through her shirt and lightweight leather, she hugged herself tightly. This couldn't be happening; it was all too unreal. Yet, strangely, Dayn seemed more real to her than anyone had in a very long time. He was bright and vivid; he drew her eyes and made her want to stare, made her want to touch. She'd felt inner sparklers when he kissed her hand. What would happen if he kissed her lips? What if he did more?

Focus. Stop transferring. You need to get out of here, not fantasize.

"Here." He dug into his rucksack and pulled out a second sweater. "Figured you'd want another layer, unless your coat is one of those fancy jobs with the really thin insulation."

"It's not." She slipped out of her leather and took the sweater from him. It was dark in color, thick and lightweight, almost airy, and the material had a faint rasp that suggested some dream-version of wool. Needing to say something that involved more than two syllables and might defuse the strangeness of wearing his clothes, she said, "Okay, so you carry a sword but you know about Thinsulate. What's the deal here?"

He hesitated, then said, "There's some travel between your realm and this one, so a certain amount of your technology has leaked over and been adapted to work here. I'm from the kingdom realm, which is pure magic. Thus, the sword."

"Is there the same sort of sharing between your realm and this one?" She was stalling, asking about things she didn't begin to believe in because she had been having sex dreams about him while he'd apparently been waiting for her to show up and lead him somewhere. And she didn't want to wear his sweater.

Except she did, because it was freezing out, and the sweater smelled like him—a mix of pine, moss and mint.

I really am losing my mind, aren't I? The thought brought a jab of new fear.

He glanced in the direction of the howls. "Things are far more complicated between my realm and this one. And we should get moving before a pack scout catches sight of us."

"Sorry." Holding her breath, she pulled on his sweater and smoothed it down her body, where it clung unexpectedly to her rather blatant curves. But she didn't care about that because she was already warmer, on the way to growing toasty. Letting out a soft sigh, she said, "Ahh, yes. That's good." Not letting herself snuggle or even take a deep breath, she nodded. "Okay. Lead on."

He made a quiet noise at the back of his throat, adjusted his burdens and headed across the track and into the moon-dappled forest. There must have been some sort of path; she couldn't see any markings, but he led her up the steep, rocky slope with a neat economy of effort, his near-silent footsteps making her feel loud and awkward in comparison. After ten, maybe fifteen minutes, he motioned for her to join him on a wide, flat ledge near a triangular cave mouth.

"Wait here. I've got some lights and other supplies inside." He slipped into the darkness. Moments later a muted glow sprang to life and he called, "Come on in."

She ducked to follow him in, found him crouched at roughly the midpoint of a low tunnel that was formed where two huge slabs of smooth, porous stone leaned against each other. In his palm he held a small rectangular unit that emitted blue-white light and a low background hum.

"The wolfyn won't come up here," he said. "After they're done with the ritual, they'll run the lowlands for the rest of the night. Moon time, you know."

She only heard part of it, though, because the moment he said "wolfyn," her stomach hollowed out and she flashed back to the woodcutting and the sly, evil creature that had seduced innocent Red. She sank down opposite him, and then leaned against the wall when her head spun. "Those were *wolfyn* back there?"

He nodded. "You'd call them werewolves. They're shape-shifters. Human. Wolf. Back again." He paused, fiddling with the little light. "I don't know what the legends are like where you come from, but you don't need to be afraid of them here. They treat guests well in their own realm. It's part of the tradition they live by."

Her heart was beating so hard her chest hurt, and her legs and arms tingled with an oncoming panic attack. A big one. *Breathe,* she told herself. *You can deal with this.* The wolfyn were just part of the hallucination. They couldn't hurt her, couldn't roofie her into sexual submission and then eat her when their other needs were satisfied. So far, all they were was just noise on the horizon. Besides, her mother's stories about them taking young girls had been allegories about not giving it up too early or to the wrong guy.

Right?

Breathe. Don't lose it. He wasn't her fantasy prince and she wasn't really in another realm. She wasn't even really wearing his sweater, even though she was far warmer now, both because of the extra layer and the intimacy of the little cave, which forced them to bump knees and kept her system on a low rev of awareness. Her racing mind was scared, confused and frustrated, but her body was entirely aware of his.

When he shifted back, so he was leaning on the opposite wall, his movements were controlled; after he settled in, he went very still, almost looking as though he wasn't even breathing. He moved like a martial artist, she thought…or a predator. A hunter. The realization stirred her blood far more than it should, and she caught herself collecting small details, like how his aristocratic nose had a faint ridge where it had been broken and just slightly offset, and the way his hands were long-fingered and elegant, yet tough and callused with hard labor.

Benz had used to tease her that she would need genetic engineering to create her perfect guy, because she wanted the whole package: brains, compassion, honor and romance in a laborer's strong, muscular body. And he wasn't far off, because that would have been a real-life approximation of her woodcutter hero… Like the one sitting opposite her now, staring out into the night.

Except that he's not really here, is he? said her logical, rational self. And the heat buzzing through her body racheted down because it was right. Her brain was tricking her, just like it had when she was a little girl and thought she heard her *maman's* voice whispering to her, sending her into the woods looking for answers. She didn't need the department shrink to tell her that.

You have to get to the vortex, logic reminded her. *He said that was the way home.* And if her mind had bought in so deeply to the illusion, then the rules of the illusion should work. Maybe. Hopefully.

But the place where the vortex formed was crawling

with wolfyn, and… Wait. "If the wolfyn are harmless, why are we hiding up here?"

He looked back at her for a moment, seeming to be measuring her mental state. Or maybe deciding how much to tell her. "There's some personal stuff between me and the pack leader. Tempers can run high this time of year, so I think it's better if he and I stay out of each other's way."

"And?" she prompted when her cop's instincts told her there was more.

He shifted, stretching his legs out beside hers, almost but not quite touching. The alignment of her battered jeans against his turned the differences in fabric and stitching from subtle to a shout as he said, "You know how I said things were complicated between my realm and the wolfyn? Well, there was a war. I don't even know what really started it—nobody here seems to, and it was a long time ago. But it was ruthless and bloody, and didn't end until a group of kingdom magic-users, the Ilth, got together and changed the nature of the vortices so that when wolfyn come through to the kingdoms they wind up stuck in the wolf form, unable to change back or cast the spell to return home. Eventually, they even lose their human thoughts, becoming purely feral." He paused. "The wolfyn came up with a counterspell, but by that time they had discovered the human realm and become fascinated with your science. For the past few generations—and my people have very long generations—contact has been limited to the few wolfyn who get sucked up into the vortices without the counterspell, and the occasional guest who shows up here, like me. In fact, the people of the kingdoms don't even believe in realm travel anymore—it's faded to legend status, just like the wolfyns' abilities to shape-shift and enthrall beautiful women."

A shiver crawled up Reda's spine as the hallucination suddenly gained an uncomfortable amount of detail that dovetailed with the stories she knew. "Can they do that? Enthrall women, I mean."

He shook his head. "They wouldn't do that to a guest, not even during the moon time. The traditions are very clear on when and how enthrallment can be used."

Which wasn't a "no." Feeling the cold more than she had been moments before, she tucked her hands under her arms beneath her jacket, warming them in a sweater that was uncomfortably peltlike all of a sudden.

He continued, "So while the wolfyn are generally tolerant, they prefer humans over kingdomites, and there are certain bloodlines from the kingdom that remain kill-on-sight."

"Which is why you don't want them to know that you're a prince," she said, remembering his earlier comment. Then, without warning, a bubble of half-hysterical laughter rose up inside her, sticking in her throat and threatening to turn into a sob. "You're a prince," she repeated. "Of course you are." She used to dream of charming princes, ethereal princesses and magical adventures, so maybe it was no wonder her mind had gone back there now, turning her fantasy man into not only the woodcutter, but also a handsome prince. She buried her face in her hands. "You're not real. *None* of this is real. Go away and let me wake up in my real bed in the middle of my real life." She felt a tug of wistfulness at the thought of leaving the dream behind, and that couldn't be good.

"It's just vortex sickness," he said soothingly. "Don't worry. Just relax—it'll all come back to you soon."

She lifted her head to glare at him. "I haven't forgotten anything, damn it. My name is Reda Weston, my father is Major Michael Weston and my mother's name was Freddy. See? No gaps. No blank spots. And this isn't real."

"By the gods and the Abyss, this *is* real." A hint of temper licked at the back of his eyes, which had gone very green in the pale illumination. His voice gained an edge. "And it's going to stay real whether you believe in it or not, so how about you chuck the 'science is God' human attitude and consider that maybe this *is* happening, and that you're here for a reason? Because unless you help me out here, people are going to die."

"I…" She stared at him, throat drying to dust. "What?"

"People. Will. Die," he said, spacing the words through gritted teeth. "I need to get my ass back to Castle Island within the next seventy-two hours, and you're supposed to be helping me."

Her throat closed, but she forced out, "I've never heard of Castle Island." Then, seeing it in his eyes, she held up a hand. "And if you say 'vortex sickness' one more time, I'm going to scream."

His expression eased. "Okay. At least you're listening."

"I'm…" She shook her head. "I don't know what I am, besides scared and confused. What's going on here? What's on Castle Island and why do you need to be there? And why does it involve me?" *This doesn't matter, anyway. It's just an illusion.*

"I don't know how you're involved, really, or why.

But I can tell you about Castle Island." He waited for her nod. When he got it, he made a rueful, bitter face, and began. "There once was a prince who thought the world should revolve around him...." Her blood chilled as he described his home being attacked by a vile sorcerer and his parents casting a massive spell that had saved him and his siblings, yet went awry, binding them to the castle and cursing the kingdom if they failed to return in time. He recited a message from his father's spirit, telling him to wait for a guide, and that when she arrived he needed to be back on Castle Island by the fourth night, to reunite with his siblings and kill the sorcerer. He paused, expression going hollow. "The next thing I knew, I was stuck here in the wolfyn realm, doing my damnedest to make them believe I'd lost my memory in the vortex and keep them from guessing that I was a member of a royal house...and all the while, waiting for my guide to show up. Then, about a week ago, I started having these dreams."

"Dreams," she whispered, body heating suddenly.

He nodded. "I saw you, Reda. Your face. Your eyes. The magic was making sure I would recognize you when you arrived."

She moved restlessly, shifting her legs away from his. "There's no such thing as magic."

"Maybe there isn't in your world. But there is in mine."

Her pulse thudded loudly in her ears. The department shrink had talked about hospitalization but in the end had signed off on an outpatient program with intensive sessions that had started off daily and tapered from there. Now, she wondered whether that had been a mistake, whether she had faked her way through her recovery, fooling even herself, until now. Was she in a hospital room somewhere, staring blankly out a window while her mind roamed free? Panic sparked in her chest as she tried to imagine it but couldn't, tried to connect with her "real" mind trapped somewhere else, but couldn't do that, either. The cave, the man and his story felt entirely real. Which would mean…

"No," she said, pushing herself up to the hunched-over crouch that was all the cave allowed, which made her feel trapped and squirrelly. "This isn't… I'm not your guide. There's been some sort of mistake."

He hadn't moved a muscle, except to follow her with his eyes. "When you first woke up in the cabin, you recognized me. I saw it in your face."

"I…" *dreamed of you, lusted after you, imagined you were all the things I haven't been able to find in a flesh-and-blood guy.* "Okay, maybe there were a couple of dreams, but there wasn't anything about me guiding you anywhere." She didn't mention waking up hot, bothered and alone. Clearly, their dreams had been very different: she had dreamed of finding love; he had dreamed of saving his people. Was that what her subconscious wanted her to see? That she was too wrapped up in her own problems? That one resonated a little too well, making her queasy. Pressing a hand to her stomach, she said, "I need to…you know. Outside."

He touched her free hand briefly in support. "Go out the back and stay close. There's a grove of borer trees on the other side of the stones, and you don't want to mess with borers."

She didn't ask why, didn't intend to find out. "I'll be back in a few minutes. I think I just need some air." And some space without him there to remind her how numb she'd been for too long, just going through the motions, stuck in her own little world.

Outside of the cave, the air was cold, stark and silent, with none of the howling of earlier. The huge moon lit her path as she picked her way over the rocks, getting clear of Dayn's sight as if looking for someplace to relieve herself. Then, with her heart pounding and fear souring the back of her throat, she looped around and headed back downhill, stumbling in her haste to get to the stones and break out of the hallucination before she did something really stupid… Like buy into it.

WITH REDA GONE, the cave was cooler and far less interesting, drained of the intense, compressed energy that practically shimmered around her. But it was also a whole hell of a lot calmer.

Dayn exhaled slowly, telling himself that it was going to be okay. This was going to work. She finally seemed ready to consider that she wasn't caught in some strange and elaborate dream, and once they got past that, he was sure her memories would resurface and she would be able to guide him. At least he hoped to the Abyss that it would work that way. He was starting to fear it might not, because a human seemed a very strange choice for someone to guide him through the magical realm of Elden. Which made him think that this part of the spell, too, had been damaged by the sorcerer's magic.

Not that *she* was damaged; exactly the opposite, in fact. She might have some human suspicions and disbelief when it came to the magic, and an apparent tendency to go wide-eyed and catatonic under fire, but she drew him, compelled him. Unlike the willowy, aloof wolfyn females he had spent the past two decades with, she was compact and curvy, and her emotions were written so clearly on her heart-shaped face. He had caught himself staring into her eyes, which reminded him of the deep blue skies of home, and basking in her voice, which was sweet, soft and wholly feminine.

Which was why she wasn't the only one who had needed a minute alone. Because he needed to get a grip on himself, needed to regain some perspective. This wasn't about him being a man and her a woman; it was about him getting his ass home and taking care of business there. And after that he would be back to being a prince of the realm, with all that the title implied. Which meant there was no benefit to him noticing how his sweater clung to the curves of her breasts and hips, and that the hitch of her breath when she caught him looking at her told him the attraction wasn't one-sided.

"Priorities," he said to himself, hearing the word echo through the otherwise silent cave, the air empty of wolf howls. The ritual was done, then, and it was time for him and Reda to head back down to the stones. Maybe she wouldn't even need to remember. Maybe her just being there would cause the vortex spell to work for him as it hadn't before.

Rising to the crouched-over crabwalk required by the cave, he eased out and straightened, calling softly, "Reda?"

There was no answer, but she wouldn't have gone far, given that he had mindspoken her to stay close.

Not long after he arrived in the wolfyn realm, he had discovered that his mindspeak powers worked on all females, regardless of what realm they came from. When he had physical contact—as he had just now, touching Reda's hand—he could implant suggestions, even orders. That was how he'd kept Keely from knowing certain things he didn't want her to, and how he'd initially pushed Candida to protect him—until she had figured out what he was doing, and went for his throat. After that, he had told her everything, and instead of killing him, she had decided to help him, instead. And thank the gods for that.

Although the pack's wisewoman hadn't been able to send him home, she had given him the vortex counterspell, and more recently had been working on some new poisons she thought would work on beings of dark magic, like the Blood Sorcerer. More, she had helped him work out the limits of his mindspeaking powers in the wolfyn realm, and they had discovered that while he couldn't make a female do something she was against or prevent her from doing something she really wanted to, he could influence other, less definitive emotions. That was why he hadn't been able to push Reda into opening up to him—she was too set against it. But given her obvious fear of the wolfyn and the fact that she was starting to warm up to him, she would obey his command to stick around. She ought to be right nearby.

Only she wasn't.

Cursing under his breath, growing increasingly anxious when there was no sign of her, he walked all the way out to the edge of the borer grove, where the ground started to go hollow. Then he backtracked and circled around the cave. And he picked up her trail heading back down the incline, beelining straight for the standing stones.

"Son of a *bitch.*" He had underestimated her mental strength, her disbelief and her determination to break free of what she thought was an illusion. Scrambling back to the cave, he grabbed his supplies and weapons, hoping to hell he hadn't just made a fatal mistake. Worse, as he pelted downhill, the horizon beyond his tree-hidden cabin started to glow.

His stomach plummeted. He was going to be too damn late.

STANDING JUST INSIDE the stone circle, Moragh threw her head back and laughed with delight as fat blue sparks leaped from one stone to the next and wind stirred her hair, fanning it out around her face.

Raising her voice to carry over the sparks and crackles of power, she called, "Oh, joyous dark gods, I knew it, Nasri! I always knew the Book of Ilth was real."

She had argued with the sorcerer's so-called scholars, who had written the text off as either fiction or a heretical interpretation of the gods and the Abyss. Granted, nothing had happened back then when she had tried the two simplest spells, but she hadn't known that location mattered. It stood to reason, though, that the separation between realms would be thinnest at certain points, the magic connecting them more active. It had taken the lost prince's spell to draw her to the right place at the right time, and the stirring of vortex wind for her to figure out that she needed to try the first of the two spells she had memorized.

It had worked then, and again just now. She was facing the beginnings of a vortex of her own, one she controlled.

"Are we going home now, Mistress Moragh?" Nasri called from where he stood outside the stones, holding the submission chain of the surviving ettin, which was still stupidly looking around for its brother.

Admittedly, she should have set both of the creatures on the prince and made sure of the kill. But she hadn't realized right away that something in this realm—gods, she was in another *realm*—would dull her connection to his father's spell, making her unable to track him beyond the immediate area of the standing stones. But no matter, she suddenly had new and wondrous options.

"Yes and no," she said in answer to Nasri's question. "I must return home and retrieve the Book of Ilth." Her heart lifted at the thought of wielding the book's power—it didn't contain only realm-travel spells, but also summoning spells more powerful than anything the kingdoms had seen in centuries, power transference spells—the possibilities were nearly limitless. "I will take the ettin with me, so you are not troubled by him, and then I shall seal this portal behind me, so the prince cannot follow." That was the second of the spells she had memorized. Sealing this particular portal might not trap the prince in the wolfyn realm—there were probably other locations where vortices could be made— but it would slow him down, giving her enough time to steal the book from the very scholars who had mocked her for believing it real.

The gnome's eyes widened. "And me, mistress?"

Satisfied that the vortex was well under way, she stepped out of the stones, froze the ettin in place with a three-word command and then turned her attention to Nasri, who had backed away a few paces when he thought she wasn't looking. And even though he had long ago stopped appealing to her, the thought of what she was about to do had her secondary canines descending easily, breaking the skin with that itchy pinch of pain she loved so much, and then gliding into place alongside her lower teeth, just touching the gums with a kiss of the wickedly sharp points.

"I have a special job for you, Nasri."

He blanched at the sight of her fangs, but the compulsion was well rooted. Even as his entire body cringed away from her, he took three jerky steps forward and raised his arm, offering her a wrist dotted with toothmarks in various healing stages.

She surged forward and took his throat instead, biting deep and hanging on as he writhed and the glorious tang of blood flowed down her throat. New connections formed; new magic came to life, and she found his weak little mind with hers. *Now pay attention. This is what I want you to do....*

REDA DIDN'T SCREAM, but that was only because she was paralyzed, stuck flat to the ground beneath a dense clump of underbrush at the edge of the clearing, where she had a perfect view of the dark-haired woman *drinking* from the neck of her small, wizened servant, and a clear soundtrack of the vampire's rhythmical sucking noises interspersed with mewls of horror from the victim.

Her gorge rose. This woman—this Moragh—was a vampire. Dear God.

She swallowed again and again in an effort to keep herself from puking at the sight of the little man's body convulsing, his hands fluttering at his sides, as if he wanted to fight her off but couldn't. Just as he had wanted to run the other way before, but had held out his arm instead. *Compulsion. Enthrallment.* First the wolfyn and now this. Was every nonhuman creature in this realm capable of inflicting its will on others? *I have to get out of here,* she thought as the breath sobbed in her lungs. *I just want everything to go back to normal.*

She had to get through that vortex, and she had to do it now, while the vampire was occupied. But she couldn't move.

Not now, she begged her body. *Please don't freeze up on me now!* But she couldn't force herself to stand and make a run for the standing stones, couldn't so much as wiggle a toe. She was vapor locked again. Immobile. Useless. All she could do was watch as the vampire let go and the little man swayed on his feet, throat drenched with blood. His eyes were glassy and unfocused, his voice monotone when he said, "I shall find the pack."

He stumbled off, headed on a tangent for the woods, seeming not to care that there was blood streaming down his front.

The vampire watched him go with a small smile playing over her bloodstained lips. "I wouldn't worry. I suspect they'll find you very soon." Moonlight glinted off her fangs as she smiled fully, horribly. Then she turned away, snagged the monster's chain off the ground and led the creature into the stones.

The vortex roared and they disappeared.

The second they were gone, Reda's paralysis snapped and she was on her feet and racing for the stones, her heart pounding as she called up the spell that had gotten her into this mess.

She was only a few steps away when Dayn burst from the trees, shouting, "Reda, *wait!*"

Hesitating, she glanced back. And as she did so, a

cracking sound filled the air and the vortex collapsed in on itself and disappeared. Seconds later, there was a brilliant amber flash and the air went utterly dead. "No!" She flew through the stones and raced to the center. "Wait, no! Take me!"

"Reda, stop." He grabbed her by the arms. "Stop. It's over. It's gone."

"No! She's sealing it off. Don't let her seal it off!" Even though she knew in her heart that it was already too late, she beat on his arms, struggling to get free, not just from him, but from this whole awful place, with its werewolves and vampires and three-headed monsters. Then, when that didn't work, she collapsed against him, grabbing his jacket to get in his face and cry, "Did you see her? Did you see—?"

She broke off when his arms shifted, their bodies aligned, and she became suddenly aware that he was hard and aroused, his eyes glazing as they locked on hers. And although it was the entirely wrong time, the entirely wrong place, heat leaped up inside her, flaring through her veins. Breath thinning in her lungs, she pressed against him, arched into him as his lips came down…parted…

And moonlight glinted off the two long, curving canines that hadn't been there before.

CHAPTER FOUR

ONE SECOND DAYN was locked on Reda's mouth with nothing in his head except: *Need. Want. Now.*

In the next, she screamed and jerked away from him, her face ashen with shock, her mouth a round O of horror as she whispered, "No. Dear God, no. You're…"

Startled, he reared back. "Reda, what—" And he felt his lips slide over his secondary canines. His *fully extended* secondary canines. The ones that were a good bit bigger than the witch's, and made for the exact same purpose. "Oh, shit. Wait. I can explain." He took a step toward her, reached for her. "It's not—"

She broke and bolted, scattering like a wild hare into the nearest section of trees, which put her headed away from both the cabin and the cave.

He went after her, but let her get ahead and moved only fast enough to keep her in sight. Not just to give her some room, but to give himself some, too. Because he was suddenly very *not* okay with what had just happened.

He'd seen the female blood drinker feeding from the gnome's neck vein, and he'd damn near lost his mind. Or maybe he *had* lost it there for a few seconds, because that was the only possible explanation for him trying to kiss Reda with his fangs up close and personal. "Wait," he called, lengthening his strides to catch up to her. "Please, just give me a minute to explain."

She threw a panicked look over her shoulder, then at the surrounding forest. And, seeing a lighter spot off to one side, swerved and bolted toward where the normal forest trees gave way to a roughly circular patch of scattered trunks whose roots overlapped and intertwined in intricate patterns.

"Reda, no!" he shouted, accelerating after her. "Stop! Those are borers! The ground isn't safe!"

But she just kept going. Either she didn't believe him, or she didn't think a tree could be worse than a vampire. She plunged into the grove, pounding across the root network, seeming not to notice how her footsteps suddenly echoed hollowly.

Cursing, Dayn followed her in, staying close to the skin-smooth trunks and leaping among the sturdier roots. The surface gave like a mattress beneath his boots and the stink of sulfur wafted up, warning that the grove was fully mature. The roots of the carnivorous trees had pushed aside the earth, creating a hollow to collect their digestive acids.

Too late, she understood. She stopped abruptly near a large parental tree, hands outstretched for balance, and looked back at him with new horror written on her face.

And she fell through.

"No!" He lunged for the ragged hole, stopping on the last sturdy root and coughing against the sulfurous stench that rose up from the torn spot. His gut wrenched. "Reda!"

Then—thank the gods—a wrist-thick root near the

edge of the hole shuddered and he heard a low cry of, "Help me!"

"I'm coming." Yanking off his sword belt, he jammed the leather-sheathed short sword into the huge trunk of the main borer, fisting it so hard that the blade sank in, leather and all. Then, hanging on to that anchor, he leaned out as far as he could without falling in himself. Which put him close enough to catch a glimpse of her wide, frightened eyes, but not close enough to grab her. Stretching out his hand, he strained to close the gap. "Move slowly and don't shift your weight when you reach for my hand," he ordered, his voice rasping with the burn of the sulfur vapors. He couldn't see her face anymore, couldn't see anything but her hand reaching up for his. Slowly. Slowly.

The ground sagged and collapsed as the smaller roots gave way, tearing, tearing... And then she screamed, lunged upward and grabbed his wrist as the rootwork around her fell away.

Dayn yanked her up and against him and propelled them both to the main trunk; then he spun them and pinned her against the tree with his body, in case she was still thinking about trying to run. Instead, she burrowed both hands beneath his jacket to wrap her arms around him and grab fistfuls of his sweater as she buried her face in his chest and clung, shaking.

And if things had been entirely wrong in his universe only a few moments earlier, now they suddenly seemed very, very right. She fit seamlessly against him and warmed him where he had been so cold. She was safe. She was unhurt. And she was in his arms.

She's your guide, dumbass, snarled a very human-sounding voice of reason. *And you're supposed to be remembering your damn priorities.*

But wasn't his guide a priority? He didn't know what role she was supposed to play in his journey, but was beginning to suspect it wasn't nearly as simple as merely showing him where to go. For now, though, it was enough that she hadn't left him stranded in the wolfyn realm, hadn't fallen to her death.

"Shh," he said against her temple, letting the subtle flowers-and-spice scent of her curly hair fill him with a touch of the feminine whimsy he had gone so long without. "I've got you. You're okay."

She sucked in a shuddering breath. "But you're, you're…"

"Not a threat to you, I promise." He pulled back far enough to give her an exaggerated smile that included only normal teeth. "See? The spares are all tucked away. I'm not going to bite you, and I can't turn you. The human legends have it wrong, Reda. I swear. I'm just another kind of man."

She shrank back against the tree, though she didn't let go of his sweater. "The woman. Moragh. She…" She shuddered, face plastered with revulsion. "He couldn't pull away. He wanted to, but he couldn't. She was controlling him. And then, after…it was like she was inside his mind."

Damn it. He hesitated, trying to find the right words, because he suddenly wanted—needed—her to understand this part of him. He cursed the bad luck that she'd seen the witch feeding from the throat in a brutal, invasive attack of mind and body rather than the way it should be, as an expression of…well, love, really.

He blew out a breath. "Blood drinking is an inherited trait like any other, but it's magic, too, so it comes with various other, um, characteristics. Most of us are stronger and quicker than average. I can heal fast, especially when I'm in fang mode. Some of us can move things without touching them, and lots of us can mindspeak to one degree or another."

"Mindspeak," she repeated, eyes going white-rimmed. "Brainwashing, you mean. That's what she did to him."

"What you saw just now was something that shouldn't have happened. A blood drinker normally feeds from the wrist or elsewhere, not the throat. There should only be throat action between consenting lovers, usually mates, because it creates a bond between them, makes them aware of each other on a different level." He paused. "Yes, it's possible for a mindspeaker to put a compulsion on someone when they drink from the throat, like you just saw. But it's just…not done. There are codes. Ethics."

It galled him to find one of his kind allied with the Blood Sorcerer, and it disturbed him deeply that seeing her feed had brought out his fangs. That was partly due to how badly Reda had inflamed his senses, but that was no better. He shouldn't be thinking of her in those terms; he couldn't be. Hadn't he learned anything from his past mistakes?

"Did you… Can you compel someone like that?"

Though it was tempting to terrorize the wide-eyed human into keeping her distance, he needed her to trust him. So he went with the truth. "I can mindspeak with my blood kin and, in this realm at least, I can compel most females when I'm touching them." Seeing her expression go blank and scared, he said quietly, "Reda.

Look at me." He waited until she focused, waited until her eyes truly met his, before he said, "I swear on my honor that I haven't mindspoken you. Though, honestly, not for lack of trying. Maybe it's a realm thing, maybe something to do with my father's spell, but I don't seem to have any effect on you."

He hadn't meant it to come out that way, but a faint rueful spark lit in her shimmering eyes and she unknotted her hands from his sweater and smoothed the wool with her palms. "I wouldn't say that, exactly. But about what happened back there."

"It won't happen again. I didn't even realize I had my secondaries down—it's been a long time since I've been around another blood drinker, never mind one who was feeding like that." He swallowed. "I overloaded on her magic for a few seconds there, and you caught the edge of it. Like I said, it won't happen again, I promise." He paused. "But I want you to promise me something, too. I need to know that you're not going to take off on me again like that. You need to stick with me, and if I say something's dangerous, I need you to believe me. Because the dreams say that we're in this together. And whether or not you believe in all this, I do. And from my perspective—" he nodded to the ragged hole "—you almost just became plant food. So promise me that you'll stick with me and let me do my best to keep you safe."

"I promise," she said immediately, somewhat to his surprise. And then her eyes filled in earnest, welling up and spilling over. Voice quivering, she said, "This is real, isn't it?"

His heart twisted for her, but there was nothing to

be gained by lying, so he nodded slowly. She nodded in return, then leaned her forehead against his throat. And burst into tears.

REDA HATED CRYING. It only ever made her feel stupid and sore afterward, not better. And if there was anything she hated more than crying, it was crying in front of someone else.

Now, though, she didn't have a choice. The emotions were too huge and overwhelming, the situation too strange, for her to hold in the tears. They erupted from her in racking, tearing sobs that hurt her throat, burned her eyes and left her helpless to do anything but hang on to the nearest solid object.

She cried over the memories she had turned away from, the beliefs she had lost. Because if this was real, if she was really here, really in another realm where magic worked and werewolves and vampires existed, then her father and the others had been wrong, her *maman,* right. She sobbed for herself, in fear and reaction. And she wept in anticipation of failure, because she didn't know what to do, how to help Dayn or even if she was really supposed to. She heard the whispered words: "To my sweet Alfreda on her eighth birthday, with the rest of the story to come when you turn sixteen." Maybe she would have known what to do if she had gotten the rest of the story. Now, though, she was lost, adrift.

Not entirely, though. Because she was anchored to a big, solid object.

Dayn was the one with the bigger problems, yet he didn't protest her tears or tell her they needed to hurry. Instead, he molded her against the strong warmth of his body, stroked her hair and was just *there,* in a way nobody had been for her in a long, long time. And when the tears finally subsided, leaving an achy hollowness behind, he waited another minute before he eased away from her. "I'm sorry you got dragged into this. We'll go to Candida—she's the wolfyn's wisewoman—and see if she knows of a way to unlock the standing stones. The witch can't be the only one who knows that trick."

Candida. The wolfyn. "The little man said something about finding the pack."

"They're more than a match for one gnome." But he moved a few steps away, to where the intertwined roots formed a path of sorts. Then he turned back and held out a hand. "Come on. Let's go see the wisewolfyn. She's a friend. She'll help."

Understanding shimmered through Reda on a surge of cold, numbing nerves. Because standing there on the pathway with his hand outstretched, painted monochromatic by the moonlight, he suddenly became one of the last woodcuttings from her book. The scene came after the woodsman had killed the wolf and saved the girl, and brought her back to the edge of the village where she lived. Then, instead of walking away, he held out his hand and asked her to come with him.

In the book, it was the beginning of a new life. Here, it was a moment of truth. A choice between conscience and cowardice.

She took a deep breath. "Do you know the story of *Rutakoppchen?*" When he nodded, she continued, "I had a copy when I was a little girl. My mother told me it was the only one in the world...." She told him the story of her book from her eighth birthday to that afternoon in MacEvoy's shop. And her inner wimp made every word an effort. He had seemed ready to send her home, and now she was buying in deeper.

What the hell was she doing?

When she finished, Dayn cleared his throat. "Thank. The. Gods." His voice was rough with emotion. "The magic brought you and the book back together after all those years because it was time." But then he paused, the light of hope that had taken up residence in his eyes dimming somewhat. "Without you knowing everything your mother would have told you, though, or even how she was related to the realm, it may not be enough."

He's right, wimpy logic said. *You should go home, leave him to his quest. You're not prepared for this place, and you're not a save-the-world kind of girl.*

Instead, she said, "There's more. In my book, you're the woodsman."

She hadn't seen him truly surprised before, she realized. "Me?"

"Your perfect likeness, even down to the pattern on your shirt. And you're not the only thing I recognize here—your cabin, this forest, it's all in there...but the standing stones aren't."

He went suddenly fierce. Intent. "There are rumors of vortices showing up in other places. Nothing confirmed, though."

Taking a deep breath, she said in a rush, "The inner back cover was carved with a picture of a huge natural stone archway between two cliffs. There was a river at the base, trees all around it and a waterfall coming down from one side." She was simultaneously terrified and relieved by the look on his face. "You know where it is, don't you?"

He nodded, shoulders easing. "About a day and a half

away. Two days, tops. It's called the Meriden Arch." His breath left him in a rush and he closed the distance between them. "Thank the gods." He took her hand, lifted it and kissed her knuckles. "And thank you, for remembering."

But he wasn't really thanking her for remembering, was he? He was acknowledging that she could have held on to her ignorance, refusing to recognize that she knew more than she thought.

She glanced down at their linked hands. "I'm not brave."

"Being brave isn't about being unafraid. It's about functioning through the fear."

"Like I said—not brave. I freeze. I don't mean to, but things happen and I just…stand there."

"If Candida knows the spell to unseal the standing stones, you don't have to come with me. You can go home from here, your duty fulfilled."

It was oh, so tempting. But at what cost? If this was all real, then so was the threat to his homeland and siblings…and to Dayn himself. And although rationality screeched at the thought, she was still drawn to him, even knowing he was a vampire. If there was a chance she could help him, she wanted to try. So she forced the words past logic and reason, saying, "Along the bottom of the picture was carved words that translated to 'Here they can part, each to their own.' Even my *maman* said it was an odd ending for the story, since the woodcutter and the girl go off together."

He nodded slowly. "It wasn't about them—it was about us. We both need to go there to get back—you to the human realm, me to the kingdoms."

The thought shouldn't have brought a twinge.

She nodded. "I should warn you, though. A good man—my partner, my friend—died a few months ago because I froze at the wrong time. You can't trust a coward like me to have your back."

If he had knee-jerked the "you're not a coward" response, she wouldn't have listened, just as she hadn't to anyone else who had said the words. She knew what she was. But instead, eyes darkening, he brought up his free hand to touch her cheek, as if brushing away a tear she hadn't shed. "Sweet Reda, you've had a time of it, haven't you? Don't worry about having my back. I can take care of us both."

Her heart shuddered at the quiet promise, which was backed up by the implacable determination in his eyes. He had so much riding on him already, yet was stepping up to take more because she needed him to, which made him a better man—vampire or not—than the others in her life, save for the partner she had lost.

Dayn, too, was lost. But he was working to get himself found.

Did she make the move? Did he? She wasn't sure of that, wasn't sure of anything except that their lips were suddenly a breath apart.

This was the moment she should hesitate, she knew, the time when freezing in place would be the smarter, safer thing to do. Here, in this strange realm, in an almost-embrace with a man who was nothing like her, she should back down, back away. But the heat that raced through her made her feel suddenly alive, when she had been numb for so long that she had mistaken it for living. And they had their endpoint already: the Meriden Arch, forty-eight hours from now.

Two days, she thought. *What's the harm?*

So she didn't back down or away, but instead held her ground as he moved in hard and fast. And kissed the hell out of her.

CHAPTER FIVE

Soft warmth against his lips. *Silky heat on his tongue. Spice and flowers. Curves.* The sensations rocketed through Dayn. Gone was any hint of reserve or control, leaving him only able to act and react, not think or plan.

Growling low in his throat, he crowded her back against the tree until their bodies were aligned, pressed together, touching from knee to chest. He kept his hands on her face, willing them to stay there with the last threads of his control, knowing that if he touched her—really *touched* her, the way he was suddenly dying to do—that he would be truly lost. Although in that moment, he couldn't remember why that was a bad thing.

It had been two decades since he had held a woman out of anything other than necessity, since he felt a burn that went beyond the physical to something more. But now, as their tongues touched and slid, as his body went tight, tense and hard, he wasn't just kissing a woman. He was kissing a dream he hadn't been aware of having.

She thought herself a coward, yet had a core of strength. She had lost someone close to her and blamed herself for it. And she didn't—couldn't—understand how much that hit home for him. He didn't know if the grief and guilt in the kiss was hers or his, but those emotions eased as the heat rose between them. And for the first time in a long, long while, he didn't feel alone.

Warm skin beneath his palms. Urgent fingers at his waist, his back, his shoulders, sliding into his hair. Heart pounding. Body tightening. A trickle of magic and moonlight, and—

"Abyss." He broke the kiss, pressed his forehead to hers. "We can't do this right now." *Priorities.*

She was breathing just as heavily as he, and her fingers dug into his wrists, but she nodded. "Yeah." And neither of them mentioned the "right now" or the way it left open the option of "later."

He stepped away, not letting himself reach for her again. "We'll stop at Candida's first. She's got some things I'll want to bring." Like the poison she had designed for the sorcerer, and maybe a trick or two that could help him keep Reda safe. Because while she couldn't be his top priority, she had very definitely become his responsibility.

The thought bumped up against the promises he had made to his father's spirit, but didn't unsettle them. He was headed where he needed to be going, with the woman who was to guide him. And when he went to Elden, he'd be going alone.

They set off along the track.

The cold, moonlit night had gone quiet, suggesting that the pack had moved on. Reda kept up easily, though she had to take three strides for every two of his. And although he told himself to think about what he needed from Candida, and the route they should take to reach Meriden Arch safely, without running afoul of the packs whose territory they would be traveling through, his thoughts kept circling back to the woman at his side.

As a younger man in Elden, he had gravitated toward the women of the queen's Special Guard and assertive, weapon-savvy guardsmen's daughters, as Twilla had been. And in the wolfyn realm he had spent most of his time with Candida or Keely—both alpha bitches, strong leaders. Not the kind of women who would weep or admit their fears. Reda, on the other hand, wore her emotions out in the open, without subterfuge. Yet, strangely, he hadn't wanted to move away when she cried, hadn't been impatient with her tears. Maybe part of that was because he understood what it felt like to be uprooted and lost, and, more, to have failed a loved one. But another part of it was less easily defined—he had wanted to hold her, comfort her, protect her, kiss her. And now that he knew her taste and the sexy sound she made at the back of her throat when they kissed, he wanted to do all that and more.

At the thought, his skin heated and his gums itched where his secondaries burned to be set free.

The response was even more discomfiting this time around, because his blood drinker's power was threatening to lock on to her, binding him more deeply than he could afford. Or was it just that drinking and sexual arousal had become inextricably linked in his mind? Maybe it was as simple as that.

He willed his secondaries far into hiding and quelled the magic. And he resolved to be on his guard.

AFTER NEARLY AN HOUR'S hike, they turned up the last narrow track leading to Candida's cave, where she lived the lone existence she preferred, close enough to the pack to mediate squabbles and provide the healing and auguring that were her specialties, yet far enough away to discourage drop-in visits.

. "Hope she's not out running," he said as they headed up the last ridge, which crested right before where the high hilltop flattened out in front of Candida's cave. "She doesn't go out with the pack every moon time, but will take a run now and then." Aware of Reda's nerves—which were understandable given that she'd been raised on the *Rutakoppchen* version of wolfyn lore—he continued, "She's an inventor, one of the best at figuring out how to take human tech and make it run off magical power cells they use for energy here. In fact—"

He broke off, blood icing as he scented smoke, thick with the rank odors of searing hair and burning flesh. Worse was the prickle of stale, foul magic.

"No!" he shouted. *"Candida!"*

He bolted over the last rise with Reda at his heels.

The entrance to the cave was a churned-up mess, with wisps of dark smoke curling around the top edge of the unlit opening. His heart hammered a sick, awful beat as he ducked inside and hit the lights, bringing up the glows strung throughout the cave and illuminating a scene of utter chaos.

And murder. Because amid the strewn wreckage of the wisewolfyn's supplies and household goods lay a huge mound of gray-buff fur. *"Candida,"* he rasped, crossing to her and going to his knees. "Gods. What did she do to you?"

The wisewolfyn's eyes were a pale, milky white, her throat torn open, her body badly burned, with patches of fur gone and the angry red flesh pitted with deeply charred stripes. A length of sword-stock metal protruded from the dying fire, suggesting the means for that torture. And torture it had been. The witch, Moragh, had hurt her, burned her, no doubt mind-raped her...and most likely all while he and Reda were hiding together in the small cave, waiting for the wolfyn to move on from the standing stones.

Again, he'd been in the wrong place at the wrong time. If he had realized the ettin hadn't stumbled through the vortex accidentally, if he'd been paying attention to the magic fluxes in the air...

"I'm sorry." Reda gripped his shoulder.

Resentment welled up, though he knew it was misplaced. It wasn't her fault they had gotten off to a rocky start; it wasn't anyone's fault. But it all sucked nonetheless.

"She was strong," he grated. "She resisted the mindspeak, tried to hold on to her secrets." Thus, the hot iron. "The magic got to her in the end, though."

"How can you be sure?"

"Her eyes." He gestured stiffly. "The white is a sign that she's been emptied out by mindspeak."

Reda sucked in a quiet breath, but didn't move her hand from his shoulder. Her grip was firm and strong; it said, *I've got your back* and *I'm sorry.* And maybe even *I'm here for you,* which was something he was very unused to.

After a moment, he continued, "The wolfyn normally revert to human form when they die. This says... shit, it says to me that Moragh stripped her all the way down to feral before she died." Which would have been a horrible fall for the proud, highly civilized wolfyn. She would have hated dying in wolf form, would've hated him seeing her like this. And she would have despised knowing that the witch had broken her.

"Should we do something for her?"

It took him a couple of heartbeats to figure out what she was asking, but far less than that to see that it was impossible. "No. We need to get moving." He pulled himself to his feet, hating the necessity. At the question in her eyes, he added, "Moragh sent her servant to tell the pack that I'm a blood drinker. Odds are, they're already on the hunt." He paused. "I'm sorry."

"Why? You didn't do this."

"I didn't stop it, either." He turned for the back of the cave. "Grab what you think you can use."

"Does she have any archery equipment?"

He stopped and turned back with a raised eyebrow.

"I was a junior archery champ three years running. The family rule was that each kid had to get good at a weapon. I think my father wanted to…" She shook her head. "Anyway, I can shoot. And I'm going to need a weapon."

"In that trunk over there," he said, gesturing. "Grab whatever crossbow bolts you can find, too, and another waterskin."

"Got it."

While she rummaged, he took a deep breath and faced the back wall of the cave. Then, tapping into the energy flow that enabled the powers of the wolfyn, he said softly, "Let that which is hidden be revealed."

The rock face shimmered and then disappeared, revealing stacked rows of brightly painted, intricately carved drawers.

Behind him, Reda gasped and something clattered.

"It's okay," he said. "It's just low-level cloaking magic. It's not a big deal."

"It is to someone like me."

Which just reinforced the fact that they came from two completely different worlds that intersected here, in this strange halfway realm. The knowledge tugged at him, but he ignored the tug and focused on the racked drawers trying to figure out which of Candida's tricks he could use to keep himself and Reda alive long enough to get to Meriden Arch, and from there, gods willing, home. And, in his case, to war.

At the thought, he reached first for the small red-capped leather tube that contained a smaller glass flask. An inch of amber syrup clung to the bottom, barely moving when he shook the carrying case.

"What's that?"

"Poison," he said without looking at her. "I'm going to use it to kill the Blood Sorcerer."

REDA DIDN'T LET HERSELF dwell on the way the things she found packed away were familiar yet not, knock-offs that were ever so slightly wrong in their details. She didn't let herself dwell on how seeing Dayn do magic had shaken her to her core and, more, how it had aroused her, as if her libido was reacting to a surge of power she hadn't felt anywhere else. But while she was so busy not thinking about all those things as she loaded her rucksack with additional provisions and strapped a dozen arrows on the outside, she had far too much leeway to think about the clash between the pretty bedding and clothes in the trunks that lined the wall…and the wolf carcass that lay nearby.

Only it wasn't just a wolf, was it? It—*she*—had used

these blankets, worn these clothes, chosen the now-broken knickknacks. *Candida,* she thought, glancing over at the motionless form, not sure if what she was feeling could be classified as pity, revulsion, confusion or all of those things at once. Probably the latter. She pitied the woman who had hung an abstract slash of color on the wall, yet reviled a species that, even in war, could enthrall, seduce, use and then discard women. *It was a long time ago,* she reminded herself. But still. The potential was there. More, the power was there.

Yet Candida had died trying to protect her blood-drinking friend.

Apparently finished gathering what he wanted, Dayn moved away from the racks to cover Candida's body with a heavy woven robe. He stood for a moment, whispering what she thought was a prayer, or maybe an apology.

Her heart bumped lightly in her chest and a new warmth moved through her, strange and unfamiliar. Tenderness.

He's a blood drinker, she reminded herself, but the warning bounced back with a rebuttal that came from deep within her: *perhaps, but he's also a prince.* Those things were both his birthrights, and both were labels that did nothing to describe the man himself. Dayn the blood drinker was dark and sexy; Dayn the prince was driven and determined to fulfill his promises. But at the same time, Dayn the man was very real.

Back home, her friends said she was too picky, that every man came with a mix of good and bad things, that she had to find a mix that worked for her rather than holding out for Mr. Perfect. What they hadn't gotten—what she hadn't been able to make them understand—was that she wasn't looking for a flawless man; she wanted one that was larger than himself, who cared about more than his car and flat-screen, and whether or not he got promoted at work. She wanted someone who combined her father's rigid code of ethics and military heroics with her mother's empathy, whimsy and lust for adventure.

She wanted the woodcutter, the storybook prince. And she had found one—for the next forty-eight hours, at least.

Finished, he turned to her, caught her watching him, but said only, "You ready?"

Standing, she slung the rucksack over her shoulder, where it joined the unstrung bow. "Did you find what you were looking for?"

He nodded. "I got the poison I wanted—which she didn't finish testing, so I have no idea if it'll work or not—along with a good supply of wolfsleep sap, which is roughly like chewing gum in your world, but also works on wounds. And this could come in handy." He dug into his battered rucksack and held out three small lumps of greenish stuff that had the consistency of putty and an oily sheen.

Reda wrinkled her nose, though any smell they might have had was buried beneath the foul smoky taste that coated her mouth and throat. "What are they?"

"Wolfsbene."

She eyed the stuff with new interest. "A repellant?"

"Not *bane*," he corrected, "*bene*. As in *benefits*. It enhances their human forms, giving them added strength, speed and stamina. It'll work for us, though not to the same degree. Think of it as rocket fuel for human forms." He tipped the lumps into a small envelope made of smooth tree bark, and handed it over. "Keep this on you. I've got more, but I want you to have your own in case we get into a situation where you need it and can't reach me." He paused. "There are side effects, so only use it when you absolutely have to."

She stilled. "What kind of side effects?"

"It doesn't just energize the body—it, ah, dials the other systems up, too."

"What is it with this realm and roofies?" she asked, flushing slightly because her first gut-level response to the idea wasn't nearly as negative as it should have been.

"What's a roofie?"

"Apparently this is." But she pocketed the envelope, because she felt suddenly very tired, as if her body had been waiting for her to notice the ache of fatigue. She didn't know how long she had been in the vortex, didn't know what time her internal clock thought it was, but she could use some rest.

That wasn't in the cards, though. If the pack was after them, they needed to move.

"Oh, and here." He held out a roll of thick laminate that reminded her of the place mats at the waterfront lobster shack back home. "In case something happens." She unrolled it and found herself looking at a map of entirely unfamiliar names and places, with Meriden Arch marked in ink and a couple of notes about trails and things to avoid. He said, "Basically, just head west, cross the canyon at the bridge and then angle almost due northwest from there at another day's hard march. The landmarks and stuff are on there."

A lump gathered in her throat, but she nodded and managed, "Thanks."

Although she tried not to think about making the trip alone, it nagged at her as they retraced their route down from the wisewolfyn's cave. She kept thinking of the furry gray body and the dead, staring white eyes, which started whispering in her mind, *It could happen to you, too.*

More, as they turned from a main road onto a narrower path that forced them to walk single file, with her following his rangy, seemingly tireless form, nerves tingled to life within her, tightening her stomach and making her want to curl up and hide.

Breathe, she told herself, hating the misfiring instincts that poured adrenaline into her bloodstream, making her too jittery to fight, to flee, to do something, anything!

The moon seemed too big, the crater shadows too irregular, the trees on either side of the trail too smooth, their joints too regular. The night crowded in on her, pressed on her.

Breathe, damn it. She focused on the trees and the darkness, the feeling of the bow on her back and the arrows she'd stuck in easy reach. *You're okay. You're doing this to yourself. You're—*

Brush crackled suddenly on either side of her and huge shapes emerged, furred, fanged and growling. *Wolfyn!*

"Run!" Dayn shouted to her. *"Go!"*

Reda gasped and whirled to bolt, but there was already one behind her, then another and another. Within seconds, she and Dayn were surrounded by more than forty of the creatures, all with their heads down menacingly and golden fur spiked down their spines.

She fell back, gaping at the terrifying beauty of

them. Candida's inert body hadn't prepared her for the shifters' sheer *presence*. The wolfyns' shoulders came up past her waist and their bodies stretched out, looking almost more like those of huge lions than wolves. Their coats had saddle marks that glowed reddish even in the moonlight; their heads were narrow triangles that made her think of wide-open spaces rather than dog parks, and their eyes were a vivid, vibrant amber.

A huge male stepped up to face her. He was the biggest among them, had the brightest markings and thickest fur. His forehead was broad, his eyes wise; they seemed to look into her and whisper, *Come to me. I can protect you, cherish you, adore you.*

Heat flared through her as she stared, transfixed.

Come to me.

She took a step toward the gorgeous creature. Reached out her hand to touch the thick, luxurious fur.

And all hell broke loose.

CHAPTER SIX

"No!" DAYN BROKE free from the betas surrounding him, grabbed Reda and jerked her behind him. Then he got right in Kenar's face and shouted, "She's a *guest!* By rights and tradition, *back off!*"

The pack surged forward, but then subsided, growling as Kenar snarled a full-throated roar and sank back onto his haunches and then sprang erect, his form blurring as he changed. When the magic cleared, he stood there in his human form—slightly shorter than Dayn, bullnecked and square-featured, with heavy, powerful muscles and boxing-glove hands. His face was flushed, his eyes narrow with hatred. "She doesn't have any rights if she's traveling with a fucking bloodsucker—and, more, a Forestal murderer. Because that's what you are, isn't it, *Prince* Dayn?"

And, just like that, twenty years of peaceful coexistence were nullified by the crimes of a long-ago war. The wolfyn surrounding him growled and scuffled, their canine faces wrinkled with hatred. They weren't just there because their alpha had led them; they truly wanted him dead. He didn't see Keely, didn't know what that meant. As for Kenar, there was hatred in his eyes, but calculation, too. He was using this somehow, or planning to.

Fumbling a little in his haste, Dayn palmed two

blobs of wolfsbene from his pack and jammed one into Reda's unresisting hand.

"Did the witch's messenger tell you that she's a blood drinker herself?" he demanded solely to buy time. Pretending to scrub his face, he gulped the wolfsbene, which was slimy going down, with an aftertaste somewhere between mint and mud. He grimaced but continued. "Or that she tortured and killed Candida?"

He heard Reda cough, hoped that meant she had taken her dose.

The pack members shifted restlessly, some whining at the news. But Kenar bared his teeth. "We killed her servant, which makes us even, claw for claw. More, he was loyal, which was more than I can say for the wise-bitch. How long had she known about you?"

The first shimmers of heat and power filtered into Dayn's bloodstream, which was good, because the pack was closing in, shifting tighter, backing him and Reda into each other. Talking fast now, he said, "You're believing the witch's messenger over Candida? Did he give you any proof, anything more than a good story?"

"Yes!" Kenar roared, and the sound was echoed by his betas. "Yes, he offered proof. He used a spell to show Keely the sick, twisted things you made her forget! She was your *lover.* How could you feed from your lover? Oh, right," the alpha sneered. "Because you're a prince of the realm and you could make her think whatever you wanted. Fucking bloodsucker, disgracing my sister like that. *Using* her."

Oh. Shit. Reda's gasp had Dayn's heart dropping, even as guilt knotted tight and sharp in his gut over what he'd done to Keely. Not just because of the feeding and the cover-up, but because he saw the politics now. "You son of a bitch. You're going to use this to boot her out, aren't you? I bet you've just been waiting for a good excuse."

The wolfsbene was flowing hard and fast in his veins now, but there was nowhere to run. He went for his crossbow, bringing it up.

Kenar's eyes lit with vicious fury. He signaled the pack forward and shouted, "By Right of Threat—*kill them!*"

Dayn nailed the closest beta in the haunch, aiming to wound but not disable. As the male went down howling and snapping at the bolt, Dayn grabbed Reda's hand. "Come on!"

They made it only a short way before the ranks closed again. Reda had his back, fending off the creatures with sweeps of her unstrung bow as he sent two more bolts into the crowd. And over his shoulder, he said, "I'm sorry, Reda."

But apologies didn't fix anything, did they? Never had.

Grief and guilt rose up within him like old friends as he pulled his short sword. "I'm going to try to make a hole. Be ready to run and hang on to that map." Because she would be running without him. There was no way Kenar would let him live now.

"Dayn." Reda's voice was choked, but that was all. And he didn't blame her for not knowing what else to say.

Roaring, he swung the weapon in a glittering arc and surged forward with her right behind him. He made it through the first rank, knocked aside a big beta in the second, and—

Without warning, an arrow seared so close that he

felt the vibration on his skin as it passed him and carved a nasty furrow across the next animal's back.

"'Ware the woods!" Kenar yelled as another arrow sang past and glanced off the shoulder of an older wolfyn in the outer rank.

Not stopping to question the rescue, Dayn grabbed Reda's hand and hauled her toward the gap that had just been punched in the line. "Come on!"

They flew across a section of open road, then across to where a huge rock face rose up thirty or so feet to a sloping plateau. With the wolfsbene flowing through his veins and the entire Scratch-Eye pack lunging after him, Dayn made it up the sheer stone face in two big bounds, dragging Reda with him.

They crested the top and charged along the downslope, which put them on a narrow ridgeline with dense scrub on either side, forcing the pursuing wolfyn to run parallel to them, howling and barking in challenge, anger and threat. But Dayn's heart pounded and his muscles burned, propelling him faster than any human, faster even than most of the wolfyn. And Reda matched him stride for stride.

They soon outdistanced the bulk of the pack, until only a few of the fastest wolfyn were keeping pace where the ridge swept lower to flat ground and the scrub thinned along a narrow plateau that ended in the canyon: a wide chasm that was spanned right at this point by a narrow rope bridge.

As they charged down the steep incline and their pursuers closed on either side, Dayn said, "Stay behind me, but keep up. If we can make it across that bridge, we can pull the pins from the other side." There were other ways across, but they involved a half day's detour.

She made a noise that might have been assent, might have been a whimper, but there was no time to stop and discuss options.

And there weren't any other options.

Dayn's pulse throbbed, thudding in his head and beneath his skin, and power seared in his veins, urging him on. When they broke from the last of the trees to the flat plateau that led to the bridge, there were only two wolfyn still following. Those two, though, closed in *fast.* Then, as if choreographed, they split and attacked, one from each side.

As they leaped, Dayn shouted, *"Down!"*

He and Reda hit the dirt and the wolfyn actually *collided* in midair. The larger one drove the smaller back and down; they landed hard a few feet away and scuffled.

Dayn dragged Reda up, ready to run again, then stopped dead as he saw that the two wolfyn weren't struggling to get up and continue the chase. They were fighting.

And one of them was Keely.

The battle was short but vicious; within seconds, she rose to her feet, leaving the other lying stunned and still. Then she shimmered and changed, becoming her familiar self. Except that she suddenly looked entirely unfamiliar—still tall, gorgeous and stacked, but...he didn't know what the "but" was, actually. It was there, though.

She looked at Reda. "You're his guide?"

"So he tells me." The women shared a look that excluded him, left him baffled.

"You knew?" he demanded of Keely. "How?" Then,

because there was only one possible answer, he said, "Candida told you."

"She wanted someone else to know, in case anything happened to her. When the witch's servant came, I pretended I didn't know, and tried to think of a way to get a message to you, warn you of what was going on, but I couldn't."

The guilt was a raw ache inside him. "I'm sorry. I would have told you everything, but...Kenar."

"Kenar," she agreed. And there was something in her voice that hadn't been there before. Anger, maybe, or defiance. He wondered whether that was new or if, like her collusion with Candida, there were layers to her that he hadn't seen.

"Thanks for helping us get away," he said, knowing that must have been her. His eyes went to the still form of the unconscious wolfyn. "Will you get in trouble?"

"I'll blame it on you." She glanced back along the ridgeline, where growing howls warned that the rest of the pack was regathering. "You should get across the bridge and pull the pins."

"That's the plan."

"Which way are you headed?"

"Northwest," he said without hesitation, giving her his full trust, though far too late. "To Meriden Arch."

She nodded. "I'll tell them you went south, then. We'll head for the log crossing down by Candle Pass."

That would put the pack a solid half day behind them. "I'll owe you one. Hell, I owe you, period." He paused. "Keels, I'm sorry about the mindspeaking. I just...I had to feed."

She shrugged, and her voice held only wolfyn practicality when she said, "I was pretty freaked out when

Candida first told me, but she helped me get over it. And in the long run, it was a fair trade—I used you for sex, you used me for blood. That's what people like us do—use each other."

It was a hell of an indictment. And he couldn't deny it.

He swallowed hard, very aware that Reda had drawn away from him; her arms were wrapped around her body as if she was freezing and she stared out over the chasm as if she couldn't look at him. He wanted to pull her aside and tell her that wasn't how it had been between him and Keely. Except that it was exactly like that—she had nailed it. They had used each other, and each been content with the deal. Now, though, with the wolfsbene running in his veins and Reda in the picture, the arrangement echoed cold and bloodless.

He didn't have the luxury of time to pull her aside, though, or even try to reason through the sudden change inside him. They needed to move now, talk later.

To Keely, he said, "Be careful, okay? And be happy."

"Go." Her amber eyes went from him to Reda and back. "And hey…you be happy, too, okay?"

He didn't know how to answer that, so he just nodded. "Thanks for everything. Business deal or not, you helped make the past twenty years bearable." He didn't kiss her goodbye, just as he had rarely kissed her hello. Theirs had never been that sort of a relationship. Instead, he nudged Reda toward where a low line of trees hid the edge of the canyon. "Come on. Keely will buy us as much time as she can, but we need to get across the bridge and drop it from the other side before the pack gets here."

She didn't say a word as they jogged toward the trees, but he didn't know for certain if that was because she was shell-shocked by the wolfyn attack, upset over the Keely thing, or something else. Or all of the above.

But he did know for certain that his arrangement with Keely had nothing to do with his feelings for Reda. One had been business and practicality, while the other was entirely impractical and ill-advised. Yet even knowing that, he couldn't keep his eyes off Reda. Part of it was the wolfsbene, yes. But most of it was her.

He wanted to crowd her, nip her, hurry her along. Instead, he stayed by her side, pacing her and guarding her flank as they reached the chasm's edge and headed for the bridge. There were enough trees that they didn't get a clear look at the spindly structure until they were nearly on top of it.

Reda stopped dead, her face going stark in the moonlight as she said, "Oh, hell, no."

"It's safe, I promise." But, admittedly, it wasn't the most inspiring sight. Four long ropes were strung from one side to the other: two suspending a sparse walkway of wooden planks that glowed nearly white in the moonlight, and two more lines at shoulder height for balance. Shorter lengths tied at gallop-stride intervals supported the fluid structure, which moved and rippled in the air currents that convected up from the depths. He nudged her forward. "You can do this. I'll be right behind you."

"No." She backed up until she bumped into him, her back to his front, stirring heat and echoes of the earlier kiss he was trying to keep at the edges of his mind. "There's got to be another way."

"There isn't."

"What if—"

Hearing the first ominous hunting howl behind them, he came around in front of her and cupped her face in her hands. "We need to keep going forward, Reda. It's the only way."

He had meant only to take her attention off the bridge, but when he touched the soft skin of her jaw, heat washed through him, and something deep inside said, *Mine*. And when her eyes came up to meet his, need tightened to a fist in his chest, and that same something said, *Now*. He didn't fight the urges, though maybe he should have. Instead, he crushed his lips to hers, swallowed her gasp and took them both under in a kiss that shouldn't have been pure perfection. But was.

ONE SECOND REDA WAS terror-stricken, and the next she was on fire.

There was no transition, no warning, nothing but the sudden press of a hard male body and the demanding shape of his lips and tongue against hers. She should have yanked away, but couldn't find those synapses amid the heat and needy, greedy desire that flared instantly through her.

Oh, she thought, as fear melted beneath the onslaught. *Oh, yes.* Was it from the wolfsbene, whose power she could feel floating in her veins? Possibly. Probably. But she suddenly didn't care.

He slanted his mouth across hers, taking the kiss deeper, and fire kindled in her blood. Something fierce and possessive welled up in her—a sharp-edged need to dig into him and leave a mark—and that had her pouring herself into the kiss, into the moment and the man. He jerked against her, his fingers at her nape and hip, hers fisted in his shirt. And in that moment, there was only the two of them and a kiss that made her heart shudder in her chest and her entire conscious self say, *Yes, this*.

This was what she had been missing with the other men she had dated, the ones she had tried to convince herself were Mr. Right, Mr. Good Enough or Mr. Prince Charming Is a Fairy Tale So Get Real. *This* was what she had been searching for: the wrenching burn of lust, the grasping inner greed that said she had to touch him, kiss him, have him. And more, *this* was the gut-deep knowledge that it was mutual, that he was going crazy with the need to touch her, as well.

"Gods." He tore away from her and stood for a heartbeat with his chest heaving and his eyes fierce and wild. Then he grabbed her by the waist, spun her off her feet and deposited her on the first of the moon-silvered wooden slats.

She gasped and grabbed for the handhold ropes, panic sparking as the whole assembly dipped and swayed and pebbles skipped off the edge of the precipice and didn't make any sound of hitting bottom. She lurched back, but slammed into a yielding wall that was as immovable as a cliff, yet warm and muscular. And she could feel his heartbeat, quick and aroused, and echoing into her where it settled in a throb of liquid need.

"Go on, you can do it," he whispered in her ear, his voice deep and sensual. Then he shocked her by nipping her neck hard enough to bring a pinch of pain that took her mind off the yawning chasm below them. He crowded her with his body, bracketing her with his arms and legs. "One foot in front of the other."

Thrown off balance when his knee nudged the back of one braced leg, she took a stumbling step forward, then another when he repeated the move on the other side. "Stop it."

His only reply was a low growl as he nipped her neck again and crowded her more, herding her along the narrow bridge.

Heart hammering, she let herself be driven. The little bites sparked an atavistic heat that stripped her of her civilized outer shell and left only her primal brain behind. And that part of her reveled in the way he was dominating her, pushing her past her comfort zone and into uncharted territory.

She was aware of the yawning drop beneath her feet, the warm updrafts that came from below and the way the bridge swayed even though he steadied it by stretching his arms and legs as wide as he could against the taut ropes. But those inputs were secondary to the pounding heat that flared through her veins, carrying a brilliant, throbbing power that came only partly from the aphrodisiac side effects of the wolfsbene.

The rest of it was him.

"Go," he urged, his voice a low growl that spoke of things other than crossing a bridge. "Faster, Reda. Hurry!"

Her head spun with vertigo, magic and the heat of the man at her back as she took a step. Felt the bridge sway. Took another. And another. The breath backed up in her lungs as the throb of fear became a hard, hot churn of excitement, then a building sense of euphoria when her feet sped up and her body started compensating for the sway.

Behind them, fresh baying broke out, becoming suddenly sharp on the night air, closing fast. The wolfyn were coming!

"Hurry," Dayn urged, but she didn't need to be told.

She flew along the rest of the bridge, her heart tapping a rapid, excited beat as they neared the far side and her strides lengthened until she was hitting every second slat, then every third. And she was across!

Solid ground felt strange and static, but she bounced on her toes as she spun back to see Dayn getting to work on the pins securing the handrail ropes to the edge. One gave, then the next.

Crouching opposite him, she copied his moves, loosening the third pin and then pulling it out. One side of the bridge sagged and the whole thing twisted in the moonlight. Her stomach dipped at the sight of the structure they had just trusted their lives to coming unraveled so easily, so thoroughly. Then he gave a hard yank, the last pin came free and the bridge sagged and fell, the moon-brightened planks making it look like a dwindling dotted line. Then it was gone.

Shadows moved on the other side as the first of the wolfyn broke out into the open, moving fast and silent.

"Follow me," Dayn said, and moved off, headed south.

She fell into step beside him without comment. And was surprised to realize that she trusted him as her leader, her alpha. She wasn't second-guessing everything he said, wasn't trying to understand it within her old framework. Instead, she was following where he led.

Be careful. You've only known him a few hours, half a day at most, argued her rational, practical, logical, *boring* self, projecting a warning that was quickly lost to the joy of running beside Dayn as he sped up. The wolfsbene power flowed higher again, as if called by the sheer relief of being free to run as they chose, with their pursuers left far behind.

He plunged into a loose thatch of trees and immediately veered in the opposite direction, heading them back north after making a fake to the south, to lead the wolfyn toward the southern crossing as he and Keely had planned.

The memory soured some of the relief. *I used you, you used me. That's what people like us do.* The bitch's words haunted Reda, because they were so unlike the man who jogged beside her…and yet, the wolfyn had known him for two decades, Reda for six hours or so.

The trail they were on widened, giving her room to move up and run shoulder-to-shoulder with him. But where before her blood had throbbed in time with their strides, now she felt like they were subtly out of sync, thrown off-rhythm by the questions circling around in her head.

He glanced over. "Go ahead. Ask." His expression was cloaked in shadows.

A chill tightened her skin. "Are you reading my mind?"

"I told you, I can't connect with you."

There was no reason for that to sting, yet it did. Which was proof positive that she needed to get a grip on herself. "Then what is it you think I should be asking?"

"Whether I drank from Keely and made her forget about it. Yeah, I did. Wolfyn blood is powerful stuff for my kind. I needed a hit once per year, just as she needed a mate one night a year, so she could have a satisfying run during the blood moon without jeopardizing her brother's leadership."

Reda's stomach gave a slow roll, not just at the idea of him drinking the wolfyn's blood—with or without her knowledge—but also because he had so easily walked away from his long-time lover without so much as a backward glance. And only a few minutes later had been kissing her, Reda, and making her feel needed. Special. Powerful.

Don't go there.

Dayn slowed to a ground-eating walk, shifting his rucksack. "I know it looks bad. Abyss, it *is* bad. Keely and I traded sex, but then I stole her blood, which makes us far from even."

Reda didn't know what to say, or even what more he could say that would ease the tightness in her chest, so she let it go. And after a while, the tightness eased on its own, and she thought that maybe that was part of being brave, too—letting things go.

They kept traveling for an hour. Two. The forest closed in on the road they were using, and she became very aware of the dark wall of trees on either side of them, the occasional rustles and crashes of startled creatures.

At the sound of a not-too-distant howl, she stiffened. "Is that the pack?"

"Just a loner looking for trouble," Dayn said, voice slightly rusty from disuse. At her look, he elaborated, "A male can get kicked out of his pack if he challenges the alpha and loses, or if the alpha thinks he's likely to challenge and wants to avoid the fight. Sometimes he can join another pack, but unless he can really suck it up and play beta, there's usually the same problem there, too. Which means he ends up on his own, except during the moon time."

Sliding cautiously into the conversation, she said, "Why then?"

"Because those are the only three days that tradition allows a wolfyn male to claim the Right of Challenge, which is the ability to fight the pack's leader for the right to rule. That's also when disputes are settled, punishments are decided, matings are formed or broken. The wolfyn have boiled most of the family stuff and politics down to these three days, leaving the rest of the year essentially peaceful."

"Does it work?"

"It seems to."

"Civilized." She frowned, trying to put that into the context of what she'd just seen of the wolfyn. "That male back there."

"Kenar. Keely's brother."

"He tried to enthrall me, but you stopped him."

"Yes."

She shook her head, trying to dislodge those few seconds when she had been utterly under the big creature's amber-eyed spell. "I thought you said they wouldn't try that in their home realm."

"Kenar is..." He paused, as if searching for the words. "Keely and I might have used each other one night a year, but Kenar uses everyone all the time. But he's smart. He makes it seem as though he's following the traditions to the letter, when he's really bending them to suit his needs. And because he's the alpha and he's kicked out the very few males who stood up to him, he can control his pack almost absolutely."

"It sounded like Candida and Keely weren't as firmly under his control as he thought."

His lips tightened and he glanced back southward. "I hope she knows what she's doing. Kenar is charming enough when he gets his own way. But he doesn't take it lightly when he's crossed."

Reda nodded. "I know men like that. Saw too many of them on the job."

He cut her a look. "What job?"

"I..." She hadn't meant to go there, didn't know how they had even come to be talking like this, like they were normal friends out for a normal walk. Or a normal first date or something.

"It's okay if you don't want to talk about it," he said. But in her heart, it jarred, made her think he was too often ready to move forward and not look back, just like the major.

"I was a cop," she said.

"A guardswoman," he said with a strange note in his voice. When she glanced over, though, he shook his head. "It's nothing. You said 'was.' What happened? This is about your partner?"

"I froze." She crossed her arms, caught herself doing it and jammed her hands in her pockets instead. "You're shocked, I'm sure. And yes, that was sarcasm." When he didn't say anything, she told herself to leave it alone, let it lie. Instead, she found herself saying, "We just went in for coffee, that's all. Benz didn't even want to—but I was cold, tired and cranky, and our shift was going to run over because a couple of guys had called in sick, so he stopped and went in for me. And he didn't come back out."

Maybe it was the wolfsbene, maybe the crazy reality out of reality she found herself in, but suddenly the memory was right there in front of her, where before she hadn't been able to remember any of it clearly.

CHAPTER SEVEN

"SERIOUSLY, BENZ, WHAT is taking so long?" Reda killed the cruiser's engine, pocketed the keys and climbed out, slamming the door harder than she really needed to. "Did you have to grow the coffee beans or milk the half-and-half cow yourself?"

More likely he was chatting up the pretty brunette who worked the counter at the Porthole Packie. Normally, it didn't bother Reda when her good-looking, easygoing partner went into casual-flirt mode, even when the flirtee was a good ten years younger than him and a coed at the nearby state college. Tonight, though, the thought set her teeth on edge. She might not have been all that into the guy who had just "it's not you, it's me"'d her, but being newly dumped—again—really ought to earn her some priority in the coffee department. Maybe even a bonus Snickers.

Which, apparently, she was going to have to get for herself. Muttering under her breath and ignoring the curious looks of a couple of passersby—what, never seen a girl cop wearing a uniform and a mood before?—she pushed through the portholed door and into the liquor store, which, like so many of the local places, had recently been forced to diversify to stay afloat, putting in a general store section that boasted damn good serve-yourself coffee.

As she came through the door, she automatically glanced up at the curved overhead mirror, which was angled toward the register area and backed up by video surveillance.

She froze at the sight of Benz standing on the wrong side of the counter with his hands up, a gun in his face and the coed cowering behind him with her eyes closed and her hands covering her ears. Then Reda looked from the mirror to the register, and saw it was for real.

In the nanosecond it took for the perp to look over, go white-eyed and start screaming for her to toss Reda's gun and lie on the floor, her brain snapshotted the scene—assessed the lines of sight, possible cover and the positions of the three other people in the store. She instantly saw herself pretending to follow orders but instead launching herself into a nearby display, saw it fall into the gunman, saw Benz come over the counter and take the guy down. It was training, planning and instinct all wrapped into one. And it didn't happen anywhere but in her mind.

In reality, she just stood there.

"Get down!" The perp jumped back a step and shifted his gun from Benz to her. She saw the panic in his eyes and knew she had to react, had to get the hell out of the line of fire, but she freaking couldn't. *Her brain wouldn't work; her body wouldn't move.*

The guy's eyes changed. And Reda saw her own death.

"No!" Benz lunged over the counter and went for the guy, just as she had pictured, but she hadn't provided a distraction, hadn't done anything.

The perp spun back and fired as Benz hit him. The .38's sharp report jolted her from her paralysis as the men went down together, but she was too slow in fumbling her weapon from its holster. The gunman got up, scrambling out from underneath Benz and bolting for the back exit.

"Stop!" she yelled. "Freeze, police!" Which just wasted time.

Besides, he was already gone, the door swinging into place behind him.

She hesitated another gutless moment—chase or stay? One look back at Benz made the decision for her. Blood pooled dark ruby-red on the hardwood floor. She grabbed her radio and called in an officer down, assistance and an ambulance needed, then crouched beside him, skidding in his blood and seeing the ragged tear in his neck.

She clapped a hand over the wound, putting on pressure like crazy, telling him to hang on, that help was on its way.

None of it mattered, though, because like the man who had killed him, Benz was long gone.

"And when the detectives started asking me about the perp, I couldn't remember a damn thing," she finished, oblivious now to the dark forest pressing in on either side of them, seeing only the liquor store, the blood, the expressions on the faces of the other cops afterward. "The other wits hadn't seen his face and the video was useless. If I could have given them something…but, no. It was all gone, *pfft*, total fog, like my mind had locked up along with my body. I couldn't even help that way. I was deadweight. Useless." She glanced over at Dayn. "Just like I have been pretty much since I got here."

He met her eyes, though his expression was lost in

the darkness of the predawn that had started lightening the horizon to a deep, rich blue. "You're expecting me to say it wasn't your fault."

Her stomach gave an ugly-feeling lurch. "You think it was."

"I think it won't matter worth a damn what I think. You've got to work it out for yourself and find a way to make peace. Or not." But although his words put up barriers, the soft rasp of regret in his voice went right through them, and reminded her who she was talking to and what he'd been through. He hadn't just lost a partner; he'd lost his family, his life, his heritage.

"Sorry," she said, blush coming on hard and fast. "You were just asking to be nice, and I rambled on, and—"

He reached over and took her hand. "Reda, stop. That's not what I meant."

She swallowed, trying not to cling too hard to his hand. "Sorry. I'm not good at reading cues. My brothers say it's because I spend too much time by myself." Or they had before they moved away to start new jobs, new families, leaving her behind.

"I'm familiar with the concept." He let go of her hand, but they were walking closer than before, their shoulders and arms brushing in rhythm as he said, "I've spent twenty years dying to get back to Elden, reconnect with my brothers and sister and kick the Blood Sorcerer's ass, not necessarily in that order. But I've also spent most of that time blaming myself for not being in the castle when the attack came."

"You wouldn't have been able to," she trailed off, getting it.

"Exactly. Right or wrong, what matters is that I feel

responsible." He paused. "There was a girl, Twilla. She was a guardsman's daughter, and planned to train for the queen's guard."

"Oh." It was ridiculous to feel a twinge. But she did.

"My parents didn't approve because she was common-born and they had plans for me. We argued and I stormed out, and was gone when the castle fell. Worse, the last things between us in their lifetime were angry words and accusations." He spread his hands; the gesture was visible now in the pink light of a new day. "I'm not proud of myself. I wish I had been a better man, a better son. Hell, a better prince. But I can't go back and change that. All I can do is be better the next time, whatever form that next time takes."

"Oh," she said again, only this time it was a softer noise, one of understanding that was what he meant when he talked about moving forward and looking ahead. He wasn't trying to get away from the past, or ignore it. He was trying to fix the future.

And in that, he was nothing like her father and brothers, who spent so much time looking ahead of themselves that they couldn't see what was right in front of them.

Her opinion of him, which was already dangerously high, notched up again. And that, combined with the wolfsbene, made her far too aware of the way their arms brushed now and then as they walked. The contact was almost undetectable through the layers of sweaters and leather, but she knew. She knew.

Yet even though the heat of arousal stayed high in her bloodstream, her energy—at least for hiking—was rapidly fading. She didn't say anything, though, just pushed onward until Dayn nudged her with his elbow and pointed to a narrow game trail leading away from the main track. "There. That's what I was looking for. It leads to a hunting cabin about a mile in." His teeth flashed. "It's Kenar's, and we know for a fact that he's way behind us. The pack will need to rest, so we should be safe. I brought a couple of wards. I'll set one down here to warn us if someone's coming up the trail, then set the other to surround the cabin."

She nodded and said, "Okay." But what she really meant was, *Thank God.*

The sun was coming up over the horizon, signaling the end of a nearly interminable night, but she didn't look around, didn't care where they were or what it looked like in the light of day. Her focus narrowed to the few feet in front of her as she followed Dayn up an incline that at times turned so steep that they were going almost vertical, using roots and rocky outcroppings as hand and footholds.

Then, finally, he crested the climb and turned back to her. "Come on. We're here."

She gave him her hand, trusting his strong grip to pull her up onto what proved to be a wide ledge at the base of a rock-strewn mountain face. Near the back, snugged up against the rock ledge, a small log cabin was nearly hidden among squat, scrubby pine trees that looked short, proportion-wise, but towered over the small structure.

Barely even registering that reminder that she wasn't in Kansas anymore, she followed Dayn to the cabin and obediently hung back at his gesture, too tired to insist on helping him scout the area and set the wards. As he rejoined her, he was mixing some sort of powder into the contents of the waterskin he'd carried over his shoulder.

As he reached her side, he tipped his head back and drank deeply.

Reda's attention was caught far too thoroughly by the way his throat worked, her eyes locking on a rivulet that escaped and tracked down. She felt the tickle against her own flesh, and the sensation reached inside her to stroke the kernel of heat that was all that was left of the wolfsbene's power.

She quivered slightly as he lowered the waterskin and offered it to her. "It's a mild stimulant. It'll clear the fog and keep you from going so deeply unconscious that you can't run if we need to."

As she took the potion, the quiver grew claws, dug in and spread through her body—a potent combination of fear and arousal that instead of freezing her in place made her want to move into him, curl against him. She didn't let her hand shake, but as she downed the mixture, which had a mellow citrus flavor but the aftertaste of too-strong black tea, she was entirely aware of Dayn staring at her, watching her as she had watched him.

She wondered whether he was feeling the afterburn, whether his skin felt singed as hers did, gone suddenly prickly and sensitive beneath her clothing.

Lowering the waterskin, she deliberately met his gaze. And was nearly scorched by it. His pupils were dilated, his body tense and somehow seeming larger than it had only moments before, as if he had puffed up with the same atavistic mating urge that suddenly surged within her.

Her face fired with an intense flush that quickly washed down her throat to heat the skin of her upper chest, then her breasts. Her nipples crinkled in an excitement that was echoed in her core, until her entire body thrummed with sensual awareness.

It's just the drug, that lame-ass, cautious part of her said, but only weakly because the reality was that it was Dayn. And she was so damn tired of being rational, practical or logical.

He wasn't the woodsman, wasn't the lover she had seen in her dreams. But that hadn't stopped her from wanting him from the first moment she had awakened and looked into his eyes. More, as they stood there on a hidden rock ledge, as safe as they could be under the circumstances, rebellion rose up within her. Greed. And, oddly, logic.

She might not be stuck in a dream, but this sure as hell wasn't her real life. And given that, as long as she guided her prince to the archway on time, what was the harm in taking what she wanted for the next forty-eight hours?

Dayn saw the change in her eyes, saw awareness followed by understanding, then determination, and knew she was going to be the smarter of the two of them, and back away. Which was probably a good thing, because now he was the one who found himself paralyzed, locked in place not by fear, but by desire. Perhaps there was some fear in there, too, brought by the knowledge that this wasn't just about the potions, at least not for him.

Yes, lust pounded through him, throbbing beneath his skin, hardening his flesh and making him want to close the distance between them and take her mouth, her body, her sex. But there was also the tenderness and respect that had come to life through the night as he watched her struggle to deal with the situation she had found herself in.

She thought herself a coward, but he saw a survivor who had been forced to rebuild her life too many times alone and had stopped believing—in herself, in luck, in faith. And that part of her reached out to the same part of him and made him feel, for the moment at least, a little less alone.

She was his guide. But she was also a woman in her own right…and that woman drew him, compelled him, made him want. And that, combined with the potions, meant that she would have to be the one to walk away.

Instead, she took a step toward him.

The breath stilled in his lungs. "Reda." That was all he could get out. Just her name.

Her lips curved; her eyes darkened to the gorgeous blue he had seen in his dreams. "Dayn."

And she took another step. One more and she could be touching him.

Even his heartbeat seemed to hesitate, and in that moment, it was like he was back in Elden woods, lying in wait for a fierce and dangerous creature that at the same time was beautiful and oddly timid. There was that same hum of anticipation in his bloodstream, that same sense of dawning wonder and the inner whisper of, *Yes, that's it. Another step or two, my beauty, and I'll have you.*

"The drug," he began, then fell silent when she took that last step, putting them face-to-face, not touching but close enough to touch. To kiss. To do more. Even through the heavy layers of his clothing and coat, he was aware of her body, her warmth.

She pressed a finger to his lips. "It's not just the drug for me. And even if it is, I don't care." Her eyes flashed. "I've been stuck in a rut, not just because of what happened to Benz, but because I haven't found what I want—in a man, a job or a life. It wasn't all bad, but I keep thinking it could be better. And now—" She broke off, pressing her lips together for a second before she said, "What matters is that, right now, I feel *alive*."

Yes, he thought. *Alive.* That was the word for the awareness that raced through him, making everything seem fresh and bright as the sun crested the horizon and a single songbird trilled from the trees surrounding the cabin. Had he spent the past twenty years sleepwalking through life, only half living because he had been waiting for her?

He thought so. Now, though, he was awake. Gods and the Abyss, he was awake.

Then, suddenly, he could move again. He wanted to rush, to wrap her around him and plunge. Because of that, and because of the way he felt his temper slip and fray, he made himself go slowly.

Achingly, sweetly, slowly.

Framing her face in his hands, he leaned in and touched his lips to hers. He lingered there, drinking in the feel of her soft skin and the way it went from cool to warm against him, hearing the faint catch of her breath, tasting magic and smelling flowers and spice.

The rising heat washed through his body and soul, making the skin at his gums itch. *No,* he said to the magic, *not now. Not with her.* The thought brought a tug because he didn't know where he would be when he next fed, or even if he would get that chance. But he knew he wouldn't be with her, because when they reached Meriden Arch, they would go their separate ways.

"Listen," he began, needing to say something but not entirely sure what. "When we get to Meriden—"

"I don't want to think about that now." She brushed her mouth across his and moved past him toward the cabin, then turned back and held out her hand. "I'd rather think about you."

Heat and need lashed through him as the sunlight brightened from dawn to day and he saw her in living color for the first time: her wild copper riot of hair catching the sunlight, her full lips soft from his own and a flush of desire on her skin.

More, her words moved through him, echoed inside him in a stark reminder that he had been many things— a son, a prince, a sibling, a hunter, a guest—but rarely himself. There were other sons, other princes, other siblings, hunters and guests. But Reda was looking at him, reaching out to him, desiring him alone.

He reached out in return. Their fingers met. Curled. Clung.

And he followed her to the cabin, feeling as if his entire existence had just shifted on its axis.

CHAPTER EIGHT

As Reda stepped into the cabin, her mind recorded the scene. The main room was maybe ten by fifteen, and had a soot-stained brick hearth at one end. A queen-size bed took up a raised platform nearby, with a big chest at the foot of the stripped mattress promising blankets against the cold. The remainder of the main space was open, save for a tall cupboard in the corner, where she guessed nonperishables were stored, maybe even an appliance or two.

All of that pretty much fit with her idea of a hunting cabin. The surprise, though, was the door on the wall opposite the fireplace, leading to what looked like a fully plumbed bathroom, including a large, multinozzle shower tiled in strange, smooth gray blocks. "What the heck?"

"Kenar had it installed a few years ago," Dayn said from behind her. "His idea of roughing it."

"A pointed reminder that I'm not in Kansas anymore." She hadn't seen a cistern, pump or solar panels, suggesting that this was another of those places where magic and science intersected.

"Kansas?"

She swallowed a laugh that threatened to turn hysterical. "Never mind," she began as she turned toward him. "I…" She trailed off at the sight of him standing backlit by a window, the yellow light of day throwing him into reddish shadows rather than the blue-white of the moon.

He had dumped his bag in the corner and shucked off his bomber and sweater, though the air inside the cabin wasn't much warmer than that outside. That left him in his shirtsleeves, standing near the doorway staring at her with eyes that seemed to see straight into her.

"'I' what?" he prompted, closing the distance between them, his eyes going very dark as he looked down at her.

"I forget," she said huskily, while her inner self said, *I'm a sucker for the woodsman.* And at the thought, new sparks raced through her, tightening her skin and making her elementally aware of the cabin around them, the bed behind them.

Shrugging her bow and rucksack strap off her shoulder, she let them fall to the floor, then brought her hands up to touch his waist, pressing her palms against the warm material of his shirt and feeling the hard strength of the man beneath.

He cupped her face in his palms in what she was coming to recognize as a habitual gesture for him—or maybe just between the two of them. Then he leaned in and kissed first one of her cheeks and then the other, then the corners of each of her eyes, which fluttered shut. She brought her hands up to grip his wrists, cuffing him in place as his lips skimmed over her face, teasing her, drawing out the anticipation of a kiss. Her blood heated sweetly, carrying a dangerous something that went deeper than lust. But at the same time, the churning desires brought by the dreams, the danger, the potions and the man himself were all mixed together now, becoming a single mating urge, a raw longing that knotted her inner muscles and brought moisture to dampen her skin.

Where only seconds before she had been cold with the realm's sharp air, now she was overheated and tingling. Though he had said he couldn't read her mind—and thank God for that—he shifted to ease her out of her leather bomber, freeing one shoulder at a time first, then sliding it down her arms, moving slowly and somehow mimicking the actions in his kiss.

Caught up in each individual sensation, she could only sway against him and make love to his mouth as he worked her out of her borrowed sweater and then her shirt, then conquered the clasp of her bra with only a brief fumble to betray the difference in technology. Then her breasts were bare to his touch, burning for it.

And they were really doing this. At the back of her brain there was a spark of shock, another of joy and an inner whisper of, *Oh, yes.*

She gasped at the first brush of a fingertip along the side of one breast, then the other. Suddenly craving the glory of skin on skin, she tugged his shirttails free and went to work on the buttons with fingers that trembled as he traced a tightening circle around one nipple and his touch ignited tiny detonations within her. Then his wide palms were covering her nipples, his long fingers shaping her breasts, and she moaned into his mouth at the hard, hot peaks of sensation that brought.

He growled something—maybe an oath, maybe her name—and kissed her again. And where before his kisses had been soft and restrained, a sort of gauzy and romantic foreplay, now his lips were hard on hers, his tongue demanding. And her body lit wildfire-bright in response.

This, she thought, *yes.* The past and future stopped mattering, stopped even existing as she kissed him back, throwing herself into the moment, into the man. Her hands shook as she got his shirt off his shoulders, his arms and sent it sailing to the floor atop their dropped bags. And then he urged her up against his body and they were suddenly, shockingly, skin on skin. His light furring of masculine hair feathered her senses as they twined together, kissing deeply, carnally.

"Gods and the Abyss," he groaned against her mouth. *"Reda."*

The raw need in his voice tugged at her, brought a prickle of tears that she willed away, focusing instead on the way her entire body throbbed in time with her heartbeat as she strained up against him, trying to increase the contact, only to be frustrated by their differences in height.

Again sensing what she couldn't make herself say, he looped an arm around her waist and lifted her up against his body. She moaned as she brought her legs up around his waist to rub herself along the ridge of iron-hard cock hidden behind the barriers of his clothing, then again when he pressed her back against a nearby wall and pinned her there, kissing her deeply as he shaped her breasts with his big, gentle-rough hands and surged his hips against her in a rhythm that should have been familiar, but felt like nothing she had ever experienced before.

She touched his bare back and found parallel scar ridges that could only be claw marks, ran her hands up the lean, cable-tough muscles of his arms to his shoulders and felt him quiver beneath her touch, history and need melding together into a man who wasn't like anyone she had ever met before, or ever would.

Tangling her fingers in his thick, rich mane of dark, wavy hair, she softened against him. *Yes,* she urged him inwardly. *Yes.*

As if he had heard her, he broke their kiss, pressed his cheek to hers and breathed, "Ah, sweet Reda. Sweet, sweet Reda. Come to bed with me?"

Her heart ached with his husky tone, her core with the need to have him buried deep within her. But she tipped her head toward the bathroom. "How about we wash off some of this road grime first?"

His eyes clouded, then cleared. "Really?" He glanced into the bathroom.

And there it was again, that gap between his life and hers. This time, though, instead of discomfort, it brought a new skim of heat and an added tug of desire. She leaned in, nipped his jaw and then touched her tongue to the spot she had just bitten. When his hands tightened rhythmically on her hips, kneading her against him, she whispered against his ear, "Then this will be a first for you, won't it?" And a memory for him to take through the Meriden Arch when they parted.

Refusing to let the heat turn bittersweet, she caught his earlobe between her teeth, then teased him with soft kisses and light tugs as he swung them away from the wall and carried her into the bathroom. There, he let her down and, when she turned to the not-quite-familiar controls, he came around behind her, cupped her breasts in his hands and bent to kiss her neck, her ear, the side of her jaw.

She closed her eyes and swayed against him as the

water came on and the streams from four nozzles intersected in the center of the glassed-in shower cube,
filling the room with the roar of the spray and an unexpected fragrance that was part pine, part citrus and
wholly enticing. Perhaps it was yet another type of
wolfyn stimulant, because as the water heated and the
glass started to fog, she felt an echo of the wolfsbene's
heat radiate from her to him and back again.

He crossed an arm between her breasts, gently holding her still as he slid his free hand down her body to
toy with the snap of her jeans, all the while kissing her
neck, driving her to a frenzy that was only increased
by the fact that she couldn't really touch him, not the
way she wanted to.

"Let me," he rasped against her throat, and for a
second she stiffened, thinking she felt the sharp point
of a tooth and, worse, knowing that if that was what he
was asking, in that moment she wouldn't have been able
to deny him. But then her pants loosened and fell away,
followed by her panties, and then he slid a hand down to
cover her mound, hesitating when he found her entirely
bare, waxed out of habit because she hadn't wanted to
admit there was no point, hadn't been in a long time.

Now, though, that habit wrung an approving groan
from him as he tightened his grip on her, pinning her
against him. She moaned, her head falling back as he
touched her, exploring and then pressing her back, so
she could feel the shape of his hard ridge against her
buttocks. She was wet for him, dying for him, yet he
held her in front of him and stroked her mercilessly,
gloriously, in and then not, his fingers sliding slickly
against her hot, swollen folds.

She tried to curl around the sensation but he held

her back against his chest so she felt every stroke of his clever, clever fingers. "Dayn," she gasped, breath nearly sobbing in her lungs as her body tightened, coiling with the breathless anticipation that presaged orgasm. "I need... God, I want..."

"Let me," he whispered again. "Let go." And he slid two fingers deeply into her, then started thrusting with an increasing rhythm that had her arching into him and clamping around him with growing intensity.

"Oh. Oh, Dayn, I—" She broke off with a low, vibrant cry, shuddering against him as heat and pleasure washed through her, coalescing to the point where he was touching her, working her.

The world seemed to draw in on itself, seemed to hold its breath and go very still for...a...single... moment...and then she went over, clenching around his fingers with a strangled moan. Then she was coming, saying his name over and over as the raw, rhythmical waves suffused her, completed her...and then ebbed, leaving her limp and boneless.

She was so boneless, in fact, that she was almost unable to support herself when he angled her into the shower stall and put her beneath the spray, but then stepped outside the bathroom for a few minutes—long enough for her to wonder where he had gone, what he was doing.

The hot water hit her with sharp enticement, bringing her all the way back as Dayn returned to the bathroom, paused to shuck off his boots and pants and then came into the shower with her.

Without speaking, he drew her up onto her toes for a raw, powerful kiss that said they weren't done. Not even close.

Her blood heated anew at the kiss and the feel of his body going wet and slick against hers as the shower spray sluiced them both. Naked, he was a dream of wide bone structure, lean, rangy muscles and an almost inhuman grace, as if he were the wolfyn-turned-man, not the others. But he was all man where she cupped him, then slid her fingers along his considerable length, very aware that her fingers couldn't completely surround him.

He groaned, pressing into her touch, at first trying to kiss her and touch her in return, but then simply leaning canted into the spray with one hand on her hip, the other bracing his big body against the wall. And while her first thought had been to pick up right where they had left off out in the other room, now that sharp heat mellowed to a softer, more gentle urge.

She wanted to touch him, wanted to make him feel good.

A small shelf within the shower stall yielded a foamy, woodsy-smelling cleansing lotion that felt cool when she first rubbed it between her palms, but then heated as if coming to life.

When she moved around him, he shifted as if to follow, but she pressed him back to where he was, and said simply, "Let me."

He subsided, leaning on his braced arms so his head was beneath one of the showerheads, directly in line with the pounding spray, and closed his eyes.

The simple act of trust fisted an ache beneath her heart. And when a shudder ran through him at the first slide of her slickened hands along the line of the claw scars, it tightened that ache even further. How long had it been since he'd been touched for the sake of touching, not as part of a transaction, but simply because the other person wanted to?

Twenty years, logic said. And for a change there was no dissenting vote. He had been in this realm for almost as long as her mother had been gone, and he had been essentially alone that entire time, forced to hide his true nature from all but Candida, who had been a loner in her own right.

Reda's heart ached as she laved his broad shoulders and arms, the back of his neck and then down again to the tight muscles of his buttocks, which clenched rhythmically as she worked on him, and then as she moved lower to his thighs and calves.

He was breathing fast, taking great, deep drafts of air that went off-rhythm when she angled one of the nozzles to rinse him, then slicked her hands down his body once more to chase the suds away.

Done with the back of him, she moved around to his front again, thinking to repeat the process, maybe steal a kiss. But he straightened away from the wall, catching her against him with one hand on her lower back, the other at her nape. His eyes, when he looked down at her, were deep and dark with emotion. "Gods. Reda." Dropping his head to press his forehead to hers, he inhaled as if to say something, but then let out a sigh and whispered simply, "Thank you."

They flowed into the kiss as naturally as breathing, and this time there wasn't just heat and desire; there was a new give-and-take, a sense that he wasn't solely trying to give her pleasure, he was taking some for himself, as well. One kiss turned to the next and the next, and then he was fumbling with the shower controls to turn off the water and bring up a strange, soft light that surrounded them on all sides.

"What— Oh!" A tingle ran over her skin from head to toe. When it was gone, she was dry. Even her hair was merely damp, and the usually unruly waves were tame and soft to the touch. "Magic," she whispered, her voice catching on the word.

"The wolfyn have some redeeming qualities," he said huskily, and scooped her up in his arms, so she was cradled against his chest.

She squeaked and struggled a little, but then subsided to nibble her way up his neck as he carried her into the main room. And she gave another small, "Oh," at the sight of thick blankets piled on the bed and a fire in the hearth. The room was warm and suddenly cheery, and the sight made her throat tighten, because he had done this for her. Even in the heat of things, he had wanted her to be comfortable.

She swallowed past the lump of emotion. "You're a prince."

"I was, once."

Hating the hollowness in his voice, she said, "You will be again. When we—"

He kissed her, cutting her off. Then, still kissing her, he lowered them both to the wide mattress, so she lay beneath him with her legs alongside his, his thighs between hers and the long length of his erection pressing against her stomach, pulsing with an inner beat that resonated deep within her.

Desire washed through her like a friend she'd only just met, feeling so much sharper and more important than ever before, building higher and higher still as they kissed and he notched one thigh between hers, creating intimate pressure as he stroked a hand from her rib cage to her knee and back again in a feather-soft caress that seared her skin and made her want to beg.

New wetness gathered, new aches sprang to life, as he shaped her, touched her, but also arched into her touch, and paused to absorb the sensations as she licked his throat, then pushed on his shoulders to roll him onto his back so she could move lower, then lower still.

"Wait, Reda. I— Ahh." He gave a full-body shudder at the first touch of her tongue along the distended vein on the underside of his shaft. *"Gods."*

He made a move to touch her, but then she took another stroke with her tongue, a long lap from base to tip, and he fisted his hands in the soft, heavy bedding instead, then groaned when she did it again, finding the places where the textures changed and he was particularly sensitive. Where in the past she had been take it or leave it on oral sex, now she reveled in it, storing up his responses and glorying in the way he was submitting to her.

Soon his body was strung tight, his hands working in the bedding, his heavy length jerking in her mouth in movements that spurred new heat inside her.

He said her name, caught her hand, urged her up his body, and then, when they were chest to chest, rolled them so he was in charge once more, pressing her into the bedding with his good, solid weight. Both of their bodies were damp with excitement, slippery with passion, and as he settled between her thighs, his slick, hard length slid naturally into position, poised for entry.

Reda shifted against him, teasing them both with the slide of his blunt head through her slick folds. But then she stiffened. "Wait," she said, almost too late remembering that this might not be her reality, but it wasn't a dream, either. "Do we need something?"

He struggled to focus through eyes gone nearly glassy. "Something?"

"Protection? For, um, diseases and other things." *Please don't make me explain this.*

"Oh." His expression cleared, turned rueful and maybe a touch sad. "No diseases for my kind, to give or get. As for the 'other things,' because of the way my mindspeak works, I must feed from my mate's throat before a child can be made." She wanted to ask, but didn't. It must have shown in her eyes, though, because he shook his head slightly. "No. Never."

Guilty at the surge of a relief she had no right to feel, she reached up to soothe the hollow echo in his voice with a kiss that started soft and almost drowsy, and shifted something inside her. The softness gained an edge, the drowsiness fled to a demand and the guilt turned to greed, and the desire not just to have him inside her, but to *have* him, to belong to him and him to her.

But knowing that was impossible, she broke the kiss, pressed her wet cheek to the faint rasp of stubble along his jaw and whispered, "Now. Please, now."

She closed her eyes, shutting out the daylight, the strange surroundings and the danger beyond, determined to be there, in that moment, with him. Then he growled low in his throat, and thrust home. And as he slid into her—stretching her, filling her and bringing a surge of emotion that she didn't dare acknowledge— she didn't need to shut out the larger world, because he did it for her. The feel of him, the perfection of the fit, eclipsed everything else in that moment.

Her mouth went round in a voiceless O of pleasure. She dug her fingers into the heavy muscles of his shoulders as he rose above her, poised there for a breathless second of anticipation...and then began to move.

It was gentle at first, the tempo slow, as if he, too, wanted to store up each individual sensation. She rocked with him naturally, the moves more instinct than volition because she wasn't thinking, wasn't planning; she was *experiencing*. She reveled in the liquid surge of his body against hers, the fullness between her legs, the way the pleasure ramped with each thrust, and the vibration of his groan as her hands dragged to his hips, dug in and urged him on.

As things sped up, there was no difference between vampire or human anymore, or between a fairy-tale prince and a disgraced cop; there were only two lost souls filling in the empty spaces for each other, no longer alone. At least for now.

Needs piled atop greed within her as the pleasure found a purchase, took root and began to grow. And where before her orgasm had been sharp and brilliant, all inner fireworks and satisfying heat, the tension that gripped her this time was deeper and more consuming, tightening her inner muscles, overtaking her senses and suddenly making the moment far more important than it was supposed to be.

This is it, her body seemed to be saying. *This is what you've been waiting for.*

Turning away from that danger, she buried her face against his neck and moved beneath him. The move wrung a groan from him, then a reverent whisper of, "Reda."

Her name had never sounded like magic before.

Willing away the tears that prickled her eyes, she kissed his throat openmouthed as he rode her, bucked against her and drove the coiling pleasure higher and higher still.

She tasted the faint salty tang of his skin, felt the throb of his pulse against her lips. It pounded in tempo with him, with the pulse of needs that drew tighter within her with each thrust, where he pressed into her inside and out, and hit that spot there, oh, yes, there.

From deep within her came the urge to bite down, to take his essence within her and bind them together. Ignoring the faint itch of disquiet, she grazed her teeth along the vein that angled along the side of his throat, nipped lightly.

He hissed, his fingers suddenly digging into her as he slammed home, setting off new sensations that carried a raw power that tempted her to shy away.

She felt him struggle for control, felt herself hesitate, tempted to duck the intensity and the possibilities. Then, because she refused to be a coward with him, right now in this moment, she found his vein again. And bit down hard. She didn't draw blood, but it was a near thing.

The last remnants of Dayn's control snapped almost audibly. He flung back his head and then bowed into her, wrapping his arms around her to anchor her body against his thrusts, which rocketed up in tempo and swing, driving them both onward.

His hold was powerful, inexorable, and Reda reveled in it. She loved his strength and intensity, loved feeling small, feminine and overwhelmed—at least here, with him. She loved the way he pressed his jaw to her temple, a kiss to her brow and whispered her name as both their bodies went tight and tense, and the pleasure gathered inside her, waiting, waiting....

He turned his head, softly grazed the side of her throat with a wickedly sharp canine, and whispered her name. Fear and pleasure were suddenly the same, sharp and brilliant, and she gasped and came for him.

Pleasure lashed through her, as keen and sharp as a sword that cut through the loneliness and apprehension and left behind strength and wonder. She arched beneath him, breath sobbing, mouth shaping his name as the waves kept coming. Then he locked himself against her, hips working as he groaned long and low in a mix of words—her name, praise, pleas—and emptied himself into her.

She imagined she felt heat warmer than her own blooming inside, caressed by her inner muscles as they pulsed, milking him of his seed. And she, who had always had a slow-ticking biological clock if at all, felt a small, wistful wish that this one could have counted that way, that they could truly be mated.

And for a change, logic and reason didn't have a damn thing to say.

He stayed locked against her while the pleasure leveled off and then faded, and the world around them started to come back into focus. She heard the *hiss-pop* of the fire, saw the brightness of the sunny day outside through her closed lids and felt the shift of the mattress when he levered up onto his elbows, taking his weight off her.

Though she would have liked to linger a moment more, she opened her eyes and met his emerald gaze. And for the first time since meeting him—and she didn't for a second want to count the hours, considering what had just passed between them—his expression was open and unshadowed. It made him look younger and a little naughty, bringing to mind the kind of man who would go for a gallop to blow off some steam, little knowing that the morning would change his life forever.

She, too, felt changed, but she didn't want to look at it too closely. Not now. Maybe not ever.

He cleared his throat. "I, uh, feel like I should say something. But I haven't a clue what."

A tension she hadn't even been aware of melted away, easing her neck and shoulders. "Me, too, and me, neither. So how about we say 'thank you' and set it aside for now?"

His face softened. "Then I thank you, dear sweet Reda, for teaching me about showers, for taking me into your bed, for touching me and for sharing your lovely, lovely body with me."

Her heart shuddered in her chest, her eyes threatened to fill, her throat to lock, and she knew she didn't dare say anything now; that if she did, she would make an idiot out of herself and make them both supremely uncomfortable. So, although it made her the coward, she just nodded jerkily and reached up to kiss his cheek.

Dayn, bless his noble heart, seemed to understand. He brushed his fingers over her cheeks as if brushing away the tears she hadn't let herself shed, then said, "Stay here and see if you can sleep. I'm going to double-check the wards."

She nodded, feeling a blush form at the strange intimacy of the moment, with the two of them strangers except in their dreams. He rose from the bed and padded, gloriously naked, to the bathroom, where he

pulled on his pants and boots, then threw on his shirt
without buttoning it. When he came back over to her,
he had one of his short swords tucked in his belt.

That shouldn't have made him even more appealing than before. She was a modern woman, an evolved
human being. But apparently that modern, evolved
woman liked men with swords.

Not men, she thought, *just Dayn.* And that wasn't
logic, reason or practicality talking. It was a fact. And
if that put her on the fast track to heartache, maybe
that wasn't the worst thing that could happen to her.
Because at least she wouldn't be sleepwalking through
life anymore.

He snagged one of the waterskins as he returned to
the main room, and crossed to the bed and offered it to
her first. "Thirsty?"

"Parched." The act of accepting water from him
shouldn't have felt profound, just as the satisfied look
in his eyes as he watched her drink shouldn't have kindled new sparks of arousal. Flustered, she handed it
back. "Thank you."

"Rest. I'll be back in a few minutes."

Nodding, she lay back and curled onto her side with
her back to the fire. With her eyes closed, the noises
around her seemed amplified. She tracked Dayn's
movements by the thud of his boots, the close of the
door at his back, the crunch of gravel outside and the
annoyed call of a bird disturbed by his circuit of the
cabin.

He returned within a few minutes, as promised, and
his clothing rustled and boots thudded as he stripped
back down before sliding into the bed with her. He

curled around her, his front to her back, and folded their hands together over her heart.

And as she drifted off to sleep with his warmth surrounding her, she found herself doubly grateful that he wasn't a wolfyn. Because if he was, she would surely be enthralled.

DAYN AWOKE NEAR NOON, when his internal clock warned that they didn't dare rest much longer, in case their pursuers were still on the road.

In her sleep, Reda had turned toward him. Now, she was nestled close to his side, her head pillowed on the arm he had curled around her. Her breath was warm on his skin, tightening his nipples and sending tendrils of reaction lower down in his body. But those physical responses were tiny trickles compared to the deep wellspring of emotion that even now threatened to fill him up and spill over.

Affection, gratitude, relief, disquiet—there was all of that and more, a complicated mix that said he probably shouldn't have made love with her, and definitely not as intensely as things had wound up getting…but at the same time he couldn't regret the decision, or his eventual loss of control.

They had well and thoroughly loved each other with no pretenses, no expectations and the knowledge that they would go their separate ways at the arch, taking with them only good memories. And if that thought brought a twinge, he ignored it and focused on how damn good he felt suddenly—refreshed and recharged, and ready to take on the world.

Or to take on a pissed-off pack and a countdown to

the night after tomorrow—the fourth night—as the case might be.

At that sobering reminder, he touched her shoulder. "Come, my sleeping beauty. It's time to waken."

He halfway expected her to jolt awake and panic at finding them in bed together. As responsive and exciting as his sweet Reda had been, he doubted she'd ever before taken a lover mere hours after meeting him, doubted she was accustomed to waking in a near-stranger's arms. Their relationship, though, had perforce been compressed, accelerated.

She must have been closer to waking than he had thought, though, because she didn't gasp or jump away from him. Instead, she smiled, eyes still closed, and said, "If I'm Sleeping Beauty, then my Prince Charming should wake me with a kiss."

"You think I'm charming, then?" Without waiting for an answer, he leaned in and touched his lips to hers, a chaste press at first, then going deeper when her lips softened and parted beneath his.

Murmuring, she shifted closer to him and slid her arms around his neck, capturing him against her. The move tugged at him, reaching inside and filling a place he hadn't even known was empty. Fierce joy raced through him as he moved over her, into her, pressing her into the mattress as he kissed her thoroughly, his body awakening to the reality of a lover, *his* lover.

Her soft moan made him want to pull her up and dance her in a mad whirl around the cabin; the gentle tug of her fingers in his hair made him want to sing at the top of his lungs, though he couldn't hold a tune; and the feeling of her beneath him, her thighs cradling him as he swelled and hardened almost instantly despite having come inside her only a few hours before made him want to race out into the forest to hunt the most dangerous foe, solely so he could bring her a talisman of the kill. Though from what he'd heard, humans could be squeamish about such things. So maybe he would pick her wildflowers instead.

The sheer ridiculousness of it was suddenly very appealing. As was the thought of slipping inside her once more and rocking them both to oblivion. He could feel the slick wetness of her cleft against him and the excited race of her pulse beneath her soft, feminine skin. And although they needed to leave the cabin, he was dying to lose himself in her, with her.

Then, suddenly, her fingers were wrapped around him, guiding him. He stiffened, broke the kiss and groaned as she teased the tip of his hard shaft along her wet folds.

Pulling his head from hers, he looked down at the spread of her coppery curls and the glint of her blue eyes. "Gods, Reda. We don't have much time."

"I know." She reached up and kissed his cheek. "So be quick." And she curled a leg around his hips, and urged him home.

Groaning, he plunged into her, then hissed with pleasure as her heated wetness snugged around him, urging him on. He was already teetering at the edge of control when she arched up to meet him, and the liquid, heated friction snapped those last thin threads that said he needed to see to her pleasure before his own.

Grating her name, he caught her by the shoulder and hip, anchoring her as he thrust heavily—once, twice, a third time was all it took before he felt the tingling, tightening sensation that presaged a climax. He didn't try to fight it, but rode it instead, pistoning twice more before the tingles became a roar of heat, the need to cut loose, and he bowed against her, thrust as deep as he could and releasing himself into her with a shattering groan.

He went blind and deaf, insensate to anything but the pleasure of coming inside her as his orgasm went on and on, seeming to last longer than the sex itself.

Slowly, he became aware of sharp prickles where her fingernails dug into his shoulders, the press of her heels into the backs of his thighs, where she had locked her ankles. And the fact that he was probably crushing her.

"Gods." He levered himself up on arms that wobbled like the legs of a newborn beast-chaser foal, and looked down at her, expecting to see... Hell, he didn't know what he expected. But it wasn't wide-eyed wonder tinged with fear.

But then again, he realized after a moment, that pretty much summed it up.

"It wasn't just the drug, was it?" she asked softly.

"No." He shook his head. "This is us, sweet Reda." He wanted to ask her if she had come, but couldn't bring himself to admit that he had been that far lost within himself. So instead he resolved that when they stopped next to rest, he would even things up. The thought put a burn of anticipation in his gut and made him look forward to that break and the next, and however many it took them to reach the Meriden Arch.

And after that...damn it, he didn't know what came after that, except that he had a vow to keep and responsibilities to fulfill. He only hoped to hell he could do all that and do right by Reda, too.

Somehow.

CHAPTER NINE

FOR REDA, THE NEXT TWO days passed in a blur, yet at the same time there were moments that were imprinted so sharply in her mind that she knew she would remember them forever.

There had been alien fairy-tale moments: like when she watched a hawk skim over the treetops, only to have it grow larger and larger as it approached, then belch smoky flame from a crocodilian head before it screeched and veered off; or when the thunder of hoofbeats called their attention to a herd moving on the other side of a low hill and, just as she turned to ask Dayn why the wolfyn and their guests didn't ride the horses, they crested to see two-dozen massive equids with coal-black coats, ember-red eyes and wickedly sharp unicorn horns that glinted in the sun.

Those moments had grown more alien still when he had told her that the demidragons were nothing compared to the true dragons of Elden legends, like the vicious Feiynd, with its black-pearl scales and assassin's instincts. Or how the wolfyn and unicorns were uneasy allies, their peace treaty based on mutual dislike, and that he—a horse lover since childhood—had tried to learn the unicorn's language, only to find that while wolfyn tongues could speak it, human forms couldn't.

There had been hauntingly beautiful moments, like

the sight of a wolfyn pack gathered on a faraway hill, silhouetted against the fat, full moon as they howled in a spine-tingling descant; and how, when they had crested the jagged ridge that separated the territories of two packs—the Nose-Claws and the Bite-Tails, both of whom they had managed to avoid by staying near concealment—a grassy green plain had spread out before them, forming a bowl-shaped crater with a nearly circular lake at its center, reflecting the pale sky and the shape of a round cloud overhead.

And then there was Dayn. He was in all of those memories and so many others from those precious two days. He was her woodsman, her prince, her lover, and in that short, precious, unselfconscious space of time, she had come to know him intimately. She knew how he moved, how he tasted, what it took to make him sigh and how far she could tease before his control snapped and his fangs came out. Literally.

His vampire heritage didn't scare her anymore; he was just a man like any other, albeit one with the powers of his realm and his heritage. He was stubborn at times, and was inexplicably fond of chewing on wolfsleep sap, which she found tasteless, with a weird consistency. But those were insignificant quirks when measured against the whole.

They hadn't used the wolfsbene again, but instead hiked under their own power, with occasional hits of the stimulant potion, which seemed to be the local equivalent of coffee, or maybe an energy drink. They had traveled steadily, talking quietly or walking in companionable silence, stopping every six or eight hours to rest…and make love. And at times she'd had to pinch herself to be sure she really wasn't dreaming, after all.

But, like a dream, the journey couldn't go on forever, and they were nearing the end of theirs.

"Ready to roll?" Dayn asked, coming out of a section of woods that ran almost all the way up to the road's edge. He carried only a single rucksack now, along with his crossbow and short swords; she was wearing the other rucksack along with the bow and arrows she probably wouldn't ever use. It was warmer today than it had been, and he was down to his shirtsleeves, with his jacket and sweater packed away.

The sight of him in his plaid shirt, pants and boots—so like the woodcuttings that had brought her to him—made her heart turn over in her chest and put a wistful lump in her throat. *If only...* she thought, but didn't bother even completing the wish.

"Let's do this," she said, pushing to her feet. By his estimation, they would reach the arch in an hour or two, well before sunset. They hadn't really talked about what they would do when they got there, but she harbored a secret hope that they could steal one last time together, maybe right beside the waterfall.

She wanted that to be the memory she rekindled when she looked at the final page of the book. Love-making, not loss. She'd had the joy; she would take the pain that came at the end of this strange magical adventure.

Still, though, her throat went tight as she came even with him on the trail. She flattened her palm on his chest and reached up on her tiptoes to kiss the side of his neck, where the blood vessels ran, and where she was oddly proud to have given him a hickey. He covered her hand with his and squeezed, but when she moved to pull away, he held on to her, trapping her hand against his heart for a moment longer before letting her go.

They started down the road together, shoulder to shoulder, in a silence broken only by the calls of different creatures. She knew them now: the deep roar of the demidragon, the high, clarion cry of the bugle beast, the deceptively sweet trill of the mudhump, which was truly repulsive in both looks and smell.

On one level, she hated the thought of leaving the magic behind, even hated the thought of leaving this strange wolfyn realm. Yet at the same time, she yearned to be back in her safe apartment, in a world where she knew how things worked and she didn't need to be looking over her shoulder all the time, didn't need to remember to be brave.

About an hour into this last leg of their journey, as they marched up the long incline of a rolling hill, Dayn spat his last piece of wolfsleep gum into the bushes, rinsed his mouth with a few sips from the waterskin they had refilled just that morning and wordlessly offered it to her.

"No, thanks, I'm good." Her voice felt rusty, her throat tight.

He tucked the skin back in his rucksack and adjusted the strap an extra time, then fiddled with his sword belt. Shrugged inside his shirt.

She glanced over and raised an eyebrow. "Are you okay?"

"Yeah." His voice, too, was husky. "It's just…we'll be able to see the arch from the top of this hill." He didn't meet her eyes as he said it.

"Oh." *Oh, God.* Her newly reawakened libido tugged at the thought of making love at the edge of the waterfall, but that pleasant flutter was quickly submerged by the thought of what would follow. Aware that her steps had slowed, she made herself speed back up. *One foot in front of the other.* "Well. I guess we made it."

He unslung his rucksack, pulled out his jacket and shrugged into it, only to yank it off seconds later with a frustrated noise. "I hate this. I hate…" He trailed off, staring at his hands. "Oh, gods. This isn't coming from me. It's the magic. The vortex is already starting up."

"No." She spun toward the crest of the hill, but didn't see anything strange about the sky or trees, nothing to say there was magic beyond. There was no glow, no noise. She couldn't even hear the waterfall.

Dayn knew magic, though. He *was* magic.

"Come on!" He tucked a piece of wolfsbene in her hand, and downed his own in a single gulp. "We'll make a run for it!"

She gulped the gritty lump, forcing it past the tightness in her throat and the pressure that made her want to cry out that it wasn't fair, that she needed more time with him. Just another hour, that was all. Though in her heart of hearts she knew even that wouldn't have been enough, and maybe it was better this way. Swallowing, she nodded. "Let's go."

They charged up the rest of the incline together, strides lengthening from moment to moment as the drug kicked in. Power raced through her veins, lighting her up and making her feel mighty, invincible…and even hotter for Dayn's body than she had been moments before. She wanted to trip him and follow him down, cover his body with hers and ride him until they were both wrung limp. She wanted to kiss him, touch him, own him, belong to him.

Instead, she concentrated on putting one foot in front of the other as they crested the top of the hill. The sound of the waterfall hit her first and then the valley opened up in front of them and she stumbled to a halt as she saw it: Meriden Arch.

Dayn stopped beside her, standing so their arms touched.

Even from the half-mile distance, she could see that it was a match to the woodcutting: a high stone archway capped the top of a waterfall that crashed halfway down an interrupted cliff face to fall in a tumbled pool that gushed to a river leading away. Heavy foliage flanked the waterway and the cliff faces, then thinned to a rolling green valley. All that was the same.

The shimmering in the air below the arch, though, was new.

He was right. The vortex was already forming.

"We need to go." His voice broke on the last word.

"I know." She reached out and took his hand. Their fingers twined together. And they ran down the hill together, shoulder to shoulder, as if they were mated, though that was only a dream.

Her eyes were burning by the time they hit the flatlands, her throat by the time they reached the edge of the pool, pausing near where a wide trail zigzagged up the cliff and led to the archway, where lightning arcs leaped from stone to stone. The air sparkled and swirled but hadn't yet begun to rotate.

They had a little time, then, to say their goodbyes. She wasn't sure if that was a good thing or not. She lifted their joined hands to her lips and kissed his knuckles, grazing the skin with her teeth and making him shudder.

"Sweet Reda." He cupped her face in his hands and bent to kiss her.

She leaned into his touch, into his kiss, feeling a poignant ache grow along with the now-familiar heat, which was made sharper by the burn of the wolfsbene in her blood. She gripped his wrists, held on to him, tried to imprint the moment on her soul.

He drew away before she was ready to let him go. But his eyes were very intent on hers, searching her face as he said, "Come with me. Come to Elden."

"Oh," she whispered as a full-body shiver ran through her; and her blood ran hot and then cold, then hot again. It wasn't like she hadn't thought about it— of course she had. But logic—and, worse, her gut instinct—said it was the wrong answer. Tears prickled, but she willed them back. "I want to," she said, forcing her voice to stay steady. "God, of course I do."

His voice, his eyes, went flat. "But you won't."

"The vortices are unpredictable and we don't know if there's a direct connection between our realms. It could be a one-way trip for me."

"Would that be so terrible?"

The question stung, mostly because, on many levels, the answer was "not really."

If she didn't return to Salem, her father and brothers would spend a couple of months trying desperately to find her, more because it was the right thing to do than because they really missed her, though, and because they would need a logical explanation for her disappearance. And her friends and coworkers would go through the motions, believing deep down inside that she had changed her name and moved to an island somewhere, as she had occasionally threatened to do.

Six months, a year from now, she would be a memory, maybe a scholarship somewhere. And how much did that thought suck?

"You think I haven't asked myself that?" she said softly. "You think I don't know that I haven't left a single indelible mark on the human realm?"

His fingers tightened on hers. "I'm sorry. I didn't mean to make it worse. But if that's the case, why go back?" His kiss was hard and possessive, and made her burn for him. "Come with me, my sweet Reda."

She wanted to; oh, how she wanted to. But for a change, logic and practicality had it right. "Say I do... then what?" *Please say you know, please say something that would make it make sense.*

But his expression went bleak. "I know it's too much to ask, too damned dangerous. There are, what? A hundred ways for things to go to hell once I get home? A thousand? Which means I'm an asshole for even asking—I should want you to be safe above everything else, right? It should be enough that I see you go into that vortex—" he pointed at where the shimmers were beginning to rotate "—and can have faith that you made it home okay. It should be enough that I've got the memories of the past few days to take with me, to remember when things turn to shit. Which they probably will."

Her throat locked, because he was saying all the things she'd been telling herself, yet she still wanted to shout, *Yes! Yes, I'll come with you.* All she got out, though, was a fractured sigh of, "Dayn."

Eyes firing, he took her other hand and lifted it, so both of her palms were pressed to his chest, folded in his hands. She could feel their heartbeats keeping time, feel the urges of the wolfsbene pounding in her veins as he said, "Maybe I haven't grown up as much as I thought, because every part of me wants to be self-ish right now, and keep you with me. Please say you'll come. I promise that I'll—"

"Don't," she interrupted, pulling a hand free to touch his lips and silence him. "You can't make promises to me. God, you shouldn't even be thinking about me."

"I know. But I can't stop." He kissed her fingers. "Come with me. I need you. I don't want to do this without you."

It was every childish fantasy come to life—the handsome, powerful prince begging her to run away from her unsatisfying life to live the adventure with him, the dream.

But dreams always ended, didn't they?

"Say everything goes according to plan," she said. "Suppose you and your brothers and sister find one another, take out the sorcerer and reclaim Elden. What then? What happens to us?"

"We live happily ever after." His answer should have seemed glib; instead, it made her yearn.

"I'm not a princess, Dayn. I'm just another guardsman's daughter."

She wanted him to look surprised, wanted to think he hadn't seen it. Instead, a spark entered his eyes. "It's no coincidence that the book came to your mother. The stories she told you are straight out of kingdom folklore."

"You think she was a guest in the human realm." She did, too. It was only logical.

"Not only that, I think she had the kind of powers that travel in royal lines, or at least the nobility. Why else would my father's spell have sent the book to her? How else would she have known how important it was, or that it was meant for you, not her?" He lowered his voice and leaned in to whisper, "Mindspeak, Reda. I think my father reached out to her the same way he did to me. And he could only do that if there was a blood-line connection, however faint."

Reda's head spun, because she hadn't taken it that far. She might have sagged if he hadn't been there to lean on. Her eyes locked on the love bite at the side of his neck. "You think I'm a vampire." She wasn't sure if her sudden queasiness was nausea or excitement.

"Half or less, and blood drinking doesn't run true. But…yeah, I think the heritage is there."

She shook her head, denying the logic more than the possibility. "You're reaching."

"Maybe. Or maybe I have faith that our feelings mean something, that all of this means something." His gesture encompassed the realm, the vortex and the two of them. "The book didn't come to you randomly. None of this is a coincidence, Reda. And we're not over. I won't let us be."

She saw the kiss coming and nearly moved away, knowing that she couldn't think clearly in his arms— or rather, that the clarity she found there wasn't always based on reason. But the wolfsbene rooted her in place and her traitorous body had her reaching for him, slid-ing her fingers up into his thick hair and opening her mouth beneath his.

They had made love only a few hours before, but heat leaped through her anew when his lips slanted across hers and their tongues touched and slid. And for the first time, something clicked inside her and a small voice whispered, *Yes. This is it. There's no way you can walk away from this.*

It wasn't the first time she had thought achingly that Dayn could be the love of her life. But it was the first time that she had thought that maybe, possibly, they could make it work. Always before, even if she could believe they would make it through the retaking of Elden, she hadn't been able to picture herself as the consort of a prince. Now, though… Her thoughts soared as he drew his lips from hers, then kissed her cheek, her forehead.

Then he took a step away from her, toward the trail leading up, and held out his hand in invitation. "Come with me, my sweet Reda. Have faith. Be brave."

She flashed on the image of the woodsman asking Red to leave everything and everyone she knew and come away with him, without making any real changes in his own life. Before, she had thought it unfair. Now, she saw that sometimes it was the only answer.

"I— *Look out!*" she screamed, catching sudden sight of a gray-buff blur flying down the lowest section of the trail toward him, then leaping.

He spun instantly to meet the attack, but he had only just started to pull his sword when the huge wolfyn hit him and took him down with a terrible snarl.

She grabbed for her bow, but it wrenched in her grip, looped across her neck, and she found herself yanked back by the strings, which cut into her. "No!" Panic hammered through her as rough hands grabbed her and dragged her away from where the huge wolfyn—she thought it was Kenar—was ripping at Dayn, tearing at him. She saw blood, heard him shout…and then, worse,

go limp and silent. She surged toward him, screaming, "Dayn!"

There wasn't any answer.

HE HEARD HER AS IF FROM afar, as if in a dream that he
didn't want to waken from, because his conscious self
was in agony. Dying. Maybe already dead.

Fight, damn it. You can't leave her to the pack. The
inner voice was his own, the sentiment a noble one,
but it seemed too late. He was drifting, his consciousness split from his physical self. He was looking down
on himself, watching as Kenar stood atop his deathly
still body, lifted his bloodstained muzzle to the sky
and howled the victory while the vortex started to pick
up speed in the background, going from air to white
vapors.

The rest of the pack stood ringing him in a mix of
wolf and human forms, with Reda pushed off to the
edge and watched by four guards, two of each form.
She was white-faced and shaking, tears running down
her face as she stared at the carnage. He looked for their
sole ally, but Keely wasn't there. Where was she? Had
Kenar figured out that she had aided in their escape?

Gods, Dayn thought. *Please. Not yet. Give me just a
little more time to put things right.* He strained toward
his body, trying to put himself back in the ragged flesh
that had once been a man.

Sensing a glimmer of pain, he pushed all his energy
in that direction, all the magic he could find within his
incorporeal self. Agony lashed through him and the
scene below dimmed as he was pulled back into the
shell of his dying body.

He tried to call more magic, to complete the connection, but he needed something more. He strained and struggled as Kenar barked a command and the pack shifted, eddying as Reda's guards brought her forward. Panic lashed through Dayn, and for a second he thought he felt a flutter of his too-still heart. *Please, gods. Put me back in my body so I can save her and fulfill my oath.*

For a second, nothing happened. Then an inner voice boomed, *Will you sacrifice your future to do it?* The voice wasn't his own, wasn't his father's, wasn't anything he had ever heard before. It was deep, powerful and terrifying, and he thought it came from the realm of the gods, or perhaps the Abyss. It was that all-encompassing.

"Yes," Dayn whispered, somehow forcing the word from between his corpse's cold lips. "Absolutely yes." This was his lesson, his warning—he had started to be the selfish man again in trying to take Reda with him. He wouldn't make the same mistake again. "I swear it."

Power flared suddenly, wrapping around him, yanking him from his distant perch and thrusting him into his dying body. Only it wasn't dying anymore. Magic washed through him, bathing his body and kick-starting his heart, which flopped for a few moments within his chest, but then took on its native, life-giving rhythm.

Pain! It hit him like a new vortex, sucking him down and threatening to send him flying once more above the agony of it all. But he dug in and gutted it out, sending all the magic he could muster toward his birthright powers. His gums burned; his secondary canines sharpened and extended, piercing the tender flesh and descending to touch the inside of his lower lip. Warmth flowed through him, knitting bones, healing flesh and organs and beating back the pain. *Faster, faster,* he chanted inwardly. *Hurry!*

Lacking his bird's-eye view, he was forced to crack his eyelids and peer through blurry eyes to see Kenar, now in human form, standing over Reda, who was on her knees, forced there by her human-form guards while the two wolf forms stood back, bristling. Dayn knew all four, knew they would follow their alpha's orders without question. And he dreaded the empty, soulless look in Kenar's eyes as he stared down at her.

"I claim the rights of a guest," she said, lifting her chin to glare at Kenar, face white and drawn. "You have to grant me shelter and safety. It's tradition."

The alpha's eyes didn't even flicker. "That would have worked on my sire, or even my softhearted whore of a sister, but not on me. I'm pack law now, not a bunch of moldy old traditions that lured a witch and her creatures to come into our realm and attack us. And my law says there are no guests anymore. There are only the wolfyn and their enemies." He turned away, tossing over his shoulder, "Kill her."

Reda screamed as the guards dragged her to her feet.

"Hold!" Dayn bellowed, lunging to his feet and yanking his short sword with one hand, his crossbow with the other. He swept the crowd and snarled, showing his blood drinker's fangs.

Reda's face lit and she gave a low, glad cry. "Dayn!"

The wolfyn flinched back, ears flat and lips pulling back in snarls of their own. All but Kenar, who rounded on him, eyes lighting with cruel joy. *"Bloodsucker,"* he hissed. "Back for more?"

The bastard had left him partly alive on purpose, testing to see if he would heal.

Not letting his hand shake at what he was about to do, Dayn pointed his sword at the alpha's throat. "I claim the Right of Challenge."

Reda's eyes widened and her lips shaped the words *Right of Challenge,* though no sound emerged.

Kenar barked a laugh. "Bullshit. A bloodsucker can't challenge to lead the pack. Only a wolfyn has wolfyn rights."

"I know." Dayn looked at Reda, and said, "Remember this if you remember nothing else good about me—I'm sorry for everything." Because what happened next would destroy the slim chance they'd had at a future. Just like the voice had said.

Exhaling against the sudden stab of pain brought by the knowledge, he did the something he had avoided since his first blood moon, when he had realized what his parents' spell had really done to him when it sent him to the wolfyn realm.

He called on his other magic. And changed.

CHAPTER TEN

REDA'S SCREAM WAS BURIED beneath the tumult that arose from the wolfyn as Dayn's form blurred, widened, shifted, shortened…and then crystallized into a huge wolfyn.

Dayn was a wolfyn. *Oh, God. No. This isn't possible. It's not happening.* But shaking her head didn't clear the sight, and she was beyond thinking any of this was a dream. Or, in this case, a nightmare.

Its—*his*—fur was dark, nearly black, which made the reddish shoulder patch and golden dorsal stripe stand out like a visual shout. And when he drew back his lips to snarl at Kenar, his canines were longer than those of any of the others, and wickedly pointed. A vampire trapped, temporarily at least, in a wolf's body.

"Noooo." The word escaped from Reda on a low, anguished moan as the structure of her unreal reality crashed to pieces around her and she saw the past few days for what they had been.

Dayn's brilliant eyes—emerald green, not the amber of the others'—flicked to her at the noise, but she couldn't find any human emotion in them. His words rang inside her: *I'm sorry for everything.*

He wasn't just talking about her being caught up in his family's magic, or even about him having kept yet another huge secret from her. He was apologizing for what he had done to her over the past two days.

The bastard had enthralled her.

Shame. Rage. Heartbreak. She didn't know what to feel, what to focus on within the huge wave of emotion that slammed through her as the pack struggled to deal with this new shift in the balance of power.

Kenar recovered quickly from the surprise. He might have paled, but his sneer didn't lose any of its oily, predatory nature. It made her think of the wolfyn in the book, the villain... And that made her see how Dayn wasn't the woodsman, after all.

He was the wolf.

He was the seducer, the tempter. And she had fallen hard for the temptation.

"A challenge?" Kenar waved the others back, and the pack members cleared out. Within seconds, he and Dayn were facing each other in the middle of a cleared circle. "You think the pack will accept you as their leader now? I don't think so. And don't look to Keely for any help this time. She was outcast for helping you. Last I saw, she was hauling ass away from a big silver loner." Kenar's sneer turned even nastier. "He's probably caught up to her by now. Wonder if she's having fun? Those loners don't get a chance at many bitches."

Dayn growled low in his throat and began circling toward Kenar, trying to flank him.

The alpha, still in human form, moved to stay opposite him, openly taunting now. "Were you planning on handing things over to my weak slut of a sister? You think that's going to be any—" He morphed abruptly, dropped to a crouch and leaped with a feral roar as Dayn did the same.

The two huge creatures thudded together midair and went down snarling in a flurry of fur, raking claws and snapping jaws. Blood sprayed and one of the combatants yowled, and then they were surging to their feet, up onto their hind legs to come together again, smashing into each other like fighting rams going for a head butt, only with gaping jaws and wickedly sharp teeth.

Growls and excited yips came from the crowd, and more than one of the human forms went wolf, as if the experience was better in fur.

Reda's stomach roiled; she had to breathe through her mouth to stem the surging nausea that came from the potent mix of fear, disgust and upset rocketing through her.

Enthralled. God.

That explained why she had fallen so hard so fast, didn't it? And even now that she knew the truth, she wasn't free of his spell. She couldn't be, because her eyes were fixed on the fight and her heart was lodged in her throat.

She hated the sight of blood wetting his thick, dark coat when he and Kenar next parted. She hated the thought of his lean, beautiful body taking on new scars. And she hated how the other wolfyn were watching him with cold, hard eyes that suggested that even if he won his fight, he wouldn't live to claim his prize. She wanted to put herself between Dayn and the others, warding them off with her body while snarling, *Mine*.

Even more, some part of her drank in the sight of him in his wolf form: how his thick black coat shimmered over his muscles and caught the light as he reared up and lunged for his enemy; and how his eyes flashed like emerald-green flame when the combatants came together chest to chest, snapping and snarling. The sight of curving, elongated and wickedly pointed canines stirred her deep inside, and the way he moved so elegantly, like a fighter, like the largest of predators, brought the same whisper of, *Mine.*

And she had to get out of here. Because if she stayed any longer, she might never escape his spell.

But how could she leave? She was surrounded, disarmed, her bow and arrows tossed aside. Mind racing, she scanned the scene. She caught a blur of motion from the trees near the waterfall, another from a stand of middle growth nearby, but then nothing, making her think it had been a bird.

Her captors were all in their wolfish forms now, glued to the fight as Dayn rose over Kenar and slammed down atop him, driving the alpha to the ground. Teeth flashed, blood sprayed and Kenar screeched in pain. When he next stood, he was panting and dragging a foreleg. Dayn, too, was injured; he was bleeding from a deep gash on his shoulder, and the blood spattering the ground beneath him said that there were other wounds hidden by his dark fur. But he lunged first, drove Kenar back and followed him down with a flash of bloodstained teeth.

The brutal, meaty crunch that followed was the most sickening thing Reda had ever heard, and she gagged as Kenar spasmed and went gruesomely limp.

And then that *slurp-crunch* instantly dropped to the second most sickening thing she had ever heard as Dayn topped it by planting his front paws on Kenar's body, lifting his blood-streaked black muzzle to the sky and loosing a terrifying and self-satisfied howl of victory.

Awwwooooooo. The noise reached inside her, making her want to scream and claw at her own skin. Or maybe that was the knowledge that she had lain with a creature, a killer. Her heart tore as she stared at him, his wolf form gorgeous, terrifying...and entirely enthralling.

He howled again and nausea flared suddenly, and she clapped a hand over her mouth and turned away. Two of her huge wolfyn guards flanked her as she ran blindly from the circle with no real destination in mind except *away*. She needed to get away from the sight of his gorgeous emerald eyes, away from the wild, feral glory in his howl, away from the burning desire to turn back.

The guards herded her toward the trailhead, near where her bow and arrows had been tossed. One nudged her toward the weapons. The other turned back to the pack, silver-white fur bristling as if he were protecting her rather than holding her captive.

Wait. Silver?

Reda looked down at the wolfyn nearest her, thought she saw something familiar in its eyes. "Keely?"

The creature nodded, then nudged her forcibly toward the weapons, the pathway. She whuffed an almost-word that sounded like, "Go."

And then there was a sudden howl of alarm, a scramble of feet, and Reda looked up to see the pack reorienting on her, Keely and the silver-backed male.

Reda exploded into motion. She grabbed her bow and arrows and bolted for the trail. Behind her, a feral snarl sounded the attack as the Scratch-Eye pack came after her, and Keely and her loner friend tried to fend them off, and only partially succeeded. They stalled some of the wolfyn, but others came on.

Reda ran for her life. Her legs and lungs hurt; the wolfsbene helped, but would it be enough? *Please, God. Gods. Whoever you are,* she thought brokenly as she hit the trail and started up with a half dozen beasts behind her and gaining.

"Hold!" The word cracked commandingly, halting the wolfyn in their tracks.

She couldn't help herself. Recognizing Dayn's voice, she stopped halfway up and looked back. Her heart shuddered at the sight of him standing over Kenar's body, both of them now morphed back to their human forms, one alive, one dead.

Dayn was wearing the same clothing he had been in when he morphed—how did that work?—and for a nanosecond he looked like the panel in her book that showed the woodsman standing over the slain wolf, triumphant at having saved the girl.

It was the truth, yet not.

Their eyes met, and even across the distance the contact struck sparks inside her. "Oh, Dayn," she whispered, heart hurting.

"For gods' sake go, Reda. Get out of here." He didn't shout the words, but she heard them clearly in her head, in her heart. And she just as clearly saw the pack orienting on him, bristling as the excitement of the fight cleared and they remembered that he was both their sworn enemy and now their leader.

This was about to get ugly, Reda thought. But even as her body—traitor as it was—sent her two steps back down the trail, a full-throated roar of sound and energy geared up above her, drowning out even her own sobbing breaths.

She didn't need to look to know what that meant: the vortex was fully formed. If she was going to leave, she had to do it now.

And, oh, dear God, she needed to leave.

Tears blurring her eyes, she spun and bolted up the remainder of the path.

She heard Dayn shout her name, but she didn't look back. Couldn't. She could only look ahead of herself.

The narrow stone bridge that formed the archway was higher than it had looked from the ground, the drop scarier, the pathway itself narrower—little more than a two-foot-wide span in places and crumbling at its sides. But where only a few days earlier she had balked at the rope bridge, now she strode across the crumbling stone archway without fear.

She wasn't sure if she was too scared to be scared anymore, having been vaccinated by repeated terror, but as she looked down into the dark center of the vortex, her only real thought was, *Well, here goes nothing.* There was no anticipation as she called the spell to mind and visualized her apartment kitchen, which seemed suddenly small and stale rather than safe. But she couldn't stay in the wolfyn realm and she didn't want to go with Dayn anymore. Not now.

She glanced over, saw the pack gathered around Dayn as if awaiting orders and felt her heart break.

And she jumped into the whirlwind that would take her away.

REDA! DAYN WATCHED her fall, felt the vortex surge deep in his bones and knew she was gone. He felt it in the emptiness inside him, the hollow spaces he hadn't even recognized until the past few days.

Agony hammered through him—not the pain that had come with the change, but from the way she had looked at him when he transformed, and again when he killed Kenar. The world was better with the bastard dead, but he wished there had been another way. There hadn't been, though, which left him with a pissed-off, leaderless pack and no time to waste.

Tearing his eyes from the archway, he refocused on the pack, not liking the way Kenar's main lieutenants were closing on him, though there seemed to be some sort of commotion going on at the back, over where Reda had broken through. Maybe he had an ally or two, after all. Too bad one or two allies weren't going to do a damn thing when the other forty-something went for his throat.

Pulse thudding sickly in his skull, he spread his hands in a "no harm, no foul" gesture. "Look, I just want to go home. If you'll just let me—"

The wolfyn closest to him shimmered and stretched to his human form to reveal Janus, a thick-necked soldier who followed his alpha's orders unquestioning and knew tradition better than he knew his siblings' names. "You won the challenge," he growled. "But we don't intend to be led by a filthy bloodsucker."

"I don't want to lead you. I just want—"

"I claim the Right of Challenge."

"Damn it, Janus, just listen for a minute. I don't want to fight you."

"Too bad." The other male blurred and retook his wolfyn form, baring his teeth in a feral snarl.

Dayn cursed under his breath, all too aware that

he only had so much time before the vortex started to die back down. Hell, the thing could collapse at any moment. Taking a deep breath, he called on his other magic, and—

"Hold, damn you!" a woman's voice called.

Every eye swung to the source, and a murmur of yips and growls rose up at the sight of Keely in human form, pushing through the crowd with a man at her side. Easily twice her mass, he had silver hair despite appearing to be only a few years older than her. He wore the heavy furs and sigil of the Bite-Tail pack, and sent Dayn a steely look as they joined him in the fight circle that had cleared at Janus's challenge.

"Who the hell are you?" Dayn blurted, but even as he said it, the Bite-Tail connection clicked and he put it together. "Roloff?"

"Aye." The big man's low growl carried enough force to quell the pack instantly. He swept the wolfyn with a look. "Keely's father promised her to me, but Kenar broke that bond and outcast me. I claim her by right of the original promise."

And to Dayn's utter shock, Keely blushed.

Not a loner, then, Dayn realized. It had been Roloff, coming around during each moon time, making himself visible and seeing if Keely was ready to go against her brother. And finally, this year, getting what he wanted.

Gods, he would never understand wolfyn politics. But at least someone had gotten what he wanted.

Dayn glanced at the vortex. *Ah, Reda.*

"Do any deny me this mate?" Roloff demanded.

Dayn met his eyes. He didn't embarrass Keely by shaking his head. But he didn't say anything, either.

Keely and Roloff didn't embrace or kiss, but the look

they exchanged said that making her an outcast had been the best thing Kenar had ever done for her.

Now, looking entirely in her element, Keely faced the pack. "By right and descent, the leadership of this pack should have come to me, not Kenar. He took control outside of tradition, which means that the challenge was not a true challenge, and this male—" she indicated Dayn "—is not your leader. I am." She swept the pack with a piercing look. "Do any challenge me on this?"

There was dead silence. Janus even looked a little relieved.

After a minute, she nodded. "Good. Then hear me. This man goes with safe passage. None shall touch him." She turned to Dayn, taking his hands and squeezing them in probably the only spontaneously friendly touch between them in two decades. "Go home, Prince Dayn of Elden. Go with my friendship, and the hope that this could be the beginning of a new era of peaceful sharing between our realms."

"You... Wow. Okay." Dayn faltered as he found himself nailed with an ambassadorship before he'd even regained his kingdom. "Yeah. That's ambitious."

"It was what Candida wanted, why she befriended you. So if you don't do it for me, do it for her."

He swallowed hard. "For both of you, then. And for the betterment of our realms, I hope."

"Good. Then go. Get the hell out of here." She kissed him on the cheek, shoved his rucksack, crossbow and sword into his hands and waved for the pack to let him through.

Roloff gave him a cuff on the shoulder that held a good measure of "and don't come back," and the rest of the pack watched him with unblinking amber eyes that said "good riddance." It would take more than Keely's goodwill to convince them—and the other packs—to give the blood drinkers a chance, but the benefits could be huge. Which was just another reason why he needed to get his ass through that vortex and get this brand-new era started.

Still, an empty hollow opened up inside Dayn as he jogged up the trail to the archway. Not because he was sad to leave the wolfyn realm, or because of the changes—and deaths—that had come because of him, or not entirely. No, the ache had curly red hair and blue eyes, and the hollowness came from knowing that the best three days of his life were over.

And the rest of it was about to begin.

His feet weighed him down as he headed out along the narrow causeway, following the line of Reda's footprints in the thin layer of grit. He stopped where she had stopped, stood where she had stood and closed his eyes for a second, trying to mindspeak her and failing yet again. Still, though, he sent his message toward the swirling realm magic, hoping against hope that it might reach her, just as a book of fairy tales once had: *Be well, sweet Reda. Be brave. Live your life.*

Then, without looking down, he stepped off the edge. And plummeted home.

CHAPTER ELEVEN

WITH DAYN'S VOICE RINGING in her ears, Reda blinked awake to find herself hanging weightless, surrounded by strange, shifting fog that was white in some places, while in others it sparkled with rainbows, lit from above with shafts of light that seemed random, yet not. She was wearing her bow over her shoulder and clutching three sad-looking arrows.

"Hello?" she called. "Dayn?" Her pulse thrummed in her ears. Part of her wanted it to be him, another part not. Maybe someday she would be able to think about him without hearing the sickening crunch of flesh and bone, the shivering howl. Not yet, though. Not by a long shot.

She had thought distance would help, time home alone.

But this definitely wasn't home.

What was going on?

Nerves prickled beneath her skin, not freezing her, but warning her that this wasn't good. She hadn't been conscious for the trip to the wolfyn realm, but based on Dayn's description this wasn't the way the vortex was supposed to work. It was supposed to suck her up and spit her out, no detours. This was most definitely a detour.

Stay calm. You can handle this. Making herself

breathe evenly, she pictured her apartment kitchen in minute detail, right down to the dishes in the sink and the book on the counter. Then she said her mother's spell. But instead of her kitchen, she got a man's voice.

Your work is not yet done.

It sounded in her head, but it came from the fog, from nowhere and everywhere. It chilled her to her marrow, though not because it was scary; it was deep and well modulated, with an abundance of that formal, faintly stiff tone that crept into Dayn's—

No. She wasn't going there. Not when it made her eyes well and her stomach heave, and filled her mind with the *squish-crack* of a broken neck, the howl of a vicious beast that was part predator, part murderer.

Aware that the voice seemed to be waiting for something, she said softly, "Please let me be done. This isn't my work. It's not my fight."

Are you so certain?

Her mind filled suddenly with horrifying images of stone walls destroyed by dozens of club-wielding ettins, armored guards cut to pieces by giant scorpions with razor-tipped tails and claws, a woman carrying a baby, racing across a flagstone floor only to be snatched up from above by a giant spider.

You are a guardswoman of the blood. You would let this happen?

"What blood? Who are you?" When there was no answer, her voice sharpened. "For God's sake, what do you want from me? I got him to the arch." She tried to spin in place, but failed. Her heart was hammered with a mix of fear and frustration. "Will you answer a direct question already, damn it! What do you want me to do?"

Help him reach the castle by tomorrow night. And help him remember his true self or all is lost.

Her stomach twisted at the dread and dismay that came with the thought of following Dayn to Elden. "And then what?"

Go home.

She flashed on the image of a rounded hill very like the one near Dayn's cottage, though without the stones. The spires of a castle were visible in the near distance beyond some trees, and there was a small shrine off to one side. And damned if it wasn't carved with a simplified version of the cover of *Rutakoppchen:* a girl traipsing through the woods while eyes watched from the darkness.

"Do I have a choice?" Her voice cracked miserably and she didn't care. She was crashing off the wolfsbene, beat-up, brokenhearted, and didn't want to have to do this.

There is always a choice, even when there seems not to be.

"Great. A frigging fortune cookie," she said.

Then she stopped, hearing her own words echo in the fog, realizing that she was snarking off at a spirit voice she strongly suspected was at least the essence of Dayn's father, the vampire king. More, she was thinking, planning, reacting, having an opinion. She wasn't paralyzed, wasn't leaning back into Dayn's reassuring presence as she had done too many times over the past few days when the going got tough.

She wasn't freezing. She was *dealing*. New strength flowed into her at the realization and, with it, came a fierce sort of joy.

You are stronger than you know, Alfreda.

A shiver ran through her. "How did you know my real name?"

Will you help him?

A few days ago, it would have seemed ludicrous for her to think she could help a man like Dayn. Even a few hours ago, blinded by her enthrallment, she wouldn't have thought he needed her help with anything save for mutual pleasure. Now, though, she was seeing things more clearly. She supposed shock could do that—either numb her out or wake her up. And now she was awake.

With clearer eyes, she realized that Dayn wasn't as evolved as he wanted to think. He had spent two decades beating himself up for having been distracted by a woman when he should have been focused on his duties the morning of the Blood Sorcerer's attack, only to fall right back into the same pattern with her. Their... relationship? flameout?—she wasn't sure what to call it—had been a distraction, a way to keep himself from focusing on the harder things. She didn't think he had been entirely dishonest with her, either...more that he had lied to himself.

She saw herself differently, too. In the rainbow fog, she suddenly saw a woman who too often waited for other people to take care of things. Granted, her childhood had shaped that, as her father and the therapists had—well meaning or not—blocked off her imagination, her initiative. But that was then and this was now, and she needed to quit being afraid, not just of danger, but of making a mistake, making a *choice*. Back home, she had stopped moving forward, and her soul had begun to wither. In the wolfyn realm, however, she had started doing, thinking, moving, deciding.

Maybe she had made a huge mistake falling for

Dayn, had almost made an even bigger one by blindly following him to Elden as his lover. But the first mistake had burned her but not killed her, and the second one wasn't going to happen. If she followed him to Elden, it would be by her own choice, and not as his lover. And if that brought a stab to fresh wounds, heartbreak wasn't fatal, after all.

"Okay," she said to the waiting voice. "I'll do it."

Good.

The fog rose up around her, curled toward her and touched her here and there, tingling where it landed. And then it started moving with more purpose, sluggishly at first and then faster and faster, she found herself hoping to hell that this wasn't going to go into the "mistake" column. She drew breath, but before she could say anything—or even really decide what she wanted to say—the world lurched around her, the fog turned dark and ominous, and *whoomp!* She suddenly found herself standing on a grass-covered hill in the middle of a dense, ominous forest.

Dayn wasn't there. In fact, she was completely and utterly alone. And in realizing that, she became aware that it was the first time she had been alone in days.

She stood for a moment, testing for signs of panic. But while she was tense and most certainly on alert, she wasn't terrified, didn't want to stand still and wait for something to happen.

Let's get moving, her instincts said. *Daylight's wasting.*

Overhead, she glimpsed a sky that was a far deeper blue than that in the wolfyn realm, making her blink at the difference. The trees, too, were strange; they were twisted and stunted-looking, though they stretched high overhead to knit their branches into a high canopy of dull brown leaves. The sunlight that filtered through those leaves was a dingy brown color, making her feel oddly dirty.

"Welcome to Elden," she said under her breath. "Doesn't look much like I expected." Both her mother and Dayn had made the kingdoms sound like lush and fertile paradises, like something out of a fantasy movie. But maybe it would get better once she was out of these woods.

Given that realm travel wasn't known in the kingdoms, it stood to reason that the access points would be hidden away, forgotten.

Thinking she'd do best with a good defense, she unslung her bow. And stared.

What before had been a plain but serviceable hand-carved bow was now a slick, high-tech compound bow of the type she had favored in the human realm, but made of a springy, unfamiliar wood and strung with a natural-looking fiber of the proper tensile strength. Her arrows, too, had transformed; she was wearing a sleek quiver that contained a dozen perfectly balanced shafts and offered hooks where she could secure the bow fully strung.

"Upgrades," she said to herself. "Nice." Better yet was the small purse of gold she found in her pocket.

Feeling more optimistic than she had moments before, she struck out in the direction where the light seemed brightest up ahead. She would find herself a village, get her bearings and go from there. If nothing else, she knew where Dayn would be tomorrow night: Castle Island.

DAYN AWOKE IN A DARKNESS so complete that he might
have thought he was still unconscious except for the
ammoniac smell of guano. It burned his eyes and si-
nuses and had him holding his breath as he pawed in
his rucksack for one of the small wolfyn hand lamps.

It lit, but only partway, emitting a bare and fitful
glow even after he dialed it to full power. *Too much science and not enough magic in the gadget,* he thought,
not daring to say the words and risk inhaling.

A quick scan showed that the vortex had dumped
him in the dead end of a cave. He thought there might
have been paintings on the walls, but the smears of
guano and the tears blurring his vision made it tough
to tell for sure. With only one way out, he didn't have
to debate his escape route; shouldering his rucksack,
he beat it for thinner air.

The cave curved and curved again before he saw reflected daylight up ahead. He paused short of the last
bend and tucked the light away. And then he stood a
moment longer, because after twenty years, the next
step was a big one.

"Elden," he said softly.

He was finally home. He could finally make things
right. And if there was a deep ache within him because he was stepping out of the cave alone, there was
nothing he could do about that now. He had made his
bargain and his sacrifice. The spirit realm had let him
save Reda and send her to safety, and in exchange he
had given up any chance for them to have a future. And
maybe, probably, that was the way it was supposed to
have worked all along.

He took a deep breath and borrowed a particularly
fitting human idiom: "Here goes nothing." If he was

lucky and the spell had his back, he would find him-self relatively near Castle Island. Better yet would be to find Nicolai, Breena and Micah camped out waiting for him. Gods, Micah would be grown now.

Trying not to lock too hard on that hope, tempting though it might be, Dayn shrugged the rucksack higher on his shoulder and set out, rounding the corner and striding out of the cave into the daylight. And stopped dead.

"Damnation." Another fitting human saying, and one that was unfortunately all too apt.

The sight that greeted him wasn't anything like what he'd been expecting, and was nothing he'd been prepared for. The forest that stretched out before him wasn't green and lush, wasn't chockful of hiding places for the forest creatures. It was brown and thin, with no groundcover and only sparse, yellowed leafy patches that hardly seemed sufficient to sustain life.

Worse, he couldn't even pretend he was at the edge of one of the southern kingdoms, near a stretch of bad-lands or desert. Because as his eyes adjusted to the painful sight, he recognized the downslope in front of him, the rise of rocky hill behind him. He even knew the cave now, though he had never before been all the way to its end due to the foulness of the air.

He was in Elden, less than a day's march to the castle. But gods and the Abyss, what had happened to his land? His forest?

Unfortunately, the answer was an easy one: the Blood Sorcerer had happened. This was what two de-cades of dark sorcery had done to his once-gorgeous kingdom, two decades of neglect. It had killed the land.

"No." Heart sinking so hard his stomach hurt, Dayn

took two stumbling steps, then went down on his knees beside a waist-high boulder, where there was a tiny scrap of green struggling to grow in the shade. It was an Elden glory—or it should have been. But instead of producing brilliant blue flowers the exact shade of Reda's eyes, this one had only a single weak bloom in a pale, sad hue.

"I'm sorry." He didn't even realize he was crying until a drop hit the dirt. It dried quickly, sucked into the parched earth so suddenly that he might have thought he imagined it, save that he found moisture on his cheeks and felt the tears in his soul.

He didn't stay there long; he couldn't. But part of him wanted to.

Any faint hope he might've had that this was a localized blight withered as he reached the edge of the forest and saw rolling hills of dusty brown leading to a yellow-hazed horizon, and his last few shreds of optimism died utterly when he hiked himself up into a nearby tree, climbing into the high, swaying branches to get a longer view.

From there, he could see other forests, scattered farms, several villages—though fewer than he remembered—and a dark smudge where he judged Blood Lake to be. And throughout it all, there were patches of brown, green, black, even some furry-looking white and bilious yellow-green, as if the land had died and been taken over by mold and rot.

"Gods help us," he whispered, soul going hollow at the confirmation that it wasn't just the forest that was blighted and dying. It was all of Elden.

And although he had already hated the Blood Sorcerer for the attack on the castle, now that rage dug deeper, grew hotter, became even more personal at the realization that the bastard hadn't just taken power, he had ruined the kingdom, leeching its energy to fuel his dark, twisted magic.

Dayn's forests, his family's people, were suffering, and from the looks of it had been for some time, and he had let it happen. If he had known he would have... The thought process ran aground there, because he couldn't have done anything differently, nothing that would have mattered to Elden. He'd had to wait for the magic to send his guide and bring him home.

Only this wasn't home. Home didn't exist anymore. Elden had become a war zone without a real war, a casualty of the royal family's abandonment, though they hadn't voluntarily abdicated.

On some level, he wished with all his heart that the spell hadn't been corrupted; that he and the others could have come together long before this to take their revenge, sparing the kingdom its torture. On another, though, he knew that it was pointless to wish history changed; he needed to deal with the matter at hand.

Right now, it wasn't about not looking back, wasn't about moving forward. It was about what happened next, about righting the course of an entire kingdom, gods willing. It wasn't about him, wasn't about the things he'd wanted or the people he'd lost.

He shimmied down the tree, feeling its inner rot in the faint slickness of its bark. Then, shouldering his rucksack once more, he hit the road.

And, as his feet carried him down the dusty track, he knew two things for certain. One, he would do whatever he could to set things right in the kingdom, even if that meant giving his life for it. And two, it was for the best that things had happened as they did in the wolfyn realm, because he never would have forgiven himself for dragging Reda into this horror, not just because there was no beauty or magic in his homeland anymore, but because there was no way he could be with her and be what he needed to be.

He couldn't be Dayn the man when Elden needed a prince so badly.

MORAGH'S NEW GNOME, Destin, tapped on the door frame of the seedy room she had rented at a grubby inn on the shore of Blood Lake, preferring to not yet be under the sorcerer's roof given that she hadn't yet told him about the possibilities of realm travel, instead keeping that gem to herself as both an exit strategy and a bargaining chip.

"Mistress?" he inquired softly.

"Yes?" she asked without moving, without even opening her eyes. It had taken her nearly an hour of careful preparation to get this far, and she didn't want to have to start over.

"I have spread the word. If the prince returns—"

"He's already here. I can feel him." The spell had reactivated an hour earlier, warning that the wolfyn hadn't managed to take care of business. She hadn't really expected them to, though, not once she learned what Dayn had become, and saw how the archaic wolfyn society worked. They were hidebound, hampered by their own foolish traditions. She had used that to her advantage, though, coercing the pack into slowing down her prey, buying her the time to come back through the stones, recover the Book of Ilth and start making plans for his return.

And the plan she had was a damn good one. It wouldn't just take care of the prince, it would announce her new prowess far and wide. The scholars who had once laughed at her would bow in awe, and the sorcerer…well, the delicious images made her smile and wet her lips with her tongue.

"Shall I send to the castle and have the beast master ready your ettins?"

"No. I'm not going out after him. I'm going to let him come to me." The ugly rumors and hints of a bounty she'd had Destin spread through his network of thieves and cutthroats might take care of the prince for her, but if not, it would slow him down long enough that she would be ready for him.

"Will that be all for now, mistress?"

"Yes. No, wait." She drew satisfaction from his hiss of indrawn breath and the sudden tension in his stillness. But lately his struggles had diminished all too quickly, his revulsion dulling to a placid acceptance that flattened her pleasure to a mere glow. She had been planning an exciting new game to play with him, but now wasn't the time—she needed raw blood energy and didn't want to have to work for it. "Send to the dungeons for a prisoner, one that nobody will miss."

He exhaled softly. "Yes, mistress."

When he was gone and the door closed, shutting out the stupidity prevalent in the corridors and common areas of any village inn, Moragh cleared her mind and cast about herself, checking the positions of the candles and lines drawn around her with a variety of powders and unguents. Then, satisfied that she was protected, she opened the Book of Ilth, turning past all the realm-travel spells to the final section, to a title page that bore a single word.

   Feiynd.

DAYN REACHED THE VILLAGE of Einharr late in an afternoon grown gray from an incoming storm. The warm air was charged with thunder, heavy with moisture and felt strange on his skin after so long in the relatively dry and cold wolfyn realm. Or maybe the strangeness came from the land's sickness; he didn't know.

All he knew was that as he walked through the open gates of the heavy wooden palisade surrounding the village, his skin felt slick and oily, and his gut churned with the deep sorrow that had only grown through the day.

He had walked past roadside ditches filled with bones, most from livestock, but some human, and of the human skulls, a too-high proportion had worn secondary canines. He had been assuming his inability to connect to anyone through mindspeak meant that the wolfyn magic he'd had thrust upon him had fouled some of his purely Elden powers. But the sight of the skull piles had made him consider that he might be the only mindspeaker in range. And that was a damned depressing thought.

He'd passed deserted farms, some burned, others just sitting there, rife with signs of a hasty exit; he wanted to believe that the farming families had fled to other kingdoms, but didn't hold much hope of it. And as he'd gotten in closer to the village proper, he'd passed clusters of small houses and seen signs of habitation, but such poor signs—a few weedy chickens scratching listlessly in the dirt, a thin dog slinking in the shadows, head down, ears flat to its skull—that his heart had hurt anew.

So now, as his boots scuffed the dirt track through the center of the village, raising no dust in the heavy air, he wasn't entirely surprised to see that Einharr, once a thriving community well known for its singing halls and honey beer, was a squalid and run-down version of its former self. Hollow-eyed children peered at him from behind doorways and around corners, flinching away when he made eye contact, and older men and women skulked in windows or on overhung porches, watching him with dull, uninterested eyes.

Twenty years ago, when last he had ridden through here as part of his parents' retinue, the villagers had packed the main street, cheering and jostling to touch the horses and carriages. Now, as he made for the third block in, where the tavern district began—or used to begin, at any rate—his presence seemed to have gone entirely unnoticed. *Seemed* was the operative word, though, because as he continued onward, his nape prickled and his instincts said someone was watching him, that he needed to be careful. Which was a no-brainer, but he needed information, and there was no place better to get it than at the local watering hole.

Picking the one with the most worn-looking steps, as had been his habit when investigating as a Forestal, he stepped up onto the slatted porch, his boots ringing hollowly as he crossed to the heavy, windowless door.

Movement blurred in his peripheral vision; he spun in a crouch, lifting his short sword, but it was just a kid, a skinny, gray-eyed boy wearing ragged homespun and grime behind his ears where he had missed washing.

He didn't duck away like the others, but rather stopped dead, eyes widening in shock and fright.

For a second, when the boy did the deer-in-headlights freeze, Dayn flashed on wide blue eyes and similar moments of fear. A searing bolt of grief rocketed through him, warning that he might have submerged his thoughts of Reda, but they weren't gone. Not even close.

Then the kid broke from his paralysis, drew breath and screamed at the top of his lungs, *"Wolfyn!"* He spun and bolted, screeching, "Mama, Papa! The wolfyn's here!"

CHAPTER TWELVE

DOORS SLAMMED OPEN on both sides of the road and club-wielding men hurtled out from the buildings and flew from around corners, boiling into the street, shouting things like "Get him!" "Cut him off!" "The money's mine!" and "Don't let him get away!"

Cursing, Dayn dodged one club swing, took another on his shoulder and leaped into the road, swinging his sword in a wide arc that was more intended to drive his attackers back rather than hurt them. His mind raced, jammed with thoughts of *Damn that witch,* and *Now what?* He was horrifically outnumbered, but he didn't want to kill the villagers. He was trying to *save* them, damn it!

Looking around frantically while he batted off club swings with the flat of his sword, he searched for a thin spot, an exit, and found—

"Now!" a voice shouted.

Too late, he looked up to see a heavily weighted net flying down at him, flinging open as it came.

"Son of a—" He spun to bolt, but it caught him hard and knocked him down.

Roaring, he lunged back to his feet, staggering as he fought the tangling lines. He got his sword arm free and slashed out, heard a cry of pain and saw the villagers shrink back for a second. But that didn't last long; they closed in just as he freed himself from the net, leaping away and flailing with his sword. He slapped for his crossbow, but it was gone.

He was surrounded, but the villagers didn't come at him, instead hesitating, keeping their clubs raised as they shouted, egging one another. For a second, their hesitation didn't make any sense. Then he realized: they were afraid he was going to change, didn't know that he'd only succumbed twice in his life and didn't intend to do it again. Not when part of his promise to his father had been to remember his true self, which wasn't wolfyn.

Heart rocketing, he went for his bloodline magic, sending his secondary canines spearing through his gums. Then he bared his teeth and roared at the nearest villager, doing his best impression of Keely on a bad-fur day.

The man shouted and fell back, stumbling into the guy behind him. They both went down and three others shied away as Dayn lunged through the small opening and raced for the open area beyond. For a second he thought he was going to make it, but then the guys at the outer edge of the crowd saw him coming and started closing ranks.

Zzzt. Thwack! An arrow whizzed past the men and sank itself in the building opposite. They shouted and fell back as a second missile followed the first, coming even closer to them before nailing a rain barrel.

Dayn didn't stop to wonder who or how; he put his head down and hauled ass for the nearest village gate.

"Close the gate!" The shout went up behind him, and up ahead, two men scrambled from a rickety guard shack and moved to comply, pushing a heavy door that slid sideways on ponderous rollers.

He wasn't going to make it.

Sudden hoofbeats pounded behind him and a familiar voice called, "Dayn!"

And his heart. Stopped. Dead.

His body might have kept running as he looked back over his shoulder, but the rest of him froze at the sight of Reda galloping toward him on a bald-faced bay horse with white-ringed eyes. She was wearing a mix of the clothing he'd last seen her in along with a few Elden-style pieces, including the close-fitting pants and boots typically worn by the members of the cavalry or elite guard. They were old, but the royal colors of his own house still shone clearly.

"Reda," he whispered through a throat gone suddenly dry with mingled joy and dismay. "Sweet gods."

The villagers scattered like blown leaves as she bore down on him. Then she was steering with her knees and weight as she knocked an arrow in a sleek compound bow and let fly, burying the missile in the village gate no more than a handspan from one of the guys who were fighting to get it shut. The two men shouted, took one look at her and dove for cover, leaving the gate half-open and unattended.

"Grab on!" She pulled even with Dayn, offered a hand and, when he locked his wrist to hers, used the bay's momentum to pull him up behind her.

It was a familiar move, one he'd done a hundred times with Nicolai, sometimes even with his father. But the bay squealed and spooked at the move, swerving and then flattening out its haunches as it accelerated to a flat-out panicked bolt that left him sprawled awkwardly on the animal's haunches, being jolted loose with every stride.

"Whoa!" Reda started to haul on the reins, but then glanced back at the villagers, thought better of it and yelled, "Hang on!"

Dayn did his best, getting a good grip on the empty bedroll straps at the back of the age-cracked cavalry saddle as Reda rode the bolt, steering the white-eyed bay through the village gate and out onto the main road, where they thundered for nearly a mile before the animal began to tire, slowing to a bumpy canter, then to a tooth-jarring trot.

Still, though, the horse was restive and upset, refusing to settle, to the point that it was all Reda could do to spin the creature in a circle as Dayn slid down. The brute kicked out and scooted away, but she hauled it back around in a few snorting, prancing whirls, and then it finally started to calm down, blowing elephant-bugle snorts at Dayn.

Who just stood there in the road, staring.

She didn't say anything, either, just met his eyes with a cool expression that didn't tell him a thing. After a moment, she lifted her chin as if to say, *Well?*

"You can ride," he said, which was dead stupid because that was far from the most important thing. But the sight of her astride the wall-eyed bay, carrying a weapon from her own realm and wearing clothes mixed from the other two, shifted his perceptions, jarring him and replacing his image of wide, scared blue eyes.

"I did Pony Club for a bit, played polo now and then in college." She paused. "That and the archery were the closest I could get to living out the fairy tales. Until now."

He had told himself he didn't want her here in this wreck of a kingdom, that he didn't have it in him to protect her and do his duty both. But now that she was here, really *here,* he wanted to fall to his knees and thank the gods and the magic, wanted to kiss her booted toe and work his way up from there, and wanted, somehow, to make things right between them. Because she was here.

The kingdom was a wasteland, Moragh had turned the villagers against him and put a bounty on his head, his siblings were nowhere to be seen and, given how much had been drained from the land, the Blood Sorcerer's powers must be immense.

But sudden, illogical joy wrapped itself around his heart as he stood there staring up at a woman who looked like something from the stories of his own childhood—a goddess of the hunt, perhaps, or a patroness of the king's elite cavalry. Yet at the same time she was the Reda he had known in the wolfyn realm, the one he had made love to, cared for, wanted beyond all reason.

His throat tightened, burning with emotion. "You used the Elden spell."

But she shook her head. "I was sent here."

His blood cooled a degree. "Then how…?"

"Your father. At least, I think that's who it was. He pulled me into limbo, told me I had to help you get all the way to the castle, and that you need to remember your true self. And that if I do that, I can go home for real."

"I know what I am and what I must be—a prince of Elden, with all that it entails." He paused, scrubbing a hand over his face. "Why did he send you with the message? Why not just talk to me while I was in the vortex?"

She looked past him. "I have a theory on that. I got here a few hours ago, bought MacEvoy here—" she indicated the bay, who had leveled off to flat-footed, eye-rolling suspicion "—and clothes that didn't scream 'outsider' quite so loudly. Then I just...I don't know. Started riding. And that gave me time to think."

He was still working to catch up with the sudden differences in her. The fear was gone—or if not gone, so deeply buried that he couldn't see it anymore. More, she was calm and competent, automatically settling her mount with a touch here, a shift of weight there, and wearing the bow naturally across her back as if it had been made for her. The Queen's Guard would have been proud to have a woman like her. And a kingdom in need of rebuilding could do worse.

Slow down, he told himself, all too aware that their entire relationship had taken place at a flat-out gallop, and that a single misstep at such speed could be fatal. "Your theory?" he prompted when she didn't continue.

Meeting his eyes, she said, "I think I'm a test."

"A... Oh." He stared at her. "No. That's impossible."

"Is it?" Looping the reins in one hand, she crossed her arms and just looked at him.

No, it wasn't impossible and they both knew it. More, it made a horrible sort of sense. He was supposed to remember his priorities and his true self. And just as the voice that had come to him as he floated out of his body had demanded a sacrifice from him in exchange for another chance, the magic—and his father—could be trying to teach him the lessons he hadn't yet learned, the ones Elden needed him to master. *Focus. Dedication. Discipline. Humility.*

Gods, no. Not this way. He wanted to make it up to her, to be with her. Their time together had been the brightest spot, not just in the past two decades, but in all the years he had been alive. With her, he had been a man, an individual, a lover, a mate.

Sacrifice.

Moving slowly, keeping an eye on the horse, he crossed to her. The bay gave a half rear, but then subsided and held its ground, nostrils flaring as he came up beside them, close enough to touch her leg, though he didn't.

He was viscerally aware of the long curves of her taut muscles beneath the cavalry breeches, though, and the familiar royal crest stamped into the leather at the top of her boot, now wearing a slash that indicated it was part of a rebellion, some sort of organized resistance. And deep down inside him where the wolfyn magic dwelled, arousal and satisfaction mingled at the sight of her wearing his family colors. He wanted to drape her in fine silks in those same colors, wanted to run their slippery softness over her body, then follow the same paths with his hands and lips. He hadn't even begun to deal with her loss, could barely comprehend her return.

But, gods and the Abyss, she could be right that this was a test, a call for him to prove that he had learned his lesson. And a reminder that Elden needed him—or rather, them—to do their duties and hold true to their roles despite their feelings.

Not to mention…what *were* her feelings? He couldn't see beyond her guarded, impassive mask, the one that seemed to say, *This is the situation. What are you going to do about it?* He knew the look from his father's elite security forces, could guess that it went with being on the humans' police force. And it drove home not only her new confidence—or, he suspected, the emergence of a deep-seated confidence that had been within her all along—but also that she had a life outside of him, duties of her own.

When he'd asked her to come with him, he had been so caught up in not wanting their gallop to end, so focused on getting what he most desired, that he'd lost sight of her needs and desires outside of the two of them. More, he had lied to her—by omission, yes, but a grave sin considering the lie. And the fact that he hadn't even considered telling her. Just as he had hidden his blood-drinking self from Keely, he had planned to leave Reda entirely ignorant of the spell-curse that had turned him into his own prey.

Son of a bitch. He hadn't grown up nearly as much as he'd wanted to think.

Aware that the silence was stretching thin, he tried to find the words, but didn't know where to start, or how. Or even whether he should try.

Yes, he needed to try. He owed that to his honor, and to her.

He touched her knee, curving his fingers around the flesh and bone, not meaning the gesture as a come-on, but rather hoping the touch would carry his sincerity to her through the fitful emotional link he had felt once or twice before.

"I got so caught up in the rush that I lost sight of my honor and your right to have the same honesty from me that you had offered me. For that, I am ashamed." He tightened his fingers on her knee. "By the gods, Reda, I'm sorry."

She went white for a second, expression stark, but then flushed hard and hot as her eyes took on a dangerous glint as she leaned down to bat his arm away and hiss, "You're sorry? You *enthralled* me, you unholy bastard."

Shock rattled through him. "I—"

"Don't you *dare* deny it. I may not know magic, but I can take a good guess what being brainwashed feels like." She straightened in the saddle and touched the reins to quiet the bay, which had lit up once more, pawing and tossing its head while its ears flipped back and forth. "When I was with you, nothing else mattered. I didn't care where we were or what we were doing, or even what was going on around us. I would have done anything you asked." She glared through the glint of tears. "Anything, damn you. An 'I'm sorry' doesn't even begin to cut it on that one."

Her words got inside him, making him profoundly wish he had been born a simple man in a simple life, that he had just met her on the street one day, without all the other chaos involved. But that was exactly the sort of thought process that had gotten him in trouble before, wasn't it?

Part of him even wondered if it might not be best to let her think that he had enthralled her. It would probably be better if she hated him—because knowing that she was, or at least had been, feeling the same crazy single-mindedness he was, that the world had threatened to disappear for her, as well, made him want to drag her out of the saddle and hold her, kiss her, talk to her until she agreed to give him—to give *them*—a chance.

But he couldn't do it. He just couldn't. He couldn't leave another lie between them.

"There was no enthrallment," he said, pressing his hand to his chest where she had liked to lay her palm and feel his heartbeat. "I swear it on my soul."

Her eyes narrowed. "There must have been."

"There wasn't." He didn't repeat the oath. She would either believe him or not. *Have faith,* he urged her inwardly. *You know me.* But did she know him enough to believe?

For a moment she didn't say anything; he could almost see the inner battle written on her face. She wanted to believe, but didn't trust him or herself anymore, didn't know what was real and what wasn't—not out in the realms, but inside herself.

He knew her. He understood her. And by the gods he wanted her to trust him. Abyss, he just damn well *wanted* her. This was a mess, *he* was a mess.

Finally, she said, "Could you have enthralled me without knowing, without meaning to?" She looked forlornly hopeful, as though she, too, knew it would be easier if they were at odds.

Or maybe he was just seeing what he wanted to see.

"I chewed the wolfsleep gum to block the wolfyn magic." Using Keely had helped, too, staving off his urges, but he didn't think it hurt anyone to keep that to himself. "What you saw was only my second change. I kept the urges strictly contained, so I would never forget who I was and what I was waiting for."

"And now?" She swept the tree line on either side of the road. "I don't see any wolfsleep trees."

"The magic functions differently in the kingdoms. I'll have to work hard to change here. And I don't intend to. All of the messages I've received from the spirit realm say that I need to be entirely true to myself if I'm going to have a chance against the sorcerer. Which means staying the hell away from the wolfyn magic."

"Yet you changed back at the archway."

He couldn't read her expression, didn't know what she wanted him to say. His better sense said to leave it alone, but he went with the gods' honest truth instead. "You were in danger and I didn't see another option."

"You…" She trailed off, then shook her head. "Never mind. And thank you. For saving my life."

He nodded, but didn't say anything. They both knew he had nearly sacrificed the hopes of an entire kingdom in the process. And what kind of a prince did that make him?

Exhaling, she nodded as if they had reached an agreement. "Right. Okay, then. We should get moving before the villagers get their torches and pitchforks and come after us." She kicked her foot free of the stirrup and shifted forward in the saddle to give him room to climb on behind her. "I'd let you drive, but I don't think MacEvoy likes you."

"He must be able to sense the wolfyn magic." Which was damned depressing, because one of the things he had looked forward to doing in Elden was once more riding a beast-chaser.

She didn't say anything, but her eyes went sympathetic as she tightened her reins in one hand and held out the other.

He hesitated momentarily, wishing he could say something that would unravel the tangle they had wound up in together, connected yet not, and with so much confusion around them. The perfect words didn't come to him, though. They probably didn't even exist.

Exhaling, he took her hand and swung up behind her, but stayed well back on the saddle skirt and held on to the cantle for balance rather than tucking himself right against her as he longed to do. And, as they rode into the first reddening of dusk, there was only silence between them. They had said what needed to be said, after all. Now they had jobs to do.

Which seriously sucks, he thought. But all of a sudden the human words didn't come as easily as they had before, as if the past twenty years were being canceled out now that he was back in his home realm.

The idea was damned disconcerting. Worse, the past three days suddenly seemed a little distant and indistinct, too, as if they had happened to someone else, in another lifetime. It was as if Reda was already gone, like he was already forgetting what they'd had together, when she was sitting only inches away.

"WE'RE COMING UP in the world," Reda commented later that night as she poked at the folding bowl she had suspended on a tripod over the small, sputtering fire. "This cave is much nicer than the last one. It even came with utensils."

"Tonight a cave, tomorrow a castle, gods willing," Dayn said from the rear of the space, where he was cobbling together a small horse enclosure from the remains of a large corral.

The huge cavern, which had been the hideout of an outlaw band that Dayn and a detachment of guardsmen had tracked and arrested just prior to the sorcerer's attack, offered a small stream, a scattering of useful items that had somehow escaped the looters, three exits that let out at various points in the forest and accommodations for the bay horse, who she was still calling MacEvoy after the shop owner, even though the stoner-quiet personality he'd originally shown her had gone right out of his furry head the second he saw Dayn.

The horse was too tired and hungry to be in full-on panic mode anymore, and had gotten somewhat used to carrying a wolfyn, but even as he hoovered down the travel cakes his seller had thrown in along with the tack and clothes, he kept a white-ringed eye on Dayn.

No wonder there weren't any normal horses in the wolfyn realm. They had probably all died of fright, or else been eaten. Or both.

Shuddering at the thought and the echoing *slurp-crunch* noise it put in her head, she glanced over at Dayn, and caught him looking at her.

They both shied away and went back to their tasks, but the already tense air between them strung itself a little tighter, as it had been doing, degree by degree, ever since he'd boosted himself up behind her and done his damnedest not to let their bodies touch.

Was it possible to simultaneously exist in both heaven and hell, or whatever this realm called them? She thought so, because she was there right now.

Part of her, idiot that it was, was basking in the glow of having rescued him so grandly, and having him right at hand now. That part of her kept reminding her that they had spent the past two nights alternately making sweet love and screwing each other blind, both equally satisfying, and it relentlessly dredged up increasingly erotic memories as the night wore on. The sensory replays tortured her, turning her insides to molten heat and putting a longing tug between her legs each time she looked at him and thought that it was nearly time for them to hit their bedrolls.

Another part of her, though, said she'd be better off sleeping outside in the cool, foggy night. That part of her was all too aware of MacEvoy's ringed eyes and flattened ears, and knew she should take a cue from the horse—prey animal that it was—and keep her distance.

"Stew's almost ready." She poked at a lump of rehydrated meat floating in a brown slick that looked entirely unappetizing, but smelled great.

"Just let me get these last three rails up."

She snuck a peek, and this time caught him turned away, which gave her a few seconds to stare at his broad shoulders as he fitted the last rails into place and lashed them with the worn rope he had salvaged. The plaid shirt she had taken off of him a dozen times in a dozen different places curved lovingly around his muscles, poignantly reminding her of how it felt to run her hands over him, how his skin tasted and how he seemed to know instinctively how to touch her, as if he really could read her mind, though he claimed he couldn't.

She wanted to believe him, just as she wanted to believe that he was telling the truth about her not being enthralled…but at the same time, without that excuse she would have to admit that she had done it all of her own free will, falling hard and fast for a fairy-tale prince who turned out to be far more complicated than she had thought.

Finished, he gave the enclosure a last check while

MacEvoy tracked his every move. Then, satisfied, Dayn ducked through the fence and headed for the fire.

Reda looked quickly away and concentrated on stirring a stew that wasn't going to get better or worse with more stirring. Her hands were trembling, her insides alight with warmth and need. She didn't want to be with a wolfyn, a liar or a manipulator, but she wanted to be with Dayn. And she couldn't have it all.

Maman, *what am I supposed to do?* The question came unbidden; it had been a long time since she stopped asking her mother's spirit for advice. But even as she told herself not to be ridiculous, she still listened inwardly for a few seconds, wondering. Because if she had truly been some part magic, maybe, just maybe…?

There was no answer, though. And as Dayn leaned too close to her and tipped half the stew into a big tin cup he had scavenged and scoured out in the river, her breath went thin and her insides tugged longingly. But at the same time, unexpected tears threatened, making her blink so hard the fire seemed to waver as a new reality solidified within her.

She had lost her *maman* and Benz. And tomorrow, one way or the other, she was going to lose Dayn. Which would she regret more, being with him tonight… or not?

"Reda," he said, voice choked, "for gods' sake, talk to me." His ragged tone brought her head up and the emerald green of his irises caught her, sucked her in.

She wanted to lose herself in his eyes, in his kiss, in the warm strength of his arms. *But then what?* logic asked, unfortunately making sense. Because if she made love with him tonight, knowing what he was and that he had lied to her, she would always know that she had caved, that she had let herself be seduced without even the excuse of enthrallment.

"I can't," she said on a shuddering breath, turning down not just a conversation but all of it, all of him.

His eyes dulled but he didn't push. He just nodded, rose and took his stew back over to the edge of the corral, where he sat with his back against the wall and his eyes on the main entrance, not on her. But he was aware of her, she knew, just as she was entirely focused on him as the night dragged on.

She was acutely conscious of him eating, then pulling a few swallows from the waterskin he'd left over there while working. She knew when he set his cup aside and when he stretched his legs, shifted his big body with the soft sigh that meant he was settling in to sleep yet staying on his guard, ready to react in an instant. He closed his eyes but didn't immediately fall asleep. She knew he was awake because she caught his faint responses when she banked the fire and curled herself into a bedroll marked with his family crest, saw a reflected glitter when he cracked an eye to watch.

Her heart told her to go to him, but her head said she needed to stand her ground and resist the temptation, or she would regret it going forward. She didn't want to go forward, though; she wanted to relive the past few nights with one more. In the end, though, she closed her eyes and listened to the *hiss-pop* of the fire because she didn't have the guts to take what she wanted when everything else was so unclear.

She might have ridden to his rescue today, but she was still a coward when it came to this.

CHAPTER THIRTEEN

THE ROYAL CASTLE OF ELDEN had been beautiful once, Reda saw through the small spyglass Dayn had found in an inner compartment of MacEvoy's saddlebag. From where they stood on the shores of Blood Lake far from the heavily guarded causeway, hidden in a scrubby patch of middle growth near the edge of the Dead Forest, she could see the classic elegance in the castle's turrets and crenellations, in the huge stone sweeps of the battlements and the gracefully engineered causeway that connected the island to the shore. Similar details made the smaller buildings beyond the castle blend in to look like part of the whole.

But although the bones of the royal seat suggested a heritage of loveliness, its current incarnation was dark and dismal, and carried a psychic stink that made her want to recoil.

"Gods and the Abyss," Dayn growled under his breath. "He'll pay for this." She saw stark pain in his eyes as he surveyed the filthy brown, polluted lake.

Here and there, swirls suggested submerged movement, though of what creature she didn't want to know. The island itself looked gray and rotten, and the castle was smog-shrouded and badly run-down, and looked somehow beaten, though she wasn't sure how that was possible. Dark figures moved here and there, some small and human, others huge and hulking, with the silhouettes of creatures she had hoped never to see outside the storybooks—or her own nightmares. Giant, razor-clawed scorpions guarded the causeway, huge crablike creatures scuttled along the battlements and ettins worked on the curtain wall, heaving huge chunks of stone like they were pebbles, though it wasn't clear if they were building it up or tearing it down.

Movement stirred near the base of the castle; squinting, she could just make out human figures walking in chains, linked together and being whipped on by a smaller man in a red-and-black uniform. All six of the prisoners were wearing royal colors and boots, but they were bent and dragging, their body language screaming of pain. Rebel prisoners, no doubt.

"Oh," Reda whispered, and then bit her lip.

"Let me see."

So she handed over the spyglass and pointed. Then she reached over, took his free hand and twined her fingers through his. He tensed and went still for a moment—she wasn't sure if it was from her touch or because he had seen the rebels. But then he exhaled and his shoulders dropped, and he gripped her hand and hung on hard.

And though there was nothing decided between them, when he lowered the spyglass and turned toward her, she went into his arms without hesitation. He clamped around her, just holding her, with his face pressed into her hair as the spyglass clunked to the ground.

MacEvoy snorted and dropped his head to graze, making the bit clink and tugging the reins from her fingers, but those inputs were so much less important than the fine shivers racing through Dayn's body and the fierceness of his grip, which made her feel as if for a change she was the one anchoring him, the one letting him lean.

"We can do this," she said against his throat. "Have faith." They still had nearly half a day to rent or steal a boat, then planned to make the crossing after nightfall.

His laugh was hollow and brittle. "I can't feel Nicolai or the others. I don't think they're here." He pressed his cheek to her temple. "I think that maybe I'm the only one left."

She closed her eyes, heart hurting for him. "You don't know that. And even so, someone has to stop the sorcerer. Things can't stay like this."

He drew away from her, looked down at her so tenderly she almost closed her eyes to capture the moment before it passed. "You're not afraid anymore, my warrior?"

She shook her head, and said, "Honestly, I'm so scared I want to curl up and hide my face in my knees. But I've decided that you were right. Being brave isn't about not being afraid. It's about continuing to function, anyway."

That was the truth she had awakened with that morning, after a long, restless night's sleep. It was a simple concept, really, and utterly logical. And she knew she'd heard it before—not just from him, but also from friends, family, coworkers, the department shrink—but for the first time she really believed it. More, she believed in herself, and knew that she wasn't going to freeze this time. Not tonight, when so much was riding on the outcome.

He framed her face in his hands and leaned in to say

against her lips, "Ah, sweet Reda. My precious warrior."

As his mouth covered hers, she knew he was a wolfyn. As his tongue touched her lips, she was fully aware that he had made love to her without telling her the worst of his secrets. And as she parted her lips and let him inside, she did it knowingly. Willingly. Greedily.

There was no enthrallment. There was just the two of them, and the connection that existed despite everything else going on around them.

She wrapped her arms around his waist and held on for a kiss that was less about arousal than about saying, *Yes, I'm here for you. We're in this together.* Because that was the other certainty she had awakened with—it wasn't about following the orders of a voice in the fog anymore; she was determined to see this through at Dayn's side. Not just because of what might or might not be between them but because it was the right thing to do. This was bigger than the two of them, bigger than anything she'd ever dealt with before. She could do it, though. And she would. She could, in her own way, help save the world. Or at least a kingdom.

Putting that certainty into her kiss, she slid her hands up his back and spread her fingers wide, covering as much of him as she could. *I've got your back,* she thought. *Let's go get this bastard.*

As if he'd heard her, he eased back with a last, lingering press of his lips to her cheek, her temple. Then he turned her so they were both facing away from Blood Lake, and pointed. "See that tall pine there with the three-way split at the top?"

It was maybe a half, three-quarters of a mile away,

and looked like a trident. She nodded. "I see it. You want to use it as an emergency meet-up point?"

"No. Your shrine is at the base of that tree."

"My...what?" She turned on him, sure she'd heard wrong.

But his eyes, which had only moments earlier been entirely focused on her, slid past her to the island before flicking back to her face. "I know who I am and what I need to do, Reda. I'm a prince of Elden, first and foremost, and I can't let anything distract me from that."

Her head spun on an inner groan of, *Nooooo*. This wasn't happening, couldn't be happening. "You can't go in there alone. They'll kill you." Her voice cracked on it, her heart bled from it. "If you're trying to protect me, don't. I can take care of myself."

Instead of answering right away, he caught her hand and lifted it to press her palm to his chest, sandwiching it there so she felt the steady beat of his heart. "We each need to live the lives we were born into." He folded their hands together, pressed a kiss to her knuckles and then let her go and stepped back. "Go home, Reda. It's where you belong."

"I..." She just stood there for a second, vapor locked, not from fear but from shock, dismay and a sudden churn of anger. "You son of a bitch. Keely was right, wasn't she? You're a user."

He didn't say anything, just stood there. And she didn't see anything that said he wanted her to stay. In fact, she didn't see anything at all.

Whatever fragile trust they had begun to rebuild—or rather, that *she* had begun to rebuild—shredded in that instant, and disappeared. *Poof.* Gone.

Done. Game over.

When something nudged the small of her back, she jolted hard and spun, which sent MacEvoy skittering back several steps, where he stood, blowing through his nose as if to say, *What's your problem?*

Her startled laugh choked to a sob as she gathered his dragging reins. She didn't look at Dayn, couldn't look at him or she would lose it. "Come on." She sighted on the trident-shaped treetop and gave Mac Evoy a tug. "Let's see if there are any decent farms between here and there." If not, she would strip off his tack and set him loose to fend for himself.

She stopped at the edge of the scrub, where it turned to a narrow track that led to the road, and turned back. Dayn stood against a backdrop of the polluted lake and the run-down castle, looking determined, distant and alone. The lone wolfyn. *Oh, God.* Her heart clutched in sudden foreboding, but what more could she say?

So in the end, she lifted a hand. "Good luck, Dayn."

A ghost of a smile touched his lips. "Same to you, sweet Reda." Then, moving with smooth, predatory grace, he slipped from the copse without looking back.

And she was left alone, save for a bald-faced horse and a heavy heart.

DAYN DIDN'T LET HIMSELF turn back, though he badly wanted to. And he didn't let himself fold inward and curl around the tearing pain that filled the place where his heart had been, though he badly wanted to do that, too. Because for a change he was doing the noble and honorable thing when it came to her: he was sending her away.

The sight of Castle Island had only confirmed the prickle of instinct that had been growing ever since they had set out that morning, the one that had said it was going to take a miracle for him to even reach the island, another for him to get inside the castle. And the odds of him surviving a fight with a sorcerer capable of wreaking so much damage, with twenty years' worth of magic and spells rooted in the castle, were brutally bad with or without his siblings, unless the decades had given them powers that far outstripped his own.

There was a damn good chance that he was going over there to die. And if that was the case he wanted her far away from the island, safely hating him in her own realm. For once, he knew he was doing the right thing when it came to her, the unselfish thing.

So instead of going after her and doing whatever it took to get that shattered look out of her eyes and put her once more back in his arms where the man in him wanted to believe she belonged, he pushed onward toward the section of the Dead Forest known as the Thieves' Woods, in search of a boat.

But as he ghosted along the edge of the Dead Forest, the sense of impending doom he'd awoken with only grew stronger, sending cold chills down his spine and causing him to look over his shoulder time and again.

Then, one of those times he caught a glimpse of movement and his gut fisted. There was something out there. Something big and nasty. And it reeked of dark magic.

Heart pounding, acting on his hunter's instincts, which suddenly screamed loud and clear, he unshipped his crossbow, hesitated and then opened the small, tightly stoppered container at his belt. Carefully—oh, so carefully—he dipped the tips of his last six bolts into the thick black liquid, coating the barbs to an oily shine.

He returned five to their spots on his belt, points hidden. He loaded the sixth onto his crossbow and started walking again, though far more stealthily than before, intensely aware of his surroundings, straining to sense a footstep or breath. Something was out there, but where?

A cloud passed over the sun, shadowing the scene momentarily and then moving on. Wind whispered overhead, sounding strange in the leaves of the dying trees. There was an open spot overhead, letting through sunlight that was dappled with another passing cloud shadow, this one moving unnaturally fast in an unseen current high overhead.

Then it curved back around and went the other way. And grew bigger.

Dayn stopped dead and stared for a split second of disbelief as the shadow grew wings. There weren't any winged creatures that big in Elden. Not unless you counted the legend of the... *No. Impossible.* He heard it in Reda's voice, and suddenly understood the wrenching disconnect of having a childhood bogeyman come to life, even before he ripped himself from his paralysis and yanked his attention to the sky.

"Gods!" The word burst from him at the sight that confronted him.

The huge dark snakelike beast undulated through the sky as if swimming. Then it screeched, swiveled, and folded its wings to plummet toward the earth with its bloodred eyes locked on him. It had small forelimbs with clawed hands, powerfully muscled hindquarters and the head of a scaled stallion. Covered entirely in black scales that gleamed dully in the sunlight, it was gorgeous and terrifying, in the way that only the worst of monsters could be.

Dayn's pulse hammered. It was a dragon. And not just any dragon; it was the Feiynd itself, the assassin of the old magi.

Moragh had summoned it to kill him.

Gods help him.

The Feiynd's mouth split in a silent gape that made it look, for a terrible instant, like it was smiling at him. Wind whistled through its wingsails, sounding like a thousand arrows in flight. And then it folded them fully and hurtled toward him, a living weapon locked on its target.

"Gods and the Abyss," Dayn whispered as his every power and instinct came together inside him at once. There was no point in running when the witch had targeted it on him, no point in hiding. He could only stand his ground and pray as he lifted his crossbow and sighted on one violent red eye.

The eyes could see. They could communicate. They were a route to the head, and from there to the heart.

Candida, I hope you knew what you were doing. And if this doesn't work, bless you for trying.

He waited a beat. Had his mark. Saw the Feiynd's mouth open wide.

And fired.

The bolt sped true, but a wing current knocked the projectile off line and it flew into the dragon's mouth, which snapped shut and then opened wide in a thin shriek of pain and anger that lifted beyond the limits of his hearing, hard and high, and so dissonant that it scraped along his nerve endings and made him want to flee like nothing in his life had done before.

Then the noise before the beast crashed through the thin canopy of yellowed leaves and hit the ground, thrown off target by the attack. It landed hard, digging its claws into the earth for purchase and screeching again as branches fell from above and peppered it— and Dayn—with debris.

Then it folded its wings and legs flat against its body and whipped into an aggressive coil, becoming a giant snake that was poised to strike.

Dayn fell back into the trees, hoping to hell they would slow the beast's attack. His heart and mind raced, bringing both fugue and clarity. There was no point in running; he would have to kill the Feiynd here and now. The eyes, he needed to go for the eyes. But they were smaller than he had realized, and set deep within scaly pits. He would have to make the shot of his life. Literally.

Deep within his soul, he whispered, *Father, if you can hear me, if you have any influence on this plane, please help me now.*

As he whipped a second bolt into place, he thanked the gods that Reda wasn't there, because there was no way in hell she could've gone up against the Feiynd. She would have tried, though, because that was who she was.

Aiming the loaded crossbow at one of those tiny, tiny eyes, he sighted. Fired.

The bolt glanced off the armor surrounding the Feiynd's eye pits. It seemed that the creature laughed at him for a split second. Then it screamed at full volume and struck. And Dayn was suddenly fighting for his life, spurred by the knowledge that if he died now, Elden would die with him.

REDA SPUN BACK AT THE sudden eruption of noise coming from the direction of the lake: roars, shrieks and the crashing of brush and trees. Her heart seized. *"Dayn!"*

The second she heard those noises, it stopped mattering whether he'd used her, or if that had been the lie instead, designed to send her running.

At a second terrible clashing noise, MacEvoy spooked and bolted, yanking her clean off her feet. She went to her knees but hung on grimly, and within a few strides, her deadweight had pulled the horse's head around and slowed him to a panting, eye-rolling stop.

"Don't you dare, you pain in my ass." Reda got to her feet, grabbed his bit and dragged his head around so she could glare into one of his white-ringed eyes and growl, "That. Is. Enough. I need you to man up, channel your inner beast-chaser, or whatever it takes, because bolting is not an option for us. Not anymore. Got it?"

She didn't know if her words got through or if it was more her take-no-crap tone, but he subsided to a shuddering standstill and let her mount.

He propped up on his hind legs in protest, but when she growled he started forward as commanded, went where she pointed. "Good choice," she said, giving his neck a quick pat.

Then, not stopping to think it through or question the logic or emotions, she kicked him toward the terrible noises, praying she wasn't already too late.

DAYN DUCKED AND SWERVED from one tree to the next, scrambling to load his last crossbow bolt as the Feiynd screeched and snapped behind him.

The Dead Forest was the only thing keeping him alive at this point, slowing the dragon and forcing it to stay in snake form because there was no room for it to spread its limbs and bring its wickedly barbed tail into the attack. But that boon was also a hindrance, as the branches fouled his aim. And there was no way he could fight the creature up close. With a boar pike and a beast-chaser, he might have had a chance. With a short sword and no armor, he would be dead before he got in his first puny blow. His wolfyn form would be no improvement; he might be able to outrun the creature on the ground, but it could fly and the witch had linked it to his life essence.

There was no hope of escape. One of them had to die.

If he could just...*there!* Up ahead there was a large tree with low, sturdy branches, and what looked like a clearing beyond.

Putting on a burst of speed that sucked all but the last dregs of his energy, even with his secondary canines extended and his healing powers maxed, he raced for the tree, leaped and grabbed the low branch and clambered up. From there, he could fire down on the dragon with no interference, maybe even a better angle.

But when he turned back, the beast was gone.

"Abyss." That wasn't good.

He was already turning toward the clearing when he heard the thousand-arrow whistle of the Feiynd plummeting from flight. The creature landed in the open meadow just short of the tree in full dragon form, with wings and limbs extended.

Screeching, it reared up on its hindquarters to tower over Dayn's position, taller even than the trees. He couldn't see its eyes, couldn't get a bead on the flexible armpit zone that was often a weakness of armored creatures. All he could see was its scaled underbelly and wide, sweeping wings as it stayed upright for nearly a full second, screaming.

Then, suddenly, it crashed down to all fours atop the tree, tearing through the branches and sending the trunk skewing wildly for a second before it fell, uprooted by the creature's great force.

Dayn tried to fling himself free, but landed just ahead of the outer branches, which came down atop him, pinning him. He ripped free, scrambled to his feet and—

A huge black mass blurred from the side as the Feiynd struck, clamping its jaws on his upper arm and partway across his chest. Its curving, barbed teeth dug in, sending white-hot pain lashing through him.

"No!" His perceptions wrenched and a terrible sense of wrongness washed over him, warning that he was badly hurt. He could smell his own blood over the creature's brimstone breath, could taste it in his mouth and feel it coming from his nose. But at the same time his focus narrowed to two crucial points: he still had his crossbow, and those tiny red eyes were suddenly very close.

He twisted his body and felt more pain, more wrongness, but that didn't stop him from bringing the crossbow up.

Without warning, he was heaved up into the air, still clamped in the dragon's powerful jaws as the beast whipped its neck. Then it let go.

Dayn's inertia tore him from the barbed teeth and he went flying. For a second he was weightless, in a state of almost-pleasure as the old pain of being chomped disappeared and the new pain of being torn up and spit out hadn't yet hit. Then he crashed into the dusty meadow and skidded several feet on the hard ground with the *boom* of impact ringing in his ears.

He tried to get up, but couldn't. Tried to raise the crossbow he still held clutched in one hand, his fingers cramped around the stock, but he couldn't do that, either. All he could do was lie there as the Feiynd reared back on its haunches again, spread its wings and roared its triumph. Then it thudded back to the ground and came toward him, swaggering in dragon form. Its piggish red eyes locked on him and its mouth split wide to show those awful barbed teeth, now stained with his blood.

It took its time, but there was no question what would come next. The stories all said the same thing, after all: the Feiynd never left its target alive.

As it closed to within a dozen of its huge paces, Dayn sought his healing magic, but it was spent. His wolfyn magic, too. He was too far gone, too depleted. His mind raced, but his thoughts were scattered and dull, his plans nonexistent. *I'm sorry, Father.* He had failed, after all. He had come so close, yet was still falling short. And in the end, he was more the man than the prince, anyway, because his last thought as the Feiynd closed to striking range wasn't of his family or Elden, but of his lover. *Goodbye, sweet Reda,* he thought, glad to know that she, at least, was safe.

But as the beast reared up over him, its eyes glittering, mouth gaping wide, he heard the thunder of hoofbeats and her voice screaming, "No!"

An arrow sang, burying itself in the Feiynd's armpit.

The dragon screeched and scissored sideways, which sent it crashing aside, away from Dayn. He simultaneously cursed Reda and blessed her, wanted to—

The Feiynd's tail lashed out, whistled through the air and came down hard on Dayn's battered body.

Darkness.

"No!" REDA STOOD in the stirrups and sent another arrow flying at the dragon as it regained its feet. "Get away from him, you bastard!" Beneath her, MacEvoy stayed steady and galloped his heart out, even though his ears were flat to his skull and his body shook with fear.

The arrow bounced, but got the dragon's attention. The thing's head whipped around and it hissed when it locked on her. It was too close to Dayn; there was no way she could get to him with the monster practically standing over his body. Worse, as they closed on the fight, she saw to her horror that Dayn was still and limp, his clothing blood-soaked, his wounds horrific. Far worse than what Kenar had done.

"No," she whispered.

In the moment between one gallop stride and the next, she flashed hard on the sight of Benz behind the counter, the gunman spinning to level his weapon at her and the plan she never executed. Divert and then attack.

A diversion!

Reda didn't stop to think or plan, there was no time, no point. She just kicked free of her stirrups, leaned close to MacEvoy's neck and said, "When I bail, get your ass out of here."

She didn't know if the bay got the message or not,

but as they blew past Dayn's body and the huge, glistening black dragon oriented hungrily on what it probably considered horsemeat-on-the-hoof, she screamed, "Go!" And then she flung herself out of the saddle.

The ground was hard, the impact crushing. She tucked and rolled, but by the time she came to a stop, her head was ringing and her right wrist hurt from being jammed, or worse.

She didn't have time to worry about that, though. As she lunged to her feet, she saw that MacEvoy had done his job—intentionally or not—drawing the dragon away. But the monstrous creature only followed the horse for a few strides before it stopped, turned back and reoriented.

Reda fell to her knees beside Dayn, horrified by the ragged, gaping wounds she could see through his torn shirt and the blood that trickled from his mouth. He was breathing shallowly, his eyes rolled back in his head. Sobs backed up in her chest, but she didn't have time for them now. She shook him slightly, hoping for a groan, but got nothing. "Dayn, wake up. We need to go!"

She couldn't carry him and MacEvoy was long gone. Worse, the ground rolled beneath her as the big black dragon headed back toward them, its beady red eyes burning with hunger and hatred.

Moving behind Dayn, she tried to lever him up, but he was deadweight. Worse, she was hurting him, probably doing more damage to his injuries, but what other choice did she have? "Dayn, please, *wake up!*"

All rationality in the world said for her to leave him and run, that the creature wanted him, not her. But logic didn't stand a chance against her feelings for him, so she stayed put, trying desperately to rouse him. His head lolled and his mouth opened slightly, revealing his fully extended secondary canines.

The sight stirred a one-two punch of heat and understanding. She didn't let herself think about it, didn't let herself hesitate. She opened his mouth, set her wrist against those two scalpel-sharp points and pushed.

She cried out at the pain, but then sucked in a breath at the wash of heat that followed, flowing through her body as he moved slightly against her, rousing. Backing her wrist off his fangs, she turned her arm so the bloody spots hit his tongue, which moved, fitfully at first and then with purpose, lapping two strong strokes and then a third.

Doing her best to ignore for now the pleasure-pain of his feeding, she leaned in and said, "Wake up. I need you."

Her heart hammered and despair threatened as the dragon reached them and reared up, shrieking and beating at the air with its wings. Then it slammed back down and snaked its vicious triangle of a head toward them, moving in for the kill, gaping its jaws wide and—

Dayn moved convulsively, jerking upright, yanking the crossbow into position and putting his bolt straight into one fiery red eye.

The dragon bellowed and yanked back, wings flailing so hard that it lifted off the ground and hung for a moment, suspended as it writhed and keened, contorting into impossible-seeming shapes in the sky. Seconds later, it went limp and plummeted to the ground.

It vanished when it hit, sent back to whatever magic had summoned it.

Suddenly, the meadow was entirely silent.

Reda stared at the place where it had been, and blew out a long breath. "Okay. We made it. That was…okay." She wasn't okay, though, because she was far too aware of the deep ache in her wrist and the echo of mingled pleasure-pain within her.

Dayn, too, was far from okay. He groaned as he tried to sit up away from her, then fell back weakly. A muscle pulsed at the corner of his jaw. "We need to get out of here. Moragh will know we killed her creature. She'll send men to find us, or come herself, and I'm in no shape to fight."

That was an understatement. It took all her effort to get him on his feet and keep him there, and he leaned heavily against her. More, as they left the meadow and headed back into the forest, he slid into and out of lucidity, his mumbled thoughts fragmented. "Don't know who I am, he says? I'll show… Wish I could've gone with you, my sweet Reda, wish you hadn't come back… Don't know where they are…"

The "wish you hadn't come back" was a theme. And where before she had told herself he had sent her away to keep her safe, now she wondered whether she was kidding herself. But for a change, instead of immediately assuming the worst, she decided she would wait and see. First and foremost, she needed to get him back on his feet. And although she thought she knew how to do it, the prospect wasn't appealing.

Or rather, it *was* appealing. And that was what worried her.

A short distance into the forest, she found a spot where a big tree had long ago fallen against three big boulders. Time and weather had hollowed out the giant trunk, creating a small sheltered area that would have to do, because Dayn was breathing hard and struggling to keep himself upright.

She eased him into the hiding spot and then walked a quick circuit, but didn't find any sign of the witch, at least nothing that she could detect with her all-too-human senses. Rejoining him, she ducked down and crawled in beside him.

The hollow was dry enough and offered good concealment, but she sorely missed the supplies that had galloped away with MacEvoy, because Dayn didn't look good at all. His eyes were closed, his breathing shallow and pain cut deep grooves beside his mouth.

The thing was, though, he didn't need anything from the saddlebags. He needed blood.

CHAPTER FOURTEEN

STEELING HERSELF, Reda looked down at her wrist. The slices were neat marks, already sealed up through some sort of vampire magic. But what made her the most queasy was the reddish circle painted on her forearm, showing where his mouth had been.

When it had actually been happening, it hadn't really bothered her. Now, though, her stomach roiled, though she couldn't have said why. It hadn't really hurt all that much, and the pleasure had far outweighed the sting. More, she didn't feel any different than she did before, and it had *saved* them, damn it. How was that wrong?

It wasn't until she didn't get an answer that she realized she was waiting for one. She wanted reason and logic to weigh in, wanted to hear from practicality, because they were the ones who could explain why her baseline human self said it was wrong for one person to drink blood from another, yet under the circumstances she couldn't think of a good reason why.

Maybe that was her answer, and the reason why the other parts of her were staying silent—because in the end this wasn't the human realm, wasn't even the wolfyn realm. They were in the kingdoms where magic—and emotion—trumped.

She had heard it all before: *love is messy, it hurts, it's not logical, it defies prediction.* But now she got why those were clichés, got why some people nodded knowingly over them while others looked blank.

Her parents hadn't made any sense together. On the surface, a fey dreamer, possibly even a realm traveler, shouldn't have had anything in common with the stalwart, conservative, linear-thinking major. Yet they had chosen each other, had made four children together. More, when she died, a piece of him had died with her—the piece that had known how to laugh, how to live, how to remember without letting the past take over the present.

Reda had long known that she was a product of her mother's death and the way her father changed. What she hadn't really grasped, though, was that she had also come from a love that had been so strong that it had drawn her parents together despite their differences, and whose absence had made her father a different, lesser man.

Which brought to mind another of those sayings: throw your heart over first and the rest will follow. He had done that and gotten burned. Had she on some level realized it and held herself at a distance rather than leading with her heart, not wanting the pain he'd lived through, not wanting to cause the pain he had experienced because of it?

When had she ever thrown herself into a relationship? More, when had she put her heart into it first? Maybe she had started to in the wolfyn realm, only to have Dayn's secrets rear up between them. But even there she hadn't given herself fully.

His test might have been proving that he could think of others before himself, but maybe hers had been to do the opposite and learn how to please herself and stop worrying about what other people—including the ones she channeled in her head—thought about her decisions.

"Got it figured out yet?"

Starting, she looked over and found Dayn watching her through heavy-lidded eyes. A flush touched her cheeks, warmed her skin and made her suddenly conscious of her own pulse. "Have I got what figured out? The way onto the island?"

"Whatever was making you look so fierce just now, like you were ready to take on the whole world by yourself. The thought of which, by the way, terrifies me."

Hearing him sounding more like himself, she took a closer look. "You're healed!"

He nodded, shifting and testing a muscle here, a move there. "I can't explain it, but that little bit of your blood helped far more than I would have expected it to. Maybe it's got something to do with whoever your ancestors were, or maybe it's connected to the part of the spell that ties my life force to the island. Who knows? But believe it or not, I'm good to go." He parted his ragged shirt to reveal his chest and flat stomach, made whole once more, save for reddish marks stamping the places where he had been torn to the bone an hour earlier.

If they had been in the outlaws' cave, separated by fences and space, it might not have happened. But she was sitting so near him in the small hollow that it was too easy to stretch her hand across and press her palm to his chest to soak up the feel of the warm, yielding muscle the steady *lub-dub* of his heartbeat.

"I thought you were going to die." She hadn't meant to say it aloud, hadn't meant for her eyes to well up.

He covered her hand with his own, holding her against his heart. "You've seen for yourself that I'm not easy to kill."

"But you could have died back there. You still might."

Reaching up with an arm that had been broken an hour before, he touched the single tear that had broken free, then cupped her cheek in his palm. "Ah, Reda. My sweet, sweet Reda. I wish I could freeze time right now. No more looking back or moving forward, just the two of us together."

She closed her eyes and felt another tear track down her cheek as he leaned in and touched his lips to hers. And although nothing was different between them, there was something new inside her as she opened her mouth beneath his.

He made a low, urgent noise in the back of his throat, almost a whimper yet so much more masculine than that, as if he, too, so badly needed this yet had been afraid that it wouldn't happen ever again. But it would happen, it *was* happening, and she poured herself into the moment, determined to take what she needed and give everything in return. There was no more second-guessing, no more inner debate; her mind was still and wholly in the moment when she wrapped her arms around his neck and he rose above her, easing her down to the dry, yielding moss. There were no more reservations, no skittering fears of too-sharp teeth or compulsions, because this thing happening between them went both ways.

She felt his wolfyn's enthrallment in the gentle rasp of his weapon-callused hands over her skin as they loosened enough clothing to find each other, and in

the shudder of his breath when she softly kissed his
cheek, his forehead, the touch saying, *I'm here, with
you, and right now nothing else matters.* She felt him
control his other, vampire self in the way he coiled tight
with pleasure and need when she grazed her teeth along
the veins at the side of his neck, nipping lightly over the
fading love bites.

And it was because of that enthrallment, because of
that control, and because of the time-faded, grief-faded
memory of her father twirling her mother across the
back lawn and the two of them racing down the wooded
path to the forest, looking back over their shoulders like
naughty kids—or mismatched lovers who had somehow matched perfectly—that there was no fear as she
shifted beneath him and guided his mouth to the side
of her neck.

He went very still. Then, with a low groan that resonated deep inside her, he opened his mouth against her
skin.

She tried not to tense but did, then relaxed when he
kissed her there, laved her with his tongue, scraped his
teeth lightly across the sensitized flesh. Then he drew
away.

Murmuring disappointment, she opened her eyes to
find him looking at her, waiting for her to look at him.
The emerald of his eyes had gone lush with passion and
his face was flushed, his dark hair tousled, making him
look younger and more carefree than she had ever seen
him before. But his expression was in deadly earnest
when he rasped, "Are you sure?"

His fangs caught the light when he spoke, and the
sight kicked new heat into her bloodstream. She wanted
them on her, in her, wanted to take the risk body and

soul, and know that a piece of her was inside him. "I'm sure. But only if you want to."

"I've never wanted anything—or anyone—more." He pressed his forehead to hers. "Reda, I—"

"Shh." She pressed her fingers to his lips. "Let's save that for after." Because for all that they were taking their moment together here and now, the immediate future pressed heavily and she didn't want either of them to make promises they might have to break.

He drew back, eyes shadowed, but nodded. "After, then." He eased in and kissed her lips, gently at first, chastely, but then parted his lips as if saying, as she had, *Only if you want to.*

And, oh, yes, she wanted to. Nerves added an edge to the excitement as she opened her mouth and kissed him back, using her tongue to explore the two long fangs that overlapped his other teeth, sliding it along one and then the other as he rumbled a deep groan that released new wetness inside her.

He stroked her body as they kissed, slid her clothes farther out of the way and cupped her, stroked her. She arched into him, parting her legs in wanton demand and then moaning when he skimmed along the outsides of her heated flesh without penetrating. But then he broke their kiss and pressed his lips to her cheek, her jaw, the soft spot below her ear.

She moved restlessly against him, would have cupped him, touched him with some inciting friction of her own, but he had angled his body away to concentrate on her. Which was so unbearably sexy she thought she would shatter. "More," she whispered. "Now. Please, now."

The nerves were gone, leaving only wild heat and

need as he grazed one fang down her neck. Pleasure shivers coiled through her until her whole body throbbed with her heartbeat, making her exquisitely aware of the blood racing through her body and running beneath the place at the side of her throat where he opened his mouth to suckle her.

His fingers mimicked the pressure of his lips, rubbing her clit with a voluptuous intensity that pulled the pressure inside her tighter and tighter. She whimpered and moved against him, and where before she might have held herself back, not wanting him to know how thoroughly she was under his control, now she gave in to the sensations, reveled in them, tangling her fingers in his hair and urging him on.

He suckled harder, worked his fingers a little deeper, so she felt his teeth on her throat, his fingers at the entrance to her body. Tingles raced through her, presaging orgasm, and she moaned his name as the pleasure gathered. Tightened. Poised...

Pain lanced through her as he bit down; pleasure rose up as he pierced her with two fingers at the same time, and she was caught amid the two for a breathless instant of shock. But then, between one heartbeat and the next, the pain became heat and the shock became a shuddering groan of "Ohh, yes," as he sucked from her on a deep and primal level while his hand surged against her with those long, elegant fingers inside her and the heel of his hand gently massaging her clit.

She clung to him, one hand buried in his hair, holding him against her throat, the other curved around his shoulder and digging in as waves of heat and pleasure rolled through her, throbbing with her pulse, and then with his, too, as their heartbeats aligned in rhythm. She felt his heartbeat, his pleasure, knew that had to be the magic of the forming bond. But instead of being terrifying or intrusive, as she had imagined, it was incredible, indescribable. It didn't take anything away from her; it gave to her, shared with her. Just like he did.

The first delicious curls of a monstrous-feeling orgasm tickled at the edges of her senses, and when he groaned deep in his chest, she knew he could feel it, too. He intensified his rhythm, working her, sucking her and gasping against her throat when she whimpered and fisted her hand in his hair, holding him against her, urging him on.

His excitement washed through her, along with a deep, possessive pleasure that whispered in her mind: *You are mine now, as I am yours. We are ourselves, yet we are also one.*

The orgasm caught her, swirled around her, inside her, and sucked her up into a vortex of pleasure so overwhelming that the rest of the world ceased to exist for her—there was only Dayn's mouth and hands, the searing heat that came through their new bond and the glory that whirled through her body.

She arched and gasped, riding the pressure and the spin, and then staying excited when the pulsing echoes faded but the pleasure didn't fade. Instead, it plateaued, as if her body, too, was saying, *Give me more.*

He groaned softly as he withdrew his fangs, bringing a pinch of pain that disappeared quickly when he licked where they had been. Then he kissed the spot, kissed her jaw, whispered her name.

"Don't stop," she whispered in return. She was replete yet still greedy, and she could feel the need inside him. He was full to bursting, hard enough to hurt, and aching to be inside her. "Come inside me."

His head came up; his eyes fixed on hers, silently asking if she knew what she was commanding. He had fed from her throat, which meant she was primed now to accept his seed.

She nodded slowly, not even bothering to check in with her inner committee. This was her life, her call. And illogical or not, it was what she wanted, what she needed. "Only if you want to," she said to him as she had done earlier.

"Gods, yes." He kissed her, fangs fully extended still, and so sensitive that he shuddered when she licked along the curve of one. As they kissed, he withdrew his fingers and looped her leg over his arm, baring her swollen flesh wide as he moved into position.

Breaking the kiss, she stared down at their poised sexes, unbearably aroused. His engorged cock was hard and heavy, and flushed a gorgeous ruddy red where it nudged her pink folds so intimately. She could feel its throb, feel her heartbeat align with the pulse.

"I want this," he said, bringing her eyes up to his. Then her eyelids fluttered closed as he pushed forward a delicious inch. He leaned in and kissed her closed lids, whispering, "I want you." He seated himself another inch, filling and stretching her. Then, voice deep and reverent, as if he was promising her the world, he grated, "I am yours." And he pushed fully home.

Colors exploded behind her eyelids, sensory rainbows that said the storm had passed, the air was clear and the past had been washed away. And for now, in this frozen moment that they had stolen for themselves, she allowed herself to believe it, because on some levels it was true.

As she surged against him, counterpointing the powerful thrusts that wrung cries from both of them, she was whole within herself, taking what she wanted and trusting her own instincts over life lessons that didn't work for her, maybe hadn't ever really worked for her. And as he clamped her hips in his hands and anchored her so he could drive deeper, so deeply that she nearly came from the pressure of him hitting her exactly right inside and out, she knew that what they had found together was separate from Elden's problems and his need for redemption. Those things might have put them in each other's orbits, but their deep connection—and now their bond—was their own.

Knowing it, believing in it and him, and this one singular moment they had stolen, she found his mouth and poured herself into a kiss that held nothing back. She was wide open to him, feeling his heartbeat and pleasure and sharing her own in return.

Emotion washed through her, tightening her body around him as a second orgasm gathered, deep and powerful, as they rocked together, not having sex or making love so much as *mating,* sealing the bond that now connected them.

Through it, she knew that he was lost in her, in the moment and the sensations, holding nothing back as he thrust and thrust again, finding a sweet, sweet spot where they fit perfectly, joined intimately. Her body tightened as he stroked harder and faster, then faster still, touching that spot, that wonderful glorious place that wrapped her up, caught her up. And sent her flying.

She threw her head back, rapt in the glory of coming

with her body, mind and heart united, and nothing held in reserve. She called his name, praised him, urged him on, drove him wild.

"Yes, Reda. My sweet Reda." He bowed his head as his rhythm hitched and his big body shuddered against her. He surged into her, pressed home, touched the place that was theirs alone, and then he was coming, too, her name reverberating in his chest as he leaned into her, against her.

The sensations washed between them, amping their responses and locking them together in protracted pleasure before leveling off and then, eventually, easing.

"Gods." He pressed his cheek to hers, his breathing still hard and fast. "Dear gods. If I had known…"

It was a first for him, too, she realized. His first time drinking from a woman's throat. His first bonding. And if she had anything to say about it, his first, last and only. She waited for panic, didn't feel any. And smiled, feeling lighter than she had in…well, forever. "I'm glad you didn't find out with anyone else."

"Only you, sweet Reda." He rolled onto his side, bringing her with him so they lay facing each other. They were no longer intimately joined, but she could feel their bond as a small kernel of warmth that moved through her, moving with her blood. It wasn't intrusive or invasive. It simply *was*.

His eyes searched hers. "I'm fine," she said, tightening her fingers on his. "Better than fine."

"No regrets?" His words were soft and slow. Hopeful.

"Not ever, no matter what happens." Her heart wanted to hurt with the prospect of things to come, but she determinedly kept her thoughts there, in the present, with him. Though from the way his lids were drooping, she didn't think she would have him with her, present and accounted for, for much longer. "You, sir, are crashing."

"Too musshh magic." His words were slurring, his eyes going unfocused. He blinked, trying to stay awake, but it was clearly a losing battle. "All that healing. Need an hour. We...we shhhould have enough time."

Whether they did or not, he wasn't going to be any use until he recharged. Fleetingly, she wished for some of Candida's clever potions, but they were long gone. "Sleep," she said. "I'll keep watch." Unlike him, she was wide awake, clearheaded and ready for action.

"Don...don't go anywhere. Not sssafe." His eyes were nearly closed now, his body relaxing toward sleep whether he liked it or not.

"I won't. I promise."

He lifted their joined hands to his lips, kissed her knuckles and then pressed them to his heart. He was smiling as he slipped into sleep, and she smiled, watching him. And in that moment, in that perfect stolen piece of the present, she felt at peace.

DAYN TIGHTENED HIS grip on Reda's hand as his older brother repeated the words that would make him the king of Elden.

Nicolai's voice rolled out across the crowds that thronged the castle courtyard and spilled beyond to the outer reaches and the greensward beyond. The sky was blue and perfect, the castle repaired, scrubbed and hung with banners old and new. Breena stood on Nicolai's other side next to a solid man with their father's features—Micah? Gods—and the sight of them warmed

Dayn, made him grateful, as he was every day since the day the sorcerer died, for the spell that had saved them and then brought them back together again, along with several others that Dayn sensed standing near each of his sibs, but couldn't see clearly.

With the vow finished, Nicolai bowed his head to receive the symbols of his reign. Dayn's eyes misted at the sight of the vestments their father had worn, but the ache was a good one, free of guilt or recrimination. "He'll be a good king," he murmured to Reda.

"He'll have a good second-in-command looking out for him," she returned.

"So will I." His lips turned up as he glanced over at her. "Or am I your second? I'm never sure."

"We can trade off, at least until our new commanding officer arrives." She brought their joined hands to the faint swell of her belly and he spread his hand, spanning their growing child as fierce love and possessiveness welled up inside him.

Nicolai moved out onto the castle balcony and the crowd erupted into cheers at their first sighting of the new king of Elden. As the noise swelled, Dayn grinned, leaned down and kissed her softly.

"There's nothing more important than this," he said, and kissed her again, silently thanking the gods and the magic that had brought her into his life.

The dream fragmented and misted away, leaving Dayn to swim back up to consciousness. Before he had even opened his eyes, he knew he had needed the rest, and the pleasant dream that he badly wanted to believe was prescience more than wishful thinking. He felt refreshed and recharged, with none of the fuzziness that had accompanied the crash.

He was a little embarrassed, though not about having wiped out so thoroughly, but because he hadn't planned for it. He'd heard of such things, but hadn't ever before used as much magic as he had over the past four days. And then to add in a bonding...yeah. Not his best planning ever.

But at the same time, it was the best decision he'd ever made. He felt the warmth of her in his veins, felt their distant connection, felt—

Wait a minute. Distant? His blood iced at the realization that she felt suddenly very far away.

Something was wrong.

"Reda?" he said as he opened his eyes, even though he already knew she wasn't there. But he got a second shock when he looked around. It was nearly dark out.

Lunging to his feet, he yanked his clothes to rights and ducked out of the shelter.

The surrounding area was undisturbed, at least as best as he could tell in the gathering darkness. There was no sign of a struggle, no evidence that she had stepped out to relieve herself and been attacked by some beast. And if she'd been taken from right there by human hands, anyone grabbing her would have seen him, and captured him for the bounty. Which meant she had left under her own power.

His pulse thudded in his ears, choppy and upset. She had promised to stay with him, yet she had disappeared and he had slept far, far too long. Gods and the Abyss. This wasn't a dream; it was a nightmare. She had disappeared and he was up against his deadline.

What had happened? Had she regretted forming the bond, maybe even been repulsed once her blood

cooled? Had the intensity of their mating sent her into
a panicked retreat?

Most importantly, had she fled to the shrine?

"No," he grated, refusing to believe it. Perhaps they
hadn't made any promises of forever, but she had fed
him, mated with him, taken his seed inside her after the
bonding. They belonged to each other now. She had to
know that.

Except he hadn't told her, had he? And when he had
started to say something along those lines, she had
hushed him and changed the subject. At the time, he
had thought she was feeling too raw and unsettled from
their other confidences to add talk of the future into the
mix. Now, though, he wondered whether she hadn't believed there would be one.

He had been so dazzled by the warrior woman
astride a fractious bay that he'd lost track that she, too,
had spent a long time alone, questioning her worth.
How had he forgotten that?

Gods. Had he lost her in truth? He quickly sought
their bond; the weak flicker had to mean she was still
in the kingdom realm. But for how long? Was she even
now working to call a vortex to carry her home?

Let her go, said an inner voice. *She'll be safer there,
alive no matter what happens on the island. Maybe you
could even travel to her when all this is over. Right
now, you need to get yourself onto that island. Time is
running out.*

He froze. Was this, then, his test? Was he to prove
himself by choosing Elden over her? Because despite
that logic, his gut said that if she left the realm, he
would never see her again. More, it said he had to go

after her now, that he didn't dare tackle the island or the sorcerer without her at his side.

Wishful thinking, came the scoff. But it wasn't really. It was faith. He had faith in his own gut, faith in the magic he and Reda made together.

Please, gods, don't let me screw this up. This time the human slang came naturally.

His heart thudded against his ribs and his stomach knotted, but when he moved, it wasn't toward Blood Lake, the island or the redemption he'd spent twenty years preparing for. Instead, he headed away, following the thin scuff-shadows that only a trained hunter would see. Seeking the bond magic, he thought with all his might, *Hang on, sweet Reda. I'm coming. Wait for me and we'll figure this out together.*

Because the dream might have been a fantasy, but it had one thing right: she was his priority. He wasn't the heir, hadn't the best of his siblings when it came to anything except his ability to hunt and ride. But with Reda—and *for* her—he had become a prince. A hero, even.

She made him better, and without her, he wouldn't be any use to Elden.

CHAPTER FIFTEEN

REDA SWAM SLOWLY UP FROM a sleep that felt too deep, with quivers in her stomach that said something was badly wrong. She was lying on a hard surface and her head hurt, but those inputs seemed strange and far away, her fragmented dreams so much more real.

Was it all a dream, after all? she thought, but wasn't sure where the inner voice had come from or what it meant.

Her thoughts scattered like a herd of identical bald-faced bay horses, snorting and blowing as they swerved and collided. Past and present mixed together: *she was a little girl of six or seven, sitting cross-legged in the woods opposite her* maman, *leaning in, wide-eyed. "Tell me more about the magic. Please?" She was a rookie cop going in low while her ride-along partner went high, and then laughing her ass off when they plugged a pair of homicide cops with red paint-ball splashes. She was ten years old, stumbling into the woods in her nightgown. "Maman? Maman, where are you?" Twenty-six, standing over Benz's grave, knowing that he wasn't in there, that dead was dead.*

The graveyard had smelled of cut grass and apple trees. Now, though, she wrinkled her nose against an ammoniac taint and the smell of animals. More, the noises were wrong. The graveyard's silence was broken by restless noises that made her think she was in a barn: sniffs, snuffles and low chuffs, the movement of big bodies in straw.

Where was she? What was wrong with her? What was going on?

She struggled to open her eyes. Then the fog started to clear…and she realized they were already open, covered by a fetid rag that was tightly tied around her head. There was another jammed in her mouth, which was dry and foul. Light and air seeped in around the edges, but just barely.

Crying out, the noise muffled and nasty, she yanked up her hands to tear at the blindfold. But chains rattled, cuffs dug into her wrists and her hands stopped short of her face.

She realized now that she had never known true terror before.

"No!" She thrashed upright, slammed against a stone wall, rolled off what proved to be a narrow cot, hit the cold stone floor awkwardly on one hip and shoulder, then got hung up on the chains. Her feet weren't bound, but her wrist shackles were fastened to the wall, giving her only a few feet of play.

Twisting so hard she felt muscles pull, she got her hands to her face and plucked at the knotted rags with weak, trembling fingers. *Breathe,* she told herself when the numbness spread and her moves slowed, threatened to stop entirely. *Damn it, breathe!*

The most recent of memories broke free: *lying curled up against Dayn while he slept; hearing a twig crack in the distance, then the voices of men talking in low undertones as they searched the forest; learning from them that Moragh had used up her magic summoning*

*the Feiynd and couldn't track Dayn by his father's spell
anymore, but knew he had to be near where the dragon
died, injured.*

Her nose was closing up from the smell, cutting off
her air, sending panic higher even as she tried to slow
her brain down. *One thing at a time. Do the gag first.
The knot is in the back.* But. She. Couldn't. Move.

More flashes: *the men moving on; her trying to wake
Dayn but failing; the debate—she had promised to stay
with him, but they would be circling back soon. Her
slipping from concealment, heart pounding with no real
plan other than to lead them away. Not into the Dead
Forest, but where? The shrine, she had thought, she
could lead them to the shrine. Would a vortex scare
them and buy her some time to double back?*

The stone was cold and hard beneath her, the knot
tight and greasy. She concentrated on those inputs,
made herself relax and suck on the thin trickle of
oxygen leaking through her gag, then try the knot
again.

The memories were coming faster now, clearer: *her
following the men, her mouth sour and her heart drum-
ming against her ribs; finding them and circling around
to where she could lead them to the trident-topped tree,
and then...*

*A blow from behind. A man kneeling on her, push-
ing her face into the dirt. A coarse, terrifying discussion about what to do with her, then the decision to
bring her unspoiled to the witch for questioning. Another blow, then darkness.*

Darkness.

She sobbed against the gag, curled around herself,
fingers useless on her bonds. The low, ragged noises

stirred the creatures around her; from a little distance, echoing as if down a corridor, she heard metal dragging on stone followed by a low, rumbling feline growl that didn't sound like anything she'd ever heard before. Then, farther down, a bugle that was part elephant, part trombone.

This was no barn. The noises belonged to creatures that would be kept in a zoo.

Or, in this realm, in a bestiary.

"No," she whispered into her knees. "Please, no." She didn't remember if the questioning had happened yet, but the too-deep sleep and numbing fog made her think of the vortex magic. Had the witch bespelled her? Had she blabbed? "Dayn?" she called, torn between equal fear and hope. "Are you there?"

There was no answer from her fellow prisoners; not even a growl. But faint warmth stuttered to life within her, moving slowly through her body, surging with the beat of her blood.

He was alive. She let the thought fill her, chasing away some of the chill and unlocking her muscles. Did he know she was on the island, captured? Or did he think she had taken off on him? She didn't know how much he could sense through the bond. Her thoughts churned with new unease: Would he turn his back on duty and come after her, or would the kingdom's needs outweigh the bond? She didn't know which she would prefer; she only knew that she hated being part of the inner war she imagined him fighting. He was an honorable male, her bound mate. Yet he was also a prince of Elden.

She should have left when she had the chance, she knew. But although that would have been the better, more honorable thing to do, all she could think was, *Hell with that.* She wanted Dayn, wanted a future with him even if she had to fight for it. Because she loved him.

"Love," she whispered softly as the small kernel of warmth unfurled from a point to a glow, and then to new strength flowing through her with the beat of her heart. *Yes,* she thought. *This.*

She loved him. Not because he was a woodsman, a prince or a hero, but because he was a vampire and a wolfyn. It didn't make any logical sense, went against everything rationality told her she should feel. But her heart didn't care about any of that. She loved him, pure and simple. She didn't need to have faith in the feeling, didn't have to believe in it for it to exist; it simply was.

That revelation spurred her, got her moving again. Her hands stopped shaking; her stomach unknotted and she uncurled herself from fetal uselessness. The chains clanked and dragged as she repositioned herself against the cot, using it to support her weighed-down wrists as she craned and went to work again on the knots, starting with the top one this time.

It gave almost immediately, and the blindfold fell away. *Success!*

She blinked against the sudden blaze of light, squinting until it resolved to rather anemic amber firelight coming from torches set in brackets outside her cell.

Because that was most definitely what it was. The space was the size of a large box stall; indeed, there was an iron hayrack in the corner, and places to hang buckets. But the door wasn't made for a horse or donkey—or none that she had ever seen before. It was made of iron bars that ran floor to ceiling, with no lock, no hinge, no nothing. Magic.

She sank back, heart thudding as bile rose.

"Oh, Dayn. Help me." Her lips shaped the words, but no sound came out. She hoped—prayed—he could sense her need through their bond, though. Because there was no way she was getting out of this one on her own.

DAYN. HELP ME!

At the sound of her voice, his head whipped up from the faint trail he'd been following. "Reda?"

His feet kept moving, but he turned inward as their bond suddenly grew stronger than before, amped by the fear he felt in her, along with an echo of hopelessness that terrified him. She was in trouble!

Adrenaline fired through his veins and his secondaries broke the skin, bringing the added aggression of his blood-drinking ancestors. "Hang on. I'm coming," he said, both aloud and in his heart. "Hang on. Don't leave. Don't—" He broke off, stopping dead at the edge of a churned-up patch of forest, where booted footprints were layered deeply and skid marks showed the impression of a human body just about her size. *"Reda!"*

The impressions were hours old, the body that had made them long gone. "No!" Gods, no. Who had taken her? Thieves, outlaws, soldiers? All equally dangerous, equally horrifying.

Pulse thundering in his ears, he sent magic into the bond, acting on instinct because he didn't know much about the connection or how it worked, especially with someone from the human realm. *Reda, where are you?*

There was no answer. Only the fear.

He took two running steps after her. But then he stopped, heart hammering. This wasn't going to work. He needed to move faster, couldn't risk losing the trail. Reda needed him, and she needed him now.

Deep within him, magic spun up. Not his blood-drinking powers, but the other. *Be true to yourself. Know your priorities.* It was his father's voice, but he wasn't sure if it was a memory or a message.

He stood for a moment in the center of the churned-up clearing, hands fisted at his sides, body shaking with the pull of the forces that were trying to tear him apart. His birthright demanded that he not give in to the lure of the wolfyn form. And his sibs, his honor and the people still living in this blighted land needed him to get his ass to Castle Island before the zero hour, which was approaching fast. Every shred of logic and rational thinking he possessed said that had to outweigh Reda's need. More, if he changed now, if he gave in to that magic, he put himself that much farther from his true self.

It felt like that was already happening, though, every time he thought about not going after Reda. She was his mate, his love, his other half. Without her, he wouldn't be living; he would be simply existing, as he had done for the past twenty years in the wolfyn realm. Without her, he wasn't himself.

He looked up into the night sky. "I'm sorry, Father. I wish I could be the kind of son you wanted, the kind of prince Elden needs. But I can't. This is who I am."

And he changed.

Pain flared through him, familiar even though it was only his third time making the transition. He gritted his teeth as flesh stretched and tore, tendons realigned and the ground grew suddenly closer to his eyes as his body reshaped itself into that of a huge wolf. A hunter. And today, if needs be, a killer. Because he would kill his own countrymen if that was what it took to keep his mate safe.

Rage and feral aggression flowed through him, calling to the beast within, and he threw back his head and howled.

Birds fled from nearby trees and several large creatures crashed in the brush, fleeing the predator that was suddenly among them. He didn't pay any attention to them, though; he was wholly focused on the scents that suddenly flooded his system as he put his nose down and bolted along the trail.

In his father's time, the smells of oiled leather, honed steel and grain-fed horses of a cavalry detachment would have been a relief. Now, though, the details coiled new fear inside him, chilling his blood and warning that she hadn't been taken by thieves or outlaws, but by soldiers.

The sorcerer had her.

He hit the road and turned toward the lake, running with his head up now, both because the scent was so strong and because he knew where he was going— which was where he'd been going all along. Not home, but to a reckoning.

He flashed on his father's memories of the castle's fall—blood splattering the stones of the courtyard, ettins fighting their way up to the second level, where the families lived, the king and queen despairing. Only it wasn't his parents he saw now; it was Reda standing alone, trying to fight her way free of the creatures that grasped and clawed at her.

In the waking dream, she looked straight at him. He didn't hear her voice, though, and the bond had gone frighteningly dim. Hurry. He had to hurry! Ignoring the panicked scatters of the villagers, he blew through a town and then blasted along the edge of the lake, body flat to the ground, claws biting into the ground, legs eating up the distance to the heavily guarded causeway. He heard shouts up ahead, saw a ragged band of men assembling, hastily armed with broken pikes and ancient-looking swords.

He didn't have time for this, didn't want to hurt them, so he just put his head down and charged, bulling through their line and sending them flying. An arrow whizzed in from the side, but he snapped it out of the air and broke it in his jaws, the moves automatic, instinctual, as if he'd always lived in this body.

Shouts followed him onto the narrow causeway and a rasping horn blared an alarm. On either side of him blurred the polluted waters of Blood Lake; up ahead, the huge, scorpionlike creatures formed ranks, clashing their claws and whipping their tails as if to say, *Bring it on!*

Hatred hazed his vision red. He had seen them through his father's eyes kill the soldiers who had been his friends, his comrades. The feral fighting instinct of an alpha male said to kill; the priorities of a mated man said to get the hell to the castle.

As he neared them, he gathered himself to leap over the huge creatures, saw their tails whip back and forth in expectation. Four strides. Three. Two. He coiled, faked a spring and ducked under the closest two, slashing at their legs on the way by.

The things screeched high, anguished screams, and

the causeway behind him exploded to slashing, clacking chaos. He heard a couple of splashes, but didn't look back. He was done with looking back.

He shouldered two bristling soldiers into the lake, and this time the splashes were followed by bloodcurdling screams. Then he was off the causeway, onto the island and charging toward the castle.

More shouts and another horn blast came, but they didn't seem to be aimed at him. The castle was stirring with movement, as if he wasn't the only unexpected arrival.

Dayn missed a step as he realized what that could mean.

It was happening, after all. He had returned in time, and unless he missed his guess, he wasn't the only one. His heart surged and he accelerated toward the castle.

A crossbow bolt thrummed toward him and buried itself in the dirt; a second carved a furrow in his haunch and he missed a few steps. But healing magic surged within him, hot and hard, as if he were suddenly drawing strength from the soil of Castle Island. Within seconds the injury had closed up and he was running once more at full tilt toward the outer bailey and—

He skidded hard, nearly falling when the trail he had been following suddenly swerved and headed away from the castle, toward the cluster of buildings at the other end of the island.

The sounds of footfalls and armor clanks rang out within the castle, calling to him. But his bond with Reda called harder. He could sense her now; he could feel her fear and despair. *I'm coming,* he sent along the bond. *Hang on!*

And he bolted away from the castle, toward the woman he loved, because he finally knew who he really was: he was hers.

CHAPTER SIXTEEN

THE TRAIL LED TO THE bestiary, which unlike the castle seemed deserted, at least of humans. Still in wolf form, Dayn slunk through the open doors at one end of the L-shaped building and padded up the long, barnlike aisle, which was flanked on either side by barred doors instead of the sliders he remembered.

The fur of his ruff bristled and his senses were maxed out. He could feel Reda's energy, but he couldn't track her using the bond. He could only look in every stall-size cell, his bile rising higher with each one as he caught sight of the beasts he had studied, the ones he had once tracked and hunted in all their wild glory, chained and contained, with much of their beauty stripped away.

A jungle liger lay chained to the wall; bare patches on its haunches showed where it had chewed its own fur away. A pair of demidragons slept huddled together in a corner, their normally dark scales bleached pale from cold and the lack of sun. A huge spider hung from the ceiling with its legs folded around its body and its multifaceted eyes glazed. The creatures seemed dispirited and uninterested...or, Dayn realized with a chill shiver, like they had been leeched of their life forces.

The sorcerer fed off everything, it seemed.

Then there was a fierce growl from up ahead, one

that had Dayn's hackles rising instinctively as he drew even with the doorway, where a smallish wolfyn male was pressed against the iron bars. The unfamiliar wolfyn's ears were flat to his head, his amber eyes crazed with hatred.

"I'm a friend," Dayn said in the simplified wolfform language Candida had taught him on the sly. "I can help."

The wolfyn didn't show any recognition. Instead, he snarled at him and then danced back to snap at the bars, dig at them, and then pressed forward again, trying to get at Dayn. There didn't seem to be any humanity left in the small male. Which, perhaps, was a blessing.

His snarls, though, had stirred up the other creatures, which stomped and shifted restlessly, starting to growl and snort.

"Hush," Dayn snarled. "They'll hear." He moved on, caught a faint whiff of flowers and spices and charged to the end of the aisle, heart rocketing. "Reda?" The word was a two-syllable chuff that sounded very like the wolfyn word for *heart.* Which was only fitting, as she had taken his.

He skidded to a stop in front of the cell that carried her scent. And stopped dead.

It was empty, the bars fully retracted into the floor and ceiling through some magical means. She was gone.

And the air beyond that point stank of fear and pain. The smell slammed into him, shutting down his senses. He couldn't scent her from there, couldn't track her.

"No." His stomach dropped. Frantically, he searched for the bond, felt her, but didn't like what he felt. There was anger, which was good because it said she was

fighting whatever was happening to her. But there was also terror and despair. And that wasn't good at all.

"They've taken her." The deep, resonant voice came from the opposite cell, and spoke a tongue he knew, though had never spoken successfully.

Heart galloping like a coal-black herd flowing over a green meadow, Dayn whirled and charged to the cell, which was so deeply shadowed that all he could see was a huge, indistinct shape in the corner. He pressed against the bars and said in the same language, "Where?"

And his wolf-form tongue said the word in a way his human tongue had never managed.

The huge shape moved, turned and came toward him, hooves ringing on the ground and striking sparks of metal on stone. The torchlight from the aisleway glinted off a long, metallic spiral and lit the blink of fiery orange eyes nearly lost beneath a long, flowing forelock.

It was the biggest damn unicorn Dayn had ever seen.

"Let me out and I'll show you." The stallion's eyes took on a hard, vicious gleam that reminded him that while the creatures might tolerate the wolfyn, they sure as hell didn't like them.

Then again, they didn't like anyone. And captivity really pissed them off. "I've got a better idea," Dayn said. And hoped to hell he wasn't about to make a fatal mistake.

"Go see what all that commotion is up at the castle," Moragh snapped in her servant's direction. "It's upsetting the beasts."

"Yes, mistress." The gnome bowed his way out.

The training hall—at least that was what Reda thought it was, based on all the open space and racked weapons—echoed with the hollow thud of the double doors shutting behind him, cutting out the distant blare of horns, the nearer snorts and stomps of the caged beasts.

The witch turned back, eyes glittering dangerously. "Now. Where were we?"

Reda just glared. Her head hurt and the large stone chamber around her kept going in and out of focus, but she held doggedly on to consciousness, clinging to the stone-cold fury that had come over her when the guards had opened her cell door and she had made a break for it, only to be struck down and dragged to her destination.

Pushed beyond fear and terror to a new place deep inside herself, where a hard and determined soldier of a woman existed, she wanted nothing more than to grab Moragh by her hair and dunk her head in the vat she was so carefully tending over a fire in the center of the big stone room. Or Reda could go for any number of the weapons displayed around the room; she wasn't picky. What she was, however, was trapped in the center of a strange symbol drawn on the stone floor in glittering powder. It generated a magical field of some sort, an invisible wall enclosing her. She flattened her palms against it now. "I don't know where you were," she said in answer to the witch's question, "but I was thinking about the scene where the wicked witch gets it, and wondering if I could get a vortex to drop a house on you."

She didn't let the bitch see the terror beneath her bravado, didn't let herself think about anything beyond stalling for time. Dayn was on the island—she could feel his nearness through their bond—and he would come for her as soon as he could. She knew that just as surely as she knew she loved him.

And that she had to stay alive and whole until he arrived.

Moragh sneered. "You've got a smart mouth on you. Must come with that royal blood of yours." She narrowed her eyes. "What are you, a quarter-bred Medinian? Can see it in the eyes." She bared her fangs and dragged her fingertips across the leather-bound book she clutched open to her chest. "All the more power for me. When I'm done with you, I'll be damn near invincible. Realm travel, magic, science—it'll all be mine."

"You…" Reda faltered. Her grandfather Medina had been a huge bear of a man, equally prone to laughter and moodiness, and everyone had said she had his eyes.

Something screeched outside, a high, keening call that raised the fine hairs on Reda's arms.

Moragh darted a glance in the direction of the bestiary. "Don't know what's gotten into them."

"The lost children are here," Reda said matter-of-factly. "They're going to kill the sorcerer." Her heart drummed against her ribs. *Hurry, Dayn!*

"Let them. Soon I won't need the Blood Sorcerer anymore." She lowered the book, scanned a page and then set the book aside to pick up a jewel-handled knife with a viciously sharp-looking cutting edge. Then, as she advanced on Reda, she recited a string of syllables in a low, sibilant tone.

"Don't—" Reda's voice cut out, her breath cut out, *everything* cut out as the magic that had held her trapped abruptly closed in on her, coating her skin.

Panic lashed—she wanted to fight, attack, retreat, do *something,* damn it—but the magic held her, controlled her.

At a gesture from the witch, the grip of the magic forced Reda to drop her to her knees, spread her arms out to the sides and tip her head back, baring her throat in a terrifying position of obeisance.

No, Reda screamed inwardly. *Nooo!*

Her mouth dried to dust as Moragh advanced on her, continuing to recite strange syllables that didn't make any sense to Reda, but coiled inside with hard, hurting intensity.

And suddenly, she wasn't cold and controlled anymore, wasn't confident, because for the first time since she had broken from her craven shell, it was painfully, elementally clear that being brave wasn't always enough.

Benz had been brave, and that hadn't saved him. He'd needed his partner to have his back.

Dayn, hurry! But she didn't know if the words got through, if anything got through. Panic bubbled in her, leaking weak tears from her eyes.

Moragh's chant rose in its intensity as the witch stopped directly opposite Reda. Her eyes were burning with power, her face frighteningly beatific as she set the knifepoint at the hollow between Reda's breasts.

Pain pricked and a drop of blood welled up. The sight made the love bites on her wrist and neck throb with memory, made the rest of her ache with sorrow. *I'm sorry, love. I tried to hold on long enough.*

The witch ended her chant with a flourish, drew back the knife and—

Bang! Moragh gasped and spun as the double doors

flew open with a gunshot crash that reminded Reda of the ettin bursting into Dayn's cabin. Only this time the creature that filled the night-dark doorway wasn't a three-headed giant; it was a huge black unicorn with a flowing mane and tail, hugely spiraled horn and murder in its fiery orange eyes.

And astride it rode a fairy-tale prince.

He wore a rebel's tunic over his shirt and brandished his short sword as the huge unicorn lunged into the hall and flew toward Moragh. The witch screeched and backpedaled, bringing up her own smaller knife.

Dayn! Reda didn't know if she managed to say it aloud or if the word sounded just in their heads, carried on the love bond that suddenly flared fierce and proud. He heard her either way; his eyes locked on hers for a brief second, with a look that said everything that she was feeling.

The unicorn swerved to miss Moragh, did a sliding stop and bumped Reda, knocking her aside as Dayn performed a flying dismount that sent him right into the witch.

The second Reda's feet left the powder-drawn symbol, the magic snapped out of existence. And she was free! She scrambled to her feet, backpedaling as the unicorn's huge head swung toward her and the light glinted off its spiral horn.

Dayn landed swinging, but Moragh ducked and spun away, coming for Reda with the knife outstretched. The unicorn oriented, lowering its massive weapon, but Dayn got there first. He flung himself on Moragh and they went down together, rolling and struggling.

And then not struggling anymore.

Reda surged forward, heart stopping for a second

and then pounding back to life when he moved, shifting to extricate himself from the witch, who lay on her back, both hands gripping the handle of her own knife, which had been driven into her heart.

"She's gone," he said, voice rough with whatever it had taken him to get to her.

Reda waited until he looked at her. Then she smiled. "I'm not."

His expression shifted, then cleared. "Ah, Reda."

And then it was easy to cross to him, reach up and touch his dear face. "You left the others to come find me." She wouldn't have asked it of him, but it mattered.

But he shook his head. "I came for you first, dear heart. I don't want to do this without you. Past, present, future—none of it matters if you're not at my side."

Her heart lodged in her throat as everything she had ever desired—even things she hadn't realized she wanted—suddenly opened up in front of her. And, even better, she didn't want to look at them yet. She only wanted to look at the man standing in front of her right then and there.

"I love you." The words weren't scary and they didn't hurt, she found. But they mattered.

His face smoothed and his eyes lit. "My sweet Reda." He drew her into his arms and kissed her, so his lips were against hers when he said, "By the gods, I love you, too. You're it for me. You're my life, my love, my one and only. I wasn't born to be the king and I don't want to play politics. I just want to be a man who's in love with his mate."

She kissed his jaw, nipped his throat and felt him quiver against her. "You're talking of kings and politics like the battle is already over. Sounds to me like it's just getting started."

"Duty calls." He broke away from her as the unicorn moved up near him, then gathered a handful of the long black mane and swung himself aboard. Leaning down, he reached a hand for her. "And it's calling for both of us. From now on, we're a team, no matter what."

As if that had answered a last lingering question she hadn't even been aware of having, the last of the tension eased her heart, leaving only the warmth of their bond—and her love for him—behind. She took his hand and settled herself gingerly into position on the unicorn's broad, powerful back. "Is he yours?"

The creature snorted disgustedly as it started out, moving easily despite the double burden and the slippery stone floor.

"I think it's closer to say that we're cautious allies."

She laughed and moved up to snuggle behind Dayn and slide her arms around his waist. As the big black creature carried them down the training hall, she asked casually. "What's a Medinian?"

"The royal family of High Reaches." He shot a curious look back over his shoulder. "Why?"

"I'll tell you later."

He smiled. "I like the sound of that. 'Later.' Yeah. That's good."

She pressed a hand to her stomach, where the warmth of their loving bond had concentrated itself in a happy glow. "My gut tells me there's going to be a later, that it's all going to work out okay."

"Mine, too. And it also says that your gut is going to be saying to you something else in the next few weeks."

"What?"

"Tell you later."

Laughing, she pressed tight to his back and wrapped her arms around his waist. "Sounds good. Now, let's help the others take care of 'now' so we can get to the later."

"Deal."

He covered her hands with his and the two of them moved in unison as the huge black unicorn cantered off, metallic hooves ringing on the stones as they headed for the castle, the coming battle...and the rest of their lives together in the magical kingdom of Elden.

* * * * *

TWIN TARGETS

CHAPTER ONE

SYDNEY WESTLAKE MADE her move a half hour before
the shift change, when the armed men who guarded
the compound on Rocky Cliff Island would be at their
least vigilant.

She hoped.

Tiberius was too smart to have a clockwork-regular
schedule for something as important as security, so the
armed forces that guarded the mansion and surrounding grounds worked randomly staggered shifts. After
eleven months on the island, though—three of them as
a prisoner—Sydney had found patterns in the random-
ness.

Today they were on what she'd dubbed "Schedule C,"
which meant the guard post located directly between
her quarters and the boat dock would change shifts at
1:40 a.m. God willing.

"You can do this," she said to herself. "You *have* to
do this. For Celeste." Her sister's name had become a
mantra, something she held on to when her bravery faltered.

At first Sydney had told herself she was helping
her ailing twin by staying on the island off the Massachusetts coast and working for Tiberius. She'd been
trying to find a cure for the insidious genetic condition that was slowly killing Celeste. The obscenely

large income being funneled into an offshore account
was an added draw, allowing Celeste to stay in their
wheelchair-friendly, restored Victorian in Maryland
with a personal aide, rather than moving to an assisted-
living facility of some sort. It had all seemed like a
godsend when Tiberius first contacted her through his
figurehead company, Tiberius Corp.

Now, though, she knew better. Tiberius wasn't a phi-
lanthropist and he wasn't a visionary. He was a monster,
a sociopath, a self-professed businessman who wanted
to use her discovery to do terrible things. Or rather,
sell it to other criminals, who would use it as a smoke-
screen, hiding their identities while they did God only
knew what.

She had to stop it from happening.

Trying not to betray her nerves, she crossed the high-
tech lab Tiberius had ordered built and outfitted to her
precise specifications. When she'd first arrived, the
huge room, filled with the latest cutting-edge biotech
equipment and analytical devices, had seemed like par-
adise. Now, it was a prison.

Sitting down at the bank of a half dozen networked
computers, each of which controlled several of the big
machines and analyzed the resulting data, she tried to
block awareness of the security cameras blanketing the
huge room, tried not to think about the men who were
undoubtedly watching her image on-screen.

She'd done her prep work well. They'd gotten used
to her returning to the lab around 10:00 p.m. and working until one or so in the morning. If she were lucky,
all they would see now was their tame lab rat pulling
up the last set of results and then powering down the
big machines for the night.

In reality, she was executing two programs she'd managed to sneak onto the island. One was an uncrackable lockdown program that would freeze all of the lab computers and machines until she typed in a password. The other would shut down all of the networked computers on Rocky Cliff Island—including the ones running power and security—for the space of five minutes, and then go back into hiding, supposedly untraceable by all but the original programmer.

Celeste had developed the routines just before she'd gotten sick; she was the techie, Sydney the bio-geek. Together, they'd used to joke, they were a nerd superhero.

Now, those powers would be put to the test.

"Okay, kids, do your thing." Sydney powered the lab computer down right after she'd fed the programs into the network. In ten minutes, the lights should go out. Then, the next time someone turned on one of the lab computers, the only thing they'd see on the screen would be a text prompt that read: Password?

If she made it off Rocky Cliff Island, she would use the password as leverage to keep her and Celeste alive long enough to grab the money out of her accounts and disappear. Then and only then, she would contact the authorities and tell them about Tiberius's plans.

If she died trying to escape, she could only hope Tiberius or his tech experts would try three wrong passwords, whereupon the worm would corrupt every piece of data on the network and fry the computers.

If she lived and was recaptured, though...

She shuddered. She'd seen what happened to people who crossed Tiberius. The image of what he'd done to Jenny Marie, the softhearted cook he'd caught sneaking emails between Sydney and Celeste, would remain burned on Sydney's retinas until the day she died. Unfortunately that day could be far sooner than she hoped, because crossing Tiberius was her only option right now. She couldn't allow him to use her scientific discovery for the purpose he intended; she had to stop him. Which meant it was now or never.

Sydney's fingers trembled as she hung her lab coat on its hook near the airlock-type passageway that was the only way in or out of the windowless lab. After pushing through the first of the pressurized doors, she touched the intercom button beside the second. "Out, please."

She'd long ago learned not to bother making small talk with the guards—it only made them suspicious. Nowadays, she stuck to her routine and they stuck to theirs, little suspecting that she was studying them and waiting for her chance to escape. Or maybe they'd suspected all along, and she was doomed before she even began.

The door unlocked with a click. Sydney held her breath as it swung open automatically, then exhaled in relief when she saw the hallway was empty. If they'd sent an escort she would've had to scrap her plan, but the armed escorts had gotten fewer and further between with every week and month she behaved herself, as she'd pretended to cooperate with Tiberius and his mad plan.

Forcing herself to breathe evenly, she stepped out into the hallway and headed for her quarters, trying to look like all she had on her mind was a few hours of sleep. When she reached the gray, featureless door leading to her two-room suite, she pressed another intercom button. "In, please."

The door clicked and opened, but instead of entering, she reached around the corner and fumbled for the thin wire she'd installed in the wall panel earlier that day, in the ten minutes she'd bought by "accidentally" blocking the view of the single camera in the main room of her suite by hanging a towel over the lens. By the time one of the guards had buzzed himself in without knocking, removed the offending item and groused at her for her continued sloppiness—which she'd carefully cultivated over the past few months—she'd done what needed to be done with the circuitry.

Concealed alongside the molding, the wire led to a simple gadget she'd Mickey Moused out of parts filched from the lab, using the diagram Celeste had sent via Jenny Marie. A sharp tug would form a bridge between the two main power lines in the wall beside the door, creating an obvious short and giving Tiberius's engineers no reason to look further for the source of the electrical failure.

At least that was the theory.

"Here goes nothing," she whispered, heart pounding. She checked her watch. Nine minutes fifty-five since she'd fed the kill program into the network. Fifty-six. Fifty-seven. As the door to her room started to close on its soundless mechanism, she yanked on the wire and jumped back.

There was a sizzle and a blinding flash in her room. Two seconds later the lights went out in the hallway, plunging her into utter blackness.

Sydney didn't think. She ran.

She heard muffled shouts and pounding feet as she

bolted along the hallway and slammed through the door at the end, where she'd jimmied the lock earlier that day.

She was out!

The night was cold and rainy, which she hadn't anticipated. Sucking in a lungful of the wet, cutting air of springtime off the Atlantic coast, she plunged down a short cement staircase and bolted past a tarped-over swimming pool. Taking the direct route she'd mapped out during her daily guard-escorted walks around the compound, she headed for the dock at the bottom of the hill. The boats were little more than a collection of shadows against a misty backdrop of rain, dark against darker in the moonless, drizzly night.

She was halfway there when the backup generators kicked in, circumventing the primary network she'd crashed. Emergency lights flared to life and alarms whooped, the noise seeming to come from nowhere and everywhere at once.

Heart pounding, legs shaking with fear and adrenaline, Sydney ran for her life.

The drizzle had slicked everything with a thin layer of water, making the cement walkway slippery beneath her sneakers. The sharp wind cut through the jeans and light turtleneck shirt she'd worn in the climate-controlled lab. She hadn't dared trigger the guards' suspicions by dressing more heavily than that, and she paid for it as she pounded down a short incline to the water. Her teeth were chattering by the time she reached the first boat.

"Stop!" a voice shouted from behind her. Booted footsteps approached from the side at a run as the guards surrounded her. Gunfire chattered, kicking up stinging pellets of concrete directly ahead and to both sides of her.

They weren't aiming to kill. Not yet, anyway.

Ignoring the warning shots, Sydney took two running steps across the dock and flung herself toward the nearest motorboat, which was one of the small, fast two-seaters the guards used for shoreline patrols. She untied the craft from the dock and clambered aboard, ducking with a terrified scream as bullets smacked into the side of the boat and peppered the interior of the craft.

Her heart rocketed in her chest and for a split second she wanted to give up, wanted to put her hands up and say, "You win, I was just kidding. Take me back to the lab."

But she didn't. She couldn't. Still, her fingers shook as she punched the ignition button—her complacence had made the guards sloppy enough to leave the console unlocked, thank God—and the engine roared to life.

Coming from the other side of the island, past the cliff-side mansion, she heard the rotor thumps of Tiberius's helicopter preparing to lift off. She wasn't sure if he was evacuating or coming after her, but the sound added to the chaos of siren whoops and shouts as a dozen guards hit the dock, running flat out toward the other boats. The gunfire was silent for the moment, though, indicating that the security detail had orders to recapture her, not kill her.

She'd figured Tiberius would consider her far more of an asset than a liability…at least until it looked like she was going to succeed in escaping. Then he'd have his men start shooting for real.

Thank God for the rain. It would give her a layer of covering fog, and hopefully spoil their aim. The idea of being shot at—of being *shot*—terrified her, but she couldn't turn back now.

She slapped the throttle forward, blessing the summer she and Celeste had spent with a foster family on Moosehead Lake, where they'd learned the basics of boating. The motorboat leapt forward, spraying the dock with a plume of water that made the guards shout and curse, sounds that were quickly lost beneath the roar of the motorboat engine and the growing thump of the helicopter.

Sydney glanced back to where the mansion rose high on the crest of the island, a dark, hulking shadow that was barely visible in the fog. Then the chopper swung up and over the building. Its searchlights cut through the mist, and the bumps of rockets were clearly visible on either skid.

That gave Sydney her answer: Tiberius wasn't fleeing. The bastard was coming after her.

Trembling with terror and adrenaline, breath sobbing in her lungs, she sent the little boat west, toward where the shoreline of northern Massachusetts ought to be. She couldn't see any town lights through the wind-driven rain, which was coming down harder by the moment. The pellets stung her face and throat, quickly soaking through her light clothing and plastering the fabric to her skin.

"Come on," she chanted. "You can do it. You can beat him." She wasn't sure if she was talking to herself or the boat, but the mantra made her feel a little better.

She almost couldn't believe that she'd gotten this far. The Sydney Westlake of a year earlier hadn't been able to fight for her university job or her project funding, hadn't been able to stand up for herself in the face of her ex's smear campaign, which had been the lowest of low academic politics.

But somehow, somewhere, she'd become the sort of woman who could plan an escape and make it happen.

Unfortunately, she'd also become a criminal, because whether or not Tiberius had coerced her—and he sure as hell had—she'd been the one to create the DNA code he considered his ultimate retail offering. Now it was up to her to make sure he never got to sell or use the engineered virus.

As she sent the boat into the gloom and the sounds of pursuit faded, hope guttered in her chest, pressing tears into her throat. She began to believe—when she hadn't really believed before, no matter what she'd told herself—that she was really going to get out of this mess, that she and Celeste were going to be okay.

Then something splashed loudly behind her, followed by a hiss and the growing thump of helicopter rotors. She turned and froze in terror. The chopper was directly behind her, and there was a dark shape in the water, churning a white wake as it sped toward her. A torpedo.

Tiberius had apparently decided she was a liability.

No, she thought. *Impossible.* Then the searchlights pinned on the boat and the surrounding water, illuminating the plume of the deadly missile speeding toward her boat and proving that it wasn't impossible at all. She was dead if she didn't move, and move fast.

Screaming, Sydney flung herself into the sea. The shock of the cold saltwater drove the air from her lungs, but she didn't have time to take another breath. She didn't think. She dove and swam down and away from the boat, kicking and stroking for all she was worth.

Moments later, the world went orange and a booming shockwave of water slapped at her, tumbling her end over end, pummeling the breath from her lungs, dazing her and making her ears ring.

She hung motionless, utterly disoriented, feeling the thud of her heartbeat in her head, in her bones.

She was vaguely aware that she was rising toward the surface, and something inside her said that was a bad thing. She couldn't seem to make her arms or legs obey her commands, though. She could only drift, longing for air as the water around her grew warmer, or maybe she got colder, she wasn't sure.

This isn't good, she thought, but couldn't seem to get beyond the thought.

Then the heavy rumble of a boat engine cut through her daze, and her brain came back online with a jolt. Tiberius's guards had arrived! Panic flared through her, chasing away the lethargy of shock, and she struck out wildly in the direction she thought was "up." Moments later she breached the surface and sucked in a gasping lungful of air. Then she was swimming, flailing her arms and legs as hard as she could in an effort to get away from the motor noise as her heart hammered in her ears and panic spurred her on.

There was a splash behind her as at least one of the guards jumped in to grab her.

"No!" She swam harder, adrenaline propelling her onward when her muscles trembled with fear and fatigue, and the numbing cold of the water around her.

Her head pounded and there was a sharp pain above her eye, suggesting she'd been cut by waterborne debris. She banged into other pieces of debris as she swam, and the air was tainted with the odor of gasoline and smoke. She wanted to cough but she couldn't spare the breath as she swam for all she was worth. She had to get away, had to—

A hand closed on her ankle, gripped hard and dragged her under.

Panic jolted and she screamed, then inhaled water and choked hard. She thrashed, fighting her captor even as she struggled to the surface and gagged, trying to get the water out of her lungs, the air in. The world spun and closed in on her, and her captor shifted his grip from her leg to her throat, clamping an arm across her upper chest while he struck out, swimming strongly with his free arm and kicks from his powerful legs.

"Let me go!" Sydney struggled against him, fouling his rhythm and dragging them both below, but he didn't fight. He simply waited until they broke the surface, then shifted his arm to her throat and squeezed until her world went gray and spun to a pinprick.

Semiconscious, she went limp against him, barely breathing even after he eased up on the choke hold. Defeat hammered through her, alongside the sure knowledge of what Tiberius would do to her now.

He wasn't just going to kill her. He was going to force her to help him sell a terrible opportunity to terrible people. Then he was going to kill her and Celeste both, very slowly. That was what he'd promised he'd do if she betrayed him, and she had every reason to believe the threat. She was going to die, and die horribly.

The realization spurred her to a last desperate attempt to escape. Knowing she had just one more chance, **she waited until** her captor reached the slick white side of a tall boat and called for others to reach down and grab her. At the moment he handed her off, she found another burst of energy and exploded, kicking and scratching at the two men who held her. They cursed and fought to hang on to her. They shouted at her, but she was too far gone to process the words.

She screamed over and over again until her voice went raw and then broke to sobs as they subdued her by grabbing her arms and legs and hanging on despite her furious struggles. When she finally went limp, they dragged her up and over the side, and dumped her onto the rain-slicked deck.

Moments later, the man who'd jumped in after her landed on the deck nearby, dripping and breathing hard.

Sydney curled herself into a protective ball, waiting for rough hands to tie her so she couldn't get away while they hauled her back to her quarters on the island—or worse, directly to Tiberius.

Instead of rope, though, a heavy wool blanket landed atop her, cutting the sting of the cold air.

She whimpered and clutched at the blanket, pulling it over her head. After a minute or two, when the warmth started to come and the men hadn't made another move, she peered out, dragging the blanket around herself as she struggled partway up on the rain-slicked deck.

Her teeth were chattering and her dark, shoulder-length hair was plastered over her forehead, covering her eyes. She slicked the strands away from her face, and when her vision cleared, she found herself only a few feet away from the man who'd pulled her from the ocean.

He was leaning back against the side of the gunwale a few feet away from her, wearing a coarse gray blanket like hers. His wet hair was short and dark, his features square and regular, his blue eyes assessing. Even soaking wet, he carried a definite aura of command.

She didn't recognize him, but that didn't mean anything. She'd only seen a few of Tiberius's guards face-to-face, but had heard the footsteps of many more. What was strange, though, was that he was looking at her with utter calm, laced with an air of speculation. He seemed willing to wait for her to speak first, which didn't make any sense.

Then her eyes locked on his blanket, which had something written on it in six-inch-high letters: U.S. Coast Gu—

It broke off where he'd tucked one side of the blanket beneath the other, but it was enough to have hope blooming viciously in her chest.

She hadn't been recaptured after all.

She'd been rescued!

She gasped and looked at the other two men standing nearby. They were burly, curly-haired guys with the shared features of brothers and coast guard insignias on their jackets.

When she looked back at the man who'd saved her, he nodded in greeting, but didn't smile. "I'm Special Agent John Sharpe of the FBI's major crimes task force, and you're on the coast guard cutter *Valiant*." He paused, expression assessing. "Whether that's good or bad news for you is going to depend on what you were doing on Rocky Cliff Island and why Tiberius wants you dead."

CHAPTER TWO

JOHN STOOD, DRAPING the blanket over his shoulders
to stave off the sharp wind, and looked down at the
woman who huddled miserably on the deck. The
drowned-rat factor did little to hide her high, angular
cheekbones or delicately tipped-up nose, or the exotic
tilt to her chocolate-brown eyes.

She was, in a word, gorgeous.

He had no clue whether she'd been Tiberius's prisoner or a coconspirator gone bad, but her looks alone
made him lean in the latter direction, because he'd seen
the file photos of the bastard's previous women and she
certainly fit the type.

Still, there was no need to head straight for "bad
cop" interrogation techniques. For now, he'd let her see
him as the rescuer, willing to play along with whatever
game she had in mind. With Tiberius and his people it
was all about the game, John knew. Move and counter-
move. A living chess match, played out on a continent-
size board, with living people as the pieces and national
security the stakes.

Not yet sure whether she was a pawn or a queen or
somewhere in between, he held out a hand to help her
up. "Come on. I don't know about you, but I could use
some coffee, a few towels and some dry clothes."

She stared at him, her lovely brown eyes stark in her

pale face. Her hand trembled when she reached for his, making him think either she was a damn good actress sent to put him off his game, or else she'd truly been running for her life. Maybe she'd double-crossed Tiberius, John mused, or maybe he'd simply grown tired of her and didn't want any loose ends returning to the mainland.

Those thoughts died quickly, though, because the moment he and the woman linked hands and he pulled her to her feet, she burst into tears.

"Oh, hell," he said. "Please don't cry." He didn't do tears.

Instead of stopping, she buried her face in her free hand and sobbed harder, her shoulders—her whole body, for that matter—shaking with reaction...or a good approximation of it.

Reminding himself he was supposed to be playing along with the illusion of a damsel in distress, John grimaced and put an arm around her in a stiff offer of comfort. He patted her shoulder. "You're safe. It's over."

She turned into him, wrapped her arms around his waist and hung on as though she never meant to let go. "Thank you," she whispered against his neck, her skin warming against his despite the chill. *"Thank you."*

Electricity jolted through him in a surge of reaction that was so unexpected, it literally took his breath away. Heat flared and his heart did a thumpity-thump number that sent up a clamor of warning bells.

Damn, she was good. Lucky for him, he'd had practice with this sort of thing, and he'd learned his lesson the hard way.

Besides, they didn't call him Iceman because he was warm and fuzzy.

"It's okay," he said, trying to disengage without making it into a wrestling match. He fleetingly wished he'd brought Grace Mears along on this run, or sharpshooter Michael Pelotti, both of whom were way better than he at comforting victims and witnesses—and suspects—while making it seem natural. Hell, pretty much anyone on his team had him beat at this sort of thing.

He looked at the coast guarders. "Can one of you help me out here?"

Dick and Doug Renfrew, the boat handlers he'd borrowed for the night's surveillance, shook their heads in unison. "Not unless you want to hang around and wait for the chopper to make another pass," Doug said. He was the talker of the two.

"Good point," John said, glancing at the gray-black sky. "You should probably get us the hell out of here."

Granted, Tiberius's helicopter had peeled off into the fog when it saw the U.S.C.G. ship approaching the scene of the explosion, and he'd heard the other motorboats cut and head back to the island, but they could swing back around for a second look at any moment.

Tiberius and his crew had probably assumed the *Valiant* was fully manned and ready to act, but the reality was that the cutter was carrying its minimum crew of two, along with one senior FBI agent—John—who was acting on a hunch that hadn't even been strong enough to justify bringing along the rest of his team.

His gut told him Tiberius was gearing up for something big, something that was focused on his private island off the New England coast. Based on that, he'd called in a few favors and gone on a semiofficial fishing expedition off the fertile ledges of George's Bank.

The good news was that he'd caught something. The

bad news was that he wasn't sure exactly what he'd caught.

Tiberius was smart enough—and devious enough—to have seen the *Valiant* on his surveillance systems, identified it through its transponder code and sent one of his people out to get herself "captured" as a diversion. It would be just like him to feed the FBI a decoy intended to distract them away from his main intent.

The question was: had he?

John looked down at the woman, who was quieting some, though she stayed leaning against him as though she found the contact as comforting as he found it disturbing.

"Come on," he said, voice unaccountably rough. "Let's get you warmed up, Ms.…." He let the sentence trail off in a prompt.

"Sydney," she said against his chest. "Just Sydney." Which could either mean she figured they should be on a first-name basis after what they'd just been through together, or that she didn't intend to voluntarily give him enough to figure out who she was for real.

He didn't recognize her name or face from the extensive files Grace and Jimmy Oliverra—the two computer jocks on his team—had amassed on Tiberius and his dealings, but that didn't mean she wasn't part of his world. Just that she hadn't said "cheese" yet and gotten her picture taken for the FBI's scrapbook.

"Okay, just Sydney," he said, playing the game. "Let's get you belowdecks, out of this wind." He disengaged and gestured her across the rain-slicked deck to the ladder that led to the cramped galley and sitting area downstairs.

She fumbled slightly when the boat sliced deeper

into the storm and the chop increased. But she looked steady enough overall, as if she wasn't going to collapse again. Was it part of an act or was it reality?

John didn't know, but he sure as hell intended to find out, ASAP.

"You can go straight on through," he said when she paused in a short hallway. "The head is to your right. There's no shower, but if you want to get out of those wet clothes and towel yourself off, I'll scrounge something for you to wear. There's a first-aid kit under the sink. When you're changed, I'll meet you in the galley. I'll fix us some coffee." *With a side of interrogation.*

She was pretty out of it, between shock and the gash on her forehead, but he didn't feel the slightest bit of remorse about questioning her. Experience had taught him that the things people in her condition said were usually more truthful than what came out of their mouths after they'd had a chance to think about their answers. And if that made him the cold, cynical SOB his teammates claimed, then so be it. His suspicious nature had kept him alive when plenty of others around him—good men and women—had died in their efforts to take down the kingpins of modern organized crime.

These days, the major crimes unit wasn't about territories or ethnicity, it was all about technology. The modern godfathers controlled pieces of science and sold them to the highest bidders...and Tiberius was king among the black-market tech dealers.

Tiberius didn't have a last name that any intelligence service worldwide had been able to find, never mind a history prior to ten years ago, when he'd appeared on the scene almost overnight. He was the worst among the worst, dealing almost exclusively in microscopic weaponry of the germ warfare variety. He'd been variously blamed for bioweapons attacks on five of the seven continents, including targeted viral assassinations in Europe and the U.S., and a series of flulike epidemic outbreaks along the conflict fronts in the Middle East.

Tiberius was bad news, there was no doubt about it. Unfortunately, he'd proved all but untouchable over the decade he'd been in business. There was no solid evidence connecting him directly to any crime and nobody would testify against him—at least not anyone who'd managed to stay alive long enough to take the witness stand. The calculating bastard lived sequestered on his private island off the Massachusetts coast when he could've been someplace warm and inviting and outside of U.S. soil. John was convinced he'd chosen Rocky Cliff Island for spite, so he could laugh at the agents who'd dedicated—and given—their lives in a series of unsuccessful efforts to put him behind bars.

Unsuccessful until now, that is, he thought as he dug through a spare clothes locker, changed into jeans, a U.S.C.G. sweatshirt and thick socks, and grabbed a slightly smaller set of the same for his mysterious guest.

Sydney—if that was really her name at all—might just be the answer to his prayers. Though his gut told him she'd probably been Tiberius's lover, he'd just tried to kill her. That might be all the leverage John and his people would need to get inside information.

Then again, she could be a clever plant. The possibility meant he'd have to be very, very careful in what he said and did around her.

He knocked on the door to the head. "There's a set of clothes for you outside the door. I'll be in the galley when you're ready."

A couple of minutes later, right about when the small kitchen space had started to take on the aroma of hot coffee, the door to the washroom opened and Sydney stepped out.

Her towel-dried brunette hair stuck up in tufts here and there, suggesting it would curl later. The borrowed clothes hung off her slight frame, and she'd cuffed the jeans so they wouldn't drag on the ground. She should've looked ridiculous in the too-large pants and sweatshirt. The fact that she didn't, that she somehow looked as though a fashion designer had chosen the outfit and told her to make it work on the runway, had those warning buzzers going off again in the back of John's brain, loud and clear.

He stared at her, seeing a drop-dead gorgeous woman beneath shock and saltwater, and thought, *Were you his lover? A customer in a deal gone bad? Are you a victim, a perp, or somewhere in between?*

As if he'd said the question aloud, she locked eyes with him. "So, Special Agent John Sharpe of the FBI… are you authorized to make a deal?"

SYDNEY SAW THE MENTAL shields come crashing down. One minute he'd been looking at her as though trying to make up his mind about her, and in the next she'd made it for him, because innocent people don't need deals.

His gorgeous blue eyes blanked and a small, sardonic smile touched the corners of his lips, which were bracketed with small creases that drew her eyes and made her wonder what he'd look like if he smiled—really smiled—at her.

"It depends on what you're offering," he said, expression giving away nothing.

She wanted to tell him that she intended to give him everything she knew, that she couldn't live with herself if Tiberius got away with what he was planning. But she had to be realistic. All she knew about this guy was that he was an FBI agent—she figured she could believe that much, because she highly doubted the coast guard loaned their boats and crew to just anyone. Well, she also knew he'd dried off even handsomer than she'd expected. That wasn't exactly relevant, but it was certainly a fact.

His hair was a rich, dark brown, thick and wavy. From his square-jawed features and the stress lines carved beside his mouth, she guessed he was in his mid-thirties, a few years older than she. Wearing a gray coast guard sweatshirt, borrowed jeans and thick socks—as she was—he should've looked casual. Instead, he exuded that same leadership she'd noticed out on the deck, that same "don't mess with me" attitude.

On one level she found it comforting. On another, disturbing.

She'd known men like him before, men who would do—and say—anything necessary to achieve their goals if they thought the ends justified the means. Hell, she'd dated one of them—almost been engaged to him—and look where that had gotten her: unemployed and forced to seek an alternative source of funding that had turned out to be far less legitimate than she'd hoped.

Thankfully, this time forewarned is forearmed, she thought grimly.

No doubt Agent Sharpe figured that the end of bringing down a man like Tiberius would justify any means. She, on the other hand, needed to protect not only herself, but also Celeste. To do that, she had to maintain whatever leverage she could get her hands on.

Knowing it, steeling herself to negotiate when her conscience was crying for her to spill every last piece of information on the spot, she stayed silent, waiting for Sharpe to start the negotiations.

Instead, he handed her a cup of coffee and gestured her to the small dining area of the galley, where there was a booth-style table and bench seats.

She sat, blew across the surface of the steaming liquid and took a small sip, welcoming the burn of heat and the bite of caffeine.

He sat down opposite her, and the booth was so cramped that their knees bumped beneath the table while he got himself settled. She moved away, all too aware of his maleness, of the way his aura filled the small space and made her think of how long she'd gone without a man's touch.

Swallowing through a suddenly tight throat and reminding herself that she needed to tread carefully, she lifted her coffee mug and said, "You'll find me in the system as soon as you run the prints off this mug— presuming, of course, that's your plan if I haven't told you who I am before we reach the U.S.C.G. station at Gloucester."

She expected the obvious question: *Why are your prints on file?* Instead, he skipped right over that and said, "In other words, you needed government clearance at some point."

She raised an eyebrow, then winced when the motion pulled at the cut she'd cleaned and bandaged in the bathroom. "You're assuming I wasn't arrested."

Again, his smile held no humor. "Consider it a hunch, based on what I know of Tiberius's women."

"I wasn't his lover." There was little heat in the denial, though she was tempted to ask why that had been his first guess. She wondered how he saw her, what she looked like to him.

After almost a year of interacting solely with the guards and Tiberius's people, it seemed suddenly strange to be speaking with a man—a tongue-draggingly handsome man—who wasn't part of that world.

But that was the point, wasn't it? He wasn't entirely out of that world—he was simply on the other side. She wasn't sure she could trust John Sharpe. She'd trusted Tiberius, and that hadn't turned out well at all.

"But you're right that I haven't been arrested," she conceded his point. "A few parking tickets and a stern warning for doing sixty in a thirty-five zone outside Bethesda, but that's it. And yes, I needed government clearance." She paused, trying to gauge how much to reveal, how much to hold back. Finally, she went with what she figured he could get from her prints and a quick background check. "My name is Sydney Westlake. I'm twenty-eight, my twin sister, Celeste, and I were raised together in foster care and we own a house together in Glen Hills, Maryland. Up until a year ago, I worked in the genetics department of the Advanced Institute of Science in Bethesda, investigating the causes and possible cures for a rare genetic disease called Singer's syndrome."

She paused when the boat's engine note changed and their momentum slowed. There were no windows in the small galley, but she thought she heard the clang of a marker buoy, indicating that they were nearing land.

"What changed a year ago?" Sharpe prompted.

"As you might guess from the fact that I was swimming like hell to get away from Rocky Cliff Island," she said drily, "I went to work for Tiberius. About a year ago my funding was cut, thanks to my lying rat-bastard of an ex-boyfriend. A few weeks after that happened, a representative of the Tiberius Corporation made me an offer I couldn't refuse. I've been working in a private lab on the island ever since, the last three months of it under lock and key until tonight."

He'd gone completely and utterly still as she spoke, making her think of a predator freezing the moment it sighted prey. His voice was inflectionless—and damning—when he said, "You developed bioweapons."

She wanted to flinch from the condemnation, but didn't because it was the truth. A far more complicated truth than he made it sound, but the truth nonetheless. "Not intentionally, and not willingly once I figured out what he actually wanted me to do…but yes, ultimately I developed a new DNA-based vector for Tiberius, and yes, under certain circumstances, it could be used for illegal purposes."

She couldn't quite bring herself to call it a bioweapon. It should've been a cure, a salvation. Instead, it was a direct threat to national security.

Sharpe set his coffee aside, very deliberately, and folded his hands on the table. "What is the target? How long do we have?"

Incongruously, she noticed that he wasn't wearing a wedding ring. Even more unsettlingly, she found that she was glad.

It's only because he's the first male nonfelon you've seen in eleven-plus months, she told herself. That, and she appreciated how he'd stayed one jump ahead of her in their conversation. He didn't repeat himself, and didn't fill the air with useless questions and chatter. He was cool and calculating, yes, but she could already tell he was extremely intelligent.

Which could make him very dangerous. He was smart, he had an agenda and he had the law on his side. It was up to her to make sure she got what she needed without pushing so far that she got herself locked up, leaving Celeste unprotected when Tiberius came for her. Because he *would* come for her. There was no question of that.

Even now, the need to get to her ailing twin sister beat beneath Sydney's skin, along with the fear that the time taken up with her rescue and the boat ride had been too long, that Tiberius would have already figured out what Sydney had done before she left.

If she were in his position she'd grab whatever her adversary held dear, demand the computer password in exchange and then disappear with the technology.

Since this was Tiberius they were talking about, he would probably do exactly that...and then once he had the password, he'd kill her and Celeste outright because she'd dared to cross him.

"Sydney, how long do we have until he sells whatever you developed?" Sharpe pressed.

"You have some time," she answered. "I corrupted the lab reagents and jammed the computers on the way out. Without the password, it'll take another scientist weeks, maybe months to re-create what I did. With the password..." She trailed off, trying not to consider that possibility but knowing she had to. "With the password, he could be up and running in a few days. Maybe less."

He muttered a curse as the boat engines cut out and the craft drifted for a few seconds, then bumped up against the dock. Above decks, they could hear the sound of tramping footsteps and men's shouts as coast guard crewmen fastened the lines and secured the cutter.

"And the target?" Sharpe asked.

Sydney kept her eyes on his, refusing to look away even though she wanted to hide her head and pretend it was all a nightmare, that she hadn't really handed this sort of power to a man like Tiberius. "The eventual target is, indirectly, the entire United States legal system."

"Go on."

Telling herself this was the only way, Sydney said, "I built a viral vector that was intended to treat the effects of Singer's syndrome. Under orders—threats, really—from Tiberius, I altered the vector so it mimics the twenty marker sequences currently used for a standard DNA fingerprinting profile." She paused, saw from his dark expression that he got it, and nodded. "Exactly. Once someone has been infected with the viral vector, any samples coming from his or her body will yield incomprehensible blurs with standard forensic DNA analysis. The police labs will be completely unable to match his—or her—DNA to crime scene samples or DNA fingerprints already on file."

He muttered a low, vicious oath. "In other words, you've single-handedly given one of the most ruthless criminal businessmen on the planet the power to render the CODIS DNA database—and a good chunk of modern forensic analysis—completely useless."

Now she did look away. "It's pointless to say how

sorry I am. I thought the job was a legit front for his other dealings. I thought I could use his money—use him—to help people." To help Celeste, and others like her who were often overlooked in favor of efforts to cure more common—and therefore more commercially lucrative—diseases.

"You're smarter than that," he said without inflection, and for some reason that stung more than all the names she'd called herself in the dark of night back on the island, when she'd realized exactly the same thing.

She wasn't just smart enough to know better, she *had* known better and she'd taken the job anyway, because she'd been so desperate to find a way to help Celeste, so obsessed with the goal of prolonging her sister's life and making up for the fact that the disease had struck one of them but not the other.

As Celeste had accused her on more than one occasion, she'd been so sure she was right, she'd bent the rules to get what she wanted.

Sharpe focused on her, his eyes gone dark with accusation, with condemnation. "Tell me more, and tell me fast. I'll need you to reproduce whatever you can remember about the vector and your work so I can kick it over to the Centers for Disease Control and Homeland Security and get them started on a counter-agent. Then you're going to sit down with me and the rest of my team, and we're going to go over the past year of your life step by step. You're going to tell me everything you can remember about the setup on the island." He paused. "Basically, your butt is mine starting now, until I say otherwise. When it's all over, if I'm satisfied that you've cooperated fully, then we'll talk about your culpability and possible charges."

Sydney was surprised and not a little dismayed to realize that the slap of scorn in his voice mattered to her, that his opinion mattered when it absolutely, positively shouldn't. He was a means to an end, nothing more.

Still, she couldn't help wishing they'd met under different circumstances, maybe even during different lifetimes. She thought she would've enjoyed getting to know John Sharpe a bit better, and figuring out what went on behind those cool blue eyes. Unfortunately, under these circumstances in this lifetime, they were destined to be at odds.

She cemented that by standing and taking the two steps needed to bring her into his personal space, then looking down at him. "I'm sorry, but that's not how it's going to work, Agent Sharpe."

He narrowed his eyes. "Excuse me?"

Reminding herself not to back off, not to back away, she inhaled a breath that contained entirely too much of his energy, and said, "This is where the deal part comes in. I'll tell you everything I know, but in exchange, I want guaranteed immunity from federal prosecution no matter what happens, and I want my sister and me placed in protective custody, effective immediately." She faltered a little. "Tiberius is going to try to get to me through her. I can absolutely, positively promise that."

Sharpe rose from the booth and looked down at her for a long moment, his eyes seeming to pierce deep inside her and see things she'd rather keep hidden. She expected more questions, and braced herself to remain mute until she had a lawyer and a signed agreement, and assurances that Celeste was safe.

She was surprised when he said only, "You disappoint me."

Then he turned and strode from the small room, his angry strides far too big for the tiny space.

When he was gone, leaving his energy to vibrate into nothingness, Sydney remained staring after him. "Yeah," she finally said, pressing a hand to her churning stomach. "I disappoint myself, too. The thing is, I'm doing my best to fix it."

Unfortunately, she didn't think he saw it that way, which made him dangerous. *Watch yourself with that one,* she told herself as she headed for the narrow ladder. *He's too smart, too sure of himself.*

If she wasn't careful, Special Agent John Sharpe could ruin everything.

She was surprised when he said only, "You might point me—"

Then he turned and strode from the small room, his angry strides far too big for the tiny space.

When he was gone, leaving his energy to vibrate into nothingness, Gwen let go of her breath. "Go after Dyan," she finally said, pressing a hand to her churning stomach. "I disappoint myself, too. The thing is,

CHAPTER THREE

JOHN KNEW HE SHOULDN'T have been surprised by what Sydney had revealed. And he wasn't really. What surprised him was the depth of his anger. She might not have been Tiberius's lover, but what she *had* done was far worse.

He'd wanted her to be innocent, he realized as they disembarked and slogged their way toward the main building of the coast guard station. Despite the fact that he damn well knew better, he'd wanted her to be innocent, which she so incredibly wasn't.

"Can I borrow your phone?" she said suddenly.

He handed it over. "Calling your lawyer?"

She sent him a look that he couldn't interpret, but that touched his skin with a skitter of warning, of want. She said softly, "Do you blame me?"

She dialed a Maryland exchange, waking what sounded from her side of the conversation like the lawyer who'd been handling her affairs while she'd been on Rocky Cliff Island. He referred her to someone local and she made a second call.

Within fifteen minutes, a fiftyish briefcase-toting blonde woman in a mint-green skirt suit strode through the front door of the coast guard station, looking wide-awake even though it was nearly 3:00 a.m.

John watched her eyes skim the room and could

practically see her thought process as she sorted through the coast guarders and himself before reaching Sydney: *pilot, pilot, swimmer, cop, ah—client.*

She made a beeline for Sydney, took up a protective position at her client's side and then turned to John, having apparently—and erroneously, at least at the C.G. station—identified him as the guy in charge. "Is there somewhere private my client and I can speak?" the lawyer asked.

John gestured to a nearby door, having already cleared it through the Renfrew brothers and their superiors. "You can borrow that office. My people are pulling together the paperwork as we speak."

Sydney looked at him, and he caught a flash of nerves and worry in her lovely brown eyes. "What about my sister?"

"The locals are already en route. They'll make sure she's safe and get her someplace protected." He'd thought briefly about using the sister as leverage, but had decided against it, not because he had any compunction against using the tools given to him, but because he knew Tiberius well enough to realize the good guys would lose that leverage if they delayed.

Instead of looking relieved, she looked discomfited, and a little guilty. "You'll need…" She trailed off, took a breath and said, "Celeste is wheelchair-bound and requires special care. You'll need to take her care provider with her, or find someone else to do the job, and you'll need a vehicle she can be wheeled onto. She shouldn't be removed from the chair."

Only his natural tendency to play his cards close to his chest kept John from cursing, not only because it meant reorganizing what was supposed to be a quick find-and-grab, but also because it proved what he'd already begun to suspect: Sydney Westlake was planning on giving him exactly as much information as she chose to, exactly *when* she chose to. This wasn't a free exchange of information. It was a damn chess game.

Worse, he was finding himself intrigued by her rather than annoyed, which was surprising, and he didn't care for surprises. In his experience, they tended to end badly.

"Let me guess," he said as a few more pieces of the puzzle connected in his brain. "Your sister has Singer's syndrome."

"My twin sister. Yes."

"Which explains why you locked the computers instead of destroying them." If he'd been a cursing man he would've let rip right then, because the information added a whole new layer of complications with the realization that her goal and his weren't the same.

He wanted Tiberius dead or behind bars, and wasn't really picky which way it went as long as the bastard was out of circulation and his operation disassembled piece by miserable piece. She, on the other hand, wanted to save her sister with a treatment that could potentially be used to topple the federal justice system, and then get her life back without any repercussions.

"Yes," she agreed, glancing away from him. "The computers were firewalled against connection to any outside network, so I couldn't email the files off the island, and Tiberius's people wouldn't supply me with a flash drive or anything I could carry with me. I kept both my main and backup files on the system, and now they're locked until either you take down Tiberius and get me back on that island, or Tiberius tortures the password out of me."

She said the words with such hollow calm that he believed her, and even felt a stir of compassion. He, too, had seen what happened to people who wound up on the wrong side of Tiberius. It wasn't pretty.

"Look," he said, "I can sympathize to a degree. If I had a sister I'd probably feel the same way. But all the good intentions in the world don't change the fact that you went to the island willingly." His voice turned hard. "I might have to accept this deal, but I'll be damned if I let you withhold valuable information in the hopes of saving your sister. Getting our hands on—or destroying—the weapon you created is our first priority. Bringing Tiberius down is our second. I'm sorry, but recovering information that might or might not cure your sister has to come behind both of those things on my priority list."

He expected her to argue fiercely. Instead, she inclined her head ever so slightly. "I know." She blew out a breath and pressed her palm to her stomach beneath the borrowed sweatshirt. "In my head I know all that. I even told myself it would be okay if I died escaping, and Celeste died because I didn't make it out and get the cure to her, as long as Tiberius couldn't use my work the way he wants to." She paused, then shook her head. "The thing is, I'm not that person. Maybe it makes me selfish or spoiled, but I'm not willing to make that sacrifice." She fixed John with a look. "It's up to you, big guy. You take what I'm willing to give you and run with it, or I'm out of here the first chance I get, and then Celeste and I are off the radar."

He should've scoffed at the threat, but damned if

he didn't think she could do it. She'd managed to lock down her work—though he had only her word on that one—and get off Rocky Cliff Island herself. Who was to say she couldn't grab her sister and disappear off the FBI's radar, as well?

His level of respect for her, which was already far too high considering they were on opposite sides of this particular issue, inched up another notch.

"Write up your terms." He gestured to the empty office. "I'll email the info to my people and get the honchos to sign off on the deal." He fixed Sydney with a look. "Then you're going to tell me everything."

She turned away, but then paused and looked back, and her eyes were dark with regret. "We're on the same side, you know. I want Tiberius put away just as much as you do."

"I highly doubt that."

"I'm sorry," she said again, so quietly he almost didn't hear her.

Steeling himself against an unexpected—and unwelcome—surge of warmth, he said, "It doesn't matter whether we like each other or not, Ms. West-lake. I have something you want, you have something I want. Let's do the deal and take down Tiberius before he sells your virus to the wrong people and they use it to bring down CODIS. Once we've done that, you can get on with your life and I can get on with the next case. It's as simple as that."

But as he turned away, effectively ending the conversation, he knew damn well that none of this was going to be the slightest bit simple.

NERVES JANGLING IN HER stomach, Sydney followed her lawyer, Emily Breslow, into the office Sharpe had indicated.

She hated how her conversation with the agent had gone, hated having to play this game, but what other choice did she have?

"It's like I always say," Emily began, waving her to one of the two chairs, which faced each other across a cluttered desk in the untidy office, "if you have to deal with the Feds, it helps to deal with a cute one."

That startled a snort out of Sydney. Her new lawyer was nothing like she'd expected. Tom Dykstra, the guy in Bethesda she'd used to set up a living trust for Celeste, had fit her sober, cynical, suited-up image of a lawyer. Emily, not so much. Though she wore a suit, it was anything but sober, and even though it was the middle of the night—closing in on morning—she was wide-awake, and her eyes held a glint of humor, as though she might laugh at any moment.

She was also, according to Sydney's Maryland-based shark of a lawyer, very good at her job. And she had a point about it being a side bonus to work with a cute Fed. The more time Sydney spent in the presence of John Sharpe, the more interesting he was getting.

"Agent Sharpe seems very…focused," Sydney said finally, though the word seemed entirely inadequate in describing the handsome, charismatic—and dangerous—man she'd gotten herself tangled up with.

"He'd have to be." Emily dipped into her briefcase and pulled out a thin folder. "Here, sign this. Standard firm contract, yadda, yadda." While Sydney scanned the document, Emily continued, "I called in a few favors on the way over and got the scoop on Sharpe— what there is of it, anyway. He's thirty-five, no siblings, parents living abroad. The FBI recruited him straight out of Georgia Tech, where he was a star on both the football team and the chess club. Go figure."

When the words on the page blurred into legalese, Sydney blinked, trying to focus on the contract. Good business practice demanded that she read and dissect it line by line, but expediency—and a lack of other options—had her signing on the dotted line of duplicate copies after only a quick skim of the document.

Besides, even though she knew it shouldn't matter, she wanted to hear the rest of the story. "So he was a brainy jock," she said, prompting Emily.

"Still is, from the looks of it," the older woman said, but more with the air of a connoisseur than someone who wanted him for herself. She continued, "He made one of the quickest rises through the ranks ever seen, and is still fairly young to be heading up a unit. He has the reputation of being dedicated and driven, even ruthless sometimes, but everyone I talked to said that his word is good. He doesn't make a promise he doesn't intend to keep."

"In other words, you think I can trust him."

"Yes and no." The lawyer took one of the copies of the signed contract and tucked it into her briefcase, leaving the other in front of Sydney. "His team has an excellent record of bringing down major criminals, and their conviction record is solid. I think you can trust him to follow whatever deal he signs off on to the letter. However, that's the key—he'll do exactly what he's promised, and no more. Watch your back and don't assume anything about him or his motivations. You heard him out there. His job is to bring down Tiberius, not protect your work…and maybe not even protect you, if you get in his way."

"I'll keep that in mind," Sydney said, pressing a hand to her suddenly queasy stomach. "And may I say that I'm blown away by how much you managed to get on him in such a short time frame."

The lawyer grinned, and for the first time Sydney saw a flash of steel beneath the pleasant exterior. "Don't worry about the overtime. You're paying through the nose for my services."

"I'm sure I am," Sydney murmured, suddenly realizing how oddly normal it felt to be talking with another woman, someone who wasn't a guard or cook, or one of Tiberius's enforcers, or the boss himself. This was possibly the least normal situation she'd ever found herself in, yet the act of speaking with Emily felt so normal, it was nearly enough to bring her to tears, driving home how much she'd left behind when she left for Rocky Cliff Island, how much more she'd lost than she'd planned on or even realized.

How much more she might yet lose.

"Okay, that was a fun bit of get-to-know-the-players, but we have work to do." Emily pulled a slim laptop computer from her briefcase, set it on the desk and flipped open the flexible screen, turning it so they could both see the display. A few taps on the keyboard woke the machine from hibernation and pulled up a document, this one written in even denser legalese than the contract had been. "This is a pretty standard skeleton for a federal immunity deal, along with some language for witness protection, either through WITSEC or protective custody. Based on the particulars of your situation, I'm going to suggest that we—"

The door opened without a warning knock and

Sharpe entered the room, filling it as much with his presence as his physical mass.

Sydney frowned, knowing she should be irritated with the interruption, but feeling something else instead, a little lift in the region of her heart, one that warned her she was well on her way to crushing on the agent, despite them being on opposite sides of too many issues.

He must've had clothes in his car, because he'd changed out of the borrowed sweats into a tailored navy suit with a crisp white shirt underneath, and a pair of oxblood shoes that were incongruously rubber-soled, as though they were business shoes intended to double for foot pursuit—which they probably were. That detail, and the glimpse of a shoulder holster beneath his suit jacket, took the look from "upscale businessman" to something else entirely.

Something that sent a quiver of nerves—and heat—through her core.

Going for bravado, she started to ask if that was it for their privacy, but something in his cool blue eyes stopped her, making her ask instead, "What's wrong?"

"The local cops just reported in from your house in Maryland. Your sister is missing and her aide and the aide's boyfriend are dead."

Celeste missing. The others dead.

The words didn't make any sense.

Sydney sat for a second as her heart beat loud in her ears and her mind refused to process his blunt words. *Impossible,* she told herself. That sort of thing didn't happen in real life. Didn't happen to people like her and Celeste.

Except it did when she made the mistake of working for a monster like Tiberius, and then compounded the mistake by double-crossing him.

She rose on legs that threatened to buckle beneath her, and took the few steps necessary to bring her face-to-face with Sharpe. "Take me there."

"We're not finished here," Emily protested, but Sydney waved her off.

"You'll have to do the best you can without me. Call me if you have any questions. I'll give you my—" She broke off, realizing she'd canceled her cell phone before she left for the island. She had no phone and no money, and her ID and credit cards were locked up. She was nobody until she retrieved her life from the safe in her bedroom at home.

A home that had been violated. Where two people had been killed.

An image flashed into her mind, that of Jenny Marie's body after it had washed up on the beach down-current from Rocky Cliff. The cook's dark hair had been matted with seaweed and sand, and blue crabs had nibbled at her fingers, toes and eyes, but that hadn't been enough to disguise the horrible things Tiberius had done to her before he'd killed her and thrown her over the edge.

This, he'd been saying to Sydney with his actions. *This is what I'll do to you if you cross me. This is what I'll do to the people around you.* Like Jenny Marie.

Like Celeste.

Tears filmed Sydney's vision and a sob caught in her throat.

"Here." Sharpe handed a business card to the lawyer. "My cell number is on it. You can call her at that number." He turned for the door, gesturing for Sydney. "Come on. We have a plane to catch."

He acted like he didn't know—or didn't care—that she was upset, like she didn't have the right because she'd brought it on herself. A kernel of bitter anger took root in her chest, kindling and spreading through her body.

"Hey." She grabbed his arm, trying to ignore the jolt of awareness that sang through her at the feel of hard muscle beneath his suit jacket. But the sensation was so strong, so unexpected, that she fumbled for a second when he turned back and looked at her.

"What?"

Are you completely insensitive? she wanted to shout. What had happened to the guy on the boat? She wanted that Sharpe back, the one who'd held her, comforted her. But she didn't ask those things, because what was the point? It wasn't his job to comfort her—it was his job to catch Tiberius, and he'd already made it clear that he didn't give a damn about her agenda or her feelings.

And maybe that was for the best, she realized, sucking in a breath. She had a feeling the sizzle she'd just felt wasn't one-sided, and that could complicate things. She couldn't become involved with him—getting involved would only serve to derail her from the important things.

She'd learned that lesson all too well before. It was her affair with Dr. Let's-share-ideas-so-I-can-steal-yours Richard Eckhart that'd led to the loss of her university position and gotten her set on this path in the first place.

So instead of asking for comfort, she said, "Why

aren't you arguing about whether or not I should be at the scene?"

Sharpe looked down at her hand on his arm, then back up, so he was staring into her eyes when he said, "Because I never fight a battle I don't think I can win, Ms. Westlake. You might want to keep that in mind."

A thousand retorts jammed her brain, a thousand reasons why she should back off, back away and sit down with her lawyer while the FBI mobilized its forces to find Celeste. Instead of giving voice to any of that, though, she said simply, "Call me Sydney."

"Okay." But he didn't offer the same in return. Instead, he gestured to the door and the world beyond, which she hadn't seen in nearly a year. "Let's go."

She went.

CHAPTER FOUR

THE FLIGHT FROM BOSTON to D.C. was a short hop, but even so, John could feel the awful tension in Sydney increasing by the minute.

He could only imagine what was going on inside her head—the guilt, the fear, the shame, the hope. He could only imagine it because he didn't have a sibling, didn't have a strong relationship with his parents... didn't really have anyone he truly loved, at least on the level other people seemed to feel the emotion. Iceman, indeed.

He had friends and coworkers, and that was plenty of attachments for him. However, that didn't mean he was unaware of the lengths other people would go to protect the ones they loved, and the agonies they suffered when those people were hurt, missing...or dead.

Sydney might have chosen her employer unwisely, and she might've let herself be pressured into doing unthinkable things with her scientific knowledge, but that didn't mean she wasn't grieving for her sister.

She sat beside him on the plane, still wearing the borrowed sweats. She had her head tipped back against the seat and her eyes closed as though she'd fallen asleep, but the tension written on her face and in the lines of her hands, which were gripped tightly together in her lap, warned that she wasn't sleeping. Maybe she was thinking of what she should've said or done differently, or maybe she was remembering happier times with her sister.

"Do you think she's dead?" she said, surprising him with the first words she'd uttered since they'd boarded.

"No."

She opened one eye and looked over at him. "I'd ask if you were just saying that to make me feel better, but I have a feeling that's not your thing."

"Good guess. I don't say things I don't mean, and I don't like repeating myself."

She closed her eyes again, and her face looked a little more relaxed than it had moments before. "You think Tiberius will keep her alive because if she's dead, he won't have anything else to threaten me with."

Except your own life, John thought. But she'd already committed to that risk when she escaped from the island. "That's the theory," he agreed.

"Which means that I should expect a ransom demand. The password in exchange for her life."

"There hadn't been any contact by the time the plane took off, and the locals were still searching the property and the nearby houses. She might've gotten away." He'd already passed on that update, but repeated the info because he thought it might help her to hear it again.

The realization brought him up short. He'd not only repeated himself, which he almost never did, but he'd also done it for no other reason than to make Sydney feel better. The very fact had faint warning buzzers going off in the back of his brain.

Keep it simple, he reminded himself. *Keep it in perspective.*

"It's unlikely she escaped," she said, her matter-offactness ruined by the hitch in her voice. "It's hard for her to get around these days, even in the wheelchair."

He heard the hollow ring of guilt, and wondered how much of it was from the immediate situation, and how much was from the fact that the disease had apparently struck one twin and left the other untouched. He imagined there could be a large burden there, and wondered what it might motivate a person to do...like sign on with a killer.

And perhaps worse?

He stared at her in repose, trying to gauge what was happening here. His gut told him she'd gone into the job with good intentions. The question was how far would she be willing to go now to reach her goal.

"I never meant for any of this to happen," she said without opening her eyes. "Please believe that, if you believe nothing else about me."

Because he never said anything he didn't mean, he didn't respond to her statement. Instead he said, "Tell me more about the weapon."

A faint smile touched her lips and then fled to a frown, as though she was proud of the work, even as she hated what it had become. But when she spoke it was to ask him, "How much do you know about DNA fingerprinting?"

He'd done a quick info dump while she'd been speaking with her lawyer. "I know the standard fingerprint focuses on twenty places where the human DNA sequence varies in length from one person to the next. Each segment by itself might be the same length in two different people, but it's statistically impossible—or close enough for government work—for two people to be the same at every one of those segments by random chance. That's why they use twenty markers, to increase the statistical power of the analysis to the 'well beyond a shadow of a doubt' point."

She nodded, eyes still closed. "That's all true, but do you know why those segments vary in length?"

"Something about repeated letters." He'd skimmed over the techno-babble, figuring he'd get back to the nitty-gritty if he needed it.

"Not letters," she corrected, "dinucleotide repeats. The letters stand for the four nucleotides that make up the DNA molecule—A, C, T and G. They can be combined in all different orders for hundreds or even thousands of bases, and the cellular machinery reads them like a blueprint." She paused. "Anyway, the segments of DNA used for fingerprinting are essentially stretches of junk DNA—that means they're not used to encode a protein—made up of the nucleotides C and A, repeated over and over again. They're different lengths in different people because the repeats let the cellular machinery slip during DNA replication, meaning that a 'CA' unit might be added or deleted. As people have evolved over time, the repeats change in length."

John more or less got that, but not how it related to her sister. "If the fingerprints are taken from junk DNA, how does a technology aimed at Singer's syndrome morph into an antifingerprinting weapon?"

"Because there are other types of repeats. In particular, some coding genes have trinucleotide repeats, like the triplet CAG over and over again, for example. When these repeats slip and get bigger, the malfunctioning proteins translated from these genes can cause serious problems, like Huntington's disease."

"And Singer's syndrome," he finished for her.

"And Singer's," she repeated sadly.

"Your parents didn't know they carried the disease?"

"They died in a car crash when we were very young." Her voice was soft and sad. "And no, they didn't know. Repeat diseases like Singer's can lurk in what's called a 'premutation' form where the repeat is longer than normal, but not long enough to cause the disease. When the sperm or egg that became Celeste was forming, the repeat expanded further, meaning that she got the disease." She glanced at him from beneath lowered lids. "We're nonidentical twins. If we'd been identical, I'd probably be sick, too, depending on when the slip occurred."

"Do you blame yourself?" he asked, surprising himself with the question.

"That would be silly." They both knew that wasn't really an answer. "Besides, that's not the point, is it? The point is that Celeste does have it and I do feel guilty on some level. I also love my sister and want her alive and able to live her life to the fullest, so I went into Singer's research. Then my funding dried up...." She paused. He had a feeling there was more to that story than she was letting on, but before he could ask, she continued, "Tiberius made me an offer I couldn't refuse, and I convinced myself it was okay to let him use me as a legitimate front, as long as my work was going to help people."

"Only it wasn't."

"Exactly." She exhaled. "After about five months, once I'd designed the vector capable of suppressing the cell's ability to transcribe the expanded region and tricking it into making a normal protein instead, Tiberius gave me twenty new repeats he wanted me to work on in parallel. The moment I saw they were di-nucleotide repeats, I knew what he was actually after."

John sent her a sharp look. "Just like that?"

She shifted uncomfortably and turned to look out the window, where the sky was starting to lighten with dawn. "Not exactly. I'd mentioned once or twice in passing that I thought repeat recognition technology could be used to block DNA fingerprinting."

He could tell from her body language she wasn't talking about a passing conversation among colleagues. "Let me guess. Research conference?"

She winced. "Worse. A review article."

He just shook his head. "Great." Now that the thought was out there, Tiberius probably wasn't the only one trying to develop the technology. Even once they took him down, they'd need some serious damage control, and probably a backup plan for CODIS.

"I'm sorry," she said softly.

He said nothing, because right at that moment he didn't have anything nice to say.

WHEN THEY REACHED D.C., one of the newer field agents was waiting to lead them to a big black SUV of the type most field offices were buying these days. The younger agent slapped a bubble light on the roof of the vehicle, and that, combined with a few strategic horn blips, was enough to get them through the city traffic and over to Glen Hills, Maryland, in under an hour.

Still mulling over what he'd learned from Sydney on the plane, John checked his messages and called for an update while they were en route.

He got his team's forensics expert, Drew Dietz. "There's practically nothing for forensics to work with,"

Drew reported. "And most of what we do have is probably going to trace back to the victims. Whoever was in here was good."

"Probably, but we're better," John said. "Keep at it." He hung up, and when Sydney looked over in inquiry, he shook his head. "Nothing yet."

She looked fragile and lost, sitting huddled against the far door with what felt like a mile between them, and for a second he was tempted to tell her everything was going to be okay.

But he didn't.

It was almost full light out when they pulled up in front of a stately old Victorian that easily dated back to the late 1800s but looked like it had been carefully updated in the years since, with modernizations that had maintained the historical charm. The shingles were painted some pale color he couldn't distinguish in the false light of dawn, the shutters and trim were accented in a darker hue and the grounds were landscaped neatly, if simply.

It might've looked like something out of a magazine, except for the police cruisers and black SUVs parked in the driveway and on the street in front of the house, in the typical hurried scatter that John knew indicated that violence had been done inside.

"Nice house." John decided he should just expect the unexpected when it came to Sydney Westlake. He would've pegged her for an ultramodern, superefficient condo. Instead, she lived in a painted lady.

"Before she got sick, Celeste wrote some seriously groundbreaking security programs. They pretty much paid for this place," Sydney said, answering his unspoken question. "The technology has moved on, though, and the residuals started drying up a couple of years ago. That was why—" She broke off, then correcting herself said, "That was partly why I took the job with Tiberius. We needed the money to keep this place up. I couldn't ask her to move, though. She's so happy here."

What about you? John wanted to ask, but didn't. Instead he said, "You ready to go in now, or would you rather wait until they've removed the bodies?"

She shuddered, but visibly collected herself and reached for the door handle. "Let's go. Maybe I'll see something that'll help us find Celeste."

As he followed her to the front door, John thought that was highly doubtful, given that she hadn't been in the house for a year, but he also knew she needed to go inside, needed to prove to herself that her sister was gone. He'd seen it before with victims' families, and would no doubt see it a thousand times more over the next couple of decades, because he was in this for life.

Major crimes—and the apprehension of major criminals—were in his blood. He hadn't gotten it from his globe-trotting musician parents, who lived for the next concert, the next party, and freely admitted they never should have reproduced. No, he'd gotten the cop gene from the uncle and great-uncle he'd visited during the short gaps between boarding school and sleep-away camp. Both of the older men had lived and died on the job, one as a cop, one as a Fed, neither married to anything but police work.

John figured he'd learned most of what he needed to know from them, including the dangers of becoming too friendly with witnesses, victims or snitches.

We're cops, not social workers, his great-uncle used to say. *Friendship doesn't change the evidence, but it can sure as hell change your perception of it. Better to leave affection out of things.*

Now, as he watched Sydney hesitate before pushing open the front door, the cynical part of John hoped she'd break down and tell him everything without waiting for execution of the immunity deal, and without withholding the parts she thought might help her if things went south. Another, deeply buried part of him—the part his great-uncle would've warned against—wished he could shield her from walking through her front door and seeing a handprint-size smear of blood on the lowest tread of the center stairwell, right beside the mechanical track her sister must've used to move her wheelchair from one floor to the next.

But he didn't shield her and he didn't stop her, and because he knew he wouldn't be able to talk her out of walking through to the kitchen, where the aide's body still lay where it had fallen, he didn't try to prevent her from heading to the scene of the crime. He walked beside her instead.

When she reached the threshold separating the kitchen and dining room, she stopped and swayed a little, but didn't back away, and John dropped the hand he'd instinctively raised to catch her if she fell.

The aide, a dark-haired twentysomething identified as Danielle Jones, lay on the tiled floor, sprawled where she'd fallen. She had two dime-size holes in her forehead, one centered, one off-center to the right and higher than the first. Both had leaked thin blood trails to the floor, where the droplets had fallen into the larger stain that spread from the exit wounds at the back of the victim's skull.

Two taps, John thought. *Professional.* According to

Drew, it'd been the same with the other victim, the aide's boyfriend, Jay Alphonse. His body was in the garage, as though he'd been nailed on his way out.

There had been no passion to the kills. They had been pure practicality, a means to dispose of obstacles. Typical of Tiberius and his ilk.

Sydney sucked in a breath that sounded like a sob, and turned to him. "Where is my sister?"

He didn't answer because he'd already told her that her sister wasn't in the house, and telling her again was pointless.

Her eyes filled with tears. "She's really gone, isn't she?"

"I'm sorry," he said.

Her face crumpled and she seemed to collapse in on herself, her hands coming up to cover her face, her shoulders folding inward and shaking with silent sobs.

When her knees buckled and she headed for the floor, he reached out and caught her.

One piece of his brain said he was simply making sure she didn't mess up the scene, but in reality the move was pure instinct, just as it was instinct that had him folding her into his arms and holding her tight as she wept.

Just then, Drew strode in through the back. He stalled hard and his eyebrows hit his hairline when he saw his boss holding a sobbing woman in his arms.

Feeling a low burn in his gut, John snapped, "Anything new?"

"No— Ah, no. Sorry." Drew gestured with the film camera he used to photograph scenes. "I was just getting started with the pictures."

"Do it."

Drew bolted and John stared over the top of Sydney's head as she burrowed against him and sobbed into his chest. This was a good thing, he told himself. It was all about expediency. He'd wanted her to break so he could get the information he needed. None of this had anything to do with the feel of her in his arms, or the way she seemed to fit naturally against him, all soft curves and woman, urging his body to soften in some places, harden in others.

Drew stuck his head back through the door and made a point of not staring at them. "I had another look at—"

The phone rang, interrupting. John and Drew turned toward the cordless unit, which sat alone at the center of the butcher-block island.

Sydney stiffened in his arms, as though suddenly realizing who she was clinging to, and maybe even wondering how that had come to be.

She pulled away, took a couple of steps into the kitchen and then looked at him for permission.

At Drew's signal that the handset had been processed, and Grace and Jimmy Oliverra had the trace and tape setups jacked into the phone line from the other room, John nodded. "Go ahead. Answer it."

She picked up the handset and hit the button to connect. "Hello?"

In the moment of silence that followed, John wished he had one of the headsets Grace and Jimmy were using to listen in. Seconds later, Sydney's whole body stiffened and she hissed a breath through her teeth before she shrieked, "You bastard. Where is she? Where is my sister? *What have you done with her?*"

John didn't need to wonder anymore; he knew. Tiberius was on the line, looking to make a deal of his own.

CHAPTER FIVE

"SHE'S FINE...FOR NOW." Tiberius's voice seemed to slither down the phone line, hissing into Sydney's ear where it curled, waiting to strike as he continued. "She'll stay that way, too, as long as you cooperate."

She didn't bother asking what he wanted. "Before I give you the password, I'm going to need some assurance that she's alive."

In her peripheral vision, she saw John surge forward a step and then stop himself, his expression dark and accusatory. He caught her eye and shook his head, mouthing, *Don't tell him the password.*

She frowned back at him. What did he think, she was stupid? If she gave up the password over the phone she'd never see her sister again.

"You're in no position to be making demands," Tiberius said, the slither turning cold and chilling her blood in her veins. "The password. Now."

Wrapping her free arm around herself and hugging the borrowed sweatshirt tight around her body, she turned away from the bloodstained kitchen and wandered out into the hall with the cordless phone pressed to her ear. She was aware that Sharpe followed, his steps nearly silent, making her feel stalked and protected at the same time.

Ignoring him, she moved into the sitting room,

which contained a small television and three walls worth of books. Interspersed amongst the paperbacks and research books were photographs of her and Celeste, over and over, just the two of them, spanning from earliest childhood to the previous year, as they'd lived their lives out together.

Tears misted Sydney's vision, forcing her to pinch the bridge of her nose to hold them back.

"I'm not giving you the password now," she said with a faint quiver in her voice from nerves at what she was about to propose. "And I'm not doing it over the phone. It has to be in person. I'll meet you—"

She broke off as her eyes locked on one photo, a special picture that showed Celeste and her kayaking in Puget Sound. It had been the summer before Celeste had gotten sick. They'd had plenty of money from the sale of her computer programs, and Sydney's new university job hadn't started until fall, so they'd worked their way across the country. It'd been the best summer Sydney could remember.

And the picture was upside down.

"Oh, hell."

"Excuse me?" Tiberius said, in a tone that indicated she'd managed to surprise the master of surprises.

"I'm not trading the password for a bluff, Tiberius. Sorry. You lose this round."

When she clicked the phone off, hanging up on the criminal mastermind, the two agents manning the phone tap gaped and squawked, and fiddled with their equipment in an effort to get the call back.

Sharpe didn't move, though. He watched her, face expressionless, as she dropped the phone and hurried to the bookcase.

Heart pounding, she grabbed the framed picture and twisted it a hundred-eighty degrees on the hidden rod that went from the back of the old frame, through the wall and into a mechanism that the contractors she'd used for the renovations thought might date back to Prohibition. Metal grated against metal and a section of wall swung inward on heavy, hand-forged hinges, revealing a dark corridor that traveled inward a few feet and took an immediate ninety-degree turn. The small bolt hole in front of them was empty. Beyond the turn, no light penetrated farther into the hidden tunnel.

But there were two parallel lines in the dust, exactly the width apart of a wheelchair's wheels.

Celeste. Afraid to say her sister's name in case she'd been wrong, in case Tiberius wasn't bluffing after all and he'd somehow gotten her after she'd made it to the bolt hole, Sydney surged forward toward the passageway.

An iron-strong hand gripped her arm, pulling her back.

"I go first," Sharpe said, and did just that, heading into the passageway with his weapon drawn. Seconds later she heard him hiss a curse.

Ignoring the others, she plunged into the darkness after him.

Two steps in, she slammed into him where he'd stopped dead. Though she'd been going full tilt, he weathered the impact easily, holding out an arm to keep her from falling. "Easy there."

"Celeste?" she whispered, clinging to his arm for reassurance, though she knew damn well he was the last person she should be leaning on.

"Yes," he said. "And yes, she's alive. She's unconscious, but her pulse is steady and her breathing seems okay. The chair seems to be wedged or something. If you back up a little, I think I can get it free."

Sydney pretty much stopped processing his words after *Yes, she's alive.* Relief shivered through her, followed by a wash of nausea and guilt. This was her fault, all of it. If she hadn't taken that job—

Stop, she told herself. Stop there. What was done was done. She couldn't go back and undo it, so she was going to have to find a way to make the best while moving forward. She was going to have to find a way to fix what she'd messed up so badly.

Still, she whispered, "Thank you." She wasn't sure whether she meant it for the man ahead of her in the secret passageway or for some celestial being looking down on her from up above, but she knew one thing for sure: she'd gotten lucky with Celeste.

The aide and her boyfriend, however, hadn't been lucky at all. Their blood would remain on Sydney's hands.

She heard the catch of metal on leather as Sharpe holstered his weapon and tried to work the heavy, mechanized chair free and drag it out into the main room.

"You've got to put the transmission in Neutral," she said, stepping forward and reaching past him to work the controls in the darkness.

In the close quarters, she had to squeeze tightly against him to reach the mechanism. They wound up pressed together, with her shoulder and arm against his torso and her leg touching his from hip to ankle. It was impossible not to notice that they lined up perfectly in all the right spots, and that he was warm and strong and incredibly male.

It might've been partly relief at finding Celeste, might've been the sensation of finally being home after so long, but the giddy rush of excitement seemed to come, not from the circumstances, but from the man. But when she found herself wanting to lean into him and stay there, she made herself pull away instead.

"There." Her voice came out high and breathy, and she forced it level before continuing, "You should be able to move it now."

She backed out of the passageway as Sharpe wheeled Celeste out of the darkness and into the light.

As he did so, her eyelids flickered.

"We'll want the paramedics in here, Grace," he said quietly to the short, dark-haired woman who'd been one of the two agents manning the phone trace.

Grace nodded and headed outside, but Sydney couldn't wait. She knelt down beside Celeste's chair and took one of her sister's cool hands, rubbing it between her own. "Celeste, hon? You in there? Knock, knock?"

It was their sad little inside joke, because Celeste was always "in there." Sometimes, though, she couldn't get out past the shell of her own body.

Singer's syndrome was a progressive debilitating neuropathy, which as far as Sydney could tell was a fancy way of saying that Celeste's mind was sharp as ever but her body was giving out on her day by day, as plaques of a faulty neural protein—the one containing the expanded trinucleotide repeat—built up along her nerve fibers. The more it accumulated, the harder it was for Celeste's brain to get neural impulses to her extremities.

She could still hold a pen on her good days. On the bad days, she had to rely on her chair, which could be operated by a press-and-puff joystick affixed at mouth-level.

At least that had been the situation when Sydney left. Now, as Celeste's eyelids fluttered open and her sky-blue eyes locked on her sister, Sydney wondered whether she'd deteriorated even further and faster than they'd both feared she would. Her hand remained cool and lax in Sydney's, and she didn't react right away, just sat there, eyes dreamy.

Then, as if she'd bumped up against a live wire, Celeste gasped, yanked upright in her chair and grabbed onto Sydney's hand.

Yet still, she didn't speak.

"Thank God." Sydney exhaled a long, relieved breath and leaned in to gather her sister close. "I was so worried." The words were completely inadequate, but what else could she say just then?

"Danielle and Jay are dead, aren't they?" Celeste whispered, voice trembling.

"Yes, they are. Thank God you made it into the hidey-hole."

"I just..." Celeste's eyes filled. "Your last email warned me to watch out, that something bad might happen."

Sharpe cleared his throat.

"Celeste, honey," Sydney said. "This is Agent Sharpe of the FBI. He needs to ask you some questions."

"Did you see the killer?" he asked quietly. Behind

him, several other agents and police officers were hard at work on the crime scene.

Celeste shook her head. "No. I'm sorry."

"Don't be sorry," Sydney responded immediately. "If he'd seen you..." She trailed off and swallowed hard, then pressed her cheek against Celeste's and repeated in a whisper, "Don't be sorry. Ever."

Celeste leaned into the embrace, but her voice was stronger and a little reproving when she said, "I'm not going to say I told you so."

"Then I'll say it," Sydney replied. "You told me so."

Celeste had wanted her to turn down the job on Rocky Cliff Island. They had argued back and forth for nearly a week before Sydney left, and the parting had been more bitter than sweet.

The homecoming was proving far worse.

Grace stuck her head around the corner to report, "The paramedics are here."

Celeste submitted to a quick vitals check, then waved them off. "I'm as fine as I get." She looked at Sharpe. "Besides, I have a feeling your Fed here wants to ask me some questions."

"He's not my Fed," Sydney said, and damned the flush that touched her cheeks.

Sharpe didn't crouch down to talk to Celeste, which gained him points in Sydney's eyes. Instead, he dropped into a nearby chair so he and Celeste were eye level with each other before he said, "Do you feel up to answering a few questions?"

Celeste glanced at Sydney and raised an eyebrow in a look of, *How much should I tell him?*

"He's okay," Sydney said. "Tell him everything you remember about what just happened."

In other words, *Don't say anything about Rocky Cliff Island or the emailed computer programs.*

Sharpe glanced at Sydney and scowled faintly. "I guess that will have to do. For now." Then he turned to Celeste. "Please backtrack as far as you're willing to go, and walk me through last night and early this morning. Tell me whatever you remember about the attacks. I'm recording this, okay?" He held up a PDA, and at her nod, keyed it to record.

She described her normal bedtime routine, then waking up and hearing strange noises, and thinking that Danielle's boyfriend was trying to sneak out before she woke up again. "I heard what sounded like silenced gunshots, you know, like they sound on TV," Celeste said. "I tried my cell phone but it wasn't working, like it was jammed or something. Right about then I figured out it was a break-in, and I got myself strapped into my wheels." She tried to pat the armrest and managed little more than a feeble flip of her hand.

That told Sydney that she was getting low on energy. She touched her sister's hand. "You should rest."

"I'm fine," Celeste snapped.

Trying not to feel the sting of a reunion that wasn't anything like she imagined, Sydney pulled her hand back and said softly, "I'm just trying to help."

"So am I." Celeste turned back to Sharpe and continued, "I wheeled myself out into the hall and used the stair lift to get downstairs. Thank God they didn't hear me."

"They?" He hadn't moved, but Sydney sensed his attention shift, focusing more precisely. "Are you sure there was more than one?"

"Positive. I saw—" Celeste broke off and swallowed.

"I saw them leaning over something in the kitchen. I saw blood…and I went the other way."

Sydney could see her sister's frustration growing, her anger at a body that let her down over and over. And though Sydney knew it wasn't her fault she was healthy and her sister was ill, guilt stung anyway.

When a tear trickled down Celeste's cheek, Sydney announced, "That's it. We're done for now."

"No, we're not," Celeste snapped. "Look, Syd, I know you're trying to help, but you're just getting in the poor guy's way." Sharpe looked mildly surprised to be called a poor guy, but kept his mouth shut as Celeste continued, "Either stop fussing and let me finish, or go sit upstairs or something."

"You're tired," Sydney said softly. "You know how you get cranky when your energy runs low."

Celeste narrowed her eyes. "Yeah, and I get cranky when you treat me like a toddler, too. I'm wheelchair-bound, not a vegetable. Give me some credit for knowing when to say when." As Sydney's mouth dropped open, she smiled a little. "You've been·gone nearly a year, Syd. Surprise." She turned back to Sharpe. "I know for sure there were at least two of them, but I only saw them from the back, and nothing really stood out. Dark clothes, dark caps, medium builds. One was shorter than the other. The one—" She broke off and swallowed hard. "The one with the gun was wearing gloves. I didn't see the other guy's hands. It was all so quick. When I realized what they'd done, all I could think to do was hide in the secret passageway. I knew they'd hear me if I tried to go out the front, and it was so late…" She trailed off. "I just…hid."

"Best thing you could've done," Sharpe said, without on ounce of coddling or softness in his voice. "The only way for you to help is to help us catch them, and you've got to be alive to do that."

Sydney knew that his blunt words probably meant more to her sister than a hundred reassurances from her.

Celeste sniffed, nodded and finished, "I'd just gotten the door shut behind me—there's another lever on the inside that locks the mechanism—when I heard footsteps going upstairs, then some banging, like they were looking for me. I just…stayed there. I heard the front door slam, like, five minutes later, but I was too scared to move. After a while, I must have dozed off."

Browned out was more like it, Sydney thought, but she didn't want Celeste to feel like she was hovering.

Over the past eleven months she'd missed her sister like crazy. They'd never been apart for more than a few weeks at a time before, and she'd pictured their reunion like one big party, had figured that after she was home everything would go back to normal.

But that was before she figured out what Tiberius really wanted from her, and how far he was willing to go to get it.

"What happens now?" Celeste asked.

"There's an agent on his way named Hugo Thornridge," Sharpe said. "He's going to take care of you."

Sydney drew a breath to speak, but Celeste silenced her with a look before saying, "Take care of me how, exactly?"

"He's a registered nurse with medic training." The agent paused. "He's also a sniper-trained sharpshooter, has a black belt in one of the martial arts and throws a hell of a punch in a bar fight." A touch of a smile suggested there was a story there. "He'll help you monitor your health, and he'll be in charge of your safety."

"You're putting me in witness protection," Celeste said. It wasn't a question.

He shook his head. "Not exactly. WITSEC is a formal program, complete with paperwork and processing. We don't have time for that, and frankly I'm not sure it's as secure as it needs to be when dealing with someone like Tiberius. You and Hugo are going underground. He'll check in with me regularly, and leave updates on your position when he deems prudent, but other than that, you two will be totally off the grid."

Sydney made a sad, pained noise. Danielle and Jay were dead. Celeste was going to be running for her life. All because she'd gone to work for Tiberius.

"Hey, Syd." Celeste made a faint motion with her hand. "You didn't do this. Tiberius did."

Sydney stifled a sob and took Celeste's hand, pressing it to her cheek. But she didn't say anything, because they both knew the truth was that Tiberius hadn't been acting alone. She had played along with him for far too long, and now she, her sister and the people around them were paying the price for her mistakes.

So much for a joyous reunion, where she brought back a cure for her sister and money for them both to live on abroad, then phoned in an anonymous tip on Tiberius and his island of horrors.

Instead, she'd returned home to two more innocent victims and a sister she barely recognized.

While Celeste and Sharpe spoke briefly, Sydney stared at her sister. She still looked the same. Her straight, midbrown hair was bobbed at her shoulders and her face was a slightly thinner rearrangement of

Sydney's own features, with the exception of blue eyes instead of brown. Her arms and legs were far too thin, due to the wasting effects of the disease, and for the most part the only motion came from her mouth and eyes, with an occasional laborious hand gesture for emphasis. There was nothing really stand-out different about her.

She was the same. Yet she wasn't. She'd gotten herself out of bed and hidden, outsmarting a pair of trained killers. And she'd snapped at Sydney not once but twice, when before she would've agreed that yes, she was tired. Yes, she should rest and not get overexcited.

Did I hold her back? Sydney wondered now. *Did I make it too easy for her to be sick?*

"Sydney," Sharpe said, his voice sharp enough to indicate he was repeating himself. "You with us?"

"Sorry." She shook her head, trying to clear it. But how could she possibly clear everything that was inside her skull at this point? It was all tangled up together in one big messy knot: the joy of finding Celeste unharmed; the hurt of seeing that she was doing okay—if not better—on her own; the pain of two more people dying because of her... "It's all too much," she whispered.

It wasn't until Celeste squeezed her hand that she realized they were still sitting close together, that she finally had her sister by her side once again.

Then Celeste said, "Hugo's here. We need to say goodbye now."

"But—" Sydney stopped herself and bowed her head to hide the tears. "I know."

A big man appeared in the front doorway, filling it

from one side to the other. He had short blond hair and pleasantly regular features, with a glint of humor in his light blue eyes. Wearing cargo pants held up by a web belt, combat boots and a khaki T-shirt stretched across his wide chest, he practically screamed ex-military, and instantly made Sydney feel better about Celeste going into hiding.

She looked up at him. "Please tell me that you're Hugo."

"My thoughts exactly," Celeste murmured from beside her, and Sydney stifled a grin, feeling a little lift beneath her heart at the realization that somehow, somewhere, she'd gotten back a part of the sister she remembered.

"That'd be me." He looked at Celeste and raised a golden eyebrow. "You ready to boogie?"

"Yes, please." Her face clouded. "I'd like to get out of here."

Sydney felt a pang at the realization that they'd probably never share their pretty little house again. Not only would she need to sell it to cover the legal bills she was no doubt racking up by the second, but she also couldn't imagine either of them wanting to live there after two people had died so horribly in the kitchen.

"Hey, sis." Celeste used her faltering strength to tug on her hand. "Take care of yourself."

"You, too." Sydney bent and hugged her sister, harder than she probably should have, but needing to prove to herself that they were both there, that they were both okay, for the moment at least.

Hugo had pulled a specially outfitted van up very close to the door, since the garage was roped off with crime scene tape. He draped a pair of Kevlar vests over Celeste for the short trip out in the open.

The precautions reassured Sydney. At the same time they made her want to throw up.

"Tell me she'll be okay," she said to the man she sensed standing directly behind her.

"Hugo's one of the best," Sharpe said. "If anyone can keep her off Tiberius's radar, he can."

She nodded. "Thank you."

He said nothing, though she didn't know if it was because he didn't want her thanks, or if his mind was already elsewhere, moving on to the next topic, the next fight.

She turned to him, battling the almost overwhelming compulsion to lean on him, just for a moment, and absorb some of the strength he seemed to wear like a second skin. "What happens now?"

He glanced down at her. "We're going to put you in a safe house under full guard. At that point I will have fulfilled my part of the bargain by getting you and your sister protected to the best of my ability. Then it's going to be your turn." His voice went low, but not in the slightest bit soft. "You're going to tell us how to fight Tiberius and keep him from taking down CODIS."

SEVERAL HUNDRED MILES away, sitting in the elegant kitchen of a renovated Vermont farmhouse that was owned under the little-used alias Kyle Cross, Tiberius slapped the phone shut with a bitter oath.

The thick-maned redhead sitting at the other end of the long breakfast bar, still wearing one of the skin-tight flight suits she favored when piloting Tiberius's chopper, looked up from buffing a chip out of one of her nails. "Problem, darling?"

"Nothing that can't be dealt with," he responded, feeling a measure of calm at the knowledge of just how true those words were. His guards might have let Sydney Westlake escape from the island—and they'd be punished for the lapse—and the contractors he'd hired in Maryland might've screwed up the sister's capture, ditto on the retribution, but that didn't mean he was entirely without options.

He tapped the computer screen of his high-tech phone, bringing up an encrypted list, and keyed in the code required to translate the names, revealing a list of key FBI personnel that he'd either found useful in the past, or who had weaknesses he knew he could exploit. A quick comparison between that list and the names he'd gotten for John Sharpe's major crimes team, followed by a brief phone call, and he had himself a new employee.

Sydney wasn't going to know what hit her.

the island without the password, short of towing each
and every computer without disrupting the networked
connections.

Sure enough, on the freaking day his followers
had torqued down on the bed and upped it of the mark-
worst and worst to be the same out. Sharpe's relaxed
through relaxed, at center... that then there to make
Those a man that hand a hidden the grace... room piece

CHAPTER SIX

SYDNEY SPENT THE NEXT four days in a safe house outside
D.C., downloading her brain into huge databases and
modeling programs run by two of Sharpe's people—
pretty, soft-spoken Grace Mears and quirky, geeky
Jimmy Oliverra.

There was no sign of Sharpe. He didn't visit, didn't
call. He might as well have taken Celeste away himself,
because she hadn't heard a peep from either of them.

Telling herself he didn't owe her an accounting of
his whereabouts, Sydney forced herself to focus on the
laptop screen, which showed a satellite photo of Rocky
Cliff Island. It was near dusk on day four, and she was
losing her edge. She was sick of the safe house, sick of
being cooped up, sick of going over the same information again and again, until it was all starting to blur together in her head.

She'd already told them everything she thought was
relevant about the DNA vector, and the computer programs currently guarding it. Now they were working on
constructing a virtual model of Rocky Cliff Island. At
first the agents had been concerned that Tiberius might
have left the island for good; none of the initial passes
of the retasked satellite had shown evidence of him
being in residence. But that didn't make any sense—
there was no way for him to get the DNA sequence off

the island without the password, short of moving each and every computer without disrupting the networked connections.

Sure enough, on the previous day his helicopter had touched down on the pad just uphill of the mansion, and word had come down from Sharpe—relayed through Jimmy, of course—that they were to model "every damn last beach plum on the godforsaken piece of rock" in case they needed to plan a raid.

Sydney was pretty sure that was close to verbatim, and she was more than a little horrified that she kept replaying the words in her mind, imagining the way they'd sound in his deep, resonant voice.

Forcing herself to focus on the job at hand, she pointed to a small white box on the extreme eastern point of the narrow, oblong island. "That's a guard shack, one of the big ones. It's got some sort of weapon on the top, hidden under a second, false roof." She glanced at the others and shrugged slightly. "Sorry, but I only saw it once on my way in. I'm not sure I can do much more with the details."

Jimmy broke off the low, tuneless whistling he maintained while working his machines. "Don't be sorry. Just do your best." That was pretty much Jimmy's attitude toward life, which made him a good match for type-A, intense Grace, who immediately began tapping away at her computer.

Within seconds, the screen in front of Sydney had the guard shack labeled as such. Next, Grace tapped a few more keys and a new page popped up, showing schematic renderings of some seriously nasty-looking turret-type guns that looked like they could take out anything from an airplane to a medium-size boat. "Anything look familiar?" she asked.

Sydney closed her eyes, trying to remember what the weapon had looked like. "It was longer and...thinner at the end, I think." They went through a few iterations before she nodded. "That's as close as I can get."

"We'll take it." Jimmy spun the image of the island on-screen, focusing their view in on another structure. "How about this one?"

Grace's e-mail program gave a *ping,* signaling incoming mail. Sydney automatically glanced at the screen. She saw *J.Sharpe* in boldface.

Grace spun the screen away from her before opening the message. She shot Sydney an uncomfortable sidelong look. "Sorry."

"You're just following orders," Sydney said softly, "It's not your fault he doesn't trust me. It's mine." What she didn't say was how much his mistrust bothered her, how much she wished things had started off differently between them.

She kept trying to tell herself it was the isolation of the safe house that had her hyperfocused on Sharpe, but that didn't play because she'd been just as isolated—if not more so—in the lab on Rocky Cliff Island, and she hadn't spent her time fantasizing about any of her guards, or thinking about her ex, Richard, or hell, imagining herself with Gabriel Byrne or one of the dark-haired hunks she usually gravitated toward in the movies.

No, she had Special Agent John Sharpe on the brain. Special Agent John Sharpe, who hadn't spoken to her in four days and twelve hours, and who, as far as she could tell, wanted nothing more from her than information.

"He doesn't trust anybody," Grace corrected. "That's why he's so good at his job."

"I'm betting it doesn't make him much of a hit in the social department," Sydney observed. She pushed back her chair at the kitchen table they were using as a workspace, and crossed the tiled floor to open the refrigerator and peer inside, just in case something interesting had magically appeared in there since the last time she'd checked. Which had been, oh, fifteen minutes or so earlier.

"Why do you ask?" Grace's look was sly.

"Just looking for a weak spot." Sydney sighed and shut the fridge before hiking herself up onto the kitchen counter. She was wearing jeans and a clingy red sweater she'd thought would cheer her up when she'd gotten dressed that morning. Her feet were laced into a pair of sneakers, even though it was doubtful she'd be going anywhere.

The shoes were a house rule, though: be ready to run, in case something bad happens.

"Sharpe doesn't have any weak spots," Grace said. "A few dents, maybe, but no gaps in the armor."

Don't ask, Sydney told herself, but did it anyway. "Dents?"

That earned her a long look, but Grace answered, "There was a woman a few years back. A witness. It ended badly."

"Ahem." Jimmy tapped the computer screen. "Not to interrupt, but…"

"I saw men coming and going from that one once, carrying things," Sydney said. "Storeroom, maybe?"

"Can you define *things?*"

"Not really. I was pretty far away." Sydney tried to concentrate, but what she really wanted to do was ask about Sharpe's ex. What sort of witness had she been? What exactly did "end badly" mean? Had it been a simple breakup that'd turned awkward, or had it been a double cross, like she'd had with Richard? Or worse, had it been a more final end, like *bang dead?*

"We need a different satellite," Jimmy groused, flipping through the views of the island. "I want thermals, high-def, that sort of thing."

"Can't do it," Grace responded. "No tasking other satellites until further notice—Sharpe wants to keep all the info gathering in-house. His paranoia has kicked in. He's got it in his head that Tiberius might be working with someone on the inside."

That froze Sydney. "Why does he think that?" *And does it mean I'm not safe here anymore? Does it mean Tiberius knows where Celeste is?*

"Because he's a paranoid bastard," a new voice said from the doorway.

Sydney gasped and spun, her heart freezing in her chest, then starting up again—entirely too fast—when she saw Sharpe standing there with his arms folded over his chest and his long, lean body propped up against the door frame.

He was wearing a dark gray suit and pale gray shirt, with a brightly patterned tie shoved in his breast pocket as though he'd worn it for a meeting and yanked it off immediately after. His eyes were dark, his expression unreadable, and the combined effect made the whole package seriously drool worthy.

A quiver took up residence in Sydney's stomach.

Damn it. She'd spent the past four days trying not to think about him—and failing miserably. Yet even at that, she'd forgotten how gorgeous he actually was.

Without meaning to, she took a step back, so she was even with Grace's chair. Glancing down at the computer specialist, Sydney realized the woman hadn't moved, hadn't reacted to the surprise.

Ergo, she hadn't been surprised.

"You could've warned me he was here," Sydney muttered under her breath.

"Could've," Grace agreed, "but I do so hate being predictable."

She casually tilted the computer so Sydney could read the brief email giving his ETA at the safe house. The note gave no hint why he was there, nor did the closed expression on his strong, elegant face give any insight into his thoughts.

Suddenly, though, Sydney had the strongest feeling that he hadn't come to speak with his teammates. He'd come for her.

"Is something wrong?" she took a step toward him. "Celeste?"

"Hugo hasn't missed a check-in," he said. It wasn't the same thing as "they're fine" but she knew it was probably the best she was going to get out of him.

Where have you been? she wanted to ask. *Have you been busy? Were you avoiding me?* But she kept those questions to herself, because he didn't owe her comfort, or an explanation. So instead she asked, "Why are you here?"

His eyes fixed on her and darkened, and there was a click of connection. Heat flared in her center, urging her to cross the short distance between them and touch the strong line of his jaw, tempting her to dig her fingers into his hair and hang on for the ride.

And from the heat that flared in his eyes when he looked at her, she wasn't the only one feeling the urge.

"Grace said you were getting stir-crazy." His voice had gone slightly rough, and the sound thrilled along her nerve endings like a caress. "She thought it'd do you some good to get out of here."

"I'd kill to," she said without thinking, then winced. "Figuratively, I mean. Sorry, I'm still not used to being around people who don't necessarily consider that a figure of speech."

"Noted." Sharpe unfolded himself from the doorway and gestured toward the front door of the heavily guarded safe house. "You want to go or not?"

Sydney hung back, sudden nerves gathering alongside the heat of excitement in her belly. "Is it safe?"

"You'll be wearing a vest and the location we're going to is secure." Again, not an absolute promise of safety. Just the facts, ma'am.

"Are you—" She broke off and swallowed hard. "Is this a plan to draw out the men who killed Danielle and Jay?"

"Would that bother you?"

"Not if I knew I was being used as bait."

He gave her a long, assessing look. She wasn't sure if he was trying to decide whether she was telling the truth, or if she'd surprised him. After a moment he said, "We already have the two men who broke into your house."

"You captured them?" If that was where he'd been, he was entirely forgiven.

But he shook his head. "We found them...or rather

what was left of them when Tiberius was through." He paused. "The prints of one of the men match the partials from your kitchen—he must've been the one not wearing gloves. The other guy had traces of blood on one of his shoes. We're running the DNA now, but I'd be surprised if it doesn't match one or both of the victims." He didn't say where they'd been found or how they died and she didn't ask.

She didn't really think she wanted to know.

"That leaves us right back where we started," Sydney said, staring at her toes on a beat of sadness. Guilt tugged at the thought of the domino chain she'd helped initiate. Yes, Tiberius was ultimately responsible for the killings, but so much of the violence had been initiated by her actions.

"Not entirely. We know more than we did before," he countered. "And Tiberius is back on the island. I have a feeling things are going to break loose in the next few days, one way or the other."

Sydney shivered, not wanting to know what "the other" might entail. "Can't you just, I don't know, blow up the island or something?"

His blue eyes glinted with a brief flash of amusement. "That's not exactly kosher in the due process department. At the moment, we don't even have enough to justify a raid on the mansion." He grimaced, his frustration evident. "That's according to our higher-ups, anyway. They want this done squeaky clean and by the books. He's slipped away too many times before. We're not taking that chance again. Besides—" now his expression turned sardonic "—I thought you wanted to protect your work. Isn't that why you froze the machines rather than blanking them completely?"

"That, and because I figured I'd need the leverage if he caught me," she answered honestly.

"You were going to trade the password for your freedom." It wasn't a question.

"Of course." Her voice went defensive. "I was going to send everything I had to the authorities the moment I thought Celeste and I were safely hidden."

"That plan has two major flaws," Sharpe pointed out. "One, you and your sister will never truly be safe from him until he's either dead or behind bars. And two, by the time you dropped the dime, he could've easily sold your bug. The damage would've already been done."

Something in his eyes alerted her. "You know what he plans to do with the virus."

He tipped his head. "We have a pretty good guess." But he didn't elaborate, emphasizing that he might be using her for information, but she wasn't really part of the team. Glancing at Grace and Jimmy, who had given up all pretense of working and were avidly watching the exchange, Sharpe said, "Speaking of which, don't you two have work to do?"

Jimmy grinned, unrepentant. "Yes, but this is way more entertaining."

Sharpe grimaced and waved in the direction of the front door, and the deepening night beyond. He said to Sydney, "Do you want to get out of here or not?"

Something in his body language warned her that it wasn't nearly that simple. "You're sure it's not a trap?"

"No. It's pizza under armed guard by yours truly. You in or out?" He said it like he didn't care which way she went, but there was a subtle challenge in his tone.

"I'm in," she said finally, wondering why it felt like she'd just agreed to more than pizza.

"Good. I'll get the Kevlar. Meet me by the front door." He turned on his heel and strode out, leaving Sydney staring at the empty doorway.

She shot a look at Grace. "Was that a little strange, or is it my imagination?"

Grace looked torn, as though she didn't want to talk about her team leader out of turn—especially with him potentially within earshot.

Jimmy had no such compunction, saying, "Yeah, this isn't his usual style." He paused and lifted one shoulder in a half shrug. "Thing is, you can trust Sharpe to say exactly what he means. If he says he's not using you as bait, then he's not using you as bait."

The statement implied he was very likely planning to use her for some other purpose she hadn't yet guessed at.

Since that lined up with Sydney's own gut check, she nodded. "Okay. I guess I'll see you guys later."

"I'm headed out." Jimmy stood and cracked his knuckles. "Hot date."

Grace rolled her eyes in a look of *yeah, right,* and said, "Don't worry. I'll be here, slaving away." She sketched a wave and bent back over her laptop keyboard.

Which left Sydney with one last question as she grabbed her jacket and headed for the front door: Why pizza?

JOHN WAS ASKING HIMSELF a similar question forty minutes later as he turned off the highway and headed his car along the outskirts of the D.C. commuter belt, toward the restored farmhouse he called home inbetween road assignments.

Why was he taking Sydney home with him? Why hadn't he just stuck her in witness protection along with her sister and forgotten about them both while he went on with the investigation?

And why, when he came down to it, had he added dinner to the mix?

He'd picked up the pizza on the way through town. The box sat on the backseat, steaming the interior of the car with the spicy smells of garlic and tomatoes, along with the greasy promise of melted cheese.

The food, along with his last-minute decision to drive his own wheels rather than a company car, made the scenario feel too much like a date. Worse was the fleeting thought of whether she'd like the place, and the hope that she wouldn't mind eating in the living room because the dining table was snowed in under a drift of psych magazines, gun journals, prison newsletters and just about anything else he could get his hands on that could give him new insight into the heads of major criminals like Tiberius.

And he was losing his mind.

He'd told himself to stay away from her. He'd even managed to follow through…for four whole days. Four days during which he'd done his job but been unable to get her out of his head. Four days of flipping open his phone intending to call her, then forcing himself to put the unit back in his pocket without dialing.

Everything she'd told them had checked out. She was who she said she was, and events prior to her leaving for the island had occurred pretty much as she'd reported. She'd lost her funding following an incident with her immediate boss that'd been clouded with enough academic double-speak to tell him they'd been lovers. The fact that the knowledge bothered him—the fact that he cared at all—was just one more warning buzzer amidst the sirens already sounding off inside his skull.

As he turned the car off the highway, he glanced over at Sydney, who'd stayed silent during the drive, lost in her own thoughts.

She stared out the window, and the passing streetlights highlighted the soft curve of her cheek and the elegant column of her neck above the bulk of the Kevlar vest. When he turned off the main road down the side street that would take them to his home, the streetlights gave way to darkness. The faint blue glow from the dashboard dials gave her profile a dreamy quality, one that made him think of bedrooms and fantasies, which should've had no place in his head.

He was willing to believe she wasn't working for Tiberius anymore. Her relationship with her sister was real, as were her initial motivations for taking the job on Rocky Cliff Island. The decision had been a poor one, but she'd learned her lessons the hard way. She was cooperating as best she could, trying to fix the mess she'd helped make.

But although she might not fall under the "suspect" category in his brain anymore, that only served to make her a witness. And he knew better than to mess with witnesses.

Which begged the question of what the hell he thought he was doing now. This was so stupid it was almost laughable, yet he'd been unable to stop himself from driving to the safe house, unable to stay away any longer.

He had, quite simply, needed to see her.

What was it about her that made him so crazy? He didn't know. Sure, she was pretty. A knockout, really, with those long runner's legs and perfectly proportioned body. And her hands—he'd never really thought about a woman's hands before, but he'd noticed hers. They were strong and capable-looking, yet tapered and feminine, and she had this way of lifting her fingertips to her face or brow as she spoke, making him want that featherlight touch on his own skin.

And that was the point, wasn't it? She'd drawn him in, wrapped him around those same fingers until, in that first crazy moment when he'd walked into the safe house and seen her for the first time in days, she could've had him with a single finger-crook.

Something had to give. Starting now. Tonight. He had to find a way to purge her from his system, a way to convince himself once and for all that he had to stay away from her, had to keep his hands to himself.

Either that or he had to have her.

Iceman, my ass, he thought, as he turned the car down the narrow, tree-lined driveway to their destination. He hated the loss of control, hated feeling as if he was spinning in unfamiliar directions, ready to snap at a touch. But at the same time, the edgy energy was tempting—dark and delicious, and so unlike his normal self that he wanted to give in, just once, and see what it felt like to be ruled by the heat.

It was full night, but the moon was out, showing the three-rail fence of the paddocks and glinting off the tin-roofed run-in sheds as he rolled the car up the dirt road to the house.

"Horses?" Sydney glanced at him. "That's pretty expensive camouflage for a safe house."

"It's not a safe house," he corrected. "And there aren't any horses at the moment. Just the sheds and paddocks."

Horses were in his long-range plans, though, along with a dog. He planned to fill the place with life when it was time for him to slow down…in twenty years or so, when he retired from the job.

He'd had a pony one summer, when camp plans had fallen through and he'd been packed off to his great-uncle's place. The neighbors had a pony their kids had long outgrown, and John's great-uncle, also named John, had borrowed the creature for the summer on the theory that every kid should have a pony at least once in their lives.

The furry, stumpy creature of unknown ancestry had tossed the younger John in the dirt as often as it let him stay aboard, and it had bitten like a viper, but it'd been there every damn day, waiting for him to spend time with it, brushing and cleaning it, mucking its stall and hauling water and hay until his back had ached and his arms had quivered with the strain.

And he'd loved every minute of it. He'd loved the responsibility, and the knowledge that the pony would be there at the gate, every day, waiting for him. He hadn't had a pet in all the years since, but always figured he'd get back to it. Someday.

He parked in front of the house, which was one of his few prides outside the job. Built in the late 1700s, it'd undergone a series of expensive—and often misguided—renovations over the years before he found it through a friend of a friend, who'd seen it as a good investment and nothing more. When John bought the place, it'd been covered in vinyl siding and faux Victorian trim, and had been inexplicably painted a weird blue-green.

Slowly, layer-by-layer, he was pulling back the changes and unearthing the charm beneath.

"Whose place is this?" Sydney asked as she climbed out of the car.

John climbed out of his side and crossed to her, but he didn't feel the need to rush her inside, out of the open. They hadn't been followed, and there was no way Tiberius could connect him to the farm. He'd made sure of that when he bought the place, needing to know he had a refuge if and when it became necessary.

"It's mine," he answered, using the remote unit on his key ring to disarm the perimeter alarms, which had started counting down from sixty seconds the moment he'd turned in the driveway. Once the motion sensors and alarms were deactivated, he reached into the car and collected the pizza, along with the plastic bag containing two six-packs of soda, one regular, one diet. "Come on in."

He headed for the side entrance, aware that Sydney hung back to give the place a once-over. He tried not to care that she'd see a house not unlike her own, with a bit of age on it, and a series of careful restorations designed to preserve the charm and character.

That's it, he thought with a slice of self-directed mockery, *charm and humor.* He didn't have much in the way of either, so he left that stuff up to his farmhouse.

He used his key to let them both through the side door, and quickly tapped his code into the security pad beside the door, telling the second level of protection to stand down.

When he turned, he found Sydney standing very near him in the small entryway, eyes shadowed with speculation. "Let me guess—this place has more surveillance gadgets than the average safe house."

He raised an eyebrow. "Are you implying that I'm paranoid?"

"No." She shook her head. "Guarded, maybe, but not paranoid. Besides," she quipped, "you know what they say about paranoids having enemies." Then her voice and expression turned serious, and she reached out to touch his arm, very fleetingly, through the material of his suit jacket and shirt. "What exactly is going on here?"

But he saw the heat in her eyes, and the acquiescence, and knew she felt the chemistry between them, too. "Don't ask the question if you already know the answer."

He very carefully, very deliberately, closed the distance between them and undid the straps of the Kevlar vest. After he'd stripped it away, he leaned in to kiss her.

She met him halfway.

CHAPTER SEVEN

IT MIGHT'VE BEEN THE fear she'd lived with for so long that heated Sydney's blood and had her diving into Sharpe's kiss even though she knew it wasn't smart. It might've been loneliness that had her pressing up against him so they touched everywhere. It might've been too long spent without a man's touch, too long spent having to be in control, having to be on guard, that had her going pliant when he spun them and pressed her against the wall just inside the door.

Whatever the reasons, it was a hell of a kiss. And then some.

He filled her senses. Color and light burst behind her closed eyelids as she feasted on him, on the taste and smell of him, and the feel of his muscles beneath her fingertips. He was utterly, completely male, and as she felt him teeter on the razor-edge divide between control and wildness, she gloried in the knowledge that he felt the same way she did, needed the same thing she did.

The thought of Sharpe wanting her so badly he'd pull her out of the safe house just to have her to himself was as erotic as the kiss itself.

Blood thundered through her, knotting her muscles to needy fists as he pressed into her, grinding against her, all hard edges and raw male strength. She fought her way through the kiss, taking as much as giving, clutching his suit coat until the material crumpled beneath her grip, then letting go so she could run her hands beneath the jacket, along the crisp cotton of his shirt, and feel the man beneath.

When that wasn't enough, she gave in to the slide of his hand down her thigh and lifted both of her legs, wrapping them around his waist and hanging on for the ride.

He said something, the words coming out harsh and low, their meaning lost in another endless, soul-searching kiss. She pressed herself against him, glorying in the sensations: the rasp of late-day beard shadow along his jaw and the crisp material of his clothes and the hot, hard flesh beneath. Even the catch of her fingertips on his shoulder holster, and the hardness of the weapon itself were a turn-on. Who knew she was a sucker for a guy with a gun?

But she wasn't attracted to just any guy with a gun, Sydney knew deep inside. She was hooked on this one.

Sharpe had rescued her from Tiberius and his men. He'd sent people to help Celeste right away rather than using her sister as leverage. He was quick on his feet and even quicker with his mind; he not only kept up with her thought processes, half the time he was a step or two ahead of her. Even better, he was about a fifteen on a scale of one to hot, and he kissed like she'd fantasized he would, only better. What was not to like?

Warning bells sounded in the back of her brain, but they were quickly lost to a flare of heat as he banded a strong arm across her waist and spun away from the wall. He took two long strides—

And froze in place.

They drew apart and stared into each other's eyes,

both breathing hard. Sydney's mind spun, and she imagined his was doing pretty much the same thing.

"Wow," she said after a long, still moment. "Wow. That was…"

"Not very smart." He relaxed his grip, letting her slide down his body as he fixed his attention on the wide-open door and the security panel, which he'd never reset. "I know. You're right."

"I was thinking unexpected, actually." It wasn't really; attraction had flared between them from the first. But she needed to say something other than *Let's lock the door and head upstairs,* because he was right. What they'd just done—and what undoubtedly would have followed if they hadn't pulled back—wasn't very smart at all.

"Unexpected works, too." But his attention wasn't on her as he crossed the room, shut the door and keyed in the security code. He was staring at the night outside, scanning the scene for signs of company.

"Nothing bad happened," she said, but knew that wasn't the point. While they'd been indulging in a little one-on-one, the door had been wide open, the security field down. It was only thanks to luck and circumstance that none of Tiberius's people had been outside to take advantage of the lapse.

His look said he knew she knew better, but true to form, instead of saying something redundant or unnecessary, he stayed silent.

He moved across the living room and looked down at the pizza. He picked up a soda, then set it down again. Without looking at her, he said, "I'm sorry. I'm not normally so impulsive. This attraction…" He waved a hand between the two of them. "Chemistry. Whatever it is, it's got me off stride. I'm all jumbled up, and I'm afraid I'm going to make a mistake because of it. I thought if we spent some time together, I could…I don't know, work it out in my head or something."

Suddenly, he wasn't the aloof, polished agent who spoke in clipped, precise sentences. In his place was someone who looked as frustrated as she felt, as his body told him one thing, his head another. The realization kindled a dangerous warmth in the vicinity of her heart.

"I know what you mean. Not exactly ideal circumstances for starting a—" She broke off and, correcting herself, said, "For getting involved."

"Go ahead and say it. Starting a relationship. That's where this seems to be headed, doesn't it?" He looked at her, and she got the feeling that he was baffled, and way outside his comfort zone.

"I don't know." She took one of the sodas, not to drink but so she'd have something in her hands, something to fiddle with. "The circumstances aren't exactly normal. Once you've got Tiberius in custody and have control of the viral sequence, and Celeste and I are cleared to start rebuilding our lives—and just stay with me on the optimism here, okay?—what's to say we'll still be interested in each other? This attraction might just be a situation-and-proximity thing."

"Do you think that's what it is?" His direct gaze caught her, forcing the truth.

"No," she said softly, nearly whispering. "I don't." Hadn't she been wishing all along that they'd met under different circumstances? Hadn't she thought they would've clicked if they'd met at a bar, or a bus stop or someplace equally mundane?

"Me, neither."

They stared at each other for a long moment while the heat built and the urges deepened. Sydney's heart beat the tempo of *do it, do it, do it,* but she'd been incautious before and it'd cost her job, and put her in the position to make the wrong choice by going to work for Tiberius. She was determined not to make the wrong choice again. Not with something that felt like it could be important, if she let it be.

"We should wait," she said softly. "It's all too complicated right now."

"Yeah." He exhaled. "You're right. I know you're right."

"But…?" she asked, hearing it in his voice.

His grin went crooked. "I don't particularly want to wait."

"Me, neither," she said, echoing his earlier words. But the tension lightened and the air between them thinned, and a bubble of nervous excitement expanded in her chest, because in agreeing that they were going to wait, they'd also agreed that there was something to wait for.

She didn't know what shape it would take, or how long it would last when it did happen, but it was something to look forward to. Something that went beyond Tiberius, who had been the focus of her life for far too long.

"So what now?" She glanced at the pizza, which he'd set on the low coffee table, and the alluring length of a long leather sofa on the other side. "Should we eat? Head back to the safe house?" *Go upstairs?* she was tempted to add, but didn't because she had a feeling he'd agree if she pushed, despite both of their better intentions.

Sharpe sighed. "It's just been a long bunch of days and I don't feel like getting right back on the road. I can hack the temptation if you can."

He sat on the sofa, flipped open one of the boxes and worked a piece of pizza onto a paper plate. He set the plate on the coffee table for her, shoved a soda beside it and put together a similar setup for himself. When he was done, he stripped off his suit jacket and slung it over the arm of a nearby chair, then tossed his holstered weapon atop it.

Then, balancing his pizza on his lap, he kicked off his shoes, put his feet up and leaned back on the sofa. Letting out a long sigh, he closed his eyes.

He was inviting her to relax with him, to be with him. To get to know him in a way she had a feeling few people did.

The sight of him stripped of some of the professional hard-ass veneer fascinated her, even as the sad lines beside his eyes and mouth, which didn't smooth out even in repose, tugged at her.

Telling herself that she could handle this—that she was an adult, they were both adults—she grabbed the plate and sat down beside him.

The couch gave under her weight, sliding her even closer to his warm bulk. She struggled for all of thirty seconds before she gave in, leaned against him and let her head fall naturally against the arm he'd thrown across the back of the couch.

After a brief pause, he sighed deeply and curled his arm around her.

They ate in silence as the old house settled in for the night around them. Unwilling to talk about what was happening between them, about Tiberius, or about how he planned to use the intel she'd given his teammates, Sydney finally said, "I like your house."

"Thanks." His smile held pure pleasure, along with acknowledgment of the neutral topic. "The previous owners 'modernized' and 'improved' the heck out of it," he said, sketching the words with one-handed finger quotes. "I bought it four years ago and have been picking away at it ever since. I'm not going all the way back to original, by any means. Outhouses are so 1800s, you know. But I'm going for the period feel."

"You're nailing it." She looked around, admiring the honey-toned wainscoting and wide-pine floors. They were king's boards, she knew, so-named because they were over twelve inches wide, and thus should've been saved for export to England prior to the Revolution. The staining around the sunken nailheads indicated that the boards were original, but their unnatural smoothness and high-gloss varnish were familiar signs from her own house, as were the faint encrustations of paint at the carved edges of the wainscoting. "Let me guess, they put down wall-to-wall, added another layer of paint to the eight already on the trim and pulled down the horsehair plaster in favor of drywall."

His chuckle transmitted to her from the places where they pressed together, with her cheek on his shoulder and their torsos aligned. "There had to be a dozen layers of paint. One of them, I swear it was creosote or something. It was this nasty black color, and it took a good four rounds of paint stripper—and a couple of layers of skin—to get it off." He shuddered. "You can't imagine."

"Trust me, I can." She grinned. "Our dining room

had a quarter-inch-thick layer of this awful middle-green color, like baby vomit or something."

Deep down inside she knew she shouldn't let herself lean. But he was so warm and solid against her, the weight of his arm such a comforting drape, that she found herself weakening and settling in, letting his warmth transmit to her and ease the places that had been so cold for so long.

While she was busy convincing herself that she could handle the attraction, that she could handle *him,* she fell asleep with her head tucked into the crook of his arm and her body nestled against his.

JOHN WAS IN SERIOUS trouble.

He held her close, watched her sleep and told himself he'd dodged a bullet when they'd agreed to wait, because he'd veered way out of his comfort zone and was speeding up, heading in the wrong direction.

Despite having brought her home on a whim, a compulsion, he didn't do flings, didn't do attractions that clicked too hard and hot, relationships that made no sense when he looked at them rationally. Worse, he wasn't doing much of anything rationally at the moment. If he was, he would've left her in the safe house. He would've stayed the hell away from her until it was absolutely, positively imperative that they share space, and then he would've kept his distance, interacting with her on a purely professional level.

Instead, he was in his own damn living room, cuddled up with her like this had been a date. And not even a first date, either. Their kiss might've had the passion of a new discovery, but their inconsequential small talk had been...

Hell, he didn't know what it'd been, other than so natural he'd fallen into it before he'd had time to think it through, and then once he had, once he realized he was teetering on the brink of another decision that'd fall squarely into the 'really stupid' category, he'd been too comfortable to move. He'd wound up watching her sleep.

And in doing so, he feared he'd already come too close to falling for her.

He knew the warning signs. Hell, he'd been in that place once before, with a woman who was at once completely unlike Sydney and very like her, and in a very similar situation—one that should've taught him not to go there ever again.

So why had he?

Maybe he had a white knight complex. Yeah, he thought, that was it. The others might think him too cold and unemotional, but somewhere deep inside he had a big old rescue fantasy that played out in his choice of women. Of course, being who he was, he couldn't have a typical white knight complex, one where he fell for damsels in distress who needed a big, strong man to fix their problems. No, that would've been too easy. He had to be attracted to the ones who didn't want to be rescued. Yep, that played. He was—and had always been—all about making his own life as difficult as possible.

Which didn't do a thing to cool his ardor when Sydney made a small noise and cuddled closer.

His flesh tightened and his blood buzzed in his veins, and for a moment he imagined himself waking her up with a kiss, pulling her against him, rolling her beneath him, pressing them both into the soft, yielding sofa cushions. Worse, he could see himself with her a week from now, a month from now. He wanted to argue with her, trade barbs with her, sink himself into her and let the world go hang itself.

And none of those feelings were real, he knew. They were illusions, his own internal construct of what affection was supposed to feel like.

He'd thought he was in love once before, and had later learned it was all a lie.

"I can't do this," he whispered against her temple, his breath stirring the fine hairs that had fallen across her lovely face.

"Mmm?" She stirred against him, frowning as though fighting consciousness when fantasies were so much better.

He didn't repeat himself.

"I said it's time to get going." He nudged her awake. "If we're gone much longer, Grace is going to send SWAT out after us." That was an overstatement—he'd checked in with the computer specialist an hour ago— but they couldn't stay where they were.

His place might be safe from Tiberius, but he was quickly learning that spending time alone with Sydney carried other, equally dangerous risks.

"Come on. Rise and shine." He got her up and moving despite her sleepy protests, and loaded her in his car. She slept most of the way back to the safe house, which was a relief, but she'd begun to wake up on her own by the time they were a few miles out.

She yawned and stretched, the motion pulling her cheeky red sweater tight across her breasts in a way he couldn't force himself to ignore—especially not after having experienced her body firsthand.

Their kiss was something he feared his brain would keep on instant recall for far too long.

Jaw set, John forced himself to face front and keep driving. "You should put the Kevlar back on."

He hadn't seen any signs of pursuit, but he also wasn't taking any chances. This was Tiberius they were talking about, and the criminal businessman didn't believe in losing. He also didn't believe in loose ends.

He would come after Sydney—it was inevitable. That left it up to John and his team to try to control the when and where, and hope to hell they got it right.

He hadn't used her as bait tonight, but that didn't mean he might not be forced to do just that in the near future. The very thought of it chilled him, made him want to pull her close and promise her impossible things.

Instead, he waved to the surveillance team sitting in a darkened car on the street outside the safe house as he drove past, and hit the button to open the door of the safe house's attached garage.

He'd phoned Grace from the road to check that everything was status quo, and had gotten the all-clear. He called through again once they were in the garage, using the prearranged signal, and got the proper counterpassword in return, indicating that it was safe to bring Sydney inside.

"Come on." He didn't draw his weapon, but stayed close to her on the way into the house, just in case. Once they were inside he took the lead, heading for the kitchen. "Grace hinted earlier that she was closing in on something. Maybe she's got something that'll—"

He broke off at the sight that confronted him.

Impressions came to him in strobe-quick flashes:

Grace bound to a kitchen chair, head lolling in a drug-induced stupor, her computer trashed and two thugs standing behind her, weapons at the ready.

Before John could react, one of them shot Grace in the temple, execution-style.

Grace! John had his gun in his hand seconds later and opened fire, his brain short-circuiting on rage and sick horror as his teammate collapsed sideways, her mouth askew, her eyes glazing in death.

His first bullet caught Grace's murderer in the upper chest, spinning the gunman away from her and sending him to his knees in a spray of blood. The second guy ducked and bolted out of the kitchen and through the back door.

For a second John was torn between his imperative to guard his protectee, and the all-consuming need to gun down the bastard who'd just killed his teammate.

Then he heard something that made the decision for him: the crash of breaking glass sounded in the front room, followed by a thump and the sound of a metal object rolling across the hardwood floor.

Grenade, his brain supplied. He didn't know if it was a flash-bang or gas, but he wasn't sticking around to find out.

Walling the grief and shock off in a small corner of his consciousness, he snapped to agent mode, processing and rejecting his available choices. He didn't dare go out the kitchen door; it was a sure bet the second gunman would be waiting, his need to finish the job no doubt fueled by the knowledge of what had happened to the last pair of killers to fail Tiberius.

That really left only one option: they had to go down.

In a reflex arc that didn't even make it to his brain

before he was on the move, John grabbed Sydney and dragged her across the kitchen, past Grace and the small blood pool gathering beneath her chair. He yanked open the door that led to the basement. "Come on!"

The lights flickered on the moment the door opened, showing a set of plain wooden stairs. He charged down them, hauling Sydney along as the seconds ticked down in his head.

Behind and above him, there were more thump-roll sounds, followed by the boom of a flash-bang stun grenade, the powerful noise muted by walls and distance.

It wasn't the flash-bangs that had him moving fast, though. He had to assume the additional sounds were gas canisters. It only made sense, because Tiberius didn't want to blow Sydney up; he wanted her alive, and in his power.

And that so wasn't going to happen if John had anything to say about it. Heart hammering in his ears, jaw set in determination, he had only one goal right now: to get Sydney out alive.

After that, it was war.

The basement was a cement cube containing a furnace and water heater but none of the usual basement clutter, because nobody actually lived in the safe house year-round. In addition to the electrical panel and other basement stuff, there was a door set in the wall opposite the furnace. John yanked it open, revealing a low, cement-lined tunnel.

The air in the basement had already started to turn with the first whiff of the gas, suggesting that Tiberius's men were using one of the newer cocktails, which readily diffused down, as well as up. Worse, footsteps sounded from above, indicating that the men had donned masks rather than waiting for the air to clear. Any moment now, they'd figure out that their quarry had gone to ground.

Muffled shouts and the quickening tramp overhead signaled they already had.

"Go!" John pushed Sydney ahead of him. Once they were both inside the tunnel, he yanked the heavy door shut and spun the lock, then urged her along the tunnel ahead of him. "Hurry!"

He was less worried about the men following through the tunnel, and more worried that they'd quickly figure out where it led.

The lights had come up when he'd opened the door. The thin fluorescent strips, which were hung on either side of the low cement tunnel, lit the way as they scrambled along. They had to crouch down, bent nearly double as they moved as fast as they could on their feet, hands, knees, whatever part of them could keep the forward momentum going.

Sydney didn't say a word, just kept going as the walls closed in on them and the air started to carry a whiff of gas that had John's head spinning. Her jaw was set, her skin very pale and he had a feeling her brain was jammed—as was his—on the sight of Grace tied to a kitchen chair, shot dead with a bullet in her brain.

How in the hell had that happened?

He'd checked in regularly. Hell, he'd even checked in from the garage. What had gone wrong? How had Tiberius found the safe house? How had his men gotten past the security system, and the surveillance teams who were supposed to be keeping watch from the outside?

Knowing that the others teams might also be dead, John felt his heart chill in his chest, felt something wither up and die within him. He stumbled and went down, the gas-tainted fumes sapping his strength, but he forced himself to struggle up and keep going, shoving Sydney ahead of him.

"There should be a door," he said, hearing his breath rattle in his lungs.

"I don't—" she said weakly, then gave a low cry. "There's a turn up ahead. Maybe that's it."

It wasn't, but once they made the turn they could see the door at the end of the tunnel, which sloped slightly upward until it ended in a metal slab that was twin to the one they'd entered through. Shuffling in their awkward crouches, laboring to suck tainted air into their cramped lungs, they hurried to the door. Sydney fumbled to unlock it, and for a frozen second John feared it was jammed on the other side, that Tiberius's men had already beaten them to the neighboring house, which was also owned by the government for use as a safe house and as an escape route.

"Got it!" She finally got the lock open, twisted the handle and moved to shove open the door.

"Wait." John grabbed her. "Me first." He couldn't let them make a foolish mistake in the mad rush to escape the bad air. Crowding past her so he led the way, weapon at the ready, he tried to gather his scrambled brain cells and cracked open the door.

For a second there was nothing but blackness. Then the swing of the door triggered the basement lights and they clicked on to reveal…nothing.

The basement was as empty as the one they'd just left. Even better, he didn't detect movement on the floor above, and the air was clean, though faintly humid with typical cellar dampness.

"Come on." Moving fast, he got her out of the tunnel and shut the door, then crossed to the stairs. He put a finger to his lips to caution silence, and they crept up the stairs with him in the lead and her breathing down the back of his neck, both of them trying not to make a sound.

Tension hummed through him. Fear, not that he'd be hurt—that was part of the job description—but that he might not be quick enough or good enough to keep the woman behind him safe.

He'd failed Grace. He didn't want to fail Sydney.

Tightening his grip on his weapon, he paused at the top of the stairs and flicked off the lights.

Sydney stiffened behind him. For a second he thought it was because of the darkness, or the shock settling in to her system. Then he heard it, too.

Footsteps.

He had a split second to consider his options, which were seriously slim. They couldn't go back into the tunnel because of the foul air, and because Tiberius's men could block them in from either end. There was another way out of the basement—a set of stairs leading to a traditional bulkhead—but odds were good that if Tiberius's people had discovered the second empty house, they had the grounds covered, too. That left him with going through the house itself.

The layout was identical to that of the house Sydney had been staying in, the furniture and placement nearly identical, as well. The footsteps were coming from the left of their current position. To the right, there should be a short hallway that dead-ended in a bathroom, with a spare room to the right. To the left of the basement door, there was another entryway leading to the kitchen, which ran the length of the back of the house.

The only thing that was different about the two houses was the garage placement. The first house had an attached garage on the left from the street-level perspective. The second had an almost identical garage, but on the right.

It was, perhaps, their one advantage.

Thinking fast, John put his lips very near Sydney's ear, and breathed, "When I open the door I want you to turn right and head through the kitchen. There's a door next to the refrigerator—go through it, and close and lock it behind you. You'll be in the garage. There should be a car in there. The keys are under the visor, along with the door remote. Get out of here." He palmed his cell phone and handed it to her. "I'll call you when it's over."

"But—"

"Don't," he interrupted. "Don't try to be a hero or back me up or anything. You'll just be in the way."

He could see the arguments in her eyes, could see the indecision, the desire to be brave warring with basic self-preservation. "Okay," she said finally. Then she turned her face so her lips touched his. "Please be careful."

The brief kiss shouldn't have warmed him, shouldn't have soothed him, shouldn't have mattered to him. But because it did warm and soothe and matter, he drew back, going for cool and in control when his heart was hammering in his chest.

"Take care of yourself," he said urgently. "Keep driving until I call—stay on busy roads where people can see you. If the men see you and follow you out, they'll be more likely to hang back if there are witnesses." He hoped. Right then, it was the best he could do.

She nodded, then stiffened.

Beyond the door, the footsteps drew closer and then hesitated, as though their owner had seen the light beneath the basement door.

John took three quick breaths, steadied himself to kill and opened the door.

He swung out and to the left, weapon at the ready, while Sydney broke right and ran for her life.

CHAPTER EIGHT

SYDNEY LUNGED DOWN to the hallway and through the kitchen, heart hammering in her ears and breath whistling in her lungs. Her legs shook with fear and adrenaline, but she forced them to carry her. Nearly sobbing with fear, she yanked open the door to the garage and plunged through.

She skidded to a halt.

The garage door was open. A man stood silhouetted in the opening, waiting for her.

A scream locked her throat, driving the breath from her body, and all she could think was that Tiberius had found her. He'd take her somewhere, torture her and then kill her once she gave up the password. It was over. Her mistakes had come home to damn her.

"No!" she screamed, refusing to believe, refusing to give in. She scrambled back through the kitchen door and into the house, bolting toward Sharpe as if he could help her, as if he could—

"Sydney!" a voice called from behind her. "Wait up! It's okay!"

She'd barely processed the words when she slammed into Sharpe coming the other way.

He let out an *oof* of surprise but weathered the impact, and his arms came up to hold her tight, to keep her from running. "It's okay," he said, echoing the other man's reassurance. "They're the good guys."

He had to repeat the words several times before they penetrated her overwrought brain. When they did, when she actually looked around herself and saw SWAT garb and badges, the fight went out of her like someone had yanked her plug, cutting off her power.

She sagged against Sharpe and burst into tears.

He caught her automatically, but there was little warmth in the embrace, as though he didn't want the others to see, didn't want them to guess at the relationship that might—or might not—be developing between them.

"Sorry." She drew away, sniffing mightily and swiping at her eyes.

"You're entitled." But his voice and expression were cool, making him look like an entirely different person than the one she'd been with the night before. This was Special Agent Sharpe, not the man she'd cuddled with on his couch.

"Sorry," she said again, backing off, then again, inanely, "I'm sorry."

She didn't even know precisely what she was apologizing for, except that all of this was her fault. Tiberius's men had come because of her. Grace had—

"Oh, God." Her eyes widened and she lifted her hands to her mouth to hold in the surge of emotion and bile that slapped at her the moment she thought of what had happened in the other house, all because of her. *"Grace!"*

"Yeah, I know." A flare of emotion crossed Sharpe's face, regret and pain and anger, but instead of moving toward Sydney in comfort, he took a step away. He gestured to two of the SWAT members. "Escort her to your van, please, and keep her there until I come for her."

"Yes, sir." They didn't salute, but they might as well have, because they snapped into action and hustled her down the hallway to the side door, and from there to the street, forcing her to keep her head down and move fast as they surrounded her with their bodies.

Sydney caught a glimpse of curious onlookers gathering in a range of nightwear and at-home casual clothes. Both of the safe houses were ablaze with light, and the first house bristled with the mechanics of murder—officers and evidence techs, and the other members of Sharpe's team, their faces etched with shock and grief, horror and rage.

I did this, Sydney thought, going numb to her soul. She hadn't wielded the hammer that'd broken Jenny Marie's fingers and she hadn't shoved the young woman off an island cliff. She hadn't pulled the trigger of the weapon that had killed Danielle and Jay. She hadn't pumped Grace full of whatever drug had loosened her enough to provide Sharpe with the "all clear" password when the situation had been far from all clear, and she hadn't shot Grace in the temple.

But ultimately she was responsible for all those things. Tiberius was sending her the same message he'd sent her once before: *don't mess with me or I'll destroy the things you care about.*

She'd gotten Celeste out of his reach—God willing—but that hadn't stopped him from killing Grace, the only woman Sydney had been friendly with since Jenny Marie's death. Which meant anyone else she was even the slightest bit close to was in terrible danger.

"Step up," said one of the SWAT team members, a

fortysomething guy with salt-shot dark hair and kind-seeming gray eyes.

Sydney blanked. "What?"

He indicated the SWAT van. "Climb in. You'll be safe in here while we get the scene secure."

"Oh. Right." She climbed aboard and found herself in a utilitarian rear compartment with sideways-facing bench seats and racks and lockers holding a variety of equipment. But as she sat on the long, uncomfortable metal bench, she realized he'd been right, whether he'd meant it that way or not. She needed to step up and start taking responsibility for her actions.

Jenny Marie had died because Sydney had used her to get information to Celeste. Danielle and Jay had died because she hadn't been smart enough when she escaped, hadn't been quick enough at getting them help. Grace had died because she hadn't given the team enough to go on, enough to justify a raid and an arrest. Four people were dead, indirectly because of her.

Sydney dropped her face into her hands. It was too much to bear.

"Hey."

Recognizing Sharpe's voice, she looked up quickly. Despite everything else, despite the situation and the danger, and the horror she'd just endured, a little jolt of electricity sped her heartbeat at the sight of him standing in the open van doors, staring at her.

His dark hair was mussed, his jaw heavily shadowed with stubble, and he still had his discarded tie wadded up in the pocket of his tired-looking button-down shirt. Beneath the gray suit jacket she could see the straps of his shoulder holster, which he'd put back on before they left his house.

He looked sexy as hell, and lethally cold. She'd never realized before how much of a turn-on the combination could be until she'd met him. Until she'd kissed him and realized that the agent's cool exterior camouflaged a warm, caring man. One she liked and trusted.

One she wanted. And that was a big problem, because if Tiberius had known about the safe house, and about Grace, then he knew about Sharpe, as well.

Which meant the agent was as much—if not more—of a target than she was.

I'll kill them, Tiberius was saying. *I'll kill the people around you, and I'll keep killing them until you give me the password.*

"Hey," she said, smiling faintly. "I'm glad you—"

"I just wanted to get my phone," he cut in. "Then I've got to get back to work."

I wasn't going to get mushy, she wanted to say, but there were other people around, so she didn't. Instead, picking her words carefully, she said, "Did something else happen I should know about?"

She didn't think his banked anger was all about Grace and the attack on the safe house. Not that he didn't have a right to be angry about those things, but this anger seemed more specific. More directed at her, like she'd done something truly terrible.

He looked at her and she nearly shivered at the contempt in his expression. "Don't bother. The game's up."

Her blood chilled in her veins. "What game? What's going on?" She reached out to touch him but he moved away. "What are you talking about?"

He looked at her long and hard, and she couldn't read a thing from his expression. Finally, he said, "Grace managed to get a message off to Jimmy before they

grabbed her. It turns out I was right. There was someone on the inside working for Tiberius. It just wasn't
who I suspected it would be."

He pulled a folded sheet of paper from the inner
pocket of his suit coat and passed it to her.

Heart thundering in her ears, Sydney unfolded the
page and scanned the contents. It was an email message, sent from a Hotmail account she didn't recognize. She recognized the destination, though. It was
one of the accounts held by Tiberius Corp. One of the
ones she'd used during their early negotiations about
her coming to work on the island.

The message was simple and damning. It gave the
location of the safe house and the positions of the surveillance teams, ending with *I trust you'll live up to
your end of the bargain.* It was signed with the same
initials that were in the Hotmail address: SEW.

Sydney Ellen Westlake.

Her fingers went numb and the paper fluttered to
the floor of the SWAT van. "I didn't send that message.
That isn't my email account."

"What was the deal?" he said, as though he hadn't
heard her. Or maybe he'd heard her and had already
judged her and found her guilty. The utter disgust in
his expression certainly suggested as much.

His mistrust cut Sydney straight to the quick. So
much for them being on the same page regarding the
attraction between them. If he was this ready to believe
the worst of her, then he wasn't the man she'd thought
he was.

Anger flared. Hurt. Confusion. "Where is this
coming from?" she said softly. "Why won't you listen?
I've done everything you've asked. I'm cooperating."

"Yes, but with whom?" He retrieved the paper, reread the contents. His voice was coldly conversational when he said, "What did he promise you? Freedom? Safety? Access to your records so you could complete the cure for your sister? More money than you could spend in this lifetime?"

"He already promised me all that," Sydney snapped, anger coming to the forefront. "And I still took my life into my own hands and escaped from the island because I refused to be involved in building a bioweapon."

"All evidence to the contrary." He folded the paper and returned it to his pocket.

"It's a fake." Her volume increased, earning curious looks from outside the van. "I'm telling you, I didn't write the email. It's not my account!"

"Grace checked that. The message traced back to the IP address on her laptop at the safe house." He paused. "What did you do, wait until she was asleep and sneak access? How'd you get around the firewalls? Something your sister taught you?"

"I didn't," she said miserably, anger losing steam as the heartache built. "I didn't sneak Grace's computer to email Tiberius and I sure as hell didn't tell him where the safe house was located. I didn't." Her shoulders sagged. "I swear. You have to believe me."

But there was no belief in his cold blue eyes, no compassion. And there was no hesitation when he turned and walked away.

JOHN STOOD ON THE SIDELINES while the evidence techs did their thing in the kitchen where Grace had died. He knew his strengths, and crime scene reconstruction wasn't one of them. Besides, he didn't need to reconstruct a damn thing. He'd been there. He'd witnessed it.

He couldn't get the sight of Grace's face out of his head, even after the techs had bagged and tagged the body and transported it away from the scene. John had lost team members before—life-threatening danger was, unfortunately, part of the job description in the major crimes unit—but he'd never before been up close and personal with premeditated murder during the actual act.

She'd been executed not ten feet away from him, which made it impossible for him not to think about what he should've done differently, and there, the answer was simple.

He should never have left the scene with Sydney. He shouldn't have taken her home, shouldn't have spent time with her alone when he could've been working instead.

While he and Sydney had been cuddling on the couch, Tiberius's hired guns had been taking out the surveillance teams—drugging them rather than killing them, thankfully—and subduing Grace. While he and Sydney had been driving back to the safe house, Tiberius's men had bound Grace and pumped her full of God only knew what for questioning.

She would've held out as long as she could, and when she broke under the combination of chemicals and interrogation—maybe worse, he didn't know yet—she would've given them as little as possible.

He hoped like hell she'd been too far gone to realize she'd given the countersigns that would lead him into the trap. He hated thinking that she'd died knowing she'd failed her team leader.

It's okay, Grace, he said inside his own skull, in case her spirit lingered nearby, or maybe because he needed to say it for himself.

Only it wasn't okay. It was far from okay.

How had he not known Sydney was still in contact with Tiberius? He should've sensed that was where her head was at, should've known she'd try something like this.

History repeated. Back at the university where she'd worked before, she'd tried to pressure the administration to reinstate her funding by accusing her ex-lover of stealing some of her work. Combine that with her decision to work with Tiberius despite knowing at least something of what he was, and there was a pattern of unaccountability. Why had he thought she'd changed?

Because you wanted her, his baser self said. And damn it, that part of him was right. He'd overlooked the history because after watching her with her sister, he'd convinced himself she'd done what she'd done out of love, and because she'd felt like she was out of other options. That didn't make it right, but it was understandable to a point.

But this...this was inexcusable. Unforgivable.

"Hey." Jimmy Oliverra came up beside John, gave him a nod and took position beside him, leaning back against the wall in a section of kitchen that'd already been processed for evidence. "They saying anything yet?"

Jimmy was the major crime unit's secondary—and now, John supposed, their primary—computer whiz. He'd spent the most time of any of them working shoulder-to-shoulder with Grace, and the grief showed in his eyes and the deep lines beside his mouth. He was a professional, though. He'd soldier on despite—or perhaps because of—the emotions.

John knew he needed to do the same, and it rattled him to know he needed the reminder.

You're the Iceman, he told himself. *Pull it together.*

"They haven't found anything we didn't already know or guess," he said, answering Jimmy's question about the evidence techs. "And we're not going to change that by sitting here and staring at them." He turned for the door. "Let's go."

Jimmy hesitated. "Can I have a minute? I'd like to… you know, say goodbye."

John didn't bother pointing out that they'd already transported the body. He nodded. "Make it quick."

AN HOUR LATER, THE MAJOR crimes unit was assembled in a conference room deep within Quantico. Sydney was in a "guest" room down the hall, with a locked door that assured she was going nowhere until John was good and ready for her to leave.

He'd had it with working around her. This time, she was going to give them everything, or he'd nail her with obstruction, conspiracy and whatever else he could think of.

"She's got immunity," Jimmy reminded him when he muttered something to that effect.

John glared. "Not anymore she doesn't. That email voids the immunity agreement. Period."

There was silence from the four teammates assembled around the table. Jimmy sat next to John. On the other side sat sharpshooter Michael Pelotti and Drew Dietz, their evidence specialist. There was an empty chair between Drew and Michael, where Grace would've sat.

John felt her loss keenly. She'd been the one to sometimes soften his rough edges, the one who'd challenged him to tread the middle ground.

Then again, the middle ground had gotten them where they were now. Maybe it was time for a take-no-prisoners type of approach.

"She might be telling the truth," Michael said, his tone thoughtful, like the man himself. Dark and lean, the sharpshooter spoke the way he fired—smoothly and deliberately. "Tiberius is clever. If he figured out he could use Sydney to put you off your game, he'd do it in a heartbeat."

"I'm not off my game," John growled. "I'm fine."

But Michael had known him a long time, longer than the others. "I don't think she's working for him, to be honest. I just don't see it. Think about it for a second—Tiberius could have looked into your background, found out about the other incident and figured a fake email implicating Sydney would be a good way to push your buttons. Even if it didn't, he could be assured you'd throw out her intel the moment you suspected she was still working for him. That'd push back any plan for raiding the island. Maybe that was his goal."

"You're giving him too much credit," John said. But he couldn't totally dismiss the possibility. First, because he trusted Michael as much as he trusted anyone, and the sharpshooter was leaning toward Sydney's side, and second because, damn it, despite his knee-jerk fury when he'd first seen the email, the more time passed the less likely he found the whole scenario.

Sydney had said it herself. She'd risked her life

to lock down her work and escape from Rocky Cliff Island. With her sister safe and an immunity deal in place, what leverage could possibly compel her to accept another offer from Tiberius? She knew what happened to his loose ends. There was no way she would've believed he'd let her walk away once it was all over.

Which suggested she was innocent—of the email, at least.

"So what's the plan?" Jimmy asked. There were deep shadows beneath the computer tech's eyes, and his shoulders sagged under the weight of his grief. The youngest and newest member of the group, he hadn't experienced the loss of a teammate before, and Grace's death had hit him hard.

"Whether or not the email is a fake," John said, trying to reorient his brain and make a new set of decisions on the fly, "and I'm not willing to say one way or the other right now, it was good enough to fool Grace. It should be enough to get permission for a raid, especially coupled with the other intel we've managed to accumulate."

That got everyone's attention. Michael said carefully, "What other intel?" His real question was obvious: Why didn't we know about it?

John spread his hands. "Sorry for the secrecy, but this was really need-to-know stuff from one of the other teams working Tiberius." And he wasn't the only one who suspected there was a leak, not in his team, but somewhere higher up the chain of command. The team leaders were keeping a very tight hold on their information as the case developed.

"And?" Jimmy prompted.

John said, "There's been some serious chatter between the island and reps of four other major players."
He named three of the country's ranking mob bosses
and a wealthy importer who specialized in drugs from
south of the border. All four had recently been indicted
and were awaiting trial, three for murder, one for rape.

All four of the cases hinged on DNA evidence.

Michael whistled. "He's lining up his buyers. Does
that mean he's cracked the computers?"

"Unknown." John scrubbed his hands across his face
and heard stubble rasp.

Exhaustion beat at him. He'd been up for... Hell, he'd
lost track of how long it'd been since he last slept. He
needed to rest; they all did. But there was no way he
was letting Tiberius get away with what he appeared
to be planning.

"I've looked at the programs," Jimmy said, making
a visible effort to focus on the conversation. "They're
good. Better than good, even. But they're not uncrackable."

"Could you break them?" Michael asked.

"Under a deadline? Fifty-fifty," Jimmy said. "But
given enough time and firepower, yeah. I think I
could."

"So if he's contacting buyers, odds are that he thinks
his people are close to breaking the code," John said.

"Or he was counting on getting his hands on Sydney
during tonight's attack," Michael countered.

In the ensuing pause, Drew spoke up. "Not to be a
total buzzkill, but how do you know he doesn't already
have Sydney's viral vector? What if he was contacting
the buyers to set up payment and drop points?"

John shook his head automatically. "He doesn't have

the bug yet. If he did, he would've left Rocky Cliff. There's no way he's staying there long-term. He's too vulnerable there. We know too much about the defenses, and he knows we…" He trailed off, realizing what he'd just said. "Oh, hell."

The logic played, which meant Tiberius didn't have the bug…and Sydney hadn't sent the email.

If she were working with Tiberius again, and had asked him to break her out of the safe house, then she would've already given him the password. He wouldn't have committed his forces without that assurance.

Ergo, Sydney hadn't sent the email. Somebody else within the organization had done so.

And he'd refused to listen to her claims of innocence. Like the cold SOB they called him, he'd automatically assumed the worst of her.

"Is it possible to send something from one computer and make it look like it came from another?" he asked Jimmy.

The tech didn't even hesitate, as though he'd been thinking along the same lines. "Yes, if you use one of those remote uplink programs, the ones that let you dial in to your home computer and use your own on-screen desktop and stuff from a remote location. It's conceivable that someone could hack in and send an email that looked like it came from Grace's laptop, under a Hotmail account they'd set up using Sydney's initials, without ever touching the machine."

"Which could mean this doesn't involve anyone on the inside," Michael observed.

"Not necessarily." John tried to talk himself out of it, but couldn't see any other way. "There has to be someone working for Tiberius, not on the team or surveillance, necessarily, but somewhere in the network. There's no other way he could've known not only the address of the safe house, but also the surveillance posts. Also, they knew they needed to get a second counterpassword from Grace. There's no way they would've known that without a heads-up. I just can't see Grace volunteering the info, regardless of what hell they put her through. She was too good an agent for that."

There was a moment of uncomfortable silence before Drew said, "So what's the plan?"

"I can only see one choice," John said finally. "We can't risk Tiberius getting the bug into circulation. We're going to have to raid the island."

"Think you can get it sanctioned?" Michael asked.

"More or less," John answered. "I'll call in a few favors, collect an insertion team I trust and get permission on the hush-hush. I can't help thinking if we do this all the way through official channels, Tiberius is going to be a step ahead of us the whole way through." He paused. "We might even think of filtering some misinformation through a few channels, and see what comes back. It'd give us an idea where the leak is coming from."

Jimmy nodded. "Drew and I will come up with some suggestions."

Michael, who was the muscle of the group, and the one with the most combat training, said, "Give me names and I'll get with the insertion team." He paused. "Are we using the intel from Sydney?"

John nodded. "Yeah. Use it. Get back to me with any questions." He paused. "Anything else?"

There were negative head shakes all around.

"Okay." John stood, body as tense as if he were going into battle. "I'll be back in a few minutes. I owe Sydney an apology."

AFTER AN HOUR OR SO sitting alone in the drab conference room, Sydney's tears had dried and she'd stripped out of the heavy, uncomfortable Kevlar vest. She folded it and used it as a pillow as she tried to nap while leaning on the conference table, but the bulletproof vest didn't rank very high in the comfort department and she couldn't calm her brain enough for sleep.

Every time she closed her eyes she saw Grace's face. And when she wasn't picturing the murder, she was imagining handcuffs and a jail cell, because there was no doubt in her mind that was where she was headed next. If Sharpe believed she'd sent that email, he wouldn't hesitate to tear up the immunity agreement.

The more she thought about it, the more she was convinced that was what was going to happen next. So much so that when the door swung open, she shot to her feet, expecting cops with handcuffs and chains.

It wasn't the cops. It was Sharpe.

Her first thought was that he looked tired, her second that even tired, he looked incredible. And the latter made her angry, because how dare he look so good when she was miserable, and how dare her body still react to him when he'd just proved he'd always think the worst of her, despite her protests to the contrary.

She lifted her chin and glared at him. "I. Did. Not. Send. That. Email."

"I know," he said quietly. "I'm sorry I didn't listen to you before."

It took her a second to process the words, longer to

comprehend their meaning. When she did, the images of handcuffs and chains vanished and she collapsed into her chair. "You know?" The question came out small and quivery, but on the heels of relief came a flare of anger. She regained her feet. "Well, good. And you *should* be sorry. You should've believed me. You can't say you're interested in me one minute, and then think the worst of me in the next. It's not fair."

She half expected him to tell her it was all off, that he'd rethought the idea of them being together and decided it was a bad idea, that he didn't want her enough to deal with the complications. And in a way that might've been a relief, because it'd take the decision out of her hands and give her a reason to hate him instead of wishing for things that seemed impossible.

But instead of saying it was over before it'd even begun, he spun one of the chairs so it faced hers, and sat, gesturing for her to do the same.

When she was seated, he said, "You're absolutely right—I should have listened to you, and I shouldn't have jumped to conclusions."

She regarded him warily. "What changed your mind?"

"We—well, Jimmy and Michael, really—stepped back and looked at that email, and finally figured out that the logic doesn't add up. Someone—most likely Tiberius or someone working for him—was trying to make you look guilty in order to complicate things at this end."

She wrinkled her nose. "Gee, you think?"

He exhaled. "I should probably explain what happened back there." He paused. "I was involved a few years ago…with someone who was part of a case."

That was so not what she'd been expecting, that it took her a moment to reorient. She also had to breathe past a hot knot of something that wasn't quite anger, wasn't quite jealousy. When she'd settled the uneasy churn in her gut, she said, "Grace mentioned that you'd been involved with a witness."

"A witness." He grimaced. "I guess that's an accurate term, albeit a kind one. Her name was Rose." He paused, and for a moment she didn't think he was going to keep going. Then, as though reaching a decision, he exhaled a long breath. "We'd been working as part of a multi-agency task force trying to bring down a major criminal working out of Boston. His name was Viggo Trehern, and he was seriously bad news. The task force had managed to get three people on the inside pretty early on—a woman who went under as Trehern's mistress, the doctor who handled his addiction to prescription meds and one of his enforcers. It wasn't my call, but none of them knew about the others, so when it went bad, it went bad fast. The woman died, the doctor's cover was broken and the enforcer dropped out of sight for a while. We needed another way in."

"Rose," Sydney said. It wasn't a question.

He nodded. "Rose. It was my job to find the weak link. I did my homework, and picked the most likely candidate for turning. She'd been Tiberius's lover, but was a good enough cook that when he got tired of her in his bed, he kept her in the kitchen. We watched her for a few weeks, got her patterns down, and I arranged to bump into her at a nightclub near the theater district."

"You seduced her to get her on your side?" Sydney said, suddenly not liking this story at all.

"No." He shook his head in an emphatic negative.

"We were friends, nothing more. She was a good person stuck in a bad situation, and I gave her a way out. A deal. Immunity for information."

Sydney's stomach did a nasty little shimmy. "Suddenly this is sounding way too familiar."

"I know. I'm sorry." He paused. "Her tips were good, and suddenly we were making more progress against Trehern than we'd ever managed before. After a few smaller takedowns, the task force leaders trusted her—I trusted her—and based on her information, we planned to close the net on Trehern for good. There was no way we were letting him wiggle out this time. We had everything sewn up tight. I thought—" He broke off and grimaced. "We had talked about after, about there maybe being a future for us."

The shimmy edged toward full-on nausea at the parallels. "Go on."

"It probably doesn't take a brilliant research scientist to guess she double-crossed me...us. She'd been working for Trehern all along, feeding us whatever tidbits of information he wanted us to have, leading us straight into a trap. If it weren't for the one remaining guy we had on the inside, the enforcer, William Caine, the whole thing would've gone to hell. As it was, I lost two good men and the total casualty count in the task force was in the dozens. We got Trehern, but the cost was high. Too high."

And he blamed himself for the deaths, Sydney realized. As far as he was concerned, those agents had died because he'd trusted the wrong woman.

The knowledge definitely helped explain his reaction to the phony email. But just as definitely, it set off serious warning bells. "I've got to tell you, I'm a little freaked out by the similarities."

"Trust me, you're not the only one."

"Did you…" She paused, trying to figure out what she really wanted to know. "Did you feel the same way about her that you feel about me?"

He took her hands in his. "God help me, I don't know the answer to that."

It wasn't what she'd wanted to hear. But one thing she knew about him was that he'd never tell her what she wanted to hear, just for the sake of placating her.

At the moment, his honesty was cold comfort.

"I wasn't brought up with a whole lot of affection," he continued, "and this isn't exactly a job that encourages touchy-feeliness. Rose brought out something in me that I wasn't used to. Something I liked. And yes, you make me feel some of the same things, but it's different. *You're* different."

"Right. Because I'm not still working for Tiberius."

He squeezed her hands in his and moved closer still. "It's more than that. You're…more of a whole person than Rose was. You're out there, making things happen. Not always the right thing, granted, but you're trying to fix what you did wrong. I admire that, even if I don't always agree with your methods."

"Was there a compliment in there somewhere?" Sydney asked. "I couldn't tell." But she felt herself softening.

She told herself not to forgive him this easily, but she could already tell it was a losing battle. He believed her. Wasn't that enough?

"Yeah." His chuckle sounded tired. "I think so. There should've been, anyway." He crowded closer, still holding her hands. Their knees bumped together and his eyes were very close to hers, and if she'd wanted to—if she'd been ready to after what'd just happened between them—she could've leaned in and kissed him.

But she didn't. She couldn't. Not after what had just happened, what she'd just learned.

"Can I trust you not to knee-jerk believe the worst of me again?" she asked quietly. "I don't want to be involved in…whatever this is, if I'm going to be constantly on the defensive. Is it enough for me to tell you, here and now, that I'm on your side? That I won't do anything to compromise you or the team?"

"Even if it means destroying your work on the island?" he countered.

She closed her eyes on a flash of pain, but nodded. "Even if that's what it means." Opening her eyes, she stared into his, willing him to believe her. "Celeste did okay without me. Better than okay, really. If she has to wait another year or two for me to scrape up the funding and replicate the work, I think she can manage it. If not…" She trailed off, hating the idea of giving up on Celeste's life, but knowing this was a battle she might not win, after all. "If not, she'd be the first one to tell me I can't give in to someone like Tiberius in order to save her. The evil he brings to the world is too big for that. We can't weigh it against one life, no matter how much I want to."

He'd watched her intently while she spoke, and now nodded. "Okay."

She paused, waiting for more. "That's it? Just 'okay'?"

"You want a marching band?" But he leaned in, and touched his lips to hers. "I'm sorry," he whispered against her mouth. "I won't assume the worst of you again."

She leaned into his warmth and whispered in return, "Thank you."

They stayed like that for a moment, each drawing strength from the other. Then she drew back. "What happens now?"

He looked her in the eye and said, "Within the next two days, my team and a few handpicked combat veterans are going to raid the island in an effort to prevent Tiberius from selling the bug to four very nasty people who are in the middle of four different trials with pivotal DNA evidence."

She appreciated that he'd trusted her with the information so soon after their tentative truce. But she frowned when the information didn't quite line up. "If the trials are already in progress, they've already got the DNA evidence. Infecting the defendants won't change anything."

"It will if they also arrange to lose, destroy or otherwise taint the existing DNA samples, necessitating the drawing of new samples," he countered. "And trust me, they will."

She looked at him for a long moment. "You don't live in a very nice world, do you?"

He seemed surprised by the question, shrugged it off. "I'm used to the scumbags. They don't get to me anymore."

I think they do, she contradicted inwardly. *You just try very hard not to show it.* Iceman, indeed. It wasn't that he didn't feel the emotions, she was coming to realize. It was that he didn't know what to do with them, so he shoved them deep down inside and pretended they didn't exist.

But she didn't think he needed—or wanted—to hear that right now, so she said instead, "Be careful on the island. It's not a very nice place."

In fact, the thought of him going to Rocky Cliff chilled her to her very marrow. She wanted to tell him not to go, but she didn't have the right. It was his job. His duty.

And he wouldn't have had to go if it hadn't been for her stupidly arrogant decisions a year ago, she knew.

"I need you," he said unexpectedly, and for a moment she thought he was finished, that he was talking about the two of them. But then he said, "The team needs you. Anything else you can tell us about Rocky Cliff, we need to know it. Anything at all." When she didn't answer right away, he squeezed her hands. "Please, Sydney."

"Don't make me go back there." A whisper was all she could manage.

"No!" He nearly shouted the word. "Hell, no. You're strictly behind-the-scenes on this one. Intel only. Okay?"

"Yeah." She nodded. "Okay. When do we start?"

He stood, drawing her to her feet. "We just did."

CHAPTER NINE

TWENTY HOURS LATER, Sydney was back on the north shore of Massachusetts, where it all began.

The team stayed in a large chain hotel farther down the coast rather than the quaint Gloucester B and B she'd used the last night before she'd departed for Rocky Cliff Island a year earlier, but that difference hardly mattered.

She leaned on the railing of the small, beach-facing deck that opened off her room and sighed, feeling as though she was right back where she'd started.

The ocean stretched to the horizon, where gray water met gray sky. It was chilly and faintly damp, and the beach was deserted save for a young man throwing a tennis ball for a wet, sand-covered black dog. In the adjoining rooms on either side of hers, Sharpe and his teammates were nailing down last-minute details. Knowing it, she should've felt surrounded and protected.

Instead, she felt very alone, just as she'd felt the last time she'd been here.

Then, as now, she wasn't sure what the future was going to hold for her. Then, as now, she was making decisions she wasn't sure were right.

A year ago, she'd been working to convince herself that the ends justified the means, that it was okay to work for a man like Tiberius if the final results would benefit the greater good. Boy, she'd been seriously wrong about that one. And that made her question whether she was doing things wrong again this time.

Sure, it was Sharpe's plan, and it would be his decision to pull the trigger and launch the raid on the island the following day, but the entire strategy was based on her inside knowledge of the compound and the guards.

What if she'd gotten it wrong? What if she'd forgotten something or remembered something wrong?

What if Tiberius captured them?

The past few days hadn't been the best of times by any means, but she'd grown fond of each member of Sharpe's team. Jimmy might be a self-proclaimed computer nerd, but he had a wickedly quirky sense of humor and a girlfriend named Sue. Drew, who'd worked with her on the maps and schematics, had made her feel like part of the team rather than an outsider. Megan, new and slightly shy, brought in to cover Grace's spot, had a dolphin's smile that tipped up at the corners and made Sydney want to smile in return. Sydney had spent the least amount of time with Michael, but he made her think of military recruiting posters, America and apple pie. She had a feeling it would be tough to feel unsafe around him. And Sharpe...

Well, Sharpe was Sharpe. On the upside, he smiled at her in passing. On the downside, she had no idea what that meant.

His mistrust was so deeply ingrained, she wasn't sure she could rely on him to believe her when it truly mattered. So why did her body come to life when he walked into the room, even though they hadn't kissed—

hadn't so much as touched—since that night at his place?

And why, in the deepest darkness of the night, when she awoke from terrible, torturous dreams so vivid she could hear Jenny Marie's screams ringing in her ears, did she find herself holding his face in the forefront of her mind as she tried to soothe herself back to sleep?

The "why" is obvious, she told herself as she stood on the hotel deck and stared out over the ocean, which was darkening with the early-spring dusk and the threat of an incoming storm. *The question is, what are you going to do about it?*

The smart answer was "nothing."

Then again, she was one of the dumbest smart people she knew.

"See something out there?" a deep, masculine voice said from behind her. She didn't need the fine shimmer of nerves and heat to tell her it was Sharpe.

She shook her head, not looking at him. "Just thinking."

"Must not be very good thoughts. You were frowning." He moved up beside her, leaned his forearms on the deck railing in a position that mirrored her own and stared out across the water.

Their forearms barely brushed, but the light contact sent liquid fire through her veins.

"Do you blame me?" She figured that was a neutral enough response. Let him interpret it however he wanted.

"Of the two of us, I'd say I have more of a reason to be uneasy. I'm the one going to the island tomorrow."

"I know," she said softly. "I wish you weren't."

"It's part of the job."

"I'll worry."

He slanted her a look. "I should tell you not to."

"Are you?"

"No." He shifted closer, so they were touching at hip and shoulder as they both leaned on the railing, staring off across the sea, which was growing choppy with the turbulence of an incoming spring squall. "Partly because you'll do what you want regardless of what I say, and partly because I think I like the idea of you being back here, thinking about me."

"I will," she said softly.

The question that loomed unspoken between them was what sort of relationship would they have when he went? It would be easy to say they were friends of a sort, with the promise of so much more, but the kindling heat inside her, and the pressure of grief and fear in her chest, warned that it wouldn't be enough for her. She wanted more. She wanted him.

When he left the next day, she wanted him to take a piece of her along, not because she wanted to go to Rocky Cliff, but because she wanted him to come back safe. If she hadn't been escaping toward Celeste, she never would've made it off the island. Was it silly to think the same might work for him, that maybe he'd be a little more careful if he was coming back to something other than the job?

They hadn't settled anything between them, not really. He'd promised to trust her, but that trust hadn't yet been tested. She'd promised to be on his side, but that hadn't been proven, either.

Still, they might not have another night. They had tonight.

She held out her hand. "Come inside."

He took her fingers in his but stayed put, looking down into her eyes. "Are you sure?"

There was no need to discuss what the invitation meant. The need for sex, the promise of it, spun out in the air separating them.

"I'm sure," she said, and willed him to see the truth in her eyes, willed him to believe her. "I don't want to wake up alone tomorrow."

They both knew what she was really saying was, *If you don't come back from the island, I don't want us to have missed this chance.* She didn't know if it'd last past tonight, didn't know if either of them were ready for it to continue onward. She did know, however, that she didn't want to live with the regret of not having taken this one night together with him.

She wanted him to have something to come back to, even if it was an illusion that dissipated once the danger was past.

"Come inside," she said again. "Please." As if in answer, the wind picked up, blowing between them, around them, and bringing the scent of the sea.

He lifted their joined hands. "Are you trying to save me, Sydney?"

Her laugh caught in her throat. "You're not a lost cause yet."

"That, sweetheart, is a matter of opinion." He closed the distance between them, and kissed her, and that was when she knew for certain. She wasn't in danger of falling for him.

She'd already fallen. She just hadn't hit bottom yet.

JOHN DIDN'T EVEN BOTHER trying to talk himself out of following her into her hotel room—he'd passed the point of no return. Hell, maybe he'd passed it days ago, while he'd sat on his own couch and watched her sleep.

Then, as now, fierce protectiveness welled up inside him. All-consuming possessiveness. She was his in a way he'd never known before, never wanted before. But now it was all about want as he slid the glass doors closed, shutting out the night. Shutting out the storm that had come in so quickly, and now announced its arrival with a sharp splatter of rain against the glass slider.

Knowing that the others were out but not how long they'd be gone, he locked the connecting doors to the rooms on either side of Sydney's. Then he turned to her, their hands still linked, and lifted his free hand to touch the ends of her dark hair and trace the soft curve of her cheek.

Her luscious brown eyes were shadowed and wary, and as fierce as they had been the first moment he saw her, dripping wet and spitting mad as she crouched on the deck of the coast guard cutter *Valiant*, ready to fight the world. Yet at the same time he saw a layer of vulnerability beneath. She was afraid for him, cared for him, and the knowledge resonated. It mattered, probably more than it should.

He needed to be focused when he led his team to the island the next day. He needed to be in charge, needed to be the Iceman, but that man seemed very far away as he leaned in and touched his lips to hers, and the layers of defense were stripped away, leaving only the man behind.

THE MOMENT THEIR LIPS touched, Sydney felt a shudder run through his big frame, as though something was changing within him. Then he slanted his mouth across hers and applied gentle suction, teasing her lips apart. His tongue touched hers, softly at first, and then with increasing pressure, and she knew she had him. He'd made his choice, and he'd chosen her.

Reveling in the knowledge, glorying in it, she lost herself in the kiss.

Fisting her hands in the fine cotton of his shirt, she leaned in and opened to him. Heat exploded inside her, muting the buzz of nerves at the thought that she was doing this, really doing this. With Sharpe. Or rather, *John*.

He pulled away and looked down at her. "What?"

She flushed when she realized she'd said it aloud. "I was practicing your name. It seems silly to think of you as Sharpe now."

"You can call me whatever feels right," he said simply, and the open invitation from a man as guarded as he was meant far more than it should have, sending a spear of emotion through her to join the heat.

She swallowed hard against the lure of affection—or more—and tried to keep it light, saying, "I'm all about doing what feels right."

Shifting her grip to the lapels of his suit jacket— navy today—she drew him down for another kiss, one that started with their lips curved in pleasure and quickly morphed to an openmouthed, searching explo- ration that detonated bombs of sensation in her finger- tips, in her core, in all the neurons between.

Murmuring something—maybe appreciation, maybe a suggestion—he slid his hands up her ribs, skimming the outsides of her breasts and causing her nipples to tighten with anticipation.

She lit up, humming with the electricity that had flared between them from the first. Her mouth turned greedy, and she tugged the tails of his shirt from his waistband and ran her hands beneath. His stomach was warm and hard beneath her fingertips, dusted with the faint irregularity of masculine hair, and though he wasn't a bulky man by any means, everywhere she touched she found muscles that coiled in hard, ready knots beneath her hands.

Sliding her fingertips higher, playing across the hard ridges of muscle and man, she found her exploration blocked by the straps of his shoulder holster, so she reversed course, stroking down along his ribs to bracket his hips with her hands, then reaching up to tug at the holster. "You're going to need to lose this."

"I was just thinking the same thing." He stepped away from her, unhooked the holster and shrugged out of it as raindrops blew in from the sea and hit the sliding glass doors with the hard rat-tat of a spring storm.

Placing the holstered gun on the dresser top, beside the hotel-standard entertainment center, he clicked off the wall lamp, plunging the room into darkness. Then he crossed to her and urged her to the glass doors, pressing her against him and wrapping his arms around her so they were aligned back-to-front, both watching the night.

He grazed his lips across one of her ears, sending a shimmery sensation straight to her core, and whispered, "Listen to the storm."

The wild fury of it raged inland, whipping the waves to frenzied whitecaps that hurled themselves onward, only to die on the beach. The wind howled off the Atlantic, rattling the windows and making the glass bow in its frame. But Sydney felt safe in John's arms. Protected. Like they were cocooned together in a moment outside of normal time, where nothing and no one could touch them.

It was an illusion, she knew, brought by the night and the storm and the feelings that bound them together.

The danger was still out there, waiting.

For tonight, though, she was safe with him.

"Will the storm change your plans if it keeps up?" she said softly, not sure what she wanted the answer to be. Part of her wanted him to say yes, for them to have another day. But that would only prolong the inevitable.

"It'll pass," he said with quiet assurance. "We'll sneak onto the island tomorrow, as planned."

They had the loan of a boat bristling with the newest in stealth technology. The Renfrew brothers, along with a half dozen coast guarders and combat-trained men, would move in on the main dock as a distraction, allowing John's team to make it to one of the less patrolled beaches of Rocky Cliff Island. That was the theory, anyway.

In reality, so many things could go wrong, it made Sydney sick to think of the possibilities. So she let the storm beat in her blood, in her heart, and she turned in John's arms, leaned up on her tiptoes and pressed her lips to his.

Finally, she eased back and said, "Then let's not waste the hours we have left."

One corner of his mouth kicked up and his eyes turned sad, as though he'd read more into her words than she'd intended, but he said nothing, simply leaned ___ ___nd kissed her. Then, without breaking the kiss, he swept her up into his arms and carried her the few steps to the bed.

The mattress yielded beneath their combined weight, and she gloried in the solidness of him pressing her down as she wrapped her legs around his, hooked her arms around his strong shoulders and gave herself up to the moment, to the spring storm, to the man.

Their kisses grew hotter and harder as the wind slapped stinging pellets of water against the glass barrier that was the only thing separating them from the maelstrom outside. The air in the small room heated with passion, with the mingling of their scents and the torturous rub of far too much clothing.

Sydney helped him wrestle her clinging pullover off over her head, then fumbled with the buttons on his shirt, parting the material so they could press skin-to-skin.

Far from being icy, he burned from within, his passion radiating outward and scorching her. She writhed beneath him as the heat built from want to an all-consuming need, until not even the storm mattered anymore, until the only thing that mattered was him—the taste of him, the good, solid weight of him and the feel of his skin against hers.

Then even that wasn't enough anymore. She parted her legs and slid her calves up his thighs on either side, opening herself to the press of his solid length as he began to rock against her.

Heat spiraled upward, breaking over them both until he pulled away, breath rasping in his lungs. He held himself there for a second, muscles so tight he was practically shaking, and in the darkness she felt him fight to master himself, to stay in control.

The thought that she could bring a man like him to the breaking point was brutally erotic, and she would have slid against him, trying to drive him beyond. But then he bent his head and touched his tongue to one of her peaked nipples, suckling her through the fabric of her bra, and all other thoughts were lost in a wave of sensation.

She arched up beneath him and cried out. Dimly aware of the people who might or might not be in the rooms on either side, she clamped her lips together, stifling further cries as he drove her up using only his lips on her breasts. His clever fingers trailed along her body, touching her. Inciting her. Promising dark delights. Teasing her beyond reason.

She pushed his unbuttoned shirt off over his shoulders, laughing when it snagged on his wrists and he reared up to yank it free. By unspoken accord they rolled apart and pulled off the rest of their clothes, with him pausing a moment to slip a condom from his billfold.

She didn't ask how long it had been there or who it'd been intended for. She was only grateful he had one, because if they'd been forced to stop now, she might've screamed in frustration.

The need for sex, the glory of it, beat hammer-loud in her blood, and sang in her ears, drowning out the fury of the storm outside.

Once he had the condom in place she reached for him, drew him down and offered herself to him, demanded he come to her and welcomed him when he did. It had been so long for her that she was tight, bringing a moment of pain as he entered her, followed by the burn of pleasure, the gut-wrenching feeling of being full, of being joined.

Of being connected. To him. Only to him.

Once he was fully seated with her, he paused and dropped his brow to hers for a second as they breathed in tandem, absorbing the moment, the sensation. An unexpectedly poignant ache fisted in her chest, just beneath her heart, and she closed her eyes tightly against the promise of tears.

If this was it for them, she thought, it would have to be enough.

Then he began to move within her, and the sadness gave way to a roar of heat and need, and the delicious, wonderful friction they created together. The mad power of it broke over them like one of the storm-tossed waves, but instead of cresting and losing momentum it kept building, kept driving them up until they were racing to the peak, gasping and hanging on to each other while he drove into her and she clung to him.

And when they got there, she turned her face into the pillow to muffle her cries of completion, and he shuddered and groaned close to her ear, keeping the moment private, keeping it hidden from the others.

Afterward, she wrapped herself around him, turned her face into his throat and clung to him some more while the world changed shape around her, and she thought, *This is it. This is what it feels like to love a man.*

At one point she'd thought she'd loved Richard, but she'd long ago realized she'd loved the idea of him far more than the reality, had loved the symmetry of being with someone from within the small world of the university. In the end, it hadn't even been much of a surprise to learn that he'd stolen some of her work and claimed it as his own, then ran to the dean's committee and accused her before she could accuse him.

It had been messy and embarrassing, but it hadn't been heartache, not really.

Not the way she felt it as she slid toward sleep, knowing that when the dawn broke, the man she loved would be going up against a monster.

HOURS LATER, SYDNEY awoke to the shrill ring of a strange phone. Groaning, she rolled over and fumbled for the thing, blearily registering the hotel room and a scattering of her belongings, and snapping to attention when she saw unfamiliar clothes slung over the desk chair—suit pants and a button-down shirt—and a holster neatly folded on the desk.

The sight made her acutely aware of the warmth at her back, and the rumble of a man's breath.

She'd slept with Sharpe. With *John*. He'd stayed the night.

Consciousness returned with a punch of heat, and the memory of them turning to each other time and again through the night, each encounter growing slower and more languid, though no less hot. More like affection than flat-out lust. Almost, at times, bordering on more. Almost like love.

Don't even go there, she warned herself, glancing over at him and stilling at the sight of him sprawled on his stomach, gloriously naked and gloriously male, with his face jammed under his pillow as if to keep the morning away a few moments longer.

Fully appreciating the desire and knowing they

damn well needed to keep their night a secret from the others, lest it disrupt the day's plan, she kept her voice low when she answered, "Hello?"

She expected one of Sharpe's teammates or maybe the front desk.

She got a smooth, silky voice that was all too familiar.

"Rise and shine, Sydney." Tiberius couldn't have sounded more charming, as if he was holding all the cards in the deck at once. "But don't—" he emphasized the word with a snarl "—even think of waking Agent Sharpe. If you look to your left, you'll see why."

Fear seized her by the throat, closing off her breath, choking her until the world spun. Shaking, afraid to look and afraid not to look, she turned her head.

The green dot of a laser-guided gun sight danced across the back of Sharpe's neck, skittered along his dark, thick hair and slid to his temple.

"Boom," Tiberius said in her ear. "That's what'll happen if you don't cooperate. Nod if you understand."

She nodded as a tear slid down her cheek and sobs backed up in her throat.

"Good girl. I want you to get up and get dressed. There's a car waiting for you outside. Do you understand?"

Another nod.

"You have two minutes. And Sydney?"

He waited for a response, forcing her to whisper, "Yes?"

"The sniper will remain in place until you're on one of my boats, headed for Rocky Cliff Island. If you do anything—and I mean anything—to signal Sharpe or the other members of his team, then he's dead. They're all dead…and they won't enjoy it."

He hung up before she could nod, but the green light shifted, crawling across Sharpe's arm and up her thigh, pausing a second to circle the area of her breasts, which were hidden by the sheet she clutched to her chest.

She batted at the light, trying to shoo it away as tears blurred her vision.

Then the green dot moved to the alarm clock as if to say, *Ten minutes, Sydney. Don't be late, or he's dead.*

She hit the ground running and told herself not to look back.

THE MORNING OF THE MISSION to Tiberius's island, the Iceman overslept. He didn't wake up until his cell phone went off with the raucous shrill he'd programmed in on the theory that only the dead could sleep through something that loud.

Even then, it was a struggle.

He felt heavy-limbed and lethargic, as if he'd been drugged or beaten up, or had a night of really great—

Sex. Oh, hell.

Shooting upright in bed, he grabbed for his cell phone. A second before he answered, he got a good look around and realized he wasn't in his room. He dropped the phone when he realized he was in Sydney's room, and odds were that his entire team knew it.

He could trust them to keep that quiet from the higher-ups, but that wasn't the point. They knew. And in a couple of hours, he was going to be leading them on a hell of a dangerous insertion, based on information they'd gotten from Sydney. From his lover.

The thought brought a wash of heat and an ache

of tenderness in the region of his heart, one that he thought he might be able to get used to over time. Despite their problems and differences, she was exactly the sort of woman he wanted at his side—clever and resourceful, tough enough to stand up to him when he got off track, tender enough to let him be tender in return.

He scratched his bare chest in the region of that ache as his phone chimed again.

"Better get dressed," he called in the direction of the bathroom. "We're about to have company, and they're not going to be happy."

Maybe the sex had dazed him or maybe he was just an idiot, because he actually expected an answer.

He didn't get one.

His stomach hit the deck in zero seconds flat. A quick look confirmed that her clothes and shoes were gone, and he knew better than to think she'd up and gone for a walk when her life was in danger.

He'd been played. Again.

Damn it.

Snapping the rest of the way awake, he erupted from the bed and yanked on his clothes, simultaneously barking into the phone, "Meet me in the spare room in sixty seconds. We've got a problem."

He hung up the phone, strapped on his holster and strode to the door.

He left his jacket behind because suits were for civilized people, and he was done being civilized.

The team was already assembled in the spare room when he got there, and from the looks of their take-out coffee cups they'd been there for a while already. He met their stares, owning every skin-crawling second of embarrassment. "I slept with her and she took off while I was zonked out. The last time I looked at the clock was four hours ago, so we can assume she's already on the island and the mission is FUBARed. Any questions?"

Michael frowned and looked at Jimmy. "Are you sure she didn't leave under duress? We could check the hotel switchboard. Maybe Tiberius called and threatened her or something."

"What's left for him to threaten?" John snapped. "We've got Celeste under wraps, and Sydney doesn't have any other close ties." At the sidelong looks, he growled, "What, she played you guys, too? Trust me, we're a means to an end, not close ties."

For a second he remembered the night before, when she'd whispered love words to him—not the big three, but endearments laced with soft, womanly affection. Acid burned his gut when he accepted that as nothing more than setting the groundwork for today.

He clenched his teeth and gritted. "I want everyone ready to roll in thirty minutes, as planned."

Jimmy frowned. "He's expecting us."

"Exactly." John nodded sharply. "We're going to use that against him and take the whole damn island with us."

"What about Sydney?" Michael persisted. "If she's there under duress, if she's innocent—"

"She's not innocent," John snapped. "Trust me on that one. And if she gets hurt, then that's no more than she deserves for serving a master like Tiberius."

His voice was harsh, his mien harsher, but as he turned away and strode from the room, grief, guilt and anger pinched beneath his heart.

He'd liked the woman she'd pretended to be, damn it. Maybe could've even loved her.

In reality, though, Sydney was no better than Rose: both traitors.

CHAPTER TEN

THE ISLAND LOOKS EXACTLY the same, Sydney thought dully as the motorboat approached the pier.

Then again, she'd only been gone a week. She was the one who'd changed. She'd escaped and she'd gotten her sister to safety as planned. But she'd also gotten involved with a man and a cause, and that hadn't been part of the plan at all.

She'd left Rocky Cliff Island looking for a way to save her own ass. She was returning in order to make things right. Or so she kept telling herself. She had a feeling John would see it far differently. He'd promised to believe her, promised to trust her, but how could a man like him trust her in the face of overwhelming evidence to the contrary?

The fact was that when Tiberius called, she'd come running. That was all John would see, she was sure of it.

Tears filled Sydney's eyes as the boat bumped up against the dock, but she sniffed and brushed them away. This was her choice, her responsibility. She'd been a coward before, hiding behind Celeste's illness, using it as an excuse to make the choices she knew in her gut weren't right. But not anymore.

This time, she was doing what was right; she was

going to undo what she never should've done in the first place.

And then Tiberius was going to kill her.

"Off," one of the guards said, and shoved her toward the dock. There were three guards on the boat, all heavily armed. They stayed stone-faced as they marched her up the ramp leading from the dock to the mansion.

Tiberius's grand house sat on the crest of the island's single large hill. The land rose up through the levels of security, past guard shacks, cameras and patrols to the main house, and then fell away on the other side in a sheer drop of several hundred feet, providing the cliffs that gave the island its name.

The sun shone on the scene with false cheer, but otherwise everything was the same as it had been when she'd escaped. The guard shacks didn't look any different, the buildings were all placed where she'd put them on the map she and Jimmy had built together. From the movements of the patrols they passed on their way up to the house, she was pretty sure they were on patrol rotation B that day.

All of which meant absolutely nothing under the current circumstances.

They entered the mansion through the front door rather than the side exit she'd escaped through.

The house was a sprawling affair originally designed in the style of the old Newport mansions, with twelve-foot ceilings and exquisitely carved moldings. The main foyer was twice that high and led to a master staircase made of pink-veined marble and granite. Instead of looking grand and lush, though, the place seemed sterile. There was no artwork on the walls, no sense that it was anything but a place of business, as evidenced by the security cameras in the corners, constantly scanning the scene, and the sense of purposeful motion elsewhere in the house.

Sydney automatically turned right, toward the lab and her quarters, but one of the guards grabbed her arm and redirected her toward the big marble staircase. "Not the lab. You're going upstairs."

The directive chilled her to her bones, proving that she wasn't nearly as calm or as brave as she wanted to think.

Prodded by the guards, she mounted the stairs. Instead of turning toward the security hub, though, they herded her down a long hall that ran at a tangent to a wing she hadn't been in before.

Nerves closed in, nearly choking her and forcing the question from between her trembling lips. "Where are you taking me?"

The guards didn't answer as they stopped her in front of a grandly carved set of twelve-foot-high double doors, inset with a normal-size door. One of the men knocked, then turned the knob and opened the normal-size door. The other two guards hustled her inside.

The room was a huge salon done in reds and golds, with lush-looking draperies and tapestries. A small dining table for four sat in one corner near a set of ornate French doors, and in the center of the room sat a claw-footed mahogany suite of sofa, chairs, end tables and a low coffee table. Several doors led from the room, all of them closed.

Unlike the rest of the mansion, the salon contained personal touches, including soft landscapes on the walls, and a man's jacket tossed over one of the chairs.

Sydney's breath froze in her lungs. She didn't need

to see into the other rooms to figure out where they'd brought her. The place fit Jenny Marie's description to a T.

She was in Tiberius's personal quarters.

But why?

The guards shoved her into one of the claw-footed chairs, turned on their heels and left. The moment the hallway door shut behind them, one of the far doorways swung open and Tiberius stepped through.

Tall and gaunt, with thinning gray hair and a Trumplike comb-over, wearing a dull gray suit that hung on his frame, he looked like a college professor, or maybe a mortician. Not a master criminal. Not a killer.

Yet he was both of those things, and so many more, none of them good.

Heart pounding, Sydney stood and faced him, trying not to show her fear even though she was so terrified her mouth had gone dry and her knees shook.

He didn't even bother to gloat, merely crossed the room and pressed some sort of mechanism. A panel slid aside in the wall and a hardwired computer station moved into view. "Give me the password."

She lifted her chin with false bravery. "No."

He smiled without humor. "You like deals, don't you? How about this one—you give me the correct password and unlock the computers. Once I've downloaded the sequence and pulled the samples from the freezers you so cleverly locked tight, we'll leave the island together." He paused and a mad glint entered his eyes. "If you try anything funny, though, like keying in the wrong word, I'll still be leaving, but you'll be stuck here, on this chunk of rock…which is set to blow in—" he checked his watch "—thirty-eight minutes and change. It's not as fitting an end as I would've liked, but the result is the same. Boom!" He made an exploding motion with his hands. He mocked a frown. "Oh, and I'm sorry about your boyfriend, by the way." At her baffled look, he smiled. "Didn't you know? He and his teammates are trying to sneak onto the backside of the island as we speak. They should be getting here just in time to watch us take off. That is, if you're as smart as I think you are."

"No." At first there was no volume to the word, so Sydney tried again. "No deal."

"What, you want better terms?" He smirked. "Don't even think I'm giving you Sharpe. It's your life for the password, take it or leave it."

A year ago, maybe even a few weeks ago, she might have been tempted, might have convinced herself it was better to live and fight another day. But meeting John Sharpe—caring for him—had changed all that, because he was a man who fought every fight, every time. And if she was on his team, could she do any less?

"I'm waiting." Tiberius crossed his arms. "The password, please."

Sydney bowed her head in submission and crossed to the computer terminal. She touched the back of the desk chair with shaking fingers, pulling it out of the knee hole so she could sit.

Then, before she could wimp out, she snatched up the chair and threw it at Tiberius. He shouted and batted it aside as she broke for the French doors, one of which was cracked open, leading out onto a carved marble veranda with a delicate wrought-iron railing.

Sydney's heartbeat hammered in her ears.

Footsteps rang out behind her, along with the sound of slamming doors and Tiberius's shout of "Get her!"

The guards opened fire. As the first bullets whizzed past and slapped into the doorway, sending up chips of wood and marble, Sydney didn't think.

Screaming, she grabbed on to the railing, swung up and over and let go, flinging herself off the second-floor balcony.

Mercifully the land sloped up beneath the house, so the fall was manageable. She landed in a beach plum bush and cried out when the thorns bit into her skin. Rolling away, she struggled to her feet and started running, heading along the side of the house, along one of the faint tracks she'd found on her guided walks during her captivity.

There were shouts from up above. Worse, she could hear one of the outdoor patrols closing in on her from the side.

Breath whistling in her lungs, she bolted for the cliff. And prayed she'd find her team in time.

JOHN WAS ABLE TO INSERT his team exactly as planned. The distraction team around the front of the island made a big, loud raid on the docks, and let themselves be repelled after a good ten minutes of gunplay. Under that cover, John, Jimmy, Michael and Drew slipped their stealth-cloaked boat into the landing spot they'd chosen.

Located a solid mile from the main compound, with twenty-foot-high rock ledges on either side of the tiny beach, the landing spot was less than ideal. In fact, it had been on the bottom of the list Sydney had come up with for possible drop points…which was why he'd chosen it.

After her disappearance, there was no way he was using one of her top choices. He still couldn't believe she'd left, couldn't believe she'd gone to the island. But surveillance cameras near the Gloucester marina had shown her climbing out of a car under heavy guard, and getting into one of Tiberius's boats.

Granted, the armed guards suggested she'd been taken under duress, and a check of incoming calls to the hotel confirmed Michael's suggestion that she'd received a call from the island, but that hardly mattered to John. She'd chosen to give in to Tiberius's pressure rather than waking him, rather than trusting him to protect her, and that galled him beyond words.

"We're going in," Michael called from the helm. "Hang on, it's going to be rough!"

The tide was on its way out, creating swirling riptides that threatened to suck the boat into the nearby cliffs, slam it into the rocks and end the attack before it even began.

Michael fought the controls with grim determination, legs set wide apart for balance, cursing under his breath and babying the powerful engine as he fought the swirling pull of water. Drew had strapped himself into one of the pilot's chairs and was backing Michael up wherever possible. Jimmy was hanging on to a sideways-facing seat, looking decidedly green. John sat facing forward, braced against the swell, his jaw locked.

He didn't feel sick, didn't feel scared. He felt…numb.

There could be no future where there wasn't any trust, and though he'd fought the realization as long and as hard as he could, Sydney's actions that morning only proved what he'd suspected from the very beginning: she had her own agenda, and wasn't above twisting the rules to suit her needs.

She might've told herself she was giving in to save him or some such nonsense, but in the end it came down to not trusting him enough to do his job, not trusting him to keep the two of them alive.

Damn her, he thought, raw hurt expanding in his chest. Why hadn't she just woken him up?

He saw Drew glance back, and though he couldn't hear the other man's words over the crashing surf and the laboring whine of the boat's engines, he read his lips as he said to Michael, "Sharpe's looking cool. We'll be okay."

I'm not cool, he wanted to say, *I'm numb.*

But because he knew his team needed him to be strong, he unstrapped himself from his chair and took up position directly behind Michael and Drew, hanging on to the back of the two captain's chairs and riding the heaving deck on braced legs. "Looking good," he said. "We're almost there."

The small gravel strip was no more than fifty feet away, but there was a vicious whip of crosscurrent in the gap, and the intersection of the riptide with the crosscurrent created an area of man-high chop. The cliffs bounced the sea breeze around, creating nearly gale-force winds in that small area, even though the day beyond was bright and sunny.

The comm device inside John's raincoat crackled with Dick Renfrew's voice reporting that they were pulling back to wait for further instructions, and godspeed to the island team.

It was time to do or die.

"Hang on!" Michael yelled, the wind whipping the words away the moment they were out of his mouth. "We're going in!"

He kicked the engines full-throttle, aiming upstream of the current in the hopes that by the time they were through, they'd be on dry land.

Or splintered against the rocks. One or the other.

John hooked his feet beneath the ankle rests of each pilot's chair and tightened his grip as the boat surged forward with a howl, leaped up the side of a wave and hung there, poised motionless for a moment, before crashing into the trough and burying its nose in the sea.

At a moment when he should've been on an adrenaline high, should've been bracing for a crash, or prepping for the fight to come, he was wishing he were somewhere else. Wishing he were some*one* else.

Suddenly, he was beyond weary of the job.

Why bother? There was always another criminal looking to wreak havoc. Every time he and his team took one down, another sprang up to fill the vacuum created. What would really happen if they all simply quit one day? Would the terrorist community eventually reach some sort of equilibrium?

You're losing it, John told himself. *Get your head back in the game.*

He needed a vacation, he thought incongruously, hanging on to the seats as a ten-foot whitecap hit them broadside, nearly turtling the twenty-foot craft. Michael and Drew fought the controls, forcing the boat to churn through the white spume. Jimmy had gone from green to gray and looked like he was praying.

Meanwhile, John was realizing there was really no

place he wanted to go. For that matter, what would he do if he up and left the Bureau? Sure, it might be fun to tinker with the house for a few months, but then what? He didn't have anything else. Didn't have anything but the job.

And damn Sydney again for bringing that painfully home inside him.

Even as he despaired in his soul, his brain stayed cool, scanning the scene and calculating options. He saw the gap and pointed. "There!"

Michael nodded and aimed the floundering boat through the patch of incongruously glass-smooth water. Like a biker skimming across hardpan after laboring through beach sand, the boat shot forward, gaining momentum enough to slew through the last section of water and fling itself up the beach with a sideways, jolting slide.

"Let's go!" Drew took a flying leap off the boat and grabbed the towline off the front. Jimmy wasn't far behind him, moving fast on shaky legs. The two quickly started looking for a stone outcropping to tie off to, or failing that, a crevice they could set an eyebolt into.

Michael stayed on board, manning the controls in case a larger wave slapped onto the beach and threatened to float the craft off. He called, "Get the line as high as you can, so the boat can move with the tide if necessary."

Don't bother, John almost said. *We won't need it past tide change.*

The way he saw it, by that time either they would've already captured the island or they'd be dead. He didn't see a viable option that involved retreat.

But he also knew that wasn't the Iceman speaking, it was someone else entirely, someone who ran on emotion rather than logic. Someone whose heart hurt in his chest. Someone who would do them no good on the mission ahead.

Focus, he told himself. *Forget the woman. Find the game.*

"We're good," Jimmy called, and tossed down the line. Once the boat was tied fast, John distributed their packs, which were loaded with the weapons and other gear they'd projected needing for the op.

By the time he'd jumped down off the boat and shouldered his own pack, he'd more or less found the calm that'd served him so well throughout his life. The moment his boots hit the gravel, signaling that it was time to roll, the questions and regrets that'd plagued him on the boat ceased to exist, or if they existed, they'd been shoved so far down into his psyche that they wouldn't interfere.

He was in the zone. Game on.

After reporting their position to the other boat in a brief burst of radio traffic—they were using a scrambled channel but still keeping the chatter to a minimum—John led his men toward the likeliest-seeming trail up the cliff face.

"There's more of an angle than I expected," he said, as much to himself as to the others. "We may not even need the ropes."

"First good news we've had all day," Drew muttered, and John couldn't disagree.

Still, it took them a few minutes to work their way up to the top of the cliff, testing their way and setting ropes as necessary. When they reached the edge, John used an angled mirror on a telescoping handle—an old technology, but smaller and lighter than the newer fiber-optic units, and fine for basic sneak-a-peek stuff—to check out what was going on above them.

"All clear," he mouthed to Drew, who was directly behind him, followed by Jimmy, with Michael taking the rear point position.

John slipped up and over the rocky lip, onto a flat promontory that was nothing but windswept rock for the first fifteen feet or so before giving way to a tangle of salt-stunted evergreens and low island scrub.

Seeing no signs of resistance, he beckoned the others up and over. As planned, they set eyehooks and climbing ropes near the edge, in case they needed a quick exit. Once that was done, they slipped into the forest of stunted evergreens, walking single file and keeping a sharp watch for hostile company.

Jimmy tracked their course and progress on a handheld GPS unit. They were still a half mile away from the main compound when John heard a noise coming from up ahead.

Senses alert, he stopped and gestured for the others to fade into the surrounding trees.

He strained to pinpoint the noise. He'd thought… there! He pointed off to the east, where a thicker stand of taller trees shaded the landscape. Michael nodded. He'd heard the footsteps, too. Moving silently, the marksman readied his weapon, knowing they couldn't let an alarm get back to the main compound.

Not yet, anyway.

The sounds grew louder as the guard approached, making straight for Michael's position and moving fast. John's heart rate increased at the thought that they'd already been discovered, but he didn't move or make a sound to indicate the suspicion, instead tensing as the noises angled away, then looped around suddenly, headed straight for his position.

Without time to pull his own weapon, and afraid that the screening trees nearby would foul Michael's shot, John didn't stop to think.

He acted.

Lunging out of his scrubby concealment, he caught the guard in a flying tackle, clapping a hand across the bastard's mouth and slamming him to the ground.

Working on icy logic and instinct rather than the mores of civilization, he had his combat knife out and was a heartbeat away from the guard's throat when he realized two things that had him pausing the final blow.

One, the guy wasn't big enough to be one of Tiberius's guards, and two, the guy wasn't a guy.

It was Sydney.

The realization flared through his gut in a burst of heat and anger that came straight from the place he'd locked away for the duration of the op. He spat a curse and rolled aside, rising to his feet before he turned back and looked down at her.

She was wearing the same clothes she'd had on the day—and night—before, and she had a faint bruise along her jaw. Her face and arms were scratched and bleeding, and she was breathing hard, as though she'd run all the way from the mansion. Her eyes were worried and scared and faintly defiant, as though she already knew what he was going to say, and didn't plan to back down.

Her eyes locked on his. "He said he was going to kill you if I didn't go with his people," she said, her voice low and rasping with the effort of her breaths. "At the hotel. There was a sniper outside the window. I saw the laser dot on your forehead."

"Don't expect me to thank you for saving my ass," John said coolly. "You should've woken me and let me do my damn job." He paused. "Did you give him the password?"

She met him stare for stare. "No, but there's something more. He's wired the island to blow. You've got maybe twenty-five minutes or so left on the countdown."

John's gut iced. "How do you know?"

"He told me."

"And then he just, what? Let you go?" He scoffed in disbelief.

"I went out the window." Her voice went low. "I'm telling you the truth."

Yeah, he thought, *but sometimes the truth isn't enough. Sometimes there's got to be trust, too.*

And that was something they apparently didn't have.

Unable to respond to her, unable to figure out how, he turned away from her, gesturing for the others to get her up. "She comes with us."

He heard her quiet sob as he walked away, but he didn't turn back. He'd already given her one too many chances.

Whether or not she was working for Tiberius, caring for her was a liability he couldn't afford right now. He had a job to do.

CHAPTER ELEVEN

SILENT TEARS STUNG Sydney's eyes as she stumbled along in John's wake. She couldn't stop looking at him, at the tense set of his shoulders and the uncompromising line of his square jaw, couldn't stop remembering the night before, when she'd run her hands over those same broad shoulders and tasted the skin along that square jaw.

Though she hadn't gone to bed with him expecting a future, she'd hoped for more than the night. Then Tiberius had called. Damn him. And damn John for not trusting her enough to hear her out, for not caring enough to try to see her side of things.

The rising burn of anger dried her tears. Her legs ached from her flight from the mansion and trembled with the knowledge that she was headed back there yet again. She knew John would keep her as safe as possible—he had a core of honor, whether he trusted her or not—but she couldn't shake the terrible knowledge that none of this was going as planned.

Or rather, none of it was going according to their plan. She suspected they were playing right into Tiberius's hands, because now if he captured the team, he'd not only get another chance to strip the password from her, he'd also have the opportunity to rid himself of a major foe in Sharpe and his team.

Or he'd just take off and hope they blew up with the island, because it sure didn't seem like John had believed her on that front, either.

Run! she wanted to say. *Let's go, let's get out of here.* But she didn't, because he wasn't listening to her.

She could only trudge along behind him, wishing she'd done things differently, wishing that she'd never taken Tiberius's damn job in the first place, or that the messages she'd managed to sneak off the island had been to the authorities rather than to Celeste.

But wishing for something was never enough to make it happen. If that were the case, her parents would've returned when they were children, Celeste would be healed and John would've known instinctively how to trust her.

Unfortunately, it seemed like all the wishes in the world wouldn't be enough to make that happen.

"We're almost there," Jimmy whispered from behind her, his voice almost soundless.

John heard him, though, and brought the team to a halt. Michael covered Sydney—his expression apologetic—while the others had a quick confab. After a minute, John gestured to the sharpshooter. "You two stay here. We're going to split up, find someplace to stash her and do a quick recon. When I get back, you can—"

A crack of gunfire cut him off, the bullet splintering the tree to his immediate left.

In the next moment, all hell broke loose.

The teammates dove for cover while Sydney stared, slow to react from the shock of it all, the strangeness of what her life had come to.

"Get her down!" someone shouted, but the voice

seemed to come from far away, muted beneath the chatter of gunfire.

"Damn it, Sydney, get *down!*" John hit her with a flying tackle, grabbing her by the waist and dragging them both to the ground.

Instead of landing flat atop her, he twisted them in midair so they landed on their sides facing each other, with his arms looped around her waist and their noses nearly touching. The hard metal of his gun pressed into her, but she barely noticed the discomfort. She was caught in his eyes, which blazed with fury and maybe something else. Something hotter and less certain, something that made her think that maybe he'd heard her, after all. Maybe a small part of him believed her.

He didn't speak, though. Instead, he scrambled to a low crouch and joined his teammates in returning fire.

But the counterattack was too little, too late. Sharpe's team was surrounded and outgunned. Within minutes, Tiberius's guards had overrun their position. They quickly disarmed the team members, stripped their gear away and secured them with zip ties.

They did Sharpe first, and they weren't gentle. Tears tracked down Sydney's cheeks as he stared at her.

She couldn't read his expression, but guilt had her blurting, "I didn't lead them to you. I didn't tell them anything."

He didn't get a chance to answer—even if he'd been planning to—because the guards who'd tied him yanked him to his feet and prodded him with his rifle butt. "Shut up and move."

As the guards herded them to the main house, John and Sydney wound up walking near each other. He bent low so he could whisper in her ear, "I believe you, about that at least. I just wish you'd trusted me enough to let me take care of Tiberius. You shouldn't be here."

Tears stung Sydney's eyes. "I'm sorry. I—"

"Keep moving." The guards shoved her ahead of the others, and then when they reached the house, hustled her down the hallway to the right, away from the others. Ignoring her struggles and panicked shouts, they pushed her through the door to her old quarters and locked her in.

"John," she shouted. *"John!"* She didn't see where they'd taken the others, but feared she could guess.

Upstairs. To the security hub.

HE HEARD HER CALL HIS name, heard her voice break on the scream, and nearly tore into the guards in an effort to get to her, but he forced aside the emotions in favor of logic. Barely.

It wouldn't help if he got himself shot in the process of getting to her. He had to bide his time. Work with his team. Think it through.

The emotion had to exist alongside logic.

Somewhere along the line he'd started to realize that the things he was feeling for her didn't have to weaken him. Far from it. Caring for her made him stronger, made him want to tear into his foe to get to her, to protect her. He needed to temper the urge with rationality, though, or he'd start making mistakes.

The guards split the team up, with three armed men marching Michael, Jimmy and Drew in one direction, while two others prodded John through a doorway.

They locked the door behind him, and the clank of metal on metal sounded very loud. Very final.

He found himself in the security hub, a large room with one wall completely given over to a flat screen, on which a shifting array of televised images showed most of the island. A bank of desks faced the displays and held computer stations manned by more of the stone-faced guards.

The agent inside John, the one that had ruled his thoughts and actions for so many years, automatically cataloged the men and armaments in the room—six men, two with obvious weapons—and mapped out his options for escape…slim to none.

He was in the middle of cobbling together a desperate plan of attack when Tiberius stepped in through a door in the far wall, and the game changed.

Wearing a mustard-colored tweed jacket and darker corduroy pants, the self-proclaimed "opportunistic businessman" looked even more like a college professor than he did in his file photos. Unlike so many of the criminals John had sought—and brought to justice—over the years, his eyes weren't dead or cold, or even angry. Instead, he carried a faintly amused, faintly downtrodden air that made him seem completely unremarkable.

That was one of the things that made him so incredibly dangerous, John knew. He appeared so trustworthy and nonthreatening on the surface. It was only when the layers started to peel back that the real evil became apparent, and by then, it was usually too late for the innocent victim to escape.

And despite the gray areas she'd strayed into, Sydney was one of them. An innocent. The blood of the dead wasn't on her hands, John finally acknowledged to himself when he'd put the guilt on her for far too long.

The dead belonged entirely to Tiberius and his peculiar brand of mad genius.

Tiberius stayed halfway across the room, keeping the guards between John and himself, and gave the agent a good, long look. "I don't have time to waste with power plays and negotiations, Agent Sharpe, so here's the deal. You get your girlfriend to turn over the password, and you two and the rest of your team are free to get back in your not-so-stealthy boat and head back to the mainland ahead of the blast that I'm sure dear Sydney told you about."

What makes you think she'd do anything I ask? John wanted to say, because she was nothing if not headstrong…which was one of the things he respected about her.

No, damn it. It was one of the things he loved about her. He loved her. There, he'd said it, if only in his head.

Now he had to get them both out of there so he could say it aloud.

He pretended to consider the deal, though he was pretty sure the other man knew it was an act. Finally, he said, "What sort of assurance do I have that you'll actually keep your word and let us go?"

"None whatsoever. It's not like you'd believe me if I gave my word, so why should I bother?" Tiberius lifted a shoulder. "Let's put it this way—once I have the password, I'm out of here. I won't be back to this island—hell, I'm thinking of being done with the States for a while. Things are getting far too complicated with you around."

"Which is a perfect reason to kill me. Isn't that your usual MO?"

"I don't like being predictable." But something

shifted in his eyes—game or not? Was the bastard lying, or did he want John to think he was? Glancing at his watch, Tiberius said, "I'm going to put you in with her now. You've got five minutes to get me that password, or the deal's off the table."

John barely heard the end of his response, though. His brain was locked on his first few words.

I don't like being predictable. It was what Grace had said, time and again, while working the computer banks in the Hoover building or over at Quantico. It had been a joke, because she'd been solid and dependable, and rarely broke pattern without checking with him first.

Or so it had seemed.

The moment the suspicion took root, it made far too much sense. He'd been too ready to blame the safe house attack on Sydney. Then, when the others had convinced him the bogus email could've come from anywhere, he'd instinctively looked outside the team for suspects.

Now he realized it could just as easily have been Grace giving Tiberius the location, Grace giving him the positions of the other agents. She would've thought herself safe, not realizing that for whatever reason, Tiberius had decided she was expendable, that she'd be more use to him dead than alive, another layer of the game.

John felt a punch of guilt, both that he'd blamed her death on Sydney, and that Grace hadn't trusted him enough to tell him she was in trouble. In making himself safe from emotion, he'd made himself so unapproachable that he'd even driven away the members of his own team.

Well, that stopped now. He was stepping up as

a leader and as a man. As soon as he figured out precisely how.

"Get going." One of the guards jabbed John with the butt of his rifle, prodding him toward the door. Two others closed around him, weapons drawn, and the three marched him out of the room while Tiberius remained in the security hub, no doubt planning to watch and listen in on everything that John and Sydney said to one another.

Fine, John thought. *Go ahead and listen. It's not going to be what you expect.*

The guards descended the marble stairs, boots ringing on stone, and escorted John down a long hallway with doors on either side. He tracked their progress against the blueprint inside his head and realized they were headed toward Sydney's old quarters, which were right near the lab space.

Something loosened inside him at the realization that she'd been stashed in relative safety, at least for the moment. But that left him not knowing where Michael, Drew and Jimmy were being kept, which could become a problem if they got free and needed to move fast.

Because he sure as hell didn't believe Tiberius. The moment the bastard got the password, they were all as good as dead.

"In here." One of the guards swiped a key card and a door swung open. The other two covered John with their weapons, making the threat clear: *one wrong move and you're a wet spot on the floor.*

But they didn't need to worry, he didn't intend to try anything. Not yet, anyway.

Still, his gut was tight as he let the guards hustle him through the door, and the panel shut behind him.

Sydney stood in the center of the room, cheeks stained with tears. She looked at him, eyes filled with a mixture of wariness and hope, as though afraid to trust him to believe, when he'd been so ready to turn on her before.

He didn't say anything, simply crossed to her, opened his arms and gathered her close. He held her tight, feeling her heart beat in time with his. Dropping his cheek to her hair, he whispered, "I'm sorry about before, in the woods. I should've acted different. I wasn't mad, I swear. I didn't think you'd led them to us, I was just—" He broke off, not even sure he could explain it to himself.

On one level he'd been overjoyed to see her, on another, so terrified for her that he'd wanted to shake her, to hug her, to touch her all over until he was sure she was okay.

All of those feelings had sort of logjammed together in his brain and he'd wound up doing nothing.

"It's okay." Her arms snuck around his waist. "You were in agent mode. I get that." She drew in a shaky breath. "I didn't get it at the time, but I get it now."

"You're sure?" He eased away so he could look into her tearstained face. "You're okay?"

"Yeah." She used her hands to swipe at her cheeks. "You?"

"I'm scared."

"Excuse me?" The look on her face might've been comical under any other circumstance.

As it was, he drew her close again, feeling their time running out as he tried to find the words, tried to let her know that he got it now, he finally understood his own heart. "I'm scared that I'm going to mess this up, that I'm going to hurt you." He paused. "But I'm more scared by the thought of losing you. I don't want that. I want us to be together. I want to learn how to be the man you need, because whether either of us likes it or not, you're the woman I need. The woman I want."

When he paused, she said softly, "Say it."

He took a deep breath. "You're the woman I love." When his heart didn't stop beating at the words, when the world kept going on around them and time kept passing, he let out a long breath. "I love you. Please tell me I'm not too late."

SYDNEY WANTED TO BELIEVE him. The need pounded in her bloodstream and spun through her soul, but she held herself back. What if this was another move in the game he'd been playing all along? What if—

That was just it, she realized. There were too many what-ifs. She could think of far too many reasons for him to say he loved her, and almost all of them seemed more plausible than believing he'd really, truly come around.

It was far more likely that he'd found another angle to play than believing he was ready to change.

"I'm sorry," she said softly, her heart breaking with the words. "I don't know how to believe you."

He closed his eyes on a wince of exquisite pain, then nodded sharply. "I understand. I can wait until you figure it out, because I'm not going anywhere this time. I promise."

Then, instead of turning away, he held her close. For a second, Sydney closed her eyes and simply absorbed the feel of him against her, and the sense of security—albeit false—that he brought her. Unable to do otherwise, she slid her hands up across his strong back and returned the embrace, pressing her cheek against his chest and letting his shirt absorb the moisture from her tears.

He brushed his lips across her temple, his lips barely moving as he whispered. "In about ninety seconds the guards are going to come back. I'm supposed to be convincing you to give up the password. He says if you do, he'll let all of us go."

Sydney stiffened. "Is that what this was all about? More games?"

He muttered a curse. "No. I was—and am—telling you the God's honest truth. About my feelings and about what's going to happen next. We don't have much time, so listen carefully. I want you to give him the password."

She started to pull away in shock, but he held her tightly, forestalling the move. That forced her to turn her face into his, so they were pressed cheek-to-cheek in a lover's embrace when she whispered, "Why?"

"Bringing Tiberius down is my responsibility, not yours. You more than did your duty by giving us all the information you did. Everything else was just…me being a blind, judgmental idiot, I guess."

A few days ago, even a few hours ago, she would've given anything to have him acknowledge such a thing.

Now it just ticked her off.

"No." She put her hands flat on his chest and pushed, creating enough distance that she could look up and glare at him. "You don't get to decide that now. You're at least partially responsible for me being back here, so you're darn well going to let me help fix what I did wrong." She leaned in and touched her lips to his in the briefest hint of a kiss, and felt the surprise vibrate through his big frame. But it was just another move in the game he'd drawn her into, because she used the kiss to murmur, "Now listen up. I have an idea, but you're going to have to trust me...."

CHAPTER TWELVE

WHEN SHE'D FINISHED explaining the plan, John growled, "No. Just give him the password and let me take care of the rest."

"Sorry," she said stubbornly. "I don't take orders from you unless they make sense. These don't. Besides, my way will work. You just have to trust me."

And there it was.

"Is that what this is about?" he whispered. "Some sort of a test? It's not enough for me to tell you I believe you?"

That made her eyes go sad. She drew away and touched his face, skimming the back of her knuckles along his stubble-roughened jaw. "Poor John. So used to being suspicious you don't know how not to be."

And then their time was up. The door slid open behind them and the guards reentered, followed by Tiberius himself.

The scholarly-looking bastard saw John and Sydney wrapped together in an embrace and his lips twitched. "Touching. Just behave yourselves and you might live long enough to do it again."

When he moved toward them, John put himself in front of Sydney.

"Don't be stupidly heroic," Tiberius advised him. "You're outnumbered and outgunned." He paused.

"Come on. Computer time." He gestured Sydney to the computer terminal sitting on a desk nearby, no doubt the one she'd used to work on her sequence late at night when she'd been unable to sleep.

John could picture her there, all alone, and his anger at Tiberius only increased.

"Not here," Sydney contradicted. "It's got to be done on the computer where the program was originally input, or it won't work."

Tiberius stared at her, unblinking. "I think you're bluffing."

"Are you willing to take that chance?"

He was silent so long John thought he wasn't going to agree. Then he did, turning away and jerking his head at the three guards. "Bring them to the lab. If either of them tries something, shoot them both. Leave the woman alive. If the agent dies, I won't be too upset."

The absolute unconcern in his voice was beyond chilling, giving a glimpse into the monster that lived within the professorial shell.

One of the guards grabbed Sydney and dragged her out into the hallway. John growled and lunged after the bastard, but the guard behind him slammed his rifle butt into John's kidneys, driving him to his knees.

"Enough," the guard behind him snapped. "Be glad there aren't any holes in your girlfriend. Yet."

The guards marched John and Sydney down the remainder of the hallway to where it dead-ended in a set of airlock-type doors that were plastered with biohazard decals and warnings. As they passed, John noticed that several of the doors were ajar, where they'd been closed and locked before. He caught a glimpse of living quarters, bare, with a scattering of debris that looked like a hasty evac.

He became aware of a low vibration running through the floor beneath his feet and the air around them. At first he thought it might be a generator running in the basement, powering the big compound. But the noise was new. He hadn't heard it before.

When they passed an exterior door that was locked and barred, the sound became more distinct. It was a helicopter getting up to temp for takeoff. Beneath the rotor-thump, he thought he heard the sound of boats motoring off into the distance, as well.

Not a generator. A full-scale evacuation.

Time was running out.

One of the guards used his passkey to open the lab doors, and John realized that was an indication that the majority of the guards in the security hub were already gone, because otherwise they would've been buzzed in remotely.

As they moved through the doors into the lab, he caught Sydney's eyes and saw the knowledge there. She nodded, and he saw fear, but no sign that she was ready to give up.

I love you, he wanted to say again. He saw her eyes widen fractionally, as though she'd read the sentiment in his expression. Even thinking the words made him feel bigger and meaner and ready to fight to protect his woman.

Before, he'd thought of love as something that would make him weaker. Instead, it was making him strong.

He could only hope it would make him tough enough to get Sydney and his team off the island before it blew.

"You said you needed the input terminal." Tiberius

gestured to a row of low desks, each holding a computer connected to one or more pieces of high-tech lab equipment. "Do your thing." He glanced at his watch. "You've got ten minutes."

"Or?" she countered.

"Or I'll have my men shoot Agent Sharpe here, and you wouldn't want that, would you?"

Responding to his boss's threat, the guy behind John reversed his rifle, so it wasn't the butt poking into his kidneys anymore, but rather the business end of the weapon. Which complicated things, but only a little.

Sydney looked over at him one last time.

"Give him what he wants," John said. "He's won." He didn't have to fake the frustration in his voice. They were too close to checkmate for his comfort. Far too close.

Eyes filming, Sydney nodded and crossed to one of the terminals. Sitting at the roll-away desk chair, she tapped the mouse to wake the screen out of saver mode. The cursor blinked against a blank field, with a one-word question glowing on the screen: *Password?*

Sydney typed in something and hit Enter. The screen blanked for a second, then the same word returned: *Password?*

She typed in a second string and hit Enter, and again the screen blanked before the password prompt returned. She typed in a third string.

Before she could hit Enter, Tiberius warned in a low growl, "Don't play games with me, Sydney. You won't like what happens."

"I know what happens," she said softly, almost whispering. "I remember what you did to Jenny Marie."

Tiberius grabbed one of the guards' weapons and

crossed to her. He pressed the gun barrel to her temple
and leaned over her. "Then what are you doing?"

John held himself still, barely breathing, fighting the
mad impulse to leap across the room and rip the bastard away from Sydney. Things only got worse when
she turned a little and glanced at him, and he saw her
lips frame the words, "I'm sorry."

Then she hit Enter.

The computer emitted a startled-sounding beep and
the screen went dark. Half a second later, the power cut
out completely, plunging them into darkness.

THE MOMENT THE LIGHTS went out, Sydney flung herself
backward in the chair. It rolled a few feet before it hit
something and overbalanced, spilling her to the floor.
She hit hard and saw stars but kept rolling, desperate
to get away from Tiberius.

Gunfire exploded in the close confines of the lab,
and she could hear equipment smashing to pieces. The
scientist in her cringed as her auto-sequencers and PCR
machines bit the dust, but the emerging patriot in her—
along with her human survival instincts—wanted only
to get out of the lab.

She heard a crash nearby, a volley of gunshots and
rapid-fire masculine cursing.

Then silence. A single set of running footsteps. The
sound of a door opening and slamming shut. More silence.

The darkness pressed around Sydney, making her
feel very small and alone all of a sudden. She huddled
up against the flat plane of a wall, barely daring to
breathe. Where was John? Was he dead? Captured?

Had he, God forbid, left her there alone, still playing his game?

No, she told herself firmly. *He wouldn't. He loves me. He said so and I believe him.*

Then, out of the darkness, his voice said, "Syd? You okay?"

Her breath exploded from her in a whoosh of relief. "I'm fine. You?"

"What did you do?"

"The first word killed the lab network permanently. The second and third together triggered another program that took the electric grid offline and FUBARed the rest of the networks on the island."

"Of course it did." But there was warmth in his voice rather than frustration. She heard the click of weaponry and clothing, presumably as he disarmed the guards he'd taken out. "Tiberius got away," he said after a moment.

Which explained the footsteps and slamming door, damn it. "Think we can catch him?"

There was a pause, and she could almost feel the internal battle before he said, "Let's find the others and get back to the boat. We'll get him another time."

"Which puts you back at square one," Sydney said. Guilt stabbed at her. "You're going to be back to hunting him without any really good connection to a prosecutable crime. I'm sorry."

"I'm not." She heard him move closer, felt his arms come around her. "And I'm not exactly back where I started, either."

Then he kissed her, leaving no doubt as to his meaning.

She leaned into him as warmth speared through her.

The darkness created warm intimacy even as the feel of a pistol in one of his hands, pressing into her back when he gathered her close against the hard wall of his chest, kept the sense of danger close by, adding to the thrill.

Heat bloomed as he slanted his mouth across hers and took it deeper, need spiraling up to become lust, desire becoming almost an obsession.

Yet alongside the physical sensations, new, scary emotions took root.

She was safe in his arms, yet exposed. She felt raw, her emotions too close to the surface, too uncertain. She'd thought she loved him, but what did she know about loving a man? He'd been a challenge, a conquest. There didn't seem to be any possible way for them to make it work. They were too different, and too alike in the wrong ways.

They were both stubborn and headstrong, and too used to running the show. If they tried to have a future, they'd probably wind up killing each other.

Then again, if they didn't get their butts in gear, their future—shared or separate—was down to twelve minutes or so.

They broke apart by unspoken accord. "Time to go," he said, voice rough with passion. He cleared his throat. "Here. Take this."

He pressed a weapon into her hand.

The small pistol was heavier than she would've imagined, and warm from his body heat. Her fingers curled around the grip and found the trigger. "Just point and shoot?"

"There's a safety." He guided her finger to the little sliding bump along one side of the trigger guard.

"Which one's off?"

"It's already off. Just leave it there for now...and yeah, with the safety off, it's point and shoot, but stick with me and it won't come to that, okay?"

"Promise?"

"I'll promise you whatever you want," he said simply.

The sentiment had her heart lodging in her throat as she began to believe he really meant it. He loved her. The very idea of it had worlds opening up before her even as the time ran out around them.

"What's the plan?" she asked, suddenly filled with renewed determination to get the hell off Rocky Cliff Island.

She'd done it once. She could do it again.

"Where do you think Tiberius is holding the others?"

She thought for a moment. "There are some wings I was never given access to." Those had been the blanks on the blueprints that they'd tried to fill in from satellite images and guesswork. "If I had to guess, I'd say he keeps his prisoners somewhere on the ground floor, north wing." She swallowed hard. "That's closest to the cliffs."

"Simplifying disposal of the bodies," he said, following her train of thought. "Right. Let's go."

He led her through the blackness. She only stumbled once when her toe snagged on the cloth-covered, yielding surface of what she could only assume was one of the guards. She didn't ask if they were alive or dead. She wasn't sure she wanted to know.

When they reached the lab door, John cracked the panel and peeked into the hallway, which was slightly lighter than the lab, illuminated by daylight refracting from the living quarters through the half-open doors.

"Looks clear," he murmured, and led her out into the hallway.

They worked their way back up to the main entrance, then took the door to the north wing. After the third time John paused to check around a corner, Sydney whispered, "It seems like everyone's gone."

"The helicopter noise hasn't changed," he whispered. "That means Tiberius is still on the island."

"And I'm betting he's furious." For a second, she flashed back on Jenny Marie's screams and suppressed a shudder. She'd come way too far to back out now. Either they found a way to locate Tiberius and take him out, or she'd be spending the rest of her life in witness protection, with or without John.

She instinctively tightened her fingers on the gun he'd given her. The feel of the bulky grip was simultaneously reassuring and intimidating. She liked knowing she could protect herself, but couldn't picture herself shooting anyone.

Then again, if Tiberius was in her sights, she might be able to deal with it.

They checked the rooms one by one as they moved up the hallway. When they reached the sixth door, the one closest to the exit, they found it locked with a manual bolt in addition to the automatic locks, which had disengaged when the power cut out.

"Stand back," John warned. When Sydney was out of range, he fired twice, then kicked the door in. He went first, then beckoned her into what was clearly a holding area—and probably served a more grisly role, as well, given the overhead sprinkler system and prominent drain in the center of the waterproofed floor.

Michael, Jimmy and Drew sat against the far wall with their legs stretched out in front of them, bound at their ankles and their arms fastened behind their backs. They sent up a quiet cheer when they recognized the figures in the doorway.

"Sydney, here." John tossed her a knife, which he must've lifted from one of the guards back in the lab.

She fumbled the catch, trying not to drop the gun in her increasingly sweaty hands. Making an executive decision, she set the safety to 'on' and tucked the gun in her waistband, hoping like heck she'd gotten the on-off thing right.

Crouching down, she went to work on the bound men while John watched the doorway.

She freed Michael first and handed him the gun. "Here. You'll have more use for this than me."

"Thanks." He took the weapon and climbed to his feet, shaking out his stiff limbs as he went. Before he joined John at the door, though, he touched Sydney's shoulder briefly. "And thanks for guarding his back."

She grimaced. "I think I've gotten him into way more trouble than I've gotten him out of."

"You know what I mean."

Before she could respond, the sharpshooter moved off to join his leader. The two had a brief, low-voiced conversation while Sydney cut the zip ties binding the rest of the men.

When they were all up and the group was assembled near the door, John said, "We've got just about eight minutes on the countdown, so we're going to split up. I want Drew and Jimmy to head straight for the boat and have her ready to go. Michael and I are going out the front and straight down to the water. We'll meet you at the ropes."

Michael said, "Obviously grab weapons if you can, but don't waste time. And keep as low as you can—the chopper still hasn't lifted off. Best guess is that the bastard is waiting for us in the helo, and is going to open fire once we get near the boat. He's not going to want to let us get off the island. If we make it off, he'll target the boat."

"Any questions?" John asked.

"Just one." Sydney looked at him sideways. "Which group am I supposed to go with?"

"You're with me," John said, and there was a wealth of meaning in the words.

She smiled faintly. "Thanks."

"Don't thank me yet. We still have to get out of here." But he reached over and took her hand, right in front of everyone, and held on as though he needed the reassurance of the touch as much as she did. "Any other questions?"

When there weren't any, the team split and moved out, with the men promising to meet up at the ropes in under five minutes. That'd be cutting it close, but it was the best they were going to be able to do.

John led, with Sydney right behind him, and Michael bringing up the rear guard. They moved quickly through the mansion, eschewing stealth for speed. There were no more boat noises, only the thump of the idling helicopter.

"Do you think they cut your boat loose?" Sydney asked as they reached the front foyer, which seemed even colder and more impersonal with the sense of emptiness that echoed throughout the mansion, and the lack of the normal blowers and low-grade beeps coming from electrical systems that'd gone dead thanks to the worm program.

"Unless you have a better suggestion, we're going to assume it's still there," John responded with a hint of an edge in his voice.

"Sorry," she said. "You're right. Don't ask unless it's something we can fix."

He blew out a breath and squeezed her hand, which he was still holding. "I didn't mean to snap. I just wish I had a better answer."

She squeezed back. "I think we're just about due for a lucky break, don't you?"

"If you say so." But he smiled and touched his lips to hers. Then he pulled away, readied his weapon and went into agent mode. "Ready?" he asked Michael.

The sharpshooter nodded. "Let's move out."

They were halfway across the cleared lawn area surrounding the mansion when the first shot rang out, coming from the direction of one of the guard shacks. John immediately spun Sydney and shoved her toward a stand of trees nearby. "Get under cover. I'm right behind you."

Heart pounding in her chest, she didn't stop to argue or ask questions. She bolted for safety, crashing through the thick brush while the men opened fire behind her, retreating along the path they'd come up only an hour or so earlier.

Sydney took two steps past the trees, stumbled and went down. The impact knocked her breath away, and she lay dazed for a second, the sound of gunfire muted by the ringing in her ears. It took her a moment to focus. When she did, she saw the tripwire that'd taken her down.

Then she saw a pair of loafers appear, topped by cabled pants and a tweed jacket, with Tiberius's face looming far above.

His mouth split in a wide, patronizing smile.

And everything went black.

CHAPTER THIRTEEN

THE ATTACK STOPPED abruptly. One minute they were taking heavy fire from three positions on the mansion side of the clearing, and the next there was a silence so complete it put John's instincts into overdrive.

That hadn't been an attack, he realized. It'd been a distraction.

He spun and bolted for the trees. "Sydney!"

There was no answer, and when he reached the clearing there was no Sydney. She was gone.

A week ago, even a day ago, his first thought would've been that she'd betrayed him, but not now. He knew her better than that, trusted her more than that, and he didn't even break stride before reversing course and returning to Michael. "Tiberius has her," he reported tersely. "They'll be headed for the helicopter."

The sharpshooter didn't hesitate. "Then that's where we're going."

They headed for higher ground, and the sound of the helicopter rotor-thump. The detour was going to take time they didn't have to spare, but there was no discussion as they melted into the trees and headed for the helipad. Sydney was one of them now, and they weren't leaving her behind.

SYDNEY'S HEAD WAS BUZZING when she regained consciousness. Or rather, there was a buzzing noise all around her, she realized as her surroundings started to come clear.

She was lying on her side against a wall of cargo netting, which held stacked boxes and trunks in place. The hard surface beneath her vibrated at an increasing frequency as the pitch of the hum increased. The whole world seemed to shudder, then sway, and the hum became the roar of an engine.

She was on the helicopter!

Panic slashed through her. She exploded into motion, only to find herself brought up short by bindings at her wrists and ankles. They gave slightly, but cut into her skin. Zip ties. And they were attached to the cargo netting, leaving her trapped, lying helpless on her side at the rear of the large, twin-rotor helicopter's cargo bay.

She was facing the forward passenger compartment and the cockpit beyond, and the light from a rolled-open side slider showed four men ahead of her: the pilot and copilot, both wearing guard uniforms, one other guard and Tiberius.

She must've made some sound while waking up, because Tiberius turned around in his seat to look at her.

He shook his head as though she'd deeply disappointed him. "Blanking the computer banks was a bad move, Sydney. And here I thought you were one of the smart ones. Turns out you're just as stupid—and idealistic—as your boyfriend." When the engine note changed again, he glanced at the pilot. "We good to go yet?"

"Almost, sir. The chips controlling the pressure gauges are just about done rebooting. I'm just lucky I logged out of the network when I did, or her program would've taken out the entire system."

Tiberius glanced at his watch. "You have five minutes to get us over the water."

The chopper dipped and spun unsteadily, and the motion slid Sydney a few more inches along the deck until she came to a stop at the farthest reaches of her bonds. Her new position gave her a glimpse out the side door, enough to let her know they were still on the island.

More importantly, she caught a flash of motion from the treeline. John.

"What are you going to do to me?" she said sharply, trying to draw Tiberius's attention.

He turned back to her and raised an eyebrow. "Well, I'm certainly not stupid. I'm going to chuck you once we're over open water."

His flat-affect delivery was equally as terrifying as the threat itself, and Sydney didn't have to fake the tremor in her voice when she said, "I can re-create the virus. I know the shortcuts now. I can do it in half the time it took me before."

"I'm through making deals with you," he said, flicking his fingers in dismissal. "You can't be trusted to stay bought. Not a very admirable quality."

She dropped her voice. "Try me. I'll make it worth your while." She paused, and when he didn't turn away immediately, said, "The technology's not just limited to DNA testing, you know. I bet I could program the vector to recognize a specific DNA fingerprint and kill just that one person. You wouldn't need to be anywhere near the target. Just leave some of the virus where he'll come into contact with it. Poof. Murder by long distance."

She had his full attention now. "You're saying you could make such a thing?"

"Imagine the possibilities," she said, trying to make him believe she'd throw herself fully on his side, if only to ensure her life. "If the target has DNA on file in one of the databases, you wouldn't even need a DNA sample. You could just lift the repeat numbers from the database, and poof. They're dead."

Frowning, he said, "It wouldn't work if the target has been infected with the other bug, right? The fingerprint would be too blurry for the virus to lock on to."

Triumph spurted. She had him considering it now. "I won't know for sure until I've tested the actual constructs, but even if that's the case, what's the downside? If someone wanted to block themselves from the fingerprint-targeting vector, they'd have to buy the fingerprint-blurring vector from you. Either way you're getting paid. It's a win-win."

She was making herself sick even thinking this way, let alone saying it aloud. Worse, John could hear her. What was he thinking as he listened in?

Tiberius's eyes flashed. "If this stuff is so easy to conceptualize, why do I need you? I should be able to give the theory to another scientist—one who'll stay bought—and have him turn it around with far less risk."

She met his eyes and willed him to see nothing but what she wanted him to when she said, "Are you willing to take that gamble?"

Before he could answer, the engine note changed to a deeper, full-throated growl, the helicopter stabilized and the pilot called, "All set, sir!"

Tiberius turned. "Then get us out of here." He was turning back to Sydney when his attention fixed on something outside the open slider. He shouted and grabbed for the guard sitting beside him.

And all hell broke loose.

John lunged onto the helicopter, followed by Michael. Just then, the craft lifted off the ground, wallowing with the added weight. The guard beside Tiberius leapt from his chair and opened fire, causing the pilot and copilot to duck and swear. The chopper dipped and swayed, bouncing off the ground and rattling the men locked in hand-to-hand combat in the passenger cabin.

John grappled with Tiberius, whose face was etched with rage. John, on the other hand, maintained his icy calm as he struggled to subdue the other man, while looking around the small cabin.

The ice cracked when he saw Sydney.

"Take him!" He shoved Tiberius at Michael, who caught the older man with a good punch along the jaw.

Then John was kneeling beside her, cutting the zip ties away and helping her up, and the only thing in his eyes was concern and love. For her.

"I didn't mean any of those things I said to him." She gripped his wrists, willing him to believe her. "I never would've built such a thing."

"I know. Don't worry about it." He touched his lips to hers. "I'll have to admit that your brain is a pretty scary place, though."

She grinned and started to laugh, but the laughter was cut off by a bark of gunfire and a sudden flurry of activity from up ahead as Michael flew backward out of the helicopter. The guard was down and unmoving, but the chopper was gaining altitude as the load lightened.

"John!" Sydney cried, her heart lunging into her

throat at the realization that they were seconds away from being trapped on Tiberius's helicopter, heading out over open water.

"Stay back," he ordered, "and get out the door as soon as you can. I'll be right behind you."

Before she could answer, he'd rushed Tiberius. His momentum drove them away from the door and he shouted, "Sydney, go!"

She dove through headfirst, not realizing that the craft was a good ten feet off the ground and rising fast. Screaming, she grabbed on to one of the skids and held on for dear life, her feet dangling in thin air. "John, *help!*"

There were three shots in quick succession, coming from inside the helicopter, but she couldn't tell who was shooting or who'd been shot.

"Sydney, let go," Michael yelled from below. "I'll catch you!"

She didn't think or argue. She closed her eyes and let go.

Her stomach jumped into her throat in a moment of free fall, and then she hit, taking Michael down in a tangle of arms and legs.

Above them, the helicopter took flight, banking and soaring away with one member of the team still on board.

"John!" Sydney surged to her feet and reached for the aircraft, though that was futile. *"John!"*

"Sydney!" Michael dragged her back. "Come on, we've got to go."

The urgency in his voice pierced the terror and anguish of seeing the chopper grow smaller, and she remembered the countdown.

How much time was left?

Seeing he had her attention, Michael started jogging downhill, toward the cliffs. "Come on!"

They fled toward the cliffs where the boat should be, reaching the ropes in under three minutes. Sydney stumbled to a halt at the sight of a man waiting for them, but it was Jimmy. One of the good guys. "Hurry!" he shouted. "Move!"

They moved. The cliff descent was a blur of gravity and burning palms to Sydney, and she hit the beach running. Drew grabbed her and boosted her up and over the edge of the boat, and the others followed moments later. Then they were casting off, and Michael was gunning the boat away from the island.

"Use the riptide," Drew shouted over the crash of waves and the laboring noise of the boat's engine. "Doesn't matter where we go, just so long as it's away from the island!"

Michael nodded and sent the skiff toward a section of flatter-looking water that was all moving in one direction, forming what looked like a river within the ocean swells. When they hit the current, the skiff leapt forward, forcing them to hang on for the ride.

Sydney hung on, but she couldn't make herself do any more than that. Her entire attention was fixed on the empty sky, while Tiberius's words rang in her ears: *I'm certainly not stupid,* he'd said. *I'm going to chuck you once we're over open water.*

Only he'd be tossing John's body, not hers.

Tears filled her eyes and grief hollowed her out until she was nothing but a shell of sadness, nothing but regret. In the end, he'd trusted her. He'd known she was lying to Tiberius about the virus, and hadn't doubted her for an instant. She should've told him she loved him right then, when she'd had the chance.

Now it was too late.

"Don't give up on him yet," Michael said, coming up beside her and dropping a blanket over her shoulders. "Sharpe is the Iceman. If anyone can gain control of the chopper and bring Tiberius in, it'll be him."

"He would've won if he hadn't been worried about rescuing me," she said softly, staring at her fingers twined in her lap. "I messed him up, made him weaker."

"Not necessarily. You gave him something to come back to." Now Michael was looking up at the stubbornly empty sky, too, as were Jimmy and Drew, but to no avail.

Then Jimmy pointed. "There! Do you see it?"

Sydney lunged to her feet and grabbed the gunwale. "Where?"

Seconds later, the island exploded behind them with the sound of a thousand subway trains crashing into each other at once.

Sydney screamed as the shockwave slammed into the boat, rolling it up on one side and leaving it poised there for a second before it hurtled back down into a trough, shuddering with the impact. Heat scorched the exposed skin of her hands and face, and shrapnel peppered down around them, large and small pieces of island debris, chunks of masonry and wood stinging her where they hit.

It took her a second to realize she was alone at the railing. "Michael!" she screamed, looking around, to where the others were picking themselves up off the deck, checking small injuries and shrapnel hits. "Where's **Michael?**"

Seconds later, Drew went over the side and struck out swimming toward Michael's motionless body, which was floating facedown in the water.

Drew was in the process of hauling Michael back to the boat, swimming one-handed, when a new sound became audible over the fading rumble of the explosion.

Helicopter rotors.

Heart lunging into her throat, Sydney searched the sky but saw nothing more than she'd seen before, save for the section of sky obscured by a thick pillar of smoke and debris pouring from the wreckage that had been Tiberius's island.

Then the noise increased and the chopper appeared from behind the smoky curtain, creating mad swirls of soot in the air.

John! she wanted to scream, but couldn't because her throat was locked on the word, on the very act of breathing as the helicopter drew near.

"Grab him!" Jimmy shouted behind her. There was a flurry of motion, and the boat tipped slightly as Jimmy and Drew struggled to get Michael on board.

"He's breathing," Drew reported, at the same moment Jimmy shouted, "Get us the hell out of here. Chopper incoming!"

Sure enough, the aircraft swept in a slow arc and headed straight for the boat.

For a split second the future hovered between salvation and destruction. Then the men on the chopper opened fire.

"Down!" Drew shouted, though they were already scrambling for the scant cover available on the sturdy boat.

With Michael down, Drew took over the controls and

sent the skiff hurtling in a series of evasive maneuvers, slewing the craft wildly from side to side and avoiding the first strafing run as the chopper passed overhead. The pilot corrected quickly, though, and lined up for another run.

"There's the *Valiant!*" Jimmy cried, pointing to a dot on the horizon.

The skiff hurtled in the direction of the coast guard ship with the helicopter right behind it, but the men on the chopper didn't fire again. Instead, the aircraft began to wallow from side to side, as though it was having mechanical difficulties.

Or someone on board was putting up a hell of a fight.

"Almost in range of the *Valiant*'s launcher," Drew called, still swerving the boat in a series of evasive runs. "One minute."

It took a moment for that to penetrate. When it did, Sydney spun to the others. "They're not going to shoot the chopper, are they? They can't! They—"

She broke off when the door in the side of the helicopter slid open and a body pitched out and fell limply for twenty feet or so to the sea. Sydney screamed, and screamed again when the helicopter suddenly swerved in the sky, seeming to be coming for them again.

"Fire, damn it!" Drew shouted, though the approaching coast guard cutter was too far away for anyone to hear, and the rotor-thump drowned out the shout as the helicopter approached.

Then without warning, it swerved hard to the left, flipped up and over and began to autorotate, spinning like a flat disk as it hurtled back toward the island. The engines screamed and smoke began to pour from the open door.

Seconds later, it slammed into the cliff below the wrecked mansion, detonated in an orange-red fireball and crashed into the ocean.

Seconds after that, it was gone, marked only by a sooty smudge on the rocky cliff face.

Someone was moaning. It took Sydney a minute to realize it was her, and to feel the bite of pain where she'd dug her fingertips into the metal side of the boat, and broken two of her fingernails away. "No," she said, "no, no, no."

But the litany of denial didn't bring the helicopter back up to the surface, and it didn't make John suddenly appear, treading water and waving for a pickup.

The sea was eerily calm.

"He jumped," Michael said, his voice ragged. He was bleeding from a cut on his head, but he was conscious and standing. "That had to be him. He got out before they hit."

Drew sent the boat toward where the jumper had landed. The *Valiant* approached the same point from the other side, and all hands were on deck, scanning the water for a swimmer.

Or a body, Sydney thought as a big shiver crawled down her spine and made her stomach pitch. *Please be there,* she thought desperately. *Please be okay.* The chant repeated itself over and over again in her head, but she saw nothing. No swimmer. No body. Just water.

Tears blinded her and broke free, tracking down her cheeks. Michael moved up beside her along the railing, Jimmy and Drew stepping to her other side, so the four of them stood together, scanning the Atlantic for the leader of their team. For the man she loved.

"Ahoy the boat."

For a second, Sydney didn't think she'd actually heard the hail, which had come from the other side of the boat, the side away from where the body had fallen.

Then she heard it again. "Hello? Anyone up there?"

It was John's voice.

Screaming his name, she flew to the other side of the boat, with the others right behind her. And there he was, treading water.

His eyes locked on her and a huge smile split his face. "You're okay."

"Yeah," she said, grinning through her tears. "I am now."

He held up a hand. "A little help here?"

Michael, Jimmy and Drew were only too happy to drag him aboard the skiff, and the team surrounded him with backslaps and congratulations, but his attention stayed fixed on Sydney, and all of his emotions were plain to see.

There was satisfaction of a job well done in bringing Tiberius to justice, one way or another. There was relief that it was over and they were both standing safely on the deck.

And there was love, shining clear as the sunlight, along with the question she hadn't yet answered.

She answered it now as he crossed to her, opening her arms to him. "I love you."

He whooped and swept her up in an embrace that might have been cold and wet from the seawater that still poured from him, but was warm where it counted—where their lips touched, and where their bodies melded together in a long, satisfying kiss.

She wrapped her arms around him, so this time,

unlike the first time they'd washed up on a deck together just off Rocky Cliff Island, they shared the same blanket.

EPILOGUE

THE SIX MONTHS FOLLOWING Tiberius's death were harder work than John had expected. He and his team had been forced to go in and dismantle certain pieces of his organization by force, and they'd been fighting a constant rearguard action to keep others from stepping into the leadership role.

Eventually someone would step up, he knew. Nature abhorred a vacuum. But the prospect didn't bother him nearly as much as it had before, because he was coming to realize that was part of the game, too. It wasn't just the moves leading up to checkmate that mattered, it was what the victor did after the game.

Before, he would've headed home for a few weeks of vacation and lasted only a few days before restlessness sent him back to the office.

Now, as he turned into the long drive leading to his house and rolled past the freshly clipped paddocks, where a pair of fat quarter horses dozed in the sun, tails swishing idly at the last of the season's flies, he knew he'd be squeezing every last drop out of this vacation, because everything was different now.

These days, he had a reason to come home.

He found her in the kitchen, cooking an army's worth of pasta and sauce with her usual combination of a scientist's precision and risk-taker's flare. When he wrapped his arms around her slim waist and pressed his lips into the curve of her neck, she leaned back into him for a moment, then turned in his arms to greet him with a proper kiss, one that had him thinking of turning down the burners and nipping upstairs.

"Company will be here in thirty," she murmured against his lips as hers curved in a smile. "Hold that thought, okay?"

Knowing it would be better for the wait—and the time to explore the ever-changing, always-blinding heat between them—he kissed her nose and grinned. "We celebrating?"

He figured he already knew the answer from her smile.

"The accelerated approval came through today," she confirmed. "We've got the go-ahead to start Celeste on the new treatment." She reached past him to give the pasta a quick stir, which involved pressing her hips against his erection, wringing a groan from him.

"Congratulations." He nibbled at her ear. "Temptress."

Her eyes glazed and her breath started coming faster, in the little puffs of excitement he loved so much. "Thanks." She tipped her head back and moaned a little as he moved to her throat and along the soft line of her jaw. "There's no guarantee it'll work, but all the early results are good. At a minimum, we should be able to stop the disease from progressing further. At best, she could get some of the feeling and strength back in her arms." She turned her lips to his and drew him into a deep, searching kiss. When it ended, she whispered, "I couldn't have done it without you."

In the aftermath of the op on Rocky Cliff Island, he'd gone to bat for her, not just to keep her safe from prosecution, but to get her added on to a government-affiliated think tank investigating ways to make—and counteract—various types of bioweapons.

He smiled against her mouth, turning down the burner when the water boiled over. "I figured the U.S. of A. was far safer with you working *for* the government rather than against it." He'd also made it a condition that the think tank had to support her side project of developing a cure for Singer's syndrome.

Her bug wasn't perfect yet, but it was getting there.

When her fingers went to his belt, he glanced at the kitchen clock. "Thirty minutes, you said?"

"Mmm." She followed the direction of his gaze. "Twenty-five now, but it's Celeste and Hugo. They'll understand if dinner's not done. And besides, I'm sure they can amuse themselves…or each other." Her eyes glittered, no doubt at the thought of the relationship that had developed between her sister and the FBI agent who'd protected her during the dangers of earlier that year.

With that, she flicked off the burner beneath the boiling water and turned the sauce down to simmer.

Then, without a word, she held out a hand and they walked up the stairs together.

As they stepped into the bedroom, he leaned close and whispered, "I love you."

She looked up at him, eyes gleaming. "I hope you know you've said that once or twice before."

He smiled, swept her up in his arms and carried her to their bed. "Then I guess that means I finally found something worth repeating."

* * * * *

PARANORMAL

Dark and sensual paranormal romance stories
that stretch the boundaries of conflict and desire, life and death.

Harlequin®

n o c t u r n e™

COMING NEXT MONTH
AVAILABLE NOVEMBER 22, 2011

#125 LORD OF THE ABYSS
Royal House of Shadows
Nalini Singh

#126 SOUL WHISPERER
The Trackers
Jenna Kernan

HNCNM1111

REQUEST YOUR FREE BOOKS!

2 FREE NOVELS FROM THE PARANORMAL ROMANCE COLLECTION PLUS 2 FREE GIFTS!

YES! Please send me 2 FREE novels from the Paranormal Romance Collection and my 2 FREE gifts (gifts are worth about $10). After receiving them, if I don't wish to receive any more books, I can return the shipping statement marked "cancel." If I don't cancel, I will receive 4 brand-new novels every month and be billed just $21.42 in the U.S. or $23.46 in Canada. That's a saving of at least 21% off the cover price of all 4 books. It's quite a bargain! Shipping and handling is just 50¢ per book in the U.S. and 75¢ per book in Canada.* I understand that accepting the 2 free books and gifts places me under no obligation to buy anything. I can always return a shipment and cancel at any time. Even if I never buy another book, the two free books and gifts are mine to keep forever.

237/337 HDN FEL2

Name	(PLEASE PRINT)	
Address		Apt. #
City	State/Prov.	Zip/Postal Code

Signature (if under 18, a parent or guardian must sign)

Mail to the **Reader Service:**
IN U.S.A.: P.O. Box 1867, Buffalo, NY 14240-1867
IN CANADA: P.O. Box 609, Fort Erie, Ontario L2A 5X3

Not valid for current subscribers to the Paranormal Romance Collection or Harlequin® Nocturne™ books.

Want to try two free books from another line?
Call 1-800-873-8635 or visit www.ReaderService.com.

* Terms and prices subject to change without notice. Prices do not include applicable taxes. Sales tax applicable in N.Y. Canadian residents will be charged applicable taxes. Offer not valid in Quebec. This offer is limited to one order per household. All orders subject to credit approval. Credit or debit balances in a customer's account(s) may be offset by any other outstanding balance owed by or to the customer. Please allow 4 to 6 weeks for delivery. Offer available while quantities last.

Your Privacy—The Reader Service is committed to protecting your privacy. Our Privacy Policy is available online at www.ReaderService.com or upon request from the Reader Service.

We make a portion of our mailing list available to reputable third parties that offer products we believe may interest you. If you prefer that we not exchange your name with third parties, or if you wish to clarify or modify your communication preferences, please visit us at www.ReaderService.com/consumerschoice or write to us at Reader Service Preference Service, P.O. Box 9062, Buffalo, NY 14269. Include your complete name and address.

*Lucy Flemming and Ross Mitchell shared a magical,
sexy Christmas weekend together six years ago.
This Christmas, history may repeat itself when they find
themselves stranded in a major snowstorm...
and alone at last.*

*Read on for a sneak peek from
IT HAPPENED ONE CHRISTMAS
by Leslie Kelly.*

Available December 2011, only from Harlequin® Blaze™.

EYEING THE GRAY, THICK SKY through the expansive wall of
windows, Lucy began to pack up her photography gear.
The Christmas party was winding down, only a dozen or so
people remaining on this floor, which had been transformed
from cubicles and meeting rooms to a holiday funland. She
smiled at those nearest to her, then, seeing the glances at her
silly elf hat, she reached up to tug it off her head.

Before she could do it, however, she heard a voice. A
deep, male voice—smooth and sexy, and so not Santa's.

"I appreciate you filling in on such short notice. I've
heard you do a terrific job."

Lucy didn't turn around, letting her brain process what
she was hearing. Her whole body had stiffened, the hairs on
the back of her neck standing up, her skin tightening into
tiny goose bumps. Because that voice sounded so familiar.
Impossibly familiar.

It can't be.

"It sounds like the kids had a great time."

Unable to stop herself, Lucy began to turn around,
wondering if her ears—and all her other senses—were
deceiving her. After all, six years was a long time, the mind

could play tricks. What were the odds that she'd bump into *him,* here? And today of all days. December 23.

Six years exactly. Was that really possible?

One look—and the accompanying frantic thudding of her heart—and she knew her ears and brain were working just fine. Because it was *him.*

"Oh, my God," he whispered, shocked, frozen, staring as thoroughly as she was. "Lucy?"

She nodded slowly, not taking her eyes off him, wondering why the years had made him even more attractive than ever. It didn't seem fair. Not when she'd spent the past six years thinking he must have started losing that thick, golden-brown hair, or added a spare tire to that trim, muscular form.

No.

The man was gorgeous. Truly, without-a-doubt, mouthwateringly handsome, every bit as hot as he'd been the first time she'd laid eyes on him. She'd been twenty-two, he one year older.

They'd shared an amazing holiday season.

And had never seen one another again.

Until now.

Find out what happens in
IT HAPPENED ONE CHRISTMAS
by Leslie Kelly.
Available December 2011, only from Harlequin® Blaze™

Harlequin®

n○cturne™

NEW YORK TIMES AND *USA TODAY*
BESTSELLING AUTHOR

NALINI SINGH

brings you the exciting conclusion
to the four-book, multi-author miniseries

ROYAL HOUSE *of* SHADOWS

Micah is a feared monster, the dark Lord who condemns
souls to damnation in the Abyss. He has no idea he
is the last heir and only hope for Elden…only the
daughter of his enemy knows. Liliana is nothing like her
father, the Blood Sorcerer who cursed Micah. She sees
past Micah's armor and craves his sinful touch. Liliana
will have to brave his dangerous lair and help him
remember his past, or all hope for Elden will be lost.

LORD OF THE ABYSS

Also available as a 2-in-1 that includes
Desert Warrior.

Available in December wherever books are sold.